Chris Haslam lived in southern Spain for a couple of years. He now lives and works in London.

Twelve Step Fandango

CHRIS HASLAM

An *Abacus* Original

First published in Great Britain in 2003 by Abacus

Copyright © 2003 by Chris Haslam

The moral right of the author has been asserted.

Excerpt from 'The Eyes' reprinted by permission of the publisher
from *Antonio Machado: Selected Poems*, translated by Alan S. Trueblood,
pp. 205, 207, Cambridge, Mass.: Harvard University Press, Copyright © 1982
by the President and Fellows of Harvard College.

Excerpt from '*La casada infiel*' by Federico Garcia Lorca © Herederos
de Federico Garcia Lorca from *Collected Poems* (Farrar, Straus and
Giroux 2002 edition). Translation by Will Kirkland © Herederos de Federico
Garcia Lorca and Will Kirkland. All rights reserved. For information
regarding rights and permissions, please contact lorca@artslaw.co.uk or
William Peter Kosmos Esq., 8 Franklin Square, London W14 9UU.

A CIP catalogue record for this book
is available from the British Library.

ISBN 0 349 11590 7

Typeset in Bembo by M Rules
Printed and bound in Great Britain
by Clays Ltd, St Ives plc

Abacus
An imprint of
Time Warner Books UK
Brettenham House
Lancaster Place
London WC2E 7EN

www.TimeWarnerBooks.co.uk

Thanks to Special Agent Kate Shaw at Gillon Aitken Associates, Top Editor Tim Whiting at Abacus, my fun-loving friend Henrique, wherever he is, and Tom Waits.

For Natalie, my dancing partner

Twelve Step
Fandango

1

Luisa was scratching mad, bouncing around the flaking kitchen like a tarnished pinball, lifting lids, sweeping stuff from shelves and scoping every surface for the legendary lost wrap, that mythical forgotten line. She cursed the Spanish in German, the Germans in Spanish, and everyone else in the most universally understood monosyllable after 'Coke'. She couldn't believe this place. She couldn't believe me, and she couldn't believe that there wasn't just one little rainy-day wrap stashed somewhere among our tattered belongings.

'*Bastardos*,' she spat, '*coños*', shaking her scraped-back pony-tail as she fumbled furiously through the pockets of a pair of my dirty jeans.

'*Scheisse!*' She hurled the ragged Wranglers against the crumbling wall and turned her desperation to me. I'd been trying to ignore her, head down in last June's *Marie Claire*, but now I realised that I'd have been better off nipping round to Dieter's Place as soon as she started pacing the room.

'You sure you have nothing?' she hissed, pushing her fringe back from her brown face and scaring me with her haunted eyes. If I had been keeping a little back, then I might even have given her half having seen the pain and frustration in those bloodshot eyes, but I had nothing, *nada*, so she would just have to wait. It wouldn't kill her. Not yet. Me, I could always scrounge a line or two from Theo, but Luisa didn't get along so

well with people these days and would have been hard pushed
to find anybody willing to cut her a share of their stash.

She sniffed. 'What about Theo?'

I stared at her like a lamped rabbit, deeply alarmed at my
apparent inability to tell the difference between thought and
expression.

'What?' I spluttered. 'Who?' I scratched my scalp to hide my
eyes, but she had already seen the gleam of guilt.

'What about Theo?' she repeated slowly, almost patiently.
'He always saves a bit.'

'Not this time.' I shook my head emphatically and stared at
the floor. 'I asked him last night. He's completely out.'

'Go and ask him again. Tell him you'll give him back
double – uncut – and bring it straight back here.' Her eyes were
alight now, burning with the optimism kindled when her quest
began.

'Go now!' she urged, pushing me towards the blanket that
hung across our doorway. I shuffled along with her – I wasn't
going to argue. I told her that I would try my luck elsewhere if
Theo had nothing. That would give me more time.

Every time I stepped outside I wished I hadn't sold my shades.
The late-afternoon sun was like the core of an arc welder's
flame, scorching the whitewashed walls and searing the shiny
tin cans we used as flowerpots. A sidewalk of shadow lay slowly
widening across the strip of rocky dirt that ran between the
houses and, blinking out my blindness, I stumbled along in its
shade. A left turn down a narrow alley took me past another
row of tiny medieval hovels built more for security than comfort by a long-displaced people. Everyone should have a castle
to run to in times of danger, and this one had provided shelter
for the past eleven hundred years. Its position atop a plug of

rock high above the farmland of coastal Andalusia assured its continuity as a sanctuary – only the refugees had changed.

Out in the empty square there was no shade but for the slowly turning finger of shadow extending from the base of the tower. Once, this parched and dusty quadrangle was the centre of castle life, the place where the *ambulantes*, the wandering salesmen, would have knocked out their stuff to the honest occupants of the village within the walls. Out here in the square is where disputes would have been settled, taxes exacted, declarations made, beneath shades and awnings of Moorish design stretched from roofs and balconies, tributes paid, whatever – all that El Cid stuff. I did some mandragora root one day a couple of years ago and wobbled up onto the walls, walking around like a stoned sentry, looking down into the square and across the *campo*. Mandragora can be risky stuff to put in your tea, but sometimes it's worth the stomach-tearing abdominal pains and the long, dark depressions that can follow a trip. This had been one of those times, for as I patrolled the perimeter, surveying the wide, sunburned fields of the Guadarranque Valley on the one side, and the narrow, bone-dry streets of the castle on the other, I saw it all in Hollywood Retrovision, and it wasn't so different. The people I had met in the thirteenth century were the same as those whom I encountered today in the streets and plazas of the villages at the foot of the mountain. Same faces, same language, same gossip, same goats and same *burros*. It was all a bit disappointing, especially since I had been looking forward to one of those Jim Morrison-type flashbacks in which I soared over Moorish Andalusia as the untamed eagle spirit of a warrior king.

The brown-eyed descendants of those busy ghosts would have been living here now had it not been for the lure of the cosy self-contained flats and maisonettes that had been built down there in the valley. I had once read that the diminishing population of goatherds and grandmothers still living in the castle in the fifties were evicted from their ancient homes and moved to the new town in the valley as punishment for their participation in acts of socialist–anarchist resistance during the war years. It was said that the castle proved to be such a thorn in the side of the railway track that runs through the valley that upon its bloody subjugation by a brutally superior nationalist force, it was declared a forbidden zone and forcibly depopulated. That was probably true of somewhere, but not here. Up here there's no running water. There's no TV, no telephone, and no chance of buying a lottery ticket. The nearest bus stop is over an hour away by *burro* and the nearest real doctor even further. In the winter the Poniente blows around the castle like ragged yachts around the Fastnet Rock and there's no wood worth cutting for an hour in any direction. *Hombre*, there isn't even a proper bar. The wrinkled Spaniards who left this ancient monument to the rooks and the hippies were old and their health was failing, but at least they were still alive, due partly to the fact that they played for the winning team in the Civil War. Those who didn't were either in the ground or had long since moved to the north where their faces didn't stand out. These days the couple of dozen or so remaining houses that stood within the Moorish walls were occupied by a suntanned and unhealthy mixture of perpetrators and victims, all of whom were running from something. We were subjects without an object, and Theo, imprisoned in the tower by his dope-induced paranoia, was our impotent king.

The ladder that led up into the tower was much, much older than me, so I always treated it with respect. Its base was anchored in the rubble of a stone staircase that had once spiralled up to the eyrie and it creaked like a rickety bridge as I took it one step at a time. I paused a dozen or so rungs from the top, the ladder bent like a longbow, and, as custom demanded, announced my arrival.

'Theo!' I called. 'It's Martin. Can I come up?'

'Er, yeah, yeah,' he replied after a moment. 'Come up.'

Leaning close to the wall I stepped off the ladder and mounted the few stairs remaining, my legs trembling with vertigo and exertion. Theo met me at the curtain, his hand extended and his shoulders squared in an attempt to prevent me seeing past him and into the room. Sadly for us both he was too skinny and I caught a glimpse of Mamout stood with his back to me on a pile of cushions, his hands fumbling with his belt.

'All right, Mamout?' I called cheerily. He half-turned and nodded weakly. I looked back at Theo, meeting his eyes and ignoring the tiny insect crawling across his brow. He was the palest man I knew, because he never went outside. He always entertained at home, balancing his agoraphobia against the vertigo of his visitors.

'How you doing, Theo?' I greeted him, smiling the most charismatic smile in my collection and squeezing his hand. This was an important moment. It was Friday afternoon and everyone knew that the only person in town with even a sniff of the white stuff was Theo. Theo knew that everyone knew that, but it was essential to my well-being that he didn't get it into his weird German head that I was up here to scrounge a line from him. It wasn't just a matter of necessity, but equally a matter of pride. I had always enjoyed a special relationship with Theo, making up for my lack of money and commodities with a surfeit of wit, intelligence and charm. I wasn't like all the other no-hope chancers, coming up the ladder with their

spurious sob stories and appeals to his sympathy and social conscience. I always made an effort, often calling round when I
didn't need a favour, just to see how he was doing and laying
the groundwork for my next visit, when I probably would
want something. I made a point of occasionally coming up
with a quarter of a gram or something and hitting him with a
line like:

'I haven't got much here, Theo, but, hell, what's mine is
yours! Let's split it down the middle.' Nine times out of ten he
would refuse to take the last of my stash and insist instead that
I assisted him in the disposal of his ten-gram bag, but even if he
did it didn't hurt too much. Let's face it – I would never have
taken my last quarter-gram up to his place if it really *were* my
last.

People like Mamout, on the other hand, traded their bodies
for drugs, but then Mamout was only sixteen and didn't have
much else to trade. He was sat on the cushions now, having
adjusted his baggy jeans, and was rolling a joint. Theo seemed
disappointed, like a man in a power-cut cinema, but sanguine.
He put his hand on my shoulder as we crossed the room to
stand at the tall, arched window.

Before us, beyond the square some hundred feet below,
beyond the gatehouse and the thick walls, the *campo* shim-
mered in the late-afternoon sun. The lengthening shadows of
the boulder-strewn sierras crept across the land like a dark tide
flowing across the golden beaches of wheat that grew on the
western banks of the sea-bound Guadarranque. Beyond the
river the fields were still sunlit, their whispering heads of grain
nodding in approval as the land rose in the gentle folds of the
coastal hills to muted groves of citrus and olive. A smudged
line of smog hung above the coast road and the ribbon city of
the Costa and further still, rising out of the Mediterranean like

a fat middle finger of colonial belligerence, the Rock of Gibraltar.

Behind the Rock the sea had turned to silver, its dazzle bleaching out the tankers and containers steaming through the Straits, and on its distant shore rose the mountains of the Atlas, the coast of Morocco, the African continent. Theo was stoned.

'It's amazing,' he breathed, 'incredible! To see so much, so far, to see another continent!' He pronounced 'another' as 'annusser'.

I nodded. 'Yeah, it's a shame we can't see Helmut and Mickey driving back from Los Molinos with my stash.' I checked his face for a reaction. He smiled.

'Yes, I think maybe they are having problems down there with the Guardia Civil. Maybe they have one truck or something parked crossing the road.'

'I bloody hope not,' I grunted, turning from the window. 'I've got a load of money invested with them tonight.'

Theo raised his wispy Aryan eyebrows. 'Don't worry. I think they are not stupid, Helmut and Mickey. They will come. So Helmut is working for you, now.'

I couldn't tell whether that was a question or not, so I ignored it. Theo took the joint from Mamout and passed it to me. I took a long pull, and then another. 'I could do with something a little stronger than this.' I passed it to Theo. He sucked, talking out of the corner of his mouth.

'You want a line?'

My heart leapt. I loved to hear those words. I loved him, up here in his beautiful tower with his dreadful Tangerine Dream collection, his long fingernails, his books on ley lines, the astral charts he had inherited from one of his mothers and his teenage smackhead rent boy.

'Hmm?'

He moved to the bookcase and took down an aluminium film tin.

'I ask if you want a line?'

I shrugged. 'Oh, go on then. I might as well.' Like I couldn't care less. I've seen people drag themselves through the gutter for a line of coke – debased and freebased – sucking the rocks from some scum-tongued dealer's mouth and licking the dust from his boots for a toot, but I wouldn't sink that low. Not yet. I treated the offer of a line like I did the offer of a *cerveza*: I accepted graciously and nonchalantly, scarcely missing a beat, but as Theo fussed over the preparation of the cocaine I noticed that the white streaks arranged on the marble slab were of unequal sizes. Theo was saying something as he rolled up the 1000-peseta note, but I wasn't listening. I was studying the three lines like an incompetent space cadet, trying to decide which of the dusty white ridges was the longest and the fattest, for I knew that Theo's Teutonic upbringing would oblige him, as a matter of courtesy, to offer the slab to the guest first. This essential etiquette would be spoiled if I accepted the slab and then spent even a moment surveying the lines, for it would appear that I was taking advantage of my host's generosity in order to take for myself the largest portion. My duty, therefore, in this illegal ritual was to have the good manners to decide which was the largest line *before* the slab was offered so that my choice would appear to be but a random selection. I licked my lips. Theo passed the slab and the straw.

'Cheers,' I nodded in a matter-of-fact way.

'I think the line on the left is slightly bigger than the others,' said Theo, in a matter-of-fact way.

I sighed and snorted the middle line. Rubbing the specks that were left into my gums, I looked up and passed back the slab.

'You have the big one, Theo,' I smiled, and there weren't many people around here who would be polite enough to do that.

With numb gums and cold noses, watching a distant firework display through a crystal cascade, we sat around on Theo's cushions and talked crap. I couldn't help wondering how much higher I would have been if I had snuffed the left-hand line, but all things considered, I couldn't complain. Mamout paced the room, tracing the outlines of the rocks with which the tower had been built by his Muslim forefathers, staring out across the plain to the snowcapped mountains of the Atlas that were his ancestral home, getting off on a real cultural buzz by the looks of things and unable to get a word in edgeways to describe it. Eventually the surging energy in his veins defeated his desire to hang out with the big boys and he whispered a giggling excuse before skipping out of the room. Theo twisted his neck to watch him leave and then looked at me, a wistful, almost fatherly smile widening his blond moustache.

'Now he goes to play football with the other boys, but he is too fast for them and scores many goals!' I stood up, crossing to the window and looking down into the square. Yeah, I thought, a real little Maradona, but what's he going to do when he gets old, like eighteen years old and too aged for Theo's fickle tastes? What was he going to do when Theo slipped him his final payment and dropped him back on the *barrio* with an expensive habit and no hope of feeding it? Maybe it wasn't worth worrying about. Maybe it was best that he just lived for the day and enjoyed his waning childhood while it lasted. Theo certainly was.

'How much of your money have you trusted to Helmut and Mickey?' asked Theo as I stood reflecting at the unglazed window. I shifted my gaze to the middle distance, across the wheat fields and along the river bed until it met the road, its assignation screened by a thicket of pine and cork oak. That was where the Guardia would be lurking, smoking Ducados and sweating as they zipped and unzipped their dark green flak vests, whispering into walkie-talkies and peeing against the trees, slipping off their safety catches and thinking up good reasons to let loose with some of those 9-mil sleeping pills. I turned away from the window and sprawled on the nest of cushions.

'"*En*trusted",' I sighed. 'It's "entrusted". And it's one-eight-o,' I muttered. Some people wouldn't presume to ask such an indiscreet question, and most of those who would were best avoided, but Theo was different.

'Thirty grams?'

'Yeah, something like that.'

'Maybe it is better for you to have other people to take the risks for you,' suggested Theo, as though it wasn't.

I shrugged. 'Helmut wants to learn the business. I don't mind teaching him. Simple as that.' My voice said, Don't push it, hippy!

I picked up the joint and relit it. 'I'll make ten into thirty and knock it out on the Costa for twelve thousand a gram.' It wasn't much, but that's the way I like to do business, and I made a good living, turning one-eighty into three-sixty in three days.

The British ravers down on the Costa were happier dealing with one of their own than with some shady local who would probably rip them off. Not that I didn't rip them off, but at least I did it with an English accent, and even if I stepped on my ten and made it forty the outcome would have been better than the crap they were used to at home. It would have been easy to expand my operation, buying fifty, a hundred, even five hundred grams at a time, but then I would have been out of my depth and would probably have ended up in the ashtray, or out in the weeds. I passed the joint to Theo. He grinned.

'Martin, my friend, you must calm yourself. You are all wound up like a brass band . . .' He frowned and looked at the ceiling.

I giggled, rubbing my eyes, then my temples, then my eyes again. 'Rubber band. It's "wound up like a rubber band", I think. I'm sorry.' I looked at him, blinking hard. 'It's just this bloody waiting around.' I was buzzing like a chainsaw and I needed to divert the coke-induced nervous energy towards some more positive end. I jumped to my feet, swaying slightly from the effects of the joint.

'Theo, I've got to get out of here. It's doing my head in sitting up here. I'm going to try and make it to Dieter's Place and see if anyone knows what's going on. Coming?'

Theo pouted and pulled on one end of his moustache. 'Nooo . . . I think not,' he finally decided.

I put my hand on his agoraphobic shoulder. 'You should get out more, man.'

A psychiatrist might have suggested to Theo that his phobia was rooted not in the great outdoors but in the route he was forced to take there. The shiny, spindly ladder curved away into the darkness, its rails seemingly held together by my white knuckles alone. Reaching the bottom weak-kneed and trembling, I crossed the square and walked down the alley to the bar. The sun never reached this low-ceilinged, flagstone-floored cavern dug out of the castle walls with its view over the reservoir hundreds of feet below. Dieter had run the place for nearly two years now, and the only sunshine in his life was reflected from the metallic strips in the notes that the rest of us passed across his bar. He did okay, too, selling cold Cokes and *cervezas* to the growing number of sightseers who stopped by on their whirlwind tour of the Real Spain by day, and by keeping the locals happy by providing music, electric lighting and cold beer at night. He was no great shakes as a barman, nor as a human for that matter, and his taste in music was worse than Theo's, but he had a generator, a refrigerator, a pretty wife whom I felt could have done much better for herself and a mature under-standing of the importance of credit.

Pulling the Moroccan curtain to one side, I stepped into the bar and stood blinking for a few moments as my eyes became accustomed to the lack of light. Dieter was sat at the bar, hunched up on a stool and reading some German news maga-zine. To his right, at the end of the bar, staring at a point two feet from the end of his nose and picking at his teeth with a fin-gernail, sat a *campesino*. To his left, under a table with his back to the wall and his worried nose pointing towards the door, was Carlito, an unfortunate dog of the parish. Apart from the whirring of the fan and the tired, wet-biscuit snap of the pages, the three sat in churchlike silence. I approached the bar and sat on a stool between Dieter and the Spaniard. The latter smiled, grunted and returned to limbo. Dieter studied a black-and-white photo of an autobahn pile-up. I lit a cigarette with his lighter and broke the silence with a cheery greeting. He turned the page, glanced at a shot of a weary fireman in a white tin hat standing beside a row of coffins, turned the page again, then turned back to the picture of the fireman. He bent low to inspect the coffins, then tossed the magazine onto the bar and looked up.

'What do you want?'

'Beer, please, Dieter,' I smiled.

He pushed his hair back from his face, pulled himself to his feet and dragged himself around the bar. Presenting the cool bottle of Cruzcampo with a sullen thud on the oaken bartop, he slouched back to his stool and dropped his head into his hands.

The Earth turned.

Down on the Costa, people were making the most of their holidays in the sun.

I looked at the Spaniard. He was still staring into space, still picking his teeth.

I sipped my beer. 'Any chance of some music?'

'Too early,' growled Dieter. 'Anyway, the likes of you should be out earning a dishonest living somewhere instead of lurking around in bars.'

If you didn't know Dieter, you might have taken that as a snide remark.

You'd have been right.

'It's the likes of me that keep bars busy on sunny afternoons,' I reminded him.

He grinned and braced his arms against the bar, leaning close enough for me to smell his reply. 'The likes of me don't need the kind of business the likes of you bring in here.'

'Oh,' I said. At least he was smiling when he said it, and he was still smiling as he turned away to celebrate his victory in private.

The fan whirred round and little droplets of moisture gathered on the brown bottle before sliding down the bartop. I took another mouthful, glancing at the Spaniard.

'How long has he been in here?'

'Who?'

I looked around the sombre cavern. 'Him at the end of the bar.'

'Oh, him,' he grunted. 'On and off since Wednesday. He

comes from Santa Ana or some other place over there. That damned dog's in here somewhere as well.'

I snuck a look at the Spaniard. He had a creased brown face and a gold tooth, thick, shiny black hair and three days' growth of beard.

'What's he doing here?' I asked. Dieter sighed miserably and mined his left ear with his little finger.

'He comes from Santa Ana and he is here because he has lost many of his goats and he cannot go home until he finds them. All right? Anything else you want to know?' People are always losing their goats around here. I like to help by butting in.

'*Senor*,' I began, breaking his thousand-yard stare, 'where did you lose those goats? Down by the reservoir?'

Still staring at his fading thoughts he smiled and swayed a little on his stool before snapping his eyes to me and shaking his head.

'No.' He wagged his finger. '*Loma de la Fuente.*' He winked, but I didn't get it.

'That's kilometres from here,' I said. 'It's right over on the other side of the mountain, isn't it?'

'*Claro*,' he nodded, 'but there is no bar there.' He lifted his thimble of thick glass and held it high as though proposing a toast to the barman. '*Uno mas?*'

I could read his mind.

He was thinking, 'That *Ingles* speaks bloody good Spanish,' and he was right. My fluency in three major languages put me in the top half per cent of the population of Europe, according to Theo. I caught the bloodshot eyes of my reflection checking me out from behind a mirror at the back of the bar. The top half per cent. I hid it well. Dieter sighed and did his death-row walk around the bar, snatching up a corked lemonade bottle from a hidden shelf.

'*Gracias Patron!*' The goatherd beamed as Dieter refilled his tiny glass with the viscous home-brewed spirit. He took a sip and turned to me, his sun-cured face creased with an exaggerated expression of satisfaction and guilty well-being.

'*Aguardiente,*' he announced. 'Take a little one with me?'

I accepted the offer graciously while Dieter glowered. It seemed that the goatherd was enjoying an unnegotiated period of unlimited interest-free credit, and Dieter, like a kid lighting matches at the corner of a wheat field, could see himself getting burned. I ignored him, proposed a toast and we introduced ourselves. Francisco herded goats, tended a small *finca*, and knew, as most people around here do, where there was buried a hoard of Arab gold. We tipped back several more, suddenly bereft of conversation, and as I helped myself to one of the goatherd's Ducados I felt the draught from the wing of the Angel of Death chill my spine. I felt my stomach squeezed in the grip of an icy hand and a dull heaviness behind my eyes as the *aguardiente* attacked and killed my buzz. I stubbed my cigarette, rose and wobbled towards the lavatory. I could feel it coming: I was going to start worrying and it would ruin the weekend. In my line of business it's good to be worried, but not the way I get worried. I locked the door and stood over the bowl, pushing my head into the crumbling white wall and breathing deeply the acid fumes of the piss-stained floor. There were serpents, said Theo, that lived in the deepest, darkest valleys of the mind. He claimed that they were blind, but found their prey by homing in on the stench of fear and paranoia secreted by a lost soul as it stumbled sobbing and whimpering through the undergrowth. If you were bitten by one of these snakes, it was imperative that you remained calm and didn't worry. If you worried, said Theo, then the venom would kill you. If you stayed cool, then you would be okay. You *would* be okay. I concentrated on the texture of the wall against my forehead, cool and powdery, and tried to build another inside my head behind which to hide. It was okay, no problems. Just the mental effect of a chemical reaction. Within the space of ninety late-afternoon minutes I had snorted up a quater-gram of coke, smoked an eighth of that blinding *kif*, and then knocked back half a pint of 80-proof home-grown *aguardiente*. It was reasonable to expect that I might be feeling a little off-centre, that my mind might take advantage of my befuddled state to play a few tricks on me. As long as I didn't worry about it, I would be fine.

I pushed myself away from the wall, wiped the cold sweat from the stubble beneath my nostrils and sank to the seat of the lavatory. Breathing in through my nose and out through my mouth, I shuddered at the reverberation of the tremor that had shaken me out there on my barstool. It was like a shadow falling across your world on a cloudless day, an eclipse of the sun unseen by anyone but yourself, a personal and specific portent of impending evil. *In through the nose and out through the mouth*. I felt a fresh scorch of sweat break out along my spine and across my upper lip, my pulse thumping in my ears as the venom surged through constricted veins. I couldn't keep thinking like this. Jesus, I'd already told myself why it had happened. Too many substances inhaled and ingested in too short a time. That, and my mental state at the time. I'd gone out worried, wound up with Luisa's pacing and scratching, my head swollen with cold turkey, and Helmut and Mickey were six hours late. No big deal. *In through the nose and out through the mouth*. The flood of panic was beginning to recede, leaving stained and broken thoughts stranded high and dry in muddy brain. There was no need to worry. *In through the nose and out through the mouth*. Give it a few minutes and it would all fade away, provided that I didn't worry.

But I *was* worried. Worried that I wouldn't be able to stop worrying, worried that perhaps I was wrong to tell myself not to worry, worried that there might be something lurking just around the next few hours that I should really be worried about. I ran through a mental list, scratching out everything that didn't matter. There were two entries left: Luisa, and my increasingly overdue thirty grams of cocaine. I stood up and rubbed my face. Maybe I'd stay away from the Costa tomorrow night. I pushed open the bog door and walked wearily back into the bar. Handclaps like tapshoes accompanied my entrance, but they weren't meant for me. They were for El Camaron, accompaniment to his smack-cracked voice and frantic guitar. Francisco had fallen across the bar, his glass out of reach, but he managed a wave in the direction of the big speakers.

'Frequencia de la Revolucion Andalus,' he announced. 'He's playing El Camaron de las Islas!' He pushed himself up from the bar, a beatific smile splitting his face and his eyes closed in stupefied ecstasy. '*Dios de la Nada!*'

The Frequencia de la Revolucion Andalus, or the FRA, was a pirate radio station hidden high in the hills with an impeccable, if somewhat dated, record collection, no apparent political agenda, in spite of its moniker, and an unusual advertising policy.

'The God of Nothing,' I nodded weakly. 'Where's his church?'

I sat at the bar and finished my beer. When it was all gone, I ordered another, since I had no intention of going home now. I was wound tighter than El Camaron's top E and I needed a little time for the bile to subside. The record ended with a hiss, and with a crafty glance at the now snoring goatherd, Dieter rose from his stool and switched off the radio. I sat at the bar for

another hour, fretting over the future and worrying about my
health, making plans and drawing maps of my destiny in the
beer spilt on the bartop. I'd never meant to stop here long
enough to be identified as one of the crusty old regulars, never
really meant to stay with Luisa. I hadn't liked her much in the
first place and I liked her a lot less now, but we needed each
other, like symbiotic parasites, two leeches joined end to end,
endlessly feeding the one from the other until a better host
came along and the stronger of us could drop the other to dry
up in the weeds. We tolerated each other's presence because we
both knew that for the time being it was the best thing on offer,
and something was better than nothing to our starved egos. It
wasn't just us: I saw the same situation in every supermarket, in
every restaurant and in every lighted window I passed in transit, and every sorry compromise sat on every dusty porch like a
locked-out dog, hanging its head in disappointment and con-
firming that love didn't live here. Inside their houses they
writhed under damp sheets, making love where there was
none, and making babies from whom to learn it. No wonder
we took drugs. The only thing we agreed on was getting high
on our own supply, and the effect left us unable to concentrate
on improving any other sphere of our trivial existence. My
life, it seemed, had slipped into a rut, but I knew that it took
only a few weeks of hard work and discipline to get it together
and split. Maybe wait until the high season, then do one big
hundred-gram run, buy a decent bike, and go. It was possible.

I looked down at the bar. The abstract symbols signifying the
motorcycle and the hundred grams were still recognisable as
wobbling pools of *cerveza*. Those representing the hard work
and discipline, however, had defeated the surface tension that
held them together and had merged to become another soggy

spillage on the bartop. I shrugged and smeared my future across the uneven surface. I was always like this on Friday afternoons.

I started as a heavy hand slapped me across the shoulder.

'I think you buy us a drink, *hombre*,' snarled a garlic voice, and I whirled around to behold the florid, sweating face of Mickey. I jumped to my feet and grabbed his fat, wet hand.

'Mickey!' I gushed. 'Nice one, *hermano*! Take a seat and I'll get the beers in.'

Mickey, however, was covered by yet another subsection of Dieter's highly selective customer services policy, for as I turned to shout up the *cerveza*, I found that he had already seen to it. I thanked him, but he didn't hear. He was too busy cueing up the C90 Mickey had tossed him.

Mickey was the kind of bloke that people name bad-looking dogs after. So fat that he looked short, with a ZZ Top beard and rotten denims held together by decomposing organic compounds, he amused children and frightened grown-ups. Club-footed and one-eyed, he wore a discreet steel plate in his head and matching pins in his nearside leg. These heavy metal accessories were affected by extremes of temperature, but the fat biker was said to control the consequential pain and confusion with huge doses of vodka and speed. It worked for him, he claimed.

In Bremen, where he was still remembered as the city's ugliest bouncer, Mickey had accidentally killed someone out of whom he had merely intended to beat the living daylights. Fleeing from the Bundesrepublik in the oft-quoted, inaccurate and somewhat cheesy belief that he was never going back inside, Mickey had bought a Belgian passport and fled to Spain, where he was quickly arrested for beating up a cop from whom he had been trying to steal a car. Now rehabilitated, his idea of a useful life involved sitting around smoking hash with Helmut, going over and over his plan to rob the casino in Marbella. It wasn't even his plan, but that of a bag-snatching market trader from Ubrique with whom he had been incarcerated in Malaga. The bag-snatcher had been released, and by the time Helmut had introduced himself as Mickey's new cellmate, it had become Mickey's plan. Just how rudimentary this plan had been before Mickey adopted it is unclear, but in its latest refined form it seemed to involve running into the casino, shooting everybody down with automatic weapons, nicking the money and running for it. On Harleys.

Helmut's wary approval of this scheme in the early days of his sentence for car theft on the Costa ensured his survival both inside and out, for far from stamping all over his head, as he felt compelled to do to all educated liberals, Mickey handed Helmut full intellectual control of the plan and devoted himself to the protection of his cellmate's brain. Two hours after his release from prison, Mickey had stolen a rental car and driven straight up to the castle, to join Helmut in his workshop.

Helmut and Mickey: Butch and Sundance for the Pepsi generation.

Helmut stooped as he entered the bar, stretched his lanky frame and wiped his oily hands on the seats of his pants. His smile was warm and genuine as he crossed the room, his hand meeting mine in a firm shake. He exhaled expressively and shook his fingers in the peculiarly Spanish gesture that signifies a close-run thing.

'*Que pasa?*' I asked.

He shook his head, pursing his lips. 'Many coppers today. Too many bloody coppers.' He glanced at the bar. 'This is mine?'

I nodded and he took a long pull on the dripping bottle. '*Skol!*' He wiped his mouth and took off his little round spectacles, rubbing his eyes with the back of an oil-stained hand. 'Too many bastards.' Helmut had clearly had a hard day.

'We drove first to bloody Christobal's house, park the truck, knock on the door and his mama comes out and tells us that he's hiding down at the *Puente Nuevo* because the police watch the house. So then we drive out of town with two, sometimes three police cars, unmarked, behind us. I say let's go home, but Mickey says no, we carry on, so we stop, and we argue, and then Mickey jumps out of the truck and starts picking up oranges and throwing them at me.' He shook his head slowly. 'So I have my hands up against these oranges and I look behind me and all these police cars are parked, watching us.' He raised an eyebrow and cocked an eye at Mickey, but Mickey had his boot in Carlito's mouth and wasn't listening to the story. Helmut frowned. 'He always attracts dogs, this Mickey, do you notice this?'

I had noticed, although I wasn't as surprised by the observation as Helmut seemed to be.

'Anyway, we drive across country to *Puente Nuevo* and these pigs cannot follow us in their little Spanish cars. When we get there Christobal is very nervous and has many guys with him. He is also very . . .' he rubbed the side of his nose suggestively, '. . . you know, what is the word, *agitated*, and angry that we have come and he says we must not leave until he says so. So we give him the money, and he gives us the weight, and then he sends some kid off on a motorbike to check if the beach is clear—'

'Coast,' I interrupted, 'to check if the coast is clear.'

Helmut frowned. '*Ja, ja, ja,*' he said impatiently. 'Anyway, the little bastard did not return until five o'clock.' He drained his beer. 'Anyway, I have your package in my pocket.'

I grinned like a delighted crowd. I had been dreading the

denouement of this tale, expecting to hear some terrible punchline that involved my stash being lobbed from the window of a pursued vehicle into the river, or being eaten by Metal Mickey. Losing both your money and your drugs was a risk you had to accept when you sent someone else to do your dirty work. If you didn't like it, then you could always go and get it yourself and take your own chances. I gulped back a couple more mouthfuls of beer and slammed the bottle onto the bartop.

'Let's go round to my place and take a look at it.' I slapped down a note, pulled back the bead curtain, and two nasty surprises arrived at once: in the foreground, Luisa, like a widowed mamba, and behind her, at the top of the alley, a face from the past.

2

I sidestepped and Luisa rushed past like a rocket-propelled grenade aimed in self-righteous indignation at Helmut and Mickey, but I missed the explosion. My attention was focused upon the sunburned grin of the figure leaning breathlessly against the crumbling wall at the top of the alley. There was a better than average chance that I had mistaken this road-soiled biker for somebody I once knew, but as he raised his hand in the casual greeting you might expect from some bloke you played pool with two or three times a week, I accepted that the odds had gone against me.

'*T'as la pêche, mec?*' he called, squinting against the falling sun.

'Bloody hell,' I exclaimed, 'Yvan!'

I fixed something indicating pleasant surprise to the front of my face and strode through shadows of doubt and fore-boding towards him. I had travelled a long, long way for a long, long time in order to be confident of avoiding exactly this sort of unexpected visit, and it clearly hadn't worked. I took his hand and pumped it in a firm, sincere shake, then turned to introduce him to the others, but they had already gone back to my house to examine my purchase. I was reluc-tant to bring Yvan in on such a private scene as this, but nor was I going to take him into Dieter's Place for a beer while they were all sitting around on my couch poking their noses into my business.

'C'mon,' I smiled, 'we'll go to my place.'

He pushed himself away from the wall, wincing as his weight fell onto his feet.

'Are you the king of this castle?' he asked, his leather armour and his mock seriousness reminding me of some medieval French interloper. I made a face like a grin, then looked down at his leg.

'What's the matter with the leg?'

'I have fallen from my *moto* down there on the corner.' He shrugged. 'S'okay, nothing broke.'

'Where's the bike?'

'It's okay too. It's at the gate.' A smile burst across his face and he hopped a little closer to me, laying his hand on my shoulder.

'Man, it's good to see you again!' he cried. 'I bet you think I never come and find you in your castle.'

'I'll drink to that!' I chuckled, playing the game. The truth of the matter was that I hadn't even thought about him in the whole time I had been here, let alone considered the possibility that he might turn up injured and out of the blue at the start of the working week. I had a feeling that he was probably *sin dinero*, broke, and I was certain that Luisa was going to hate him.

Only the uppermost orange tiles on the shallow roofs were illuminated against the deep blue of the cloudless sky as the setting sun sank beyond the sierras. Below, dusk crept through the overgrown streets as we made our way along the dirt path to my place. To my relief the others had only just arrived as I pushed through the blanket and stepped into the room. The FRA was playing '2000 Light Years from Home'.

'Right,' I announced, 'first things first: Helmut, Luisa, Mickey, this is Yvan. He's French, he's a bastard and that's all you need to know.' Surprisingly, everybody laughed politely, enabling me to press my advantage. 'Luisa, if you would care to attend to our guest's every need, I will rejoin you all in a *momentito*.' I smiled at her and shot up the ladder that led to our bedroom like a rat up a drainpipe. Helmut followed, dropping my packet on the dressing table and crossing to the window to let in the last of the light.

'You believe in God?' he asked, sweeping aside the blanket that served as a curtain and revealing a sunset so exhilaratingly beautiful that, in the time it took a late pigeon to cross the frame, my usually fluid atheism had been turned into a pillar of salt.

'Course I do,' I replied, clearing a space on the dressing table. 'This is the altar at which I worship.'

Dios de la Nada.

The cocaine had been weighed into the severed corner of a white carrier bag, a neat, bowl-shaped receptacle that sits nicely in the palm of the hand. The edges had then been gathered together and sealed with a flame to form a bud-shaped package about the size of a drought-shrunken mandarin. I sliced through the molten tip and the bud began to unfurl, exposing the icy white pollen within. I smiled at Helmut and switched on my electronic scales, breathing hard into the dish and buffing the acrylic before scooping the crystalline powder into it with the tip of my blade. When the digits were agreed my little pile of livelihood weighed in at twenty-seven and a bit grams, nearly ten per cent short. Somebody had taken their cut somewhere along the line. I sighed. What could I do?

'It's okay?' asked Helmut, poker-faced.

I smiled. 'Yeah, it's fine. A little under, maybe.' My words said, Unconcerned. My voice said, Pissed off.

'Maybe Christobal weighed it out in its wrap,' suggested Helmut.

I shrugged. 'Yeah, it's possible.' It was also possible that the missing weight had gone up the noses of the two *muchachos* I had engaged to do my fetching and carrying, just as it was possible that they hadn't seen a cop all day and had spent it getting wrecked on my rocks and playing pool with Christobal. I dragged my knife tip through the edge of the pile, separating enough for a quartet of decently sized lines.

'Maybe the quality will make up for the quantity.' I glanced up at Helmut and he nodded. I started chopping. It was a crying shame, but the most dangerous side effect of this otherwise wonderful substance was that it turned the habitual user into a lying, conniving, cheating, thieving, smarming, scheming, suspicious paranoiac. Helmut, for instance, was a thoroughly decent bloke. An educated, cultured polyglot with scarcely an ounce of ego on his lean frame, he was friendly, helpful, polite and made exceedingly good cakes. Introduce the cocaine alkaloid to this winning formula, however, and see how the shade and the structure of the character is changed. I divided the chopped pile into lines and beckoned to him.

'Here,' I said, passing him a rolled-up lottery ticket, 'have a toot on this.' If he had any conscience, he wouldn't enjoy it.

3

As darkness fell and a sliver of moon hung like a silver cradle before Venus we stumbled like lost goats through the smoky alleyways of the castle and fell into Dieter's Place. My mood had improved as my intake of stimulants had increased, and the anger I had felt at the shortfall had since been outweighed by my wonder at the excellent quality of this week's purchase. It had been heavily cut, but it had been cut *well*. Tomorrow morning I would turn ten into thirty and head down to the Costa, *no problemos*, but tonight I would party with my friends. The ambivalence I had felt towards Helmut had been dissipated by my admission to myself that had I been in his position, and he in mine, then I would have ripped a few lines from him. Furthermore, the fact that if I had stolen cocaine from his stash I would have made up the missing quantity with Dextrose, Mannitol or chalk made me more insidious than him and thus reaffirmed my faith in his overall decency.

Yvan, too, had excelled, being in possession of both money and hash, but I was right about Luisa. Hanging from my arm she whispered that there was something spooky about my French friend, that he unnerved her. She looked up at me, her eyes already like full moons but widening further still in terror, before exploding in a fit of the giggles and scampering off to disrupt the Danes. Yvan limped across with a couple of Scotches and glanced over to where Luisa was reminding a party of Danish hippies of their exact position in the European Superiority League Tables.

'She's okay,' he smiled, like he had the right to comment. Behind him a lost tourist, all catalogue leisure wear and sunburn, pushed his head into the bar like a man probing a rat's nest. He gave me a look that said it was all my fault before retreating into the night. I chinked Yvan's glass with mine in appreciation of the drink and the compliment.

'Wanna buy her?'

Like nearly everybody here but me, Luisa had missed her vocation. She should have been selling landmines in sub-Saharan Africa, or conducting medical experiments in Stuttgart. She was wasted as a hippy, although she had a reputation for kindness to animals. Eight out of ten of the cats living in the castle owed their lives to Luisa, but only because she was planning on wearing fur next winter.

Somehow, on a subconscious, autonomic level, the very thought of our relationship brought about a subtle, unwelcome change in my blood chemistry, so I changed the subject. I tried hard to entertain Yvan with tales from my eccentric life in the castle, and he tried hard to be amused. Cocaine had made me think I was interesting. I shrugged and changed the subject again.

'Like the music in here?'

He hadn't really noticed. He came from a big city with so much music in the air that one tended not to notice it, and a local golden-oldies station with an announcer who sounded like a sedated Eeyore didn't raise his pulse by much.

We drank and stayed high until the eastern sierras rolled back round to the sun. We spoke of the day we had first met, our backs bent beneath a burnished Bordeaux sky as we struggled up dusty slopes between rows of twisted, stunted vines, our baskets on our hips. Born and ill-bred in Bercy, Yvan knew about as much about grape-picking as I, and he implausibly explained his presence in this ancient and isolated rural valley by way of a general disenchantment with city life. We had been employed by a small cooperative, and due partly to the paucity of the harvest and principally to the unwillingness of the *viticulteurs* to spend any more money on the outrageous twentieth-century salaries demanded by itinerant agricultural workers, we were the only outsiders engaged. This and our mutual horror at the terms of our contract served to bond us together in something that was initially an alliance, developed into a friendship, and, over the weeks we were together, like a pot plant bought from a garage forecourt, became a bit of a disappointment. He never trusted me enough to admit his heroin addiction and I never respected him enough to tell him that I knew. Our eyes didn't meet as we said our farewells.

The next time we met was two years later, on the other side of the same country. I was kicking my heels behind an Alpine bar, and he was stalking skiers with an Olympus OM-1. It seemed to me, as we celebrated our chance encounter, that he knew everybody in town. Not everybody, he had laughed as I refilled his glass, but those he did know were always pleased to see him. Before the week was out I had joined him, adding ecstasy and weed and hashish and speed to the other intoxicants on offer behind my bar. At first I worked on a commission basis alone: taking the orders to Yvan and delivering the goods to the customer, but as soon as I had saved enough *sous* to buy in we became equal partners, sharing the risks and running the town, or so we thought, for three and a half glorious, affluent months. Unfortunately for Yvan, it emerged that it was the gendarmerie who ran the town, and although they were never able to prove his involvement in any criminal activity, their investigation and interrogation were intimidating enough to scare him off. He lost his job at the photographer's – not much

of a job but a great way to meet people who want to buy drugs –
and found it impossible to find another. It seemed that everybody
in town knew him, and nobody was pleased to see him.
Although shaken by the police investigation, my interests had
remained undetected and unaffected, for I dealt exclusively to
foreigners – British, mainly. I could charge a little more than they
paid at home – the altitude premium – sell them a little less for
their money – the metric system – and tell them to sod off if they
didn't like it. British tourists were the ideal customers: nobody
wanted to end up in a foreign jail for drug possession, so they
were always more cautious in their consumption than they might
have been at home. Furthermore, since they were only in town
for a fortnight at most, and had spent the best part of the first
week trying to find somewhere to score, they were never around
long enough to be a threat to my security.

In the meantime, however, the knives came out for Yvan. He
lost his apartment when the owner called the letting agent from
Paris and insisted that his property was vacated by the end of the
month due to unforeseen holiday arrangements. Yvan moved in
with me – what else could I have done – but his reputation and
his freedom to deal were severely impaired by an official ban
placed on him by almost everyone in town. There remained a
couple of bars on the edges of the resort where he could count
the bottles and sip a *trente trois* or a *cinquante et un* of an evening,
but they were hardly where it was happening, so as the season
matured and the days lengthened, Yvan stayed in a lot, watched
TV, and smoked a lot of smack. When he did go out, it was in
the late morning or the early afternoon, but I never asked him
where he'd been or what he'd been doing. I already knew. It was
only the discovery at the bottom of my airing cupboard of a carrier bag stuffed full of chequebooks, ID cards, passports,
cashpoint cards, driving licences and other such items of which

he had been loath to dispose that turned my misplaced, confused sympathy for this pilfering little junkie to outraged indignation. It was snowing hard when I dragged him from the apartment, the flakes whirling around the streetlights like a plague of Arctic moths as I dropped his feebly protesting body in the road. It was still snowing in the morning, the cars in the street buried beneath huge drifts, but Yvan had gone.

And now he was here, and the past was all sunny. Maybe we really had been mates: maybe the likes of Yvan were the only sorts of friend I could expect to have; and maybe the likes of Luisa were the only sorts of girlfriend I deserved. Far off, in the overgrown, abandoned corner of my mind where I had dumped my childhood, I could still see the ruins of my destiny. The future was not what it used to be. I rubbed my eyes and tipped back my *aguardiente*. Yvan was still rattling on about all the good times we had shared, and when, splashed by his wave of drunken nostalgia, I tried to apologise for tossing his half-clothed, smacked-out, semi-conscious body into a snowdrift in the middle of a howling Alpine blizzard, he just smiled a wet-eyed smile and draped a limp arm around my shoulders.

'You did me a great service, my friend,' he slurred, 'a great service.'

A sunny Saturday morning had laid siege to the castle by the time Yvan decided to call it a night, and leaving him grunting and wheezing on the sofa in my house I rolled down the mountain in the Transit, my stash cut and pasted into thirty tiny envelopes for posting on the coast.

I spent a searing day beneath the smog of the N340, drinking brandy and coffee in the sophisticated squalor of the Torremolinan tourist traps. Fortune shook her head in pity and left me an expensive pair of sunglasses on a barstool in the

Bar Salsa. I experimented with them in the mirror behind the bar. Without them, I looked seedy and illegal, like a friendly Glaswegian in a foreign bus station. Wearing them, I looked seedy and illegal and rather cool. I left them on. Trigger, the barman at the Bulldog with whom I had a trading agreement, said they made me look like a drug dealer.

'It's not just the shades,' he explained. 'It's the general Freak Brothers look that goes with it. You must be the only bloke on the coast who still wears cowboy boots!'

That wasn't strictly true, but I took the glasses off anyway so as not to upset him. With the charter jets circling like pregnant vultures over the shimmering runways of Malaga airport, there were plenty of people on their way to the Bulldog Bar who would do that. I swallowed my sixth brandy of the day and sold my last two wraps to a trendy couple of city-hippies sporting middle-class tattoos. I showed them mine, but they were too nervous to appreciate it.

'This better be good,' warned the girl, her silver-ringed fingers caressing the wrap as I pocketed her money.

I frowned, truly confused. 'What's the procedure if it isn't?'

'They could write a letter to *Time Out*,' suggested Trigger.

'Is it any good?' he asked, when they had gone.

'It's okay,' I shrugged, digging a film can from my pocket. 'This is better, though!' Leaving Trigger all sparkly and excited about the coming evening, I drove west along the 340 and into the setting sun.

Luisa was drinking with Helmut when I returned. She held out her hand and I gave her some money. Our greetings hadn't always been like this.

'Your friend's not so good,' she told me. 'He can't walk. You can't expect me to stay at home with him in the house. You'll have to get rid of him.'

I closed my eyes and sighed.

Luisa shot back her Scotch. 'He's got to go. Pay up. I need a big hit and I don't want to have to share it.'

We walked around the glowing ramparts to my house, Luisa ten paces in front of me. She waited outside the house, gripping my arm as I arrived. 'I want him gone,' she announced. 'Today.'

'He'll be all right,' I reassured her, but when I saw him spilled all over my sofa it became clear that he wouldn't. He was as white as cocaine and the familiar apologetic smile that cracked his wan face was iced with yellow scum. I had no time and no sympathy for this.

'Crap skag again?' I sneered.

He sighed and shook his head. 'No man, I swear.' He sighed again and shook his leg gently with his hand. 'It's this fucking leg.'

I stuffed my hands in my pockets and glanced at his scuffed kneepads, immediately and sadly aware that this wasn't going to go away.

'Maybe you should take those trousers off and let some air get to your skin.'

'He can't,' said Luisa. 'He says it hurts too much.'

I groaned. It was Saturday night, I'd had a good day down on the Costa and all I wanted to do was drugs. Yvan read my mind and shrugged.

'I'm sorry, man, but don't worry.' He shifted himself awkwardly into a semi-upright position, gasping tight-eyed at the effort. 'Leave me for a while – you two go out. I'll be okay.'

Both the situation and Yvan's cod-dramatic representation of it were pitiful, and I should have gone out and left him, but something soft and illogical wouldn't let me.

'Fuckit,' I hissed. 'Let's get his trousers off at least.'

I struggled with the sweat-soaked, grease-stained, blood-caked leather pants for ten minutes, but the leg had swollen to become so hot and tight that I could peel them down only as far as the knee. Finally Luisa stopped holding her breath long enough to step forward and suggest that we cut them off.

'No way!' cried Yvan. 'These cost nearly five thousand francs a pair – they use these for Paris–Dakar!'

'Yeah, well you can always nick another pair,' I muttered. 'Luisa, get the scissors.'

'Don't you start giving me orders,' she warned, moving away from the sofa. 'Anyway, we only have nail scissors, and they're mine.'

Yvan struggled to sit up. 'Don't cut my trousers up, man, please!'

I pushed him back down and growled at Luisa. 'So get *your* bloody nail scissors.'

She stood her ground and narrowed her eyes. 'Don't you dare take it out on me. He's your stupid friend – you get the scissors and cut his stinking trousers off.'

Yvan squirmed. 'You don't need to cut them – just pull them off, for God's sake!'

I kicked his leg and he yelped. 'Shut up,' I hissed, 'I'm the doctor.' I turned to Luisa and spoke as calmly as my rising bile would allow. 'Please would you fetch your nail scissors for me so I can cut my stupid friend's trousers off?'

'I can't believe you just kicked him,' she cried. 'You're a stinking pig!'

'For Christ's sake!' I cried, leaping to my feet. 'I'll use a sodding razor blade.'

'Look, this is not necessary,' pleaded Yvan as I climbed the ladder to the bedroom, and as I descended moments later with my rock-chopper he was making a last-minute effort to re-enlist Luisa's assistance. 'Just pull from the ankle, please. Please don't let him cut me!'

Luisa wrinkled her nose. 'No way – you smell too bad.'

I sat down on the edge of the sofa. 'Right then: stop struggling or there'll be tears.'

As I grabbed the ankle hem of his pants he moaned and put both hands to his head.

'*Oh merde!* This is not necessary,' he whined.

I dragged the blade through the thick, double-stitched leather, sawing back and forth to split the seam. I snatched at it and it ripped a little. I took the blade to the next stretch.

'These are very high-quality pants, you know,' I remarked, 'tough as hell.'

Maybe it was a knee-jerk reaction to my jibe as he suddenly cried out and wrenched his leg from my grasp. I looked down and saw blood on the leather, on the blade and on my thumb. My blood. 'Remember the blizzard?' I hissed, showing him my thumb. 'Now we're even.'

I slashed through the seam to the knee and ripped the trouser leg apart. Beneath the leather the limb had festered to a blue-blotched yellow, fat and shiny like some bloated insect larva. It stank.

'You dumb fuck,' I whispered, shaking my head. 'Look at the state of this.' I stood up, wrapping my bleeding thumb in my T-shirt. 'You got to see a doctor, man.'

Yvan looked worried as he wriggled into a sitting position. He didn't look down. 'Is it bad?'

I rubbed my stubble, considering my response as Luisa approached from the darkening corner of the room and peeked over the back of the sofa.

'Oh my God!' she yelped, clamping a hand over her mouth. She looked at me like it was all my fault. 'What are you going to do?'

I shrugged. 'I suppose we'll have to take him to the doctor.'

She shook her head and shrank back into the shadows. 'I'm not going anywhere – you'll have to take him yourself.'

I strode towards her. 'Why can't you come with me? Huh? Why not?'

She tried to walk away but I blocked her path.

'How long are you going to carry on this agoraphobic junkie-chick routine? How long? You're gonna end up like Theo – and he started out like you, pretending to have left the big bad world behind because he thought it looked cool . . .'

'You shut your mouth!' barked Luisa. 'It's easy to take the piss, isn't it? How dare you say that I'm pretending?'

'Yeah?' I countered, my face close to hers. 'So why is it that any time we need to go somewhere you come up with this "Oh I'm too fucked up to handle the world" routine? Supposing I caught it too, hey? Who would get the coke in? Who would buy the booze?'

'It's not that bad,' interrupted Yvan.

'Shut up,' cried Luisa, unsure of whose cause his comment was allied to.

'Yeah, stay out of it, Yvan,' I added.

'My leg, you bastards, my leg is not that bad. I've looked at it. It'll be okay.'

'Good,' I declared, punching through the bead curtain. 'Fucking brilliant. Let's go dancing.'

As I stormed through the lengthening shadows to Dieter's Place I took deep, deep breaths in an attempt to flush the darkness from my mind. Yvan had brought his own malevolent spirits with him but it was Luisa's that had taken the tightest hold upon my shrivelled soul. One afternoon, eight, maybe nine months ago, she had decided that she shouldn't leave the castle in daylight. Bad vibes, she said, digging her heels in, and in our business it paid to listen to one's inner chicken. Then, a week or so later, she had refused to drive across the valley with me to a midnight *feria*, claiming that the roads were too dangerous by night. The next day she had upset the last remaining female in Andalusia with whom she was not fighting a blood feud by refusing to join her on a cheese run to Gibraltar, because of a recurring car-wreck nightmare. There were few enough people around who would request the pleasure of her company, and the fact that this tiny number was diminishing still further seemed of no consequence to her. She seemed to be quite happy – although happy was probably the wrong word – to sit around stoned alone. It looked to me as though the only thing Luisa would be doing from now on would be drugs, and I was damned if I was going to stick around to play valet to the Acid Queen. I kicked a rock down the weedy street. One of these days I'd buy me a bike and split.

In Dieter's Place I encountered an international selection of wasters, skivers and misfits drinking beer and waiting for the revolution, which, according to rumour, started at closing time. Neither Helmut, Mickey, Henrique nor his miserable brother Octavio would have understood the joke, so I didn't bother to explain. They were far more interested in the contents of a little brown bottle with a white label.

'Sarafem,' frowned Helmut. 'What is this, then?'

'What's "*that*", then?' I corrected, without thinking. 'It's the Hindu God of Crazy Women, known to some as Prozac.' I grabbed the bottle, clocking the address of a pharmacy in Newtownards, Co. Down, then chucked Henrique a hard look. 'Where d'you get these?'

'Found them,' he shrugged.

'In whose car?' I asked.

He sent back a look of hurt indignation.

'How is your friend?' asked Helmut, chewing the flesh from a fat, green olive.

I pulled a cold Cruzcampo across the bar, peeling its wet label.

'I dunno,' I groaned. 'I mean, his leg is fucked right up, broken or something, and he won't go and see a doctor.' I sucked on my bottle. 'I've offered to take him but . . .' I left it at a shrug.

'So drag him there,' suggested Mickey.

I shook my head. 'Nah. Sod him.'

I sat on the same stool for six hours. Luisa appeared twice, I bought her two drinks, we had two rows and twice she stormed out. I tried getting pissed, attempted to get stoned and giggly and had a crack at making myself pale and interesting with line after line of coke, but the sides of the cold crevasse of anxiety into which I had blundered were too slippery to scale. The harder I tried to climb out, the deeper I slipped into the cold, crushing depths of unjustifiable despair. I watched miserably as Helmut had a busy night, slipping in and out of the smoky bar with nervous teenagers from the valley while their less confident mates skulked at the corner tables nursing drinks that they didn't really want. One in ten of these kids would would fall like a broken bottle onto the shattered heap of *La Coca*'s scorned lovers, having given all and lost everything for the sake of her haughty caress. Some would be gone in a couple of years, others in less than a decade. It all depended on how much time and money they were willing to invest in their own destruction. I stared at some pimply kid in a Black Candy T-shirt until he reddened and turned away. Christ, I was a miserable sod tonight.

Henrique slapped my back and knocked the self-pity from my dehydrating head. If, as some people suggested, Carlito the flea-bitten mongrel was a human trapped inside a dog, then this lanky streak of hair gel and bumfluff was a puppy trapped inside a youth. Some time in the recent past, at the age of nineteen years, high on pollen and buzzing like a fridge on poor-quality cocaine, Henrique had worked it all out. He'd had some help, of course. Long nights of national service on low alert on the Portuguese border had taught him a few tricks. From a Castilian corporal he had learned, during a number of unofficial incursions into Portuguese sovereign territory, how to break in to and steal from Portuguese cars. He had examined the weak points in the security apparatus of the capitalist state ideology with a Catalan intellectual who should never have been allowed into the Fuerzas Armadas, and he had been told by a Majorcan cook that a dribble of olive oil would stop the butter from burning. Since leaving the army and returning to his village his life had become a little more confusing, but he was making an effort to shape the world according to his understanding. He bought me a Whisky Coca because he wanted a line, so we slipped into the candlelit bog and I passed him my wrap. He passed me a package wrapped in a bandanna in return.

'What's this?'

He pulled his knife and wiped the blade on his jeans. 'Have a look,' he replied.

I unwrapped the bundle to reveal two British passports, a UK driving licence, some sort of insurance documents and a blue nylon wallet. Henrique grinned below his wispy moustache like he'd just potted the black off the cushion. He bent to snort up his line.

'You thieving little bastard!' I hissed. 'Where did you get these?'

He rubbed his gums and then his nostrils. 'Found them.' He addressed the remaining line, snorted, and in a strained voice said, 'Want them? They're free.'

I couldn't condone this sort of behaviour. I gripped his shoulder. 'You can't go breaking into tourists' cars, not here, Jesus! You'll bring the Guardia down on us!' I shook my head in desperation. 'You *loco* or something?'

Henrique's mullet was shaking harder.

'I didn't,' he protested. 'Not up here, anyway. It was parked by the river, outside La Mirador.' He rubbed his nose again, haughtily, like a wronged nobleman. 'They were having lunch inside, so it's okay.'

I stuffed the stolen docs down the front of my jeans as Henrique cut me a line.

'Well that's all right then,' I decided, sagely. 'Just as long as you don't bring the cops up here.'

'Whatever,' he shrugged. 'Anyway, tell me: how much you got left? To sell, I mean.'

'Enough for you, *hermano*,' I replied, between snorts. 'How much you want?'

He pouted. 'Ten, fifteen, whatever you've got.'

As if.

I stared at him, waiting for the punchline. None came. I bent to the remaining line and sniffed hard. 'I got nothing till this time next week. Show me the money, and I'll make an exception.'

'Fair enough,' he nodded, 'I'll catch you later.'

I waited for the appropriate period and followed him into the nicotine-rich atmosphere. I had been heading back to my stool but I kept on walking as soon as my ringing ears heard Nina singing '99 Luftballoonen'. It seemed that Germans had captured the FRA.

Outside the warm Andalusian night was still and scented with the sweet smell of the refinery at Algeciras, although as I climbed the crumbling steps to the ramparts of the east wall a breath of something sweeter still, like the scent of a passing Sevilliana, whispered down from the north. Up there, in the thick-forested mountains, where wolves still took daft goats and bad kids, all was black beneath the waxing moon, but down there, across and beyond the twinkling valley and its shouting hounds, blazed the Costa del Sol, its trillion-watt rig backlighting the sierras and outshining the stars as another high-season Saturday night slipped into fifth and tore screaming down the N340, cranking up the stereo and tossing Eurodollars out of the window. I lit a fag and pulled the stolen documents from my waistband. Here was a couple who were not having such a wild time down on the Costa tonight.

William Murphy, born 26.02.64, and Sarah O'Connor, born 19.08.67, would have spent the past few hours trying to report their passports, driving licence and God knows what else Henrique had lifted from their hire car as stolen. The chances were that they would have done what the brochures and the guidebooks recommended and driven to the nearest Guardia post to do so, thus discovering just how unhelpful and unin-terested a hard-core paramilitary police force can be when your country won't give them back their rock and their monkeys.

Something big and black – more likely a bat than the Angel of Death – swooped soundlessly overhead and I shuddered at its passing. The effects of something I had eaten, snorted, smoked or drunk were obviously wearing off, allowing my fears to come rumbling and creaking through the smokescreen I had laid down. I stood up, looking around me. I couldn't face my worries now, not at this time of night, not out here, so I shuf-fled back home, whistling a nervous tune, dropped a Mogadon and fell asleep in an empty bed.

4

I awoke alone, with the feeling that I had gained a day on my pursuers, but only because I'd been running all night. Sniffing and grunting and wheezing and scratching like a toothless old *campesino* I wobbled down the ladder and into our living room. I smelt it straight away. It was warm and sweet, obscene and repugnant. It was Yvan's leg.

I pulled the neck of my beer-stained T-shirt up over my nose and mouth and crept around the sofa on which he was sprawled. He was whey-faced, blinking fast and smiling, but as I lifted the blanket to look at the leg he sighed and tipped back his head.

'*C'est pas grave*,' he whispered.

'Oh yes it bleeding is,' I replied. I'd never seen gangrene before, not in real life, but if gangrene was sort of purple and yellow and swollen and rank, then that's what Yvan was wearing on his dead left leg, from the calf to halfway up the thigh. Tendrils of subcutaneous blackness reached further up through the clammy, lard-like skin, reaching for his heart, and something else was going on in his hands and his wrists. Not being medically qualified, it was difficult for me to determine the exact cause of the skinny Frenchman's infection, but my diagnosis was that he was fucked. His breathing was shallow and ineffective, his lips were the colour of sloes and his pupils were big enough to fit on your finger.

'I have got to get you to a doctor,' I told him. 'You're not healthy.'

He shook his head. 'Uh-uh.'

I nodded mine. 'Oh yes.'

He grabbed my wrist and pulled me back. Beads of sweat hung like condensation on his clammy forehead and the erratically pulsing veins on his neck stood out as he leaned forwards.

'I will not go to the doctor!' he hissed through clenched teeth. 'Do you understand? I cannot go to see a doctor.' He stared long and hard before releasing my wrist and dropping back exhausted. 'Please, Martin, *je t'en prie*, understand me, hear me.' He sucked in air and closed his eyes. 'I would for you do the same, so please do not call the doctors.'

'I don't understand you.' I waved my arms around in exaggerated confusion. 'You're fucked, you're in agony, and you stink. If you stay here – which you won't, by the way – you will lose that leg and you will probably die.'

Yvan held up a hand, his eyes still closed, then let it flop. 'I say again . . .' only this time weaker still, 'please, Martin, no doctors. I can't.'

'Am I speaking a fucking foreign language to you or something?' I exploded, realising as I said it that indeed I was. 'How clear do I have to make it before you get it into your stupid, thick, Frog skull that you are fucked, *foutu*, that you are going to die.' I took a deep breath and sank to his level, speaking slowly and loudly like an Englishman abroad. 'Without a doctor, you will die. With a doctor, you will live. Now then, do you want to live or do you want to die?'

He raised that limp wrist again and tried to push me away.

'Please, Martin, no doctors. It is . . .' He paused, considering his words. 'What's the point?'

I shook my head. 'Bollocks to you. I'm going to get help.' I grabbed my fags off the table and stepped into the street, the sun's searing reflection off the *cal*-coated walls reminding me that I'd left my new shades somewhere.

Dieter's Place was closed, so I swung down the narrow alley-way that led to Helmut's lair. His was the strangest house in the castle: two vaulted dungeons hacked out of the black volcanic rock upon which the castle had been built. Past tenants had included Moors and Crusaders, Inquisitioned Jews, Republicans, Nationalists and the entire cast and crew of a German S&M porno outfit. The two westward-facing windows looked out across the Sierra de Montecoche, and when the sun dipped below the ridge, the walls were washed in blood. There were no bars on the cell windows – the drop was close on three hundred feet – but Helmut had made some lovely curtains.

I had always thought that his occupation of the dungeon was indicative of the effect that prison had had upon him, but Theo had argued more convincingly that as a bloke from the black, throbbing, industrial heart of Germany, Helmut had simply chosen the dwelling that best replicated a two-room flat in a concrete tower block. Either way, it was where he felt safest, and he had decorated it in a fashion best described as Deutsche Hippy, with rugs from across the Straits, bits of embroidered cloth from Rajestan, incense candles, little silver bells from Nepal, and at the bottom of a chest he had bought in Ronda, all wrapped up in Yasser Arafat's dishcloth, a cheap Russian 9mm pistol and a small box of Astra ammunition. He didn't know that I knew that he had a gun, for I had found it under circumstances too low down and scummy to go into, and for all I really knew, it might no longer have been there. Shame if it wasn't, though, I thought as I banged on the door. It might have taken Yvan's mind off his leg.

'Who's there?'

'Me,' I announced, 'Martin.'

I could hear the FRA broadcasting 'White Rabbit', and I hummed along with Grace as I waited for the door to be opened.

'Martin, can you do me a big favour?' he called. The door was still closed. 'Can you get my spare glasses from my car? I lost my other ones last night, and I'm blind as a bear without them.'

'It's "bat",' I yelled back. 'Where's your car?'

A crack appeared in the doorway and Helmut's lanky nudity filled it. Even his face looked naked without his glasses. 'Here's the keys,' he smiled, blinking hard. 'It's next to the workshop.'

Ten minutes later, with Helmut's glasses in my hand, I knocked again. Bolts slid back and I stepped into the darkness, as blind as my host until my eyes adjusted.

'Martin, you look like shit!' laughed Helmut, his bony white buttocks glowing as he bent over to fiddle with his camping stove. 'Some coffee?'

'Er, yeah,' I replied, averting my gaze as my eyes grew used to the half-light of the cell. For all my years in Europe I had never attained the level of comfort and self-confidence apparent in Europeans when confronted with nakedness. 'You know that . . .'

Helmut silenced me with a raised hand. 'Hang on,' he interrupted, 'listen to this: Alberto's got new ads.'

'So you're driving in your car,' announced Alberto the DJ, 'and this man comes on the radio, and he is telling you more and more, about some youthful information that's supposed to fire your imagination and stuff and he says you can't be a man because you don't smoke the same cigarettes as him. How often does this happen? Too often, eh? I tell you, my friends, you smoke Winston and it won't happen. Smoke Winston. Be a man.'

There was a clatter as something plastic fell on a distant floor. I looked at Helmut.

'That sucked,' I said.

'Shush,' he replied. 'There's more.'

'Okay,' declared Alberto. 'Who's that skinny dog? All bones and skin, raiding bins and eating fruit because someone's too mean to feed him and he's too dumb to catch rabbits. Send that skinny dog to the farm of Fernando Leon Nero and let him feast on horse! This offer is for a limited period only. Terms and conditions apply. Call Fernando Leon Nero for details. Now, er, Stevie Harley and Cockney Rebel . . .'

'What the fuck was all that about?' I asked Helmut.

'I'm thinking it is a dead horse,' he replied. 'Down in the valley. So what were you saying?'

'You know that French bloke who's staying round my house?' The floor was smooth and rounded by the anxious pacing of long-dead prisoners. Helmut passed me a cup of coffee. He moved behind me and sat down on the bed.

'Yes, Yvan,' he replied. 'So?'

I sipped the coffee. No sugar. 'He's in a very bad way.' I took another sip. It would do. 'He seems to have hurt his leg and now it stinks and I think it might be gangrene.'

Helmut sucked in his breath. 'You must take him to the doctor.'

'He won't go.'

'Well he must.' Helmut sounded quite annoyed. 'Does he wish to die?'

I looked out across Montecoche and swallowed my coffee. 'That's the weird thing. I don't think he cares if the leg kills him. All he's worried about is staying away from doctors – that's all he keeps saying: "No doctors, no doctors."'

'Maybe he has secrets,' mused Helmut.

'Maybe he has,' I agreed, 'but he'll take them to the grave if I don't get him some attention.'

Helmut rose and wrapped one of his Rajastani cloths around his waist. Perhaps he had at last sensed my embarrassment at his heathen nudity. He picked up the enamelled coffee pot and refilled our mugs.

'You cannot take him to a doctor if that is not his wish. These are the ethics of medicine.'

'Hmm,' I nodded slowly, wisely. Ethics were unknown quantities to me. 'So I just leave him to rot, do I?'

'Do you feel a sense of responsibility towards him?' he riposted.

I sighed. It was too early to get involved in one of these conversations. I turned and leaned against the windowsill. 'I dunno. All I know is that he's as sick as a pig, he stinks, and Luisa is going to go ballistic if I don't do *something* with him.'

Helmut polished his little round specs with the corner of his loincloth, replaced them and stood before me with his hands behind his back, looking like Gandhi in the Gestapo. 'I tell you what you must do,' he announced. 'You must take your friend to see the witch.'

It was worth a try. Antonita La Buena cropped up in conversation every now and then, and although I had never met her, her reputation as a healer could not be questioned in these parts. Everybody knew somebody whose uncle's *burro*, sister's baby or neighbour's syphilis had been cured like a *jamon negro* by this weird old woman in her rocky hovel. Henrique himself claimed to have been saved by her magic powers. Swollen and breathless, written off by the doctor, he had been carried by his father through the boulder-strewn gorge in the dead of night to Antonita La Buena's house. They had never made it – Antonita met them down by the river where she was charming the fish or something and told Henrique's father to take him home, because there was nothing wrong with him. Sure enough, the infant Henrique was fine, and to prove it he grew up to be a fine young man.

Yeah, it was definitely worth a try. Maybe she could have a look at Luisa at the same time.

I shared a joint with Helmut and moonwalked back to my house feeling comfortably stoned and confident, the swooping fears of last night now far behind me. I stepped through the curtain, pulled my T-shirt up over my face and approached my gasping liability.

'*Hombre*, it's sorted,' I announced. 'We're taking you to see a witch; you know, *une sorcière*.'

He closed his eyes tighter still and groaned. I pushed my advantage.

'Wait here and I'll get you some medicine for the journey.'

He began to protest as I climbed the ladder to the bedroom but it all came out in French and I ignored him.

Luisa was lying wide-eyed and angry in bed, a scarf tied around her face and her headphones on her ears.

'That stinking bastard has to go,' she shouted, in what she might have thought was a loud whisper.

'He's going,' I replied. 'Where have you been?'

'Out,' she replied. 'Why?'

I shrugged. 'Just wondered. I lost track of you last night, that's all.'

'Oh yes?' she replied archly. 'So you're tracking me now, are you?'

I shook my head wearily. It was too early in the day for combat. 'Never mind,' I sighed.

My stash was lying on the dressing table, the wrap considerably lighter than I'd left it. Luisa had taken her breakfast in bed, but was it worth complaining? I chopped up two fat ones and a skinny one. The first two were for me, so I took it easy coming back down the ladder.

'Here you go,' I smiled, 'and there's another one waiting for you at the van.'

He leaned forward awkwardly, snorted up the skinny one and glared at me. 'Still I don't go.'

He said the same thing, or variations thereof, all the way to the van. Helmut, Mickey, Mamout and I carried him on a chair through the empty streets like some gouty prince on a tour of his ruined city. We laid him down, his lips like bruises and his face like ash, on a mattress in the back of the van, and shared a joint in the shade.

'So who's coming with me?' I asked my friends when they had finished my joint. They stared at the dust and mumbled. Mamout seized the initiative and stuck his hand into the air.

'Me, no,' he announced. 'See you all later,' and he was gone.

I looked at Mickey. He looked back and shook his head. 'Can't, mate,' he said. 'I'm not supposed to go near witches.'

'How many witches have you known, then?' I challenged.

His eyes never wavered. 'Loads and loads,' he said. 'I'll catch you later.' He held up a fist. 'Rock!'

We watched him limp across the square. 'Did he say "Rock"?' I asked Helmut.

He nodded wearily. 'He says that quite a lot. It's like "goodbye" or something.'

It took me ten minutes to persuade Helmut to come with me. He had arranged a rendezvous with an unnamed lady and was reluctant to stand her up. However, he and I had entered into an unwritten agreement whereby I would do what I could to help him establish his own little drug-dealing enterprise in return for a little help here and there. Today, I told him, I needed a little help.

Twenty minutes later as we drove through the still-shaded valley we realised we had left the chair behind.

'We'll manage without it,' I decided.

'How?' asked Helmut. 'How are we to carry him for three or four kilometres through the gorge?'

'Oh, I dunno,' I shrugged. 'We'll take it in turns or some-thing, or we'll make a stretcher out of some wood and stuff.' I lit up a fag. 'All you need is two poles and a blanket.'

Helmut was miserable now. 'We have neither,' he muttered, but his pessimistic pragmatism wasn't going to spoil my day out. I was cruising along, in the sunshine, a lovely little buzz on, the radio cranked up and a nice day in the country ahead of me. Fair enough, I had a gangrenous Frenchman in the back of the van, but one couldn't have it all ways.

'Have you been messing with the radio station?' I asked, to stop him brooding.

'You mean the FRA?'

'Yeah,' I confirmed. 'Free Radio Alberto. You been messing with him?'

Helmut tried to be cool. 'What do you mean by "messing"?'

'I mean influencing the output of this station. Who, for example, is this singing now?'

'Münchener Freiheit,' replied Helmut.

'From . . .?'

'Germany,' he said.

'Exactly. He was playing bloody "Ninety-Nine Red Balloons" last night, and doing adverts for Heckler & Koch.

Free Radio Alberto is no longer free. He's been compromised by the Kraut.'

Helmut grinned and turned up the volume. 'Maybe we're part of the revolution,' he suggested.

We parked the van at the mouth of the gorge an hour or so later and I skinned up a couple for the journey while Helmut knocked on a few doors to ask directions.

'There is a route along the valley side and a route along the valley floor,' he announced upon his return. He pointed up the gorge, his finger indicating a path that zig-zagged up the left-hand side before disappearing into dense pines.

'That way is harder to start with, but then it gets easier. The other way is always hard.'

I walked to the edge of the first obstacle on the low route: a six-foot drop down onto the path. It snaked off into a wide, riverside garden of thorn and scrub, landscaped with boulders as big as the Transit and criss-crossed with goat tracks that could lead you right up the creek.

'We'll take the high road,' I decided. Helmut shrugged.

We found a piece of four by two with which to make a seat for the invalid floating in a foam-flecked pool at the riverside. My plan was to sit him in the middle and for Helmut and I to carry him from each side, but before we had advanced ten yards from the van the wet wood slipped from my hands, dumping Yvan in the dirt and somehow reopening the cut on my thumb. Yvan exhaled a thin, high-pitched whimper.

'You have got to carry him,' opined Helmut.

I couldn't, however, carry him piggyback, for it meant holding on to the nastiest-looking part of his leg, so I put him over my shoulder in a fireman's lift. The only pleasant surprise I ever got from Yvan was his weight, and as I strode towards the first turn in the narrow, powdery track I felt that I would be able to take him right to the top without dropping a beat or catching my breath. Halfway to the second bend, I fell over, my thighs seared with acid and my lungs burning tar. When I looked up, Yvan was smiling.

'I'm sorry, man,' I gasped, 'that's twice now.'

'Three times if you count the snowdrift,' he replied, his voice seeming stronger now, his eyes somehow brighter. 'Don't worry about it.' He grimaced as something hissed through his nervous system, then smiled, blinking fast. 'It's nice to come out to the countryside, to smell the air.'

Helmut caught up, and bent breathlessly to lift the broken Frenchman. He waved him away.

'It's okay. I can walk a little.' He struggled into a sitting position. 'Help me up.'

Helmut's eyes narrowed slightly but he pulled him to his feet and I wobbled to mine, sucking the dust from the reopened wound on my thumb. Yvan's torn trouser leg flapped fashionably in the resin-scented breeze.

'Get me a stick,' he demanded, like a crotchety pensioner. 'Where are we going?'

I put my hands on his shoulders and stared into his sunken, half-bearded face. 'How come you can walk all of a sudden?'

He raised one shoulder and both eyebrows, pouting as the French do. 'It has stopped *hurting*.'

He looked away and spat. I watched where it landed, splattering onto a chalky limestone boulder like a memory of the Civil War, half black and half red. Something fluttered in my stomach and no one else noticed the sun go dark. I wiped the scum from the corners of my mouth.

'Let's go,' I muttered.

Yvan made it to the next bend, and from there Helmut and I took turns to drag him up the ridge. As we rested in the shade of a pine, Helmut slipped away to scout ahead. He returned moments later and pointed to a coil of smoke rising from the valley. 'Should have taken the bottom road,' he commented, in a Germanic approximation of a Scottish accent.

'"The low road",' I sighed. 'They say "the low road".'

I wiped the sweat from my eyes and squinted into the scrub until I saw a chimney, then scanned the foreground. A well-worn track zig-zagged down through the herbs and the shrubs, its junction with the ridge trail marked by a tiny, well-kept shrine to some painted saint.

'Look.'

'Ah yes,' nodded Helmut, 'the Witch's Path.' He smiled and shook his head. 'I can't believe it! A real Witch's Path!'

I looked at Yvan. He didn't know what was going on either.

'What's the big deal about a path?'

The German looked at me in pity and amazement. 'It's not *a* path. It's a *Witch's Path*. Don't you see?'

It wasn't worth pursuing.

'Come on.' We followed the Witch's Path in silence, tip-toeing over rocks and stepping around the dry sticks that lay across the steep and narrow trail. I tried to breathe in the atmosphere of the occasion, but could recall only one fairy tale and I wasn't even sure that it featured a witch. Might have been a troll, but I didn't mention it to the others. After all, if they had Witches' Paths, then they probably had Troll Bridges.

The edge of Antonita La Buena's property was marked by no more than a pair of *cal*-painted rocks, each the size of a football. The house was still unseen, somewhere over there in the bushes, and the path wound onwards towards it, its progress across the valley floor marked now by more white rocks. The witch felt close, and my companions distant. I looked back. They were.

'*¿Que quieras?*'

I started, scanning the brush for the wizened owner of that harsh voice.

'Er, hello!' I called. 'We've come for some help.'

'Have you brought money?'

I hadn't thought of that. I edged forward on the path, peering into the dry, shimmering scrub. My mouth was dry, my tongue swollen and muddy with the dust. I swallowed hard. This was ridiculous.

'Can I come and see you?' I called, sounding like a patronising social worker.

'I will not see anybody unless you have some money!' yelled back the old crone.

I shuffled forwards, a tension headache rising from the base of my neck as I rounded the final bend and saw the old woman's house. A low wall of *cal*-painted rocks enclosed the single-roomed dwelling and a small garden of some sort. In another walled corral a pair of satanic-looking goats tinkled about in the shade of an ancient olive tree. Near by, somewhere off to my right, beyond the avocado tree and a small orange grove, the roar of a river falling over rocks could be heard. If you enjoyed solitude then this would be a lovely place to be on your own. Antonita La Buena thought so, too.

She waddled from the shaded step of her house and across her garden to block me at the gate. She was dressed in the style of an Andalusian geriatric with thick stockings under a heavy woollen dress, an apron and a cardigan. She also wore a shawl around her shoulders to keep the chill off – altogether enough layers to avoid hypothermia above the snowline and to boil the blood of anybody else down here on the baking valley bottom.

She was tiny and fast and brown and ancient, and as she clattered towards me in her iron-shod boots I began to question the aptness of her epithet. Maybe I had only heard the first half of her name, the shortened version. Maybe her full name was Antonita the Good at Killing Visitors and Burying Them in Unmarked Graves by the Guadiario. I took a step backwards, squinting at the flash of malice glinting in her wrinkled eyes.

'I know of you,' she growled, wiping her hands on her apron.

'I know of you, too,' I replied reverentially. Bullshit wasn't going to work here, but even as I realised the truth, my mouth was moving and crap was coming out. 'We have travelled a long way to find you and your famed wisdom. We have heard from many—'

She cut me dead, looking around me and back down the track. 'I know of him, too.' She jerked her chin towards Helmut who smiled and gave a happy 'Hello Granny!' wave.

'*¡Coños!*' she declared. '*Y hijos de putas,*' as an afterthought.

'Señora Antonita,' I began, 'I have a friend, well, not really a friend, just someone I know, a bit . . .'

'How much money do you have?'

I shrugged. 'Some. Not much.'

She laughed, I think, or maybe she just barked. 'You have lots of money. You stink of money – of dirty money, of money from the sale of drugs and pornography!'

Blimey, I thought, like a salesman whose colleague has just tipped him off about his body odour. Do I?

Antonita wagged a finger at me. 'Don't lie to me, boy, because I see you for what you are. I see you for the thief, for the liar, for the adulterer that you are.'

The adulterer bit wasn't right, at least, not in the sexual sense, but I was accustomed to criticism and I let her carry on.

'You are a thief of lives – a murderer of minds and of bodies. I know what you do – what he does – with these *putas* up there in the castle, with your aristocrats and your actresses – but that is not enough for you, is it?' She shook her head and smiled knowingly, dangerously. 'Ah, no.' She shifted her weight and lashed a boot at an innocent chicken.

'You need fresh blood. You need the sons and the daughters of honest *campesinos*, to entrance them and to entrap them, to take their money and their souls and their emptiness with your poison.' She stopped her ranting abruptly and pointed her nose at me, banging on her ribcage with a bony fist. 'What beats in here?' she hissed.

I shrugged, but if what she had said about me was right, it would take a silver bullet or a stake to stop it. I looked at my feet and started mumbling. It seemed to be the appropriate response.

'I know I've done some bad things,' I admitted. The bullshit alarm was going off at maximum volume in my head, but all the exit doors were locked and I was trapped. 'All I need is a chance to do some good and . . . and this is why I have brought this man here to you. Please just take a look at him. He's hurt his leg.'

Antonita spat into the dust in disgust. '*Coño!* One of these days that north wind will blow a spark onto your wickedness and turn your evil realm to ashes. Mark my words!' She glanced up at the sky and I followed her gaze. A single cloud, as dirty and as dense as a doss-house pillow, was on course for the sun.

'Five thousand pesetas and you can bring him in,' she decided.

The price seemed reasonable – I wasn't sure of the going rate for occult consultations – and I took it from the money we found in Yvan's wallet, pocketing what was left over for safe keeping.

We carried Yvan through the rat-gnawed door and into the pungent murk of Antonita's hovel. A single, virtually sheer shaft of dust-dancing sunlight lit the room like a spotlight, revealing a single bed, a round table covered by a heavy, carpet-like tablecloth that reached the floor on all sides, and a stool. Sweet-smelling joints of home-cured meat hung from the low ceiling with bundles of brittle herbs and straw-wrapped bottles of dark liquids. More of these stood by the door, their contents crystallized around the slender necks of crude green glass. Antonita stood with her hands on her hips as we lowered Yvan onto the stool, then held out her left hand.

'*Cinquo mille.*'

I handed over the notes and stepped aside to let her examine the patient. Outside, the sun climbed higher and the tempera-ture rose. The indignant protests of a disturbed bird shrieked in sharp contrast to the indolent tinkling of the goats. Antonita advanced upon Yvan, her right hand outstretched to touch his clammy forehead, and I noticed that the river could not be heard from here. Helmut stood with folded arms, his head bent low to chew on his thumbnail. Antonita's fingertips brushed Yvan's brow, and she yelped. Yelped like someone burned, and leapt backwards, her eyes widening as she looked from Yvan's bemusement to her healing hand. She backed away farther, muttering and shaking her head, then turned and fled from the house.

I looked at Helmut. 'What the fuck was all that about?'

He looked worried and confused. He shrugged and shook his head at the same time. I followed Antonita into the sunshine.

She was kneeling at the water's edge, bent forward on a tiny beach of silver sand.

'*Señora*, what's happening?' I asked. 'Is everything all right?'
I moved closer, close enough to see that she was washing her
hands with the urgency of a murderess, scrubbing them with
sand in a quivering panic. 'Is everything all right? Is my
friend . . .'

When she turned, I saw her true age. I saw the horror and
the terror in her eyes, and I saw that her hand was bleeding
from the abrasion of the sand.

'You take your friend away from me. You take your friend,
and your money, and . . . and you go.' Her hands were clasped
together in supplication, something silver glinting in her grasp.

I started to reply a couple of times, looking around at the
rocks and the river as though some explanation might be
coming downstream. 'Look, can't you at least give him some
herbs or something – I dunno, something to make him feel
better – before we go?'

Antonita pulled a bitter smile. 'You are as stupid as you are
evil. I can do nothing to make your friend feel better.' She
opened her bleeding hand and held out a blood-stained crucifix for me to see. 'He can do nothing to make your friend feel
better – no one will make your friend feel better because your
friend is already dead. Now go and leave me.'

I looked at her for a few moments and then she turned back
to her scrubbing. I walked back to the house, a sudden drop in
air pressure and temperature that no one else would have perceived sending a chill through my veins. Sod her. She was
crazy, and I was stupid for even considering her. Now we were
going to have to lug the undead back down the valley and
back up to the castle.

I snatched the money from the table and pulled Yvan
upright.

'This was a bad idea,' he moaned. 'We should have gone to

a witch where we could have parked outside.' He looked exhausted. 'What did she say about me, anyway?'

'Nothing I didn't already know,' I muttered. 'Come on, let's get out of this shithole.'

Yvan had fallen into a deep sleep as we drove out of the valley, so we left him in the back of the van and ducked into a bar.

'To the doctor?' suggested Helmut, brushing the dust from his short hair and raising the frosted, dripping glass to his cracked lips.

I raised my glass. 'To the doctor!'

Helmut sighed and shook his head. 'It was not a toast. Your friend is very sick. I think we should just take him to the doctor.'

'You ever seen *Ice Cold in Alex*?' I replied.

He shook his head impatiently and ordered another round. 'I mean, how will you feel if he, you know . . . died, or something?' asked Helmut.

I sucked a long draught of lager. 'Apparently he already has,' I sighed. My mind was made up. 'Let's take him back to the castle.'

5

Luisa's reaction to Yvan's return was loud and entirely predictable. That I had taken all the drugs in the house for a day out in the country goaded further her already vicious mood, so I took the unusual course of attempting to placate her.

I held out my stash tin in one hand and the film can in the other. '*Cannabis sativa* or *Erythroxylum novogranatense*?'

'Prick!' she replied, snatching both and scurrying out of the house.

I lit a joint and sat on the wooden chair opposite Yvan. He awoke and asked for some water.

'So how long were you in Morocco for?' I asked, pouring the dregs from a cracked plastic bottle into a stained mug.

'Morocco?' He frowned, but I couldn't tell if it was from confusion or pain. 'Why do you think I've been to Morocco?'

I shrugged. 'Just a hunch. Thought you might have been down to grab some pollen.'

He smiled. 'If I had made it to Marrakesh I would never have returned, especially not to visit you.' He tried to laugh, to let me know he was joking, but he could manage only a spittle-splattered splutter. 'I would have loved to have made it to Dar el Baida.'

'Is that up in the *rif*, in the hash-growing zone?' I asked, still fishing even though it was clear that the pond was stagnant.

Yvan sighed. 'Martin, there is more to Morocco than *shite*, you know.' He held out his fingers like a bedridden hypochondriac aunt. 'Give me some of that *pet* for my pain.'

Despite my growing and as yet undeclared concerns about leprosy, I passed him the joint. It was his hash, after all. He took a long suck, coughed weakly and sighed the smoke back into the room.

'Dar el Baida is the name the Arabs give to Casablanca. It is a port, very romantic, like Marseilles, only busier.'

'So what's the point of going there? They got lax Customs or something? You want to see Rick's Bar, play it again, Sam, and all that?'

He shifted his weight and grimaced. 'There is no "Rick's Bar",' he snorted disparagingly. 'It was made up for the film.' I had forgotten just how fond and tedious the French could be about American culture. 'Did you also know that the line "Play it again, Sam" was not in the script of *Casablanca*?' he added, smugly. Did he know how little time I had for dying pedants? He drifted like a junkie, swinging on greasy fingertips between worlds, and I let the matter drop into the void between.

The white Andalusian sun had had all day to infiltrate its heavy heat through the thick walls of the *casa*, and by late afternoon the air in my front room was viscous and oppressive. The dust on my T-shirt had turned to mud where it had soaked up the sweat on my back, and my dope-addled brain had turned into a swamp. As an explorer I would have realised that there was no point in continuing along this route, beset as it was by an unnavigable expanse of thick black mud and brackish, stinking pools wherein lurked those blind serpents and other monsters of the mind that Theo so rightly feared. I closed one eye and looked at Yvan, suddenly knowing that as surely as love dies and cannot be resurrected, so would he, and I didn't know why. Whether his leg had ceased to emit that nauseatingly sweet odour of putrefaction or whether I had become used to it I could not tell, but the visual evidence of his decline was irrefutable. His fingers, once long and bony, ideal for the *vendage*, had swollen and gone black at the fingertips, and his lips, once so admired by the schoolgirl ski trippers for their ruby sensuality, had become thin, cold and blue. A yellow film played across his corneas and seeped into the gutter of his eyelids and a tight, maggoty-white waxiness had stretched the skin across his cheekbones. His head lolled to one side, and his eyes rolled around to meet mine.

'Do you think I've had too much fun?' he whispered, licking his lips with a yellow-carpeted tongue.

I grunted and looked away. 'I dunno. Do you think you've had enough?'

He raised an eyebrow and looked back to the movie of his life that was playing across the ceiling. I lit up a fag, wishing that I could get up, walk out and come back in an hour to find that he had gone.

'My *moto*,' he said, during a boring bit of his biopic. Despicable, I know, but it was something I had already considered. 'Should I not need it, then it is yours.'

It was nice to have his permission. I studied the floor. 'That's very kind, but stop talking such nonsense.'

I pride myself on being an accomplished liar, having practised and refined my art since I was old enough to talk, but this one came out like a Tory manifesto.

'You're looking better already,' I added. 'Give it another night and you'll be up and running, off across the Straits upon the Marrakesh Express. Wait and see.'

Yvan closed his eyes. '*T'es très gentille, mais c'est pas necessaire.*'

Something raced through his veins, dragging its nails on every nerve-end before popping out through his forehead. He screwed his eyes tighter still and whimpered. I stood up and moved away. This was horrible.

'Listen: how about some painkillers? I know a bloke who's got some DF118s – how about a handful of those?'

He nodded, his breathing short and fast, his black hands opening and closing as though he were trying to pump the blood out of his body.

'Just hang on – I'll be back, and I'll bring some water too.'

He lifted a hand to stop me. 'Martin, wait. Wait just a moment. There's something you should know, something about the *moto* . . .'

I nodded quickly. 'Yeah, yeah, I know all about the *moto*. Tell me more when I get back.'

I met Theo's friend Mamout as I rushed to the square, and told him to take some water round to my house. A wagging finger in the back of my reeling head scoffed at my stupidity and scolded me for failing to take the febrile Frenchman to the doctor. None of my excuses seemed pertinent now that it was almost too late, and I knew that as a last resort I could stick him in the back of the van and dump him outside the *Urgencias* department at the Costa hospital. That's what I would do, I decided, just as soon as I'd mellowed him out with some of Theo's opiates.

I started to climb the ladder, feeling calmer now that I had chosen a constructive course of action, and yelled up to Rapunzel from the thirteenth rung.

'Theo! I need some of those DFs! Can I come up?'

'*Ja*, *ja*, *ja*,' he replied, meeting me at the door with an enormous joint. 'Try this,' he uttered, his smile dripping like a melted ice-cream. 'You will see into the heart of Africa,' he claimed, as I took a tentative toke on the oily cone.

I needed to sit down. 'What is this?' I wondered, as cool mountain streams were diverted through my veins and high cirrus strata drifted above the gullies of my throbbing mind.

'Is it not incredible?' laughed Theo. He never tired of the view from his tower. 'Come here and look at the ocean,' he beckoned. 'You can see the fishes.'

I wobbled across to verify his claim, my feet as cold as if I had taken hemlock.

'Blimey!' I cried. 'Look how close Morocco is! I can see people there, for fuck's sake!' It was true. I could. Theo put his hand on my shoulder and pulled me closer.

'Look there.' He pointed at the Rock, at the cloud forest of antennae sprouting from the summit. 'They can surveille us, you know.' I could smell his sweat.

'"Put us under surveillance",' I replied. '"They can put us under surveillance."'

He released me and moved back from the window. 'They already have.' He exhaled a huge cloud of smoke. 'Cameras, microphones, radar, everything. They know who we are.'

I looked down at the courtyard below, wondering how long it would take, and how much it would hurt. Theo was going to start talking about aliens any moment now, and I was too stoned and too weak to take any preventative action. I couldn't even leave, at least not until I had come down a little bit from that outrageous hashish, or else I would be sure to discover exactly how long and how much.

'I saw more lights last night . . .' I stopped myself, but too late. Bringing up the subject of aliens was an effective way of ensuring unlimited access to Theo's drug stash for as long as the discussion could be maintained, but there was no need for it now.

'Where were they centred?' asked Theo. 'Over the Alguedias again?'

I nodded, then neatly sidestepped discussing the threat of alien invasion by remembering that I had a dying friend to attend to – a fantastic excuse – and left with a handful of 30-mg DFs, going straight home via Dieter's Place, where I washed down half a dozen of the bitter little pills with a cold Cruzcampo.

As I returned home Luisa was standing outside, smoking someone else's cigarettes. She looked worried, and vulnerable.

'Martin, he's really sick, you know,' she insisted, between deep, deep drags on a soggy Ducado. 'He's going to die – we have to get him out of here.' We – I liked that, but let it go. Sometimes I could see something in her eyes, in her mouth, in the nape of her neck or the twist of her hips that I could love and care for. I studied the down on her cheeks for the briefest of moments, just to see if it was hidden there, before she caught me looking.

'I know,' I replied. 'I'm going to sort him out right now.'

As I pushed through the blanket it was clear that I wasn't. Mamout was sitting on the floor, his legs crossed and his hands clasped together as though praying to the God he didn't know. Yvan was the colour of a city sky with a thunderstorm brewing, his eyes opening and closing in a manner too slow to be called blinking, his tongue fat and yellow against his lower lip.

'We've got to move him out of here,' I told Mamout. 'I'm going to drop him at the hospital.'

Mamout rolled his wet brown eyes towards me and shrugged. He clearly thought it was too late for that – but then again, he was a sixteen-year-old rent boy so what the fuck did he know about anything?

He reached across and gently lifted Yvan's swollen, lolling hand, placing it neatly across his chest.

'He has been in the Atlas? In Morocco?' he asked quietly.

'Er, not yet, but that's where he's heading,' I replied. Dropping those DF118s had probably not been such a good idea. My mind and body seemed immersed and supported in a gradually warming, gently thickening liquid duvet, and I couldn't be bothered to decide whether to sharpen up the edges with a couple of snorts or simply to enjoy the smacked-out opiate buzz for a while.

'Shit, that reminds me!' I pulled a fistful of painkillers from my jeans. 'Let's give him a dozen of these.'

Mamout picked the pills from my palm with his long brown fingers. 'I have seen men like this before, at home, after they have been into the mountains,' he said. He lifted Yvan's head with a mother's tenderness, and cradling the delirious Frenchman in his arms, placed the pills in his mouth and brought a mug of water to his bruised lips. He lowered Yvan back down to the cushion and turned to me

'The tribesmen are very bad peoples. They prey upon travellers coming from the north to buy *kif*.'

Yvan sighed, long and tired. Mamout traced circles in the dirt on my floor as he spoke.

'You say, "I want to buy the best *kif* – many kilo." These peoples say, "No problems, please, come to my house as my guest. Come please and see my farm and my fields where my *kif* grows. I show you the best." So you go, and you see the fields and the plants and then you chew and you do business, and then when you have made the business, this peoples say, "We are brothers! Now I make big feast to honour my brother and our business." And that night you go, and you eat big feast and you drink whisky and then . . .' He stopped drawing and looked straight into my eyes. 'Then you die. These peoples have poisoned you because they want your money but they don't want to give you their *kif*. Sometimes they make too little poison, and you wake up alive the next day, so they must give you the *kif*, and then they must follow you and pray to Allah that maybe you die later, before you leave the mountains.'

It was a good story. He saw my expression and mistook the effect that the opiates had had upon my facial muscles for slack-jawed disbelief.

'It's true!' he insisted, sounding like a lying schoolboy. 'I promise!'

'Yeah, right,' I sighed.

Mamout pouted and rocked on his haunches, and I collapsed into the wooden chair. I felt tired and stressed and, perversely, highly content. A joint laced with coke would have made things better, but I couldn't be bothered to fetch my stash. Dusk continued to seep into the house, and if I had owned a clock, I would have listened to its ticking. If I had possessed a tap, I would have listened to its dripping, but all I had was Yvan's laboured respiration. I dropped my eyes upon his face and was spooked to see him looking straight back at me.

'How's it going, *mec*?' I whispered. 'DFs kicking in yet?'

He whispered something in French that I didn't quite understand. It sounded like he had come from the past to fuck up my future, or maybe he had simply observed that in the past, the future hadn't been so fucked up.

Whatever.

I smiled and nodded.

A dribble of saliva welled on his lip and began rolling south before Mamout leaned forward and wiped it away with his thumb. His eyes remained locked on mine, maybe looking at me, or into the gully that gaped between us, or maybe even seeing right through me and out the other side. A prickle of unease penetrated the blanket of opiate protection in which I had wrapped myself and sent a trickle of brine dribbling down my spine.

'I think it's time we got you sorted,' I declared. 'I'm just going to skin a couple up for the journey, and then we're out of here.' I leaned forward and looked into his face, but the bit that responded to external cues had long since retreated from the front. I stood up. 'How about some music while you're waiting? Yeah?' I walked quickly to the cassette player and rummaged among the tapes. There had to be something here that appealed to a Frenchman's unevolved taste in rock. I slotted a TDK into the machine and pressed PLAY.

'You'll like this one.'

The wop wop wop *Apocalypse Now* song filled the room, and I was halfway to the ladder before I realised the awful appropriateness of my random, careless choice.

'This is the end, my only friend, the end,' sang the Lizard King, but I stopped him before he could elaborate and punched the radio into life. Maybe Free Radio Alberto would play something for his non-German listeners.

'You're everywhere and nowhere, baby, That's where you're at . . .' sang Jeff Beck as I climbed the ladder, and it was hi, ho, silver lining, as the first line cleared my head and the second brought it all back, but in order. It was simple: round up some help, carry Yvan back out to the van, give him another handful of DFs, drive down to the hospital on the 340 and drop him where it said *Urgencias*, then split before anyone could ask me any questions. It was the easy and most convenient way to manage a crap situation, and no one could say that I was abandoning a friend, because, number one, he was no friend, and, number two, I was saving his life. Furthermore, number three, I was removing him from the house and thus acceeding to Luisa's wishes. I was on a roll now – I quickly chopped up a short one, just in case reasons numbers four, five and six needed a little encouragement before doing a subterranean homesick blues across my brain.

As I descended the ladder Guns N' Roses welcomed me to the jungle, and I would have loved to have taken the tour, but I needed to move things along now – it was time for Mamout to go and round up some assistance. I reached into my pocket for another couple of DFs and turned to the teenager. He was standing now, having risen and moved away from the couch. He raised his hands and placed them gently over his mouth, so that I could hardly hear what he had to say.

'I think he has gone now.'

Something landed heavily in my stomach as something else, something vital, left the room. I looked at Mamout, then followed his gaze down to Yvan's face. My tongue was thick and dry, and I had to swallow. The song ended, swifts screeched before the setting sun, and a car horn sounded urgently, excitedly, in the valley. I looked back at Mamout.

'What do you mean?'

The boy looked at me as though I were the child, and Alberto, high in his mountain hideout, wished his listeners goodnight.

'I mean,' said Mamout quietly, 'that your friend is dead.'

'*This is the sound of the Frequencia de la Revolucion Andalus wishing you a pleasant evening and reminding you all that the lights are always on . . . Vaya con Dios!*'

6

Henrique wasn't distraught, and Mickey didn't look particularly grief-stricken.

'I can't believe you played "Hi Ho Silver Lining" to a dying man,' he guffawed. 'You are such a prick!'

'Do you think he's gone cold yet?' asked Henrique. I shook my head and passed the joint. As a wake, this was weak, but it was probably all that the late Frenchman deserved. I blew a cloud of smoke over the corpse.

Unusual, probably unique, as this bizarre situation was, it seemed somehow appropriate that I was spending a Sunday evening, the most depressing time of the week, in the company of some friends and a cadaver. Mamout had placed a cushion over Yvan's face, and I had squeamishly added a blanket.

'We've got to get rid of him,' I said. 'He can't stay here. What am I going to do?'

'We could have a fire,' offered Mickey.

'Next of kin,' suggested Henrique. 'That's what they do in the army. You have this form, and on it you have what's called next of kin, and you put someone's name there, like your mum, and if—'

I held up my hand. 'I know what next of kin is.' Henrique didn't know that his nickname was El Stupido. 'Good idea, though.'

That I had Yvan's thick wallet in my pocket was of little

shame to me: he owed me that much for destroying my week-end. I sat up and began to pull it from my back pocket, then changed my mind.

'Got any *coca*?' I asked my guests. They stuck out their lower lips and upturned their palms. Standard response.

'I'll go and chop us a couple of lines,' I suggested, moving to the ladder. Mickey crossed to the radio.

'Music?' he offered.

'You know where it is,' I sighed, and climbed into the bedroom.

As the Scorpions rocked the house I inspected the contents of Yvan's wallet and found six thousand francs, close on seventy thousand pesetas, two credit cards with his name on and two telephone numbers with Paris area codes.

Six hours later, as the sun rolled into a curved steel sky, I dialled from the payphone in Paco's bar down in the valley. A long, long way away, over the Pyrenees and beyond the Massif Central, north of the Loire and under, I fancied, a smog-grey sky, a fax machine responded to my call. I swore and hung up, then dialled the second of Yvan's carefully copied numbers. The long French ring tone was replaced shortly by a chirrup of electronic beeps and pulses that would have convinced me that I had called another fax, had it not been interrupted by a hard, nervous human voice.

'*Oui?*'

I stared at the *corrida* posters on the wall behind the phone. I hadn't really thought about how this conversation was likely to progress, and the absurdity of the respondent's opening question had completely thrown me.

'*Qui est là?*' demanded the voice, becoming more urgent, almost angry. I began to flap.

'Er, yeah, um, you don't know me, I don't think, anyway, but I'm calling about Yvan, er, Yvan Auneau.' I was sweating now. 'I think he might be your son, or something.'

'And who are you?' replied the voice, its tone now calmer and more in control. This last moderation was somehow disturbing. He didn't need to know who I was.

'I'm Martin, I'm a friend of Yvan's.'

'Where are you calling from, Martin?'

This didn't seem right to me. I felt as though I was talking to some kind of professional, someone somehow used to taking information over the phone, like an AA man, or a cop. He was trying to control the conversation, and I wasn't going to let that happen.

'Where I'm calling from doesn't matter,' I replied assertively. 'What's your name?'

'My name is Jean-Marc, Martin,' he replied easily. Fair enough.

'And where are you, Jean-Marc?'

'I am in Paris, Martin, in the nineteenth.'

'Okay, Jean-Marc, do you know Yvan?'

'Of course I do, Martin.' I was taking control of this conversation now, but he was still holding a little back and I didn't have enough coins to play this game for long.

'Look,' I stated firmly, 'I'm calling from a payphone as a service to my friend and I don't have enough cash to hang around. Just tell me how you know Yvan. Are you his dad, or his brother, or what?'

'I am his cousin,' replied Jean-Marc. 'Listen, Martin, give me your number and I'll call you back.'

A cousin. That was okay, I supposed. I gave him the number and he read it back to me, puzzled.

'This is not a Paris number,' he guessed.

'No: Spanish,' I replied. 'Algeciras area code. Call me back.'

He did, almost immediately, and without going into too much detail, I hit him with the bad news about his cousin. His emotional devastation was difficult to detect over 1400 kilometres of copper wire, but he seemed to be grateful for my call and promised to drive down to the castle without delay to take his cousin's ripening corpse off my hands. Today was Monday, and he reckoned that he would arrive on Wednesday night.

I sat and drank a *cortado* with a couple of shots of *aguardiente* by way of celebrating this minor accomplishment, and even the contemptuous stares of the half-dozen or so unemployed shell suits and their great-grandads with whom I shared the bar failed to undermine the feeling of control that I had brought to bear. I now had two days within which to work out what questions had been left unanswered by Yvan's death. It was clear now that he had been a bloody sight sicker upon his arrival on Friday night than he had let on, even to the extent of knowing that a grim reaping was imminent. That explained his reluctance to be examined by a doctor – he didn't need a weatherman to know which way the wind blew. I knocked back my *aguardiente*, lit a fag and considered that last assumption. It seemed to me that he would refuse to see a doctor only if he were sure that there was nothing that could save him, and to be that sure he would have to know more or less exactly what was wrong with him.

A nineteen-year-old ex-national serviceman with nothing better to do at eleven-thirty on a Monday morning than to get pissed and play pool spat on the floor, very close to my feet, so I picked up the van keys and left. Driving back up the mountain, past invisible, tinkling herds of goats hiding out in the shade of the cork oaks, I wondered if there were any special, sinister reason why Yvan had chosen to end his days in my company, since I was sure now that he had known he wouldn't be leaving the castle alive. Something worrying, like a half-heard threat from a stranger in a crowded bar, echoed in the back of my head, but I couldn't be sure of its pertinence. Yvan and I had never really been friends, yet, the blizzard-blown snowdrift incident apart, nor had I ever really given him a motive for vengeance. He was just some bloke with whom I'd passed some time, and as far as I could see, there was nothing more to it.

I stirred around the gearbox until I found second and shook my head, attempting to dismiss the paranoia. It was interesting that I felt neither remorse nor sorrow over his lonely, painful, undignified death, just a morbid curiosity that verged on disgust at the way his short life had trickled away. Everything he had accomplished, every detail of the infancy, childhood and never relinquished adolescence of the life that I imagined he had led amounted now to nothing. It was sad, I supposed, in a way, but I could feel no pity for him. At least he seemed to have a caring family, to whom, at the very end, he had still managed to bring grief.

The road emerged from the shadow of the corks and out into the noonday sun. I lit the long roach I'd left in the over-flowing ashtray, switched on Free Radio Alberto and sang along with the Ramones, fairly and fondly certain now that the leather-clad junkie thief would cause me no more trouble.

Henrique loved the bike. He walked in respectful circles around it, moving forwards, moving backwards in the dust but not yet touching, in the same way that his gypsy ancestors might have admired an Arab stallion. He knew all about it as well, spouting off incomprehensible nonsense about brake horsepower, engine cooling and modified suspension. He would have loved to have mounted the dusty widow, but respect for the dead held him back on a fraying leash.

'Do you have the keys?' he asked, a soggy joint hanging from his lip.

'No,' I scowled, 'as in yes, but no.'

He shrugged.

'We can't,' I added. 'It's not right.'

He stuck out his lower lip and nodded in agreement.

I sighed. 'We can't. We really can't. I mean, the poor bastard's only been dead less than a day. It would be like . . . I dunno.' I spat in the dust. 'We just can't. Not yet, anyway.'

He nodded again and rubbed his wispy chin. 'Okay, *si, no problemos, comprendo*. When?'

'Later,' I promised.

He danced away, tripping along the bleached alleyway and leaving me alone with the bike. I skinned up, watching the machine as though it might let me into a secret. This time yesterday Yvan had still been alive, and now he was dead. It was as simple as that. His life was over, finished, his consciousness expired, yet still some part of him lived and radiated from the painted steel.

I stood up, swaying slightly, and approached his steed. The impression of his leathers could still be seen along the lower edges of the tank, and the grease of his palms glistened on the grips.

'You're not quite gone, are you?' I murmured, half expecting to see his grin reflected from the wing mirrors. I ran my palm over the seat, then the speedo, and took a long suck on my roach.

'You are a *nice*-looking bike,' I schmoozed, 'but where did you come from?'

My wandering hand drifted across something hard at the back of the seat, fiddled with it, and succeeded in releasing some sort of catch. I pulled the seat, and up it came, its underside lined with thick polythene. Polythene? I looked under the seat.

'Fuck!' I gasped.

Yvan's legacy was taped under the hollowed-out seat of his motorbike. I looked around like a shoplifter and dropped the vinyl back to the horizontal.

'Fuck!' I whispered again. My adrenals went into spasm. For months my idle fantasy had been to line up a couple of kilos, buy a bike and hook up with St Christopher, and now, in one hit, I had scored what looked to my professional eye like five kilos and a bike. I started to sweat – not the usual indolent perspiration of the underworked and overheated, but the pungent lather of a worried man. I wanted to take another look at the five carefully wrapped parcels, but I was scared of some hippy dopehead wandering into the realisation of my nosecone fantasy.

'Shit!' My vocabulary seemed insufficient to express my awe.

How could he have been so cool about it? Crazy Frog bastard. How much time would getting caught with that much have cost him?

My heart rate soared with the swifts while my mind scuttled like a rat into the shadows to consider its next move. This score was mine. I needed to shift it to a safer place while I worked out how to dispose of it, how to turn it into luxury and cocktails.

I've never been much of a biker. Back in the UK I used to drink in biker pubs, go to biker parties and lust after biker birds – some of them, anyway – but I always arrived in the back seat of someone else's car. I had ridden a motorcycle before, but, sitting astride the wide tank of this muscular mare, my cluelessness surprised me.

I turned the key, my feet barely touching the dirt, and

pushed the black button. The horn worked fine. I looked around again and pressed the red button. There was a highly tuned clatter like an aero engine, a satisfying fart, and then the big bike settled down, humming softly, psychotically, like a sedated, straitjacketed psychopath. I pulled in the clutch, twisted the throttle, tapped the gear lever down until its click was matched by a subtle clunk from within, and slowly released the clutch.

And stalled.

I repeated this procedure until I was entirely familiar with it through all five gears, and then I switched the machine off, my carbs flooded with frustration. I dismounted and lit a fag while I waited for my head to clear, remembering Yvan mentioning that he had taken a tumble on the way up the hill. Maybe something had broken in the accident.

'Heyyy, Mikey-boy!'

I jumped, and spun round to confront two of the Danish ecowarriors who lived on the other side of the castle. I forced my face to grin. 'Lars! Henrik! I'm Martin, remember?'

They nodded as though it didn't matter and shuffled closer, all open-toes and Guatemalan pants.

'Oh yeah – Dr Martin.' They still thought that was funny. 'Nice bike, man. Where d'ya steal it?'

'I inherited it.'

'Cool!' Henrik, big, blond, rich, tanned and pig-ignorant, strode across to the horse and swung his leg over the seat. 'Feels good.' He twisted the throttle and let it go, squeezed the clutch and then the brake, then pressed down with all his considerable strength on the front forks. 'Yeah, nice.' He had, I recalled, given Luisa the same kind of examination shortly after being introduced, but he seemed to like the bike more.

'I'm glad you approve,' I muttered.

Henrik looked over the side, his hand slipping below the tank and fiddling around above the cylinder casing. I stood up and walked to the bike. He was becoming a little too intimate with my machine now, and she and I had a secret that I didn't yet trust her to keep.

'Give me the keys,' he said.

'No way,' I laughed, trying to keep it friendly. The keys were in the bike, and the idiot hadn't seen them.

Lars sat down on the wall and lit up one of those pattern-perfect Danish joints.

'C'mon, man,' urged Henrik. 'I'll show you how to do a wheelie!'

'Yeah, right,' I nodded, placing a proprietorial hand on the rump of my machine, 'and then I'll teach you how to do a three-sixty aerial. How's that?'

I had no idea what a three-sixty aerial was and nor, it seemed, did he. He looked down, unsure of how to persuade me to let him ride my bike. A shadow of déjà vu slid across the scene as I remembered an identical situation that took place in a playground twenty-odd years ago involving a Raleigh Chopper and two kids from another village. That time I got a kicking.

Henrik, however, had no need to resort to violence for he had seen the keys. He pushed her buttons and she responded. His mock-apologetic grin said, John, I'm only dancing, and I knew that no matter what I said now, I had lost another battle of wills. I smiled, though, as he stalled her, and raised my eyebrows as he stalled her again.

'Off,' I said. 'This bike is too big for you.'

He ignored me, stalled it again and yelled to Lars in Danish. Lars shrugged and replied in Danish, and Henrik started to run his hands along the dusty flanks of the fickle machine. The memory of how easily I had found the seat-release catch spurred me and I pulled the keys from the ignition.

'C'mon,' I said. 'Off it.'

Henrik's tone became petulant. 'Ah, come on, man! Just tell me where the gas switch is.'

I shook my head. 'Dunno what you're on about. Get off.my bike.'

He sighed and climbed off. 'The thing you switch the gas on and off with.'

'There isn't one.' There was, there had to be. 'You just ain't man enough to get her going!'

'Yeah, fuck you,' he laughed, meaning it.

I found the switch a few moments after the Danes had sloped off, and a couple of minutes later I wobbled through the gates, my departure witnessed only by Carlito, who was leaving at the same time. He crossed the road in front of me, low and fast like a conscript under fire, and took cover from the backfiring bike in the shade of a jasmine bush. I tried to raise a hand to wave to him, but I didn't yet trust my ride. By the time I rounded the third hairpin, she and I were comfortable in each other's company, and by the fifth, I was in love. I had been driving up and down this hill for so long that I no longer saw or remembered the route, but out here, on the back of this bike, diving in and out of the shaded pools of cool air that I had never known to exist, I felt like a wide-eyed, wild-haired tourist with five kilos of coke and a future so bright that I'd have to wear shades. God, and on the other side Yvan, only knew how fast this bike could go, but right now I felt no need for speed. I hummed along the cracked tarmac, heading as far as the next shimmering heat haze, seeing and feeling the road and the *campo* as I had never experienced it before. At the foot of the mountain, in a shady grove, the road crossed a bridge and climbed gently up to the main highway. A right turn before the bridge led along a broken track on the north bank of the river towards the dam. Scared of the blacktop, I took the track, steering my latest flame between the potholes and the boulders with accelerated confidence. I had been down here once before, writing the track off as another dead-end road with no way out, but the view from behind the handlebars offered a new perspective.

Somewhere around here, not far from the dam, there was an abandoned *finca*, its walls of crumbling *cal* surrounded by dead and dying citrus and smug, squat succulents, reclaiming their promised land. I couldn't be entirely sure that I hadn't simply dreamed of its existence, for my recollections of the orange roof, the smoke-blackened walls, the terracotta pots half-hidden by a carpet of Russian vine and the heavy ironmongery of the wooden door were unconnected, as though I had seen these details as individual photographs. It was at times like this, important times, that I rued the effect of drugs upon my dehydrated mind. If it existed, the broken-down house would have been an ideal hiding place for my stash. It was remote, and unless anybody was watching me, it was pretty much impossible to suss it as a cache. More certain than not that the ruined house was real, I parked the bike at the end of the track and lifted the seat.

Now, for the first time, I could spend some quality time making the acquaintance of my five white sponsors. Weighing the first of them in my hand I noticed first the quality of the presentation. Well packed is half sold, as an old Jew of Gibraltar had once observed, and how right he had been. Professionals had wrapped this thousand-gram brick of cocaine hydrochloride, and it was a joy and a privilege to handle their work. Under ordinary circumstances, the likes of me would never have been this close to the top of the bush, never so near as to touch the source, but these were extraordinary times. With the dumb numbness of a lottery winner, I pulled the remaining four bricks from their hiding place and cradled them in my arms, grinning into the *campo* and wishing that someone had arranged for an official photographer to record my joy. As it happened, the only photographer I had ever known was Yvan, but he was indisposed, standing in a long queue somewhere, leaving me on Earth to manage his estate.

Still holding the shiny white bricks, I slipped out of my T-shirt and used it to wrap up the booty, then, with the sun hard in my face, I set out on foot through the waist-high chaparral to find the ruin. I found it where I had imagined it would be, an overgrown enclosure of *cal*-painted walls with spindly trees thrusting through the stripped roof and piles of dusty rubble forming where the earth was claiming it back.

Inside, breathless with excitement, I stabbed through the thick polythene of the first package with a blade of broken glass. A fine spray plumed around the jagged tear as the shard sank into the powder. I pulled it back out, and, like a good guy from *Miami Vice*, rubbed a little of the shimmering dust into my gums. The effect was instant cold, clear and organic, with none of that artificial procaine freeze. It was *muestra*-quality coke, packed by pharmacists and of pristine purity − if this stuff had been snow, yuppies would have rented helicopters to reach it. Trembling, I used the glass to scoop ten grams or so into an emergency wrap made from a twisted paper napkin, my mouth like tundra and my ears quivering with paranoia. Hiding the remainder seemed to be the most sensible action to take, although the idea of leaving it all on its own terrified me. There was, however, no question of my being able to secrete five bundles the size of Bibles in the back pocket of my jeans, so with a heavy heart I pulled my T-shirt tightly around them and buried them beneath a pile of rubble in the corner of the crumbling room. I took a long, looping route back to the unburdened bike. The only people likely to use the track were fishermen heading up the dam, but I sold drugs to fishermen. One leisure activity didn't necessarily preclude another, and anglers seemed especially fond of that Friday feeling. Anyone seeing me return to the bike would have assumed I had descended from the high ground to the north, up where the rock-climbers hung out.

7

I pushed my nose past the blanket that was my front door and took an apprehensive sniff.

'Seems okay,' I decided, 'so let's get on with it.'

I turned and looked expectantly at the duty undertakers. Francisco the assetless goatherd had been tracked down by his brother-in-law Jesus, who, instead of following orders and dragging Francisco's pickled hide back over the mountain to Loma de la Fuente to assist his wife with her enquiries, had elected to spend the weekend in Dieter's Place on the off-chance that the missing goats might drop in for a pint and a game of darts. Our collaboration was the result of a syn-chronicitous confluence of needs and abilities. I had a corpse to shift, and they had stumbled over the edge of Dieter's Flat Earth of Infinite Credit. They had strong arms and a prag-matic, indifferent appreciation of death, and I had Yvan's wallet.

'If we just get him down the street and into the Red House,' I said, 'he can stay there until his cousin turns up. All right?'

'*Claro*,' shrugged Francisco, like he really cared.

'But you pay us now,' insisted Jesus.

If I had possessed even a couple of vertebrae, the shortest of backbones, I would have pointed out to him that I was the boss, it was my cadaver, I called the shots, and they would be paid when the undertaking had been undertaken. But I was spineless.

'There you go,' I muttered. 'Ten grand each.'

They were good, though, and well worth the money. While

I popped upstairs to cut another couple of lines they wrapped Yvan's remains in a blanket, bound the bundle with cord, found an old plastic bottle of *vino mosto* and broke a pot that Luisa had bought in Ronda. Then, as I led the way, they carried the dead man along the street and into the Red House, where they laid him out on the floor.

'*Vaya con Dios*,' muttered Jesus softly to the corpse as we backed away.

On the way back to Dieter's Place we bumped into Luisa.

'Oh, so where the fuck have you been?' she said, by way of a greeting.

'Moving Yvan,' I replied, by way of an excuse. I had already lost whatever row was about to break out. I didn't know how but she managed it every time. When we first started living together, nearly three years ago, she would walk through the door at four in the morning, pissed out of her head and leading a posse of German bikers, wake me up and complain that I had drunk all the wine. Even then, when my head was reasonably uncontaminated by the effects of pharmaceuticals, she managed to make me feel guilty. These days I had no chance.

'Moving Yvan?' she parroted, her dark eyebrows raised at my two employees.

I started to explain, but she shook her head. I was boring her now.

'I need some blow.' She stood with one hand upturned, cupped, and the other on her hip. It was almost alluring.

'Er, don't have any,' I shrugged. ''S all gone.'

'I need some blow!' she repeated, each word a little longer now, enunciated to express the urgency of her requirement.

'It's all gone,' I repeated. 'What's happened to yours?'

'What do you fucking think?' she hissed. 'You have to get some more.'

'That's exactly what I'm doing now.' I sidestepped her, keeping my eyes on her all the time. 'I'll see what I can do, all right?'

'It had better be,' she replied bizarrely. She slunk off, hugging herself. 'Steal it if you have to,' she advised.

Tuesday died of good intentions and slipped away on a funeral barge bedecked with stoned dreams and cocaine promises, and on Wednesday morning I awoke with the terrible feeling that I had spent the last two nights telling both locals and complete strangers the most comprehensive load of bollocks ever heard in these parts. Snatches of last night's many cocaine-induced conversations came back to me in nauseous waves, like the half-heard nonsense of the dickhead two rows behind you at the cinema who thinks he's funny.

I sat up, lit last night's dog-end and unfolded a wrap of my inheritance.

'Do me one,' groaned Luisa.

I chopped away, almost certain that I had kept my secret. These days, however, it was hard to know when thoughts ended and speech began, so I said a desperate little prayer as I addressed the first line of the new day: Lord watch over my garrulous mouth.

'*Allo?*'

My heart stopped, then adrenalin met cocaine hydrochloride and started it up again, faster, though not necessarily better, than before.

'Who the fuck is that?' cried Luisa, in a loud whisper. I hid the wrap and reached for my jeans.

'*Allo? Monsieur?*'

There was someone downstairs, a Frenchman betrayed by his pronunciation. My pulse rate decreased a little. I peered through the hole in the bedroom floor.

'Hello, who's that?'

He looked up, and smiled, holding out his hand in greeting. '*Monsieur?* I'm Jean-Marc, the cousin of Yvan.' He wrapped his French in an affected accent, like a market trader at a garden party.

'It's okay, it's Yvan's cousin,' I reported to Luisa. She cursed and buried herself beneath the duvet.

There was little family resemblance between the skinny, scabby, worn-out corpse bloating gently in the Red House and this urbane *Charles Henri*, with his designer jeans and tailored jacket. He seemed like the kind of lizard who often entered people's homes without knocking and always got away with it, hiding his wormy carcass beneath a thin veneer of moral superiority and polishing it with a shallow, shiny charm.

I climbed down the ladder, wishing that I had a clean T-shirt with which to impress my house guest. We shook hands. Jean-Marc had the upper one. He looked me over, then began inspecting my front room, and when I suggested that we took coffee at Dieter's Place, he gave the idea a moment's thought, then declined.

'We have driven a very long way and we do not wish to stay here any longer than is absolutely necessary.' He replaced my snowshaker, starting a voodoo blizzard in Seville, and turned to face me. 'I am sure that you, too, are very busy.'

'Er, yeah, yes, I have a few things to do,' I nodded.

'Right!' he smiled. 'Let's get on with it.'

I was searching for another fag when he tossed me a soft-pack of Marlboro. Now I was in his debt.

I lit one up. 'Who'd you come down with?'

He was looking through the hole in the ceiling as he replied. 'Oh, just some friends – they're waiting in the van.'

'Oh. Right.' I crossed the room and flicked my ash into the fireplace, sucked on the butt, then flicked it again. Just as the world had turned and brought the sierras to the dawn, so had I been brought once again to a situation beyond my control. Last night I had been determined to sit quietly in Dieter's Place, with a couple of beers, and work out a plan whereby I got to keep both the cocaine and the motorcycle. That Yvan had bequeathed his bike to me in his dying hour was irrelevant, for his will was unwritten and my will was too weak to argue my ownership. I was, however, an accomplished liar, and I was confident that if I could persuade myself that Yvan had turned up on foot, then I could deceive anybody except a cop with that story. All I had to do was to invent the facts and test their plausibility upon myself, and I hadn't even managed that. Like some sad lost goat from Aesop's fables, I had spent the night telling pointless lies to inconsequential strangers for no gain whatsoever. Now the wolf was at my door and I was unequipped to outwit him.

'Shall we go?' smiled the wolf.

I led the way along the street to the Red House. It was still early, and I was glad of the support of my crystalline breakfast. I felt that I should find out more about Jean-Marc.

'So you're Yvan's brother, right?'

'No,' he replied. 'I'm his cousin. His mother is my mother's late brother's wife. We are, I suppose, second cousins.'

'"Were",' I corrected. 'Did you hang out together much as kids?'

He laughed. 'We were never kids together. I was much older than Yvan, and only knew him from quite recently.'

'So you never got to stay with him in Brittany?' As far as I knew, Yvan had never been to Brittany, but I had my reasons for suggesting otherwise.

Jean-Marc shrugged. 'I never even knew he had lived there. Ours is not the closest of families, and, as I said, we only knew each other recently.'

Maybe that was why he was so cool about Yvan's death. I pulled open the ancient oak door of the Red House and stood aside to let Jean-Marc in. He pulled a handkerchief from a designer pocket and held it against his face. It was a strangely familiar gesture, and as he moved past me into the dank gloom of the derelict cottage I realised where I'd seen it before. Cops did it in movies before they saw a corpse – it was a habit of those used to dealing with dead bodies. He crunched across the broken plaster and squatted beside the formless bundle huddled on the debris-strewn floor.

'Need I look?'

I shrugged. 'It's up to you.'

He touched the blanket and hesitated.

'There's nothing wrong with his face,' I added, 'it's his leg that was nasty.'

He stood up, rubbing his hands together. 'We'll do it outside.'

It was only as we emerged blinking into the climbing sunlight that I realised that I had been holding my breath. Jean-Marc slipped on a pair of city-slicker sunglasses before glancing up and down the weedy street.

'You wait here – I'll fetch my colleagues.'

Colleagues, now, were they? I flicked him my Travis Bickle, hitting him hard in mid-turn. He winced.

'Sorry.' He held up his hands in conciliation. 'How rude of me.' His smile was deprecatory, but the shades stayed on. 'You don't mind waiting here while I bring the van around, do you?'

I pulled out a fag. 'Nah, but don't be long. Like I said, I got things to do.'

He nodded and strode away. I watched him until he turned the corner. The last vehicle that had made it down this street was Henrique's brother's 2CV, and if my Transit couldn't go around the corner then whatever he was driving wouldn't either. Still, there was no harm in letting him try, for the longer he spent attempting to provide a door-to-door hearse service, the longer I would have to work on my story. I hadn't expected him to arrive until this evening, and thus I hadn't bothered to hide the motorcycle last night. It was parked at the top of the alley leading down to Dieter's Place, its Parisian licence plate catching the early-morning sun and reflecting it right back across the square to where Jean-Marc's pals were probably waiting. A strange thumping noise came from the square, but it was too low and too irregular to be the bike. I sucked a lungful and stubbed the half-smoked Marlboro. I was becoming stressed, feeling that giddy sensation of the world being pulled from under my feet, seeing the baby fall screaming from beyond my grasp in a cascade of bathwater, tasting the salt of my sweat in the tongue-prickling stubble of my upper lip. I was losing control of the situation, and as this realisation became more focused, so my loser's resignation deepened. Let him have the bike. *Que sera, sera*, and that was the extent of my wisdom. I pulled Yvan's wallet from my back pocket and removed the thick, slightly damp wad of cash, peeled off about thirty quid's worth of pesetas and replaced them between the stained satin folds of the dead man's wallet. The rest went deep into my front pocket. So what do you want to know about your distant cousin, monsieur? Yeah, he turned up on Friday night, limping but happy. Yeah, he said was off to Morocco to visit Rick's Bar or something. No, he didn't say where he'd stayed – we mostly talked about the old times, you know, reminiscences about the glory days. Oh, by the way, here's his wallet – that's all he had, which is probably why he ended up crashing here. No, I never really knew him that well, but I liked him, and it's a terrible,

terrible thing that has happened. I feel so sorry . . . It was plau-
sible, but there were many things about Jean-Marc that weren't,
that made me suspicious, that needled me and then tattooed the
word 'bollocks' across his forehead. He didn't act like a man
who had taken time off work to drive south and pick up his
auntie's kid's corpse. He acted like a man *at work*, a man taking
care of business. Jean-Marc, I realised, with sudden breathless-
ness, was a gangster, and he was going to see through my story
like it was a one-way mirror.

I sidled along the wall into the shade and took a deep breath.
I had fallen into hot water, and while I could stay afloat in the
shallows close to the shore, I was not cut out to be a long-
distance swimmer. I was scared of sharks, for one thing. I
looked up the alley, but it was still quiet. I could do a runner, I
supposed, but it took a certain special courage to chicken out
in such a positive manner, and I wasn't up to it this morning. I
could have given them half of the coke, or left half of the
bricks taped under the seat, or I could have given them all of
the coke and kept the bike. Jean-Marc didn't give me enough
time to think about it.

'They can't drive this van past that corner,' he said, shaking
his head and sharing his disgust with me. 'They'll have to carry
the body round.'

He leaned on the wall beside me.

'*Merde!* Do you have a cigarette?' I passed him one of his
Marlboro and he lit one for me. He dragged and coughed.
'What do you think about taking him through the street? Is it
safe?'

I started to answer but he cut me short.

'This place is a little bizarre. What is it? Some sort of commune, *quoi*? There are some hippies banging drums in the
square, but they are not Spanish. What do they do here?' He

sucked smoke then turned to look at me, his shiny nose a hand's length from my cheek. 'What do you do here?'

I gave him the standard reply.

'I'm just taking a little time out from real life, from the rat race, you know?'

He chuckled and nodded. 'Nice life if you can afford it. How long have you been here?'

I looked as though I was thinking about it. 'Few months, I s'pose, but you don't need much to get by up here. We all help each other out, swap stuff, grow our own food, keep chickens and things.'

'And this also,' he smiled conspiratorially, rubbing his fingers against his thumb, 'social security?'

'Some try for it,' I shrugged, 'but it's a lot of effort.' I pushed myself away from the wall, and from him. 'Are your mates coming?'

He glanced up the alleyway. 'They should be. They're loading up the *moto*.' He looked right at me. 'It was parked in the square.'

I held his gaze for a moment, then looked away, something weak crumbling away in my belly.

'Yeah, I know. The place where I was going to take you for coffee is just down the alleyway from there.' *Que sera, sera.*

Jean-Marc's assistants were exactly what the darkest, most negative, most pessimistic lobe of my brain had imagined: Bill and Ben the Gangster's Men after a Marseillais childhood and a Scrubs education.

'Where is it?' grunted the taller, his pink, pock-marked skin reddening with the effect of too much fresh air and sunshine. He should have been inside on a day like today, and up until recently, he probably had been. Jean-Marc jerked his head towards the Red House and they ambled inside, the second of them, a shell-suited apprentice of eighteen or nineteen with more than a drop of the Moor in his veins, throwing me a look of intense, unnerving curiosity. I listened to them banging around in the ruined house, then jumped as Jean-Marc touched my sleeve.

'Come on, let's go and get that coffee. You shouldn't have to watch this sadness.' It was said with such tenderness and feeling that I could only nod weakly in reply, and I let him lead the way to Dieter's Place.

We passed Helmut in the alley. I gave him a look that said don't ask, and he gave the Frenchman a nod that was on the curt side of ambivalence. Helmut didn't like men in suits, even when they weren't.

'There is an Englishwoman asking about you,' he warned me.

I waved him away. 'She'll have to get in line.'

A face like a snakeskin handbag turned to greet me as I entered the bar. Bloody Mary, a wizened, middle-aged ex-pat with a past more tragic than most, was clearly looking to score. Normally, we met in a bar in Matamoros on a Saturday night, but she had lately been into less stimulating substances that had caused her to miss our last two rendezvous. I had heard that she was trying to give up her smack habit, but right now she looked as though the horse had kicked her.

'I've been looking for you,' she growled.

I stilled her tongue with a finger and a look. 'Later, Mary,' I said. 'I'm busy.'

She read the message and ignored it. 'I need to see you. It's important.'

Bloody Mary took orders from no man, and later wouldn't do – she needed something more certain around which to organise her empty day. 'I'll come to your house,' I promised. 'About two, three hours' time. Okay?'

She looked at a shiny watch on a skeletal wrist with blood-shot eyes. 'Two hours.'

'Two hours,' I agreed, over my shoulder.

'Girlfriend trouble?' smirked Jean-Marc.

We ordered a couple of shots and a couple of *cortados* and sat by the narrow, unglazed arch that overlooked the reservoir.

'To Yvan,' he declared, and I raised my *aguardiente* to his, chinking glasses to the insincere memory of one of our own.

I lit a fag and took several long drags. 'You still haven't asked me how it happened.'

'Two hours,' called Bloody Mary, slipping from her stool and heading home to watch the clock.

Jean-Marc raised his eyebrows and leaned across the table to help himself to one of his cigarettes. He smiled and showed me his palms. 'You know, I have been expecting this for a long time, and I know what happened.' He watched me for some reaction, taking a sip on his coffee and exhaling through his nose. 'He was fine to start with, right? A little tired, a little short of breath, but for the most part okay, in his sickly way? Yeah? And then he became sick, and then sicker, and before you knew it he wouldn't get out of bed, and he wouldn't see a doctor, and by the time you decided to take him to the hospital it was too late. Am I right?'

Not quite, but I was impressed all the same. I shrugged. 'It was something like that, yeah. He turned up on Friday, on the bike, tired, like you said, but hurt, too. He'd piled the bike up somewhere and bashed his leg. Otherwise, it's like you said.' I leaned forward. 'So how do you know?'

Jean-Marc leaned forward to meet me, a cloud of his exhaled tobacco smoke enveloping us like a conspirator's fog.

'He was predictable, my cousin. He did crazy things, but he did nothing surprising. A sociologist could have predicted his every move without ever once meeting him. He was a model

Frenchman, a child of the projects, a born loser with ambition.'
He shrugged and sat back. 'But it's the same the whole world
over.' He pointed at me. 'You knew about his habit, didn't you?'

'Uh-huh,' I nodded.

'It was expensive, and dangerous, but he said it kept him
young.'

'Well,' I mused, 'he was right in that respect. Now he's forever young.'

Jean-Marc smiled and shook his head. 'Wasn't the *hero* that
snuffed his light, though. It was the virus.'

I didn't know what he was talking about. He knew that I
didn't know, so he told me. '*La SIDA*, what you call it? The
Aids, that is what killed your friend.'

Jean-Marc wanted to stay sober, but I needed a drink, and a
fag, and a joint, and probably something pharmaceutical. I settled for another *aguardiente*.

'What do you mean, Aids?' I blustered. Yvan's ghost passed
smiling across Jean-Marc's face. 'You mean the disease Aids?'
He had come to Spain to die of Aids on my sofa, and all
because I threw him out into the snow for taking too many lib-
erties. The mad bastard. 'You sure it was Aids?' I needed
verification.

'Absolutely,' shrugged Jean-Marc. 'Did he say where he'd
been before he came here?'

'No, and I didn't ask. Wasn't that interested. We just talked
about the old times, you know, up in the mountains.'

Jean-Marc nodded slowly, dissatisfied. 'So he didn't mention
anywhere he might have stopped off before coming here?'

I looked up at the rough, nicotine-stained ceiling. It made
no sense to smuggle cocaine to Morocco, so he must have
planned to sell it before he crossed the Straits. Jean-Marc was
waiting for an answer. I hoped I hadn't already given him one.

'Nope. Why's that?'

'Oh, it doesn't matter,' he said, airily, although it plainly did. 'It's just that he was gone for a long time, and I thought perhaps . . . I'll get you another drink, it will be good for your nerves.'

I stood up and walked to the window, looking out over the distant reservoir while considering my position. There was no doubt at all in my mind now that Jean-Marc was rotten, and that the cocaine I had found on the motorcycle was in some way related to him. Nor was there any doubt that he had little interest in Yvan's fate. What mattered to him was what he believed had been the fate of those bundles of white powder, and there were several possibilities, some of which involved me. A wave of nausea-inducing vertigo so intense that it caused me to reach out for the wall to steady my body crashed over my back as I perceived for the first time the true implications of this deceit into which I had so casually entered. In the criminal ecosystem I inhabited, I was very, very close to the end of the food chain. Jean-Marc, on the other hand, was some species of shark, used to trawling the bottom and chewing on the shrimps that were too dumb to avoid his jaws. I felt his approach and turned to meet him, my hand outstretched to take the shot glass of *aguardiente*. He looked past me and smiled. Bottom-dweller, maybe, but now I was out of my depth. I sipped my drink and reached for my fags. I could have ended it all now by giving back the cocaine, by telling them that Yvan had tried to sell it to me but I couldn't afford to buy it. They might even have given me some of the stash as a reward for my honesty, and then they might have pissed off back to Paris and left me in peace to continue with my deeply unwholesome and unfulfilled lifestyle.

Or they could have killed me. It happens in movies all the time to the bit-part players, the extras and the unknowns whose deaths give life to the story. The only person guaranteed to live is the star, and I had long been resigned to the fact that I would never be the leading man in anybody's drama. This, however, was not a movie, and as I tried to light another cigarette and decide how to play the scene, Jean-Marc's assistants burst in and stole it.

'*On s'en va*,' suggested the spotty one, with a raised eyebrow that added, 'Know what I mean?'

Jean-Marc nodded, then smiled at me again. 'Okay, Martan, it is a shame we should have met under such sad times . . .'

'"Circumstances",' I suggested.

He nodded. 'Exactly. Anyway, *comme tu dis*. We must go and make the necessary arrangements with the authorities.'

I pulled the wallet from my back pocket. 'Here, you'll need this. There's his *carte d'identité*, and some cash – that's all he had, which is probably why he ended up crashing here.'

Jean-Marc took the wallet, looked at it, and then at me, as though he had just seen a rat fetch the mail. 'Thank you, Martan, you have been very kind and I am sorry for the intrusion and the destruction.'

I hoped he meant 'disruption'.

'I hope to see you soon, before we go back to France.'

'Yeah, right,' I smiled. 'You know where to find me.'

I watched the van pull out of the courtyard, then headed back to the house. Luisa met me halfway, half-dressed and distressed.

'Where the fuck have you been?' she screamed, her eyes red and puffy with fresh tears, her hair awry, her shoulders shaking. I reached out and grabbed her, holding her at arm's length.

'What's happened? Come on, what's happened?'

She shattered in my grasp, falling as an uncatchable cascade of crashing sobs. 'They smashed up the house,' she managed, eventually. 'Those men smashed up our house.'

I could hear the blood rushing through my ears as the walls closed in and the knives came out. I swallowed. 'Which men? The French men?'

'Of course the fucking French men,' she screamed, shaking herself from my grip.

'*Your* fucking French men! They smashed up our fucking house!'

8

They must have waited for their boss to lead me around the houses before going in. Luisa, buzzing away beneath the covers with Joni Mitchell in her headset, had heard nothing, or so she said.

'Jesus Christ! Can't I even sleep in my own house any more?' she asked, as though she ever did. 'I look out of my bed and this Arab is leering at me through the hole in the floor. I called you, and where the fuck were you when I needed you? Fucking drinking in a bar!'

She kicked a cushion and shook her head in despair. 'Look at what they've done. Who are these bastards?'

I'd seen this scene dozens of times before, but never in real life. Although it was hard to maintain an objective eye, the damage, and the malevolence with which it had been wreaked, compared pretty well to anything I'd seen on TV. My cassettes were scattered across the room, cases crushed and tape exposed like funereal ribbons. The deck lay face down on the floor, its back broken and its shiny electronic guts exposed, its shattered flanks hidden beneath paperbacks that lay in loose piles like the tiles from a wind-wrecked roof. The sofa – Yvan's deathbed – had been kicked onto its back, its greasy cushions slashed and its lining ripped. Robbed of its magic, the Sevillean snowshaker sat cracked in a pool of glittering water amid the remains of our mantelpiece ornaments. I swallowed back a throatful of panic, and hopped from one foot to another like a kid who needed to

pee, too scared to stand still and too chicken too move any further into the room. Everything was broken. Even our
underused pots and pans had been bounced across the flags, and
I found it hard to believe that Luisa had not heard any of this.
I also wondered why the Arab she had described hadn't
knocked the ladder out of the hole, thus trapping her in the
bedroom and giving them more time to search our house. It
wasn't that I didn't believe what she'd told me . . .

Luisa punched me hard on the arm. 'Who are these
bastards?'

I rubbed at my triceps. 'That hurt. You got the bone.'

'Like I care. Tell me who did this.'

'Frenchmen,' I replied. 'Friends or relatives of Yvan. That's
all I know, except that they'll be back, and they'll probably torture us or something.' I shrugged like a useless hippy and
fumbled for a fag. What I wanted to do was call the police, fill
out an insurance claim and go and stay with relatives until the
perpetrators had been caught, but I had chosen a cut-price life
that didn't offer those facilities. I looked around for something
to pack. 'We've got to split, right now, before they come back.'

'Why?' demanded Luisa. 'What have we done to them?'

'Just go get some stuff and meet me by the van.'

'Why should I?'

Luisa hated being told what to do and, unusually for a vam-
pire, she hated being kept in the dark. I was doing both, and I
didn't care.

'Do what you like,' I muttered, slipping into the sunshine.
'I'm leaving in ten minutes.'

'Bastard!' she yelled as I scurried away.

A spray of bright orange sparks arced out of the shadows,
singeing my hair and pricking my face as I entered the screaming

confusion of Helmut's Vulcanic workshop. Mickey's big club-foot lay stiffly in a pool of shiny black oil, the huge leg to which it was attached disappearing beneath the chassis of a hearse-like vintage Mercedes, his angle grinder sending yet more bouquets of burning steel through the empty aperture where the car's engine had once been. Helmut stood with his back to me, an aura of heavenly light surrounding his silhouette as though he were witnessing an act of creation. If there had been anything at all worth nicking in the workshop I could have had it, for they were entirely oblivious to my presence.

Hitmen must love getting contracts on mechanics.

'Have you got a minute?' I shouted, my hand on Helmut's shoulder. The tip of his welder burned as blue as the sky outside, and just as hot. I looked away – arc-eye hurts. He nodded, closed the valves on his gas bottles, dropped his gloves and pushed his goggles onto his forehead.

'Outside,' he shouted back, polishing his glasses with an oily rag. We stood in the shade at the foot of the castle walls and Helmut pulled a joint from the pocket of his filthy dungarees.

'You find that pretty blonde?'

He was trying to be funny, but it was wrong to joke about something as scary as Bloody Mary.

'You need new glasses, mate,' I advised him. 'Now listen, without me going into too much detail, who do you know who I don't who could sell me a very large score of cocaine?' Anybody who can sell heavy weights can buy them.

Helmut looked surprised. 'You're asking me?'

I grabbed the joint from him and lit it up impatiently. 'Yeah, I'm asking you.'

He couldn't help smiling. 'Locally?'

'Of course not locally. Somewhere else – a city, maybe.'

'Where are you thinking of?' he frowned. 'Malaga? Granada? Sevilla?

I shrugged. 'Wherever's best, but it's got to be someone you can vouch for, someone I can trust, you know what I'm saying?'

He passed me the joint and rubbed his chin. '*Ja, ja*, naturally. Let me think . . .'

'Someone who could sort out, say, ten, fifteen kilos,' I added.

He raised his eyebrows, but that was all.

'I know a friend in Cadiz,' he mused. 'He works for a big guy there, a businessman, he is involved in some sort of local politics or something . . .' He was looking at my scuffed boots, my ripped jeans, my sweat-stained T-shirt, and my unwashed hair. 'I'm trying to think if I know of anybody else.'

'Obviously there would be a consultancy fee for you,' I confirmed, by way of jogging his memory.

'Of course,' he acknowledged, deadpan. 'But the only person I can think of would be this gentleman from Cadiz, and I think perhaps he is not the right person for you to be doing business.' He frowned. I passed him back the joint. 'He is, you know, a very elegant man . . .'

'Helmut, I don't mind, I really don't. Write me a letter of introduction, vouching for me, and I'll go and see him.'

He grimaced. 'I can't – I don't know the guy. I only know my friend, his bodyguard.'

'That'll do,' I said. 'Write to him.'

Helmut was in an uncomfortable situation. 'Listen, you must, er, change those clothes, maybe I can lend you a disposing razor . . .'

'Helmut, please.' I reached out my hand to allay his fears. 'Don't worry. It's business – I'll change my jeans and I'll wash my hair. Just write me that note and I'll see you all right for a few thousand. And it's "*disposable*", by the way.'

He sighed, and I led him to Dieter's Place. Carlito was coming out as we went in, moving fast as though pursued by a wasp. We took a seat by the big window, and while I plied him with beer, cigarettes and a long line of Yvan's legacy, he tore a page from his notebook and wrote a short letter introducing me to his old friend on the Atlantic coast.

'Listen, Martin,' he pleaded as I folded the letter into my wallet, 'this guy will do no business with you if he thinks you are a bum. Do you understand? I think maybe you should take a long shower and buy some new clothes before you see him. Okay?'

I grinned and patted him on the back. '*¡No problemos, hombre!*'

He stopped me as I was leaving.

'Where will you stay in Cadiz?'

Did it matter? 'Why?'

'You taking Luisa?'

I nodded. 'She could do with a break.'

He smiled. 'Then stay at the Hotel Zipolite, on the right, just before the city gates. It's good.' He smiled. 'I recommend it.'

'Fair enough,' I nodded impatiently. I needed to be history and Helmut's tourist information was holding me up.

'If you can't get into the Zipolite, try the Trianes, just down the street. They're the only decent places in town, unless you—'

'Cheers,' I interrupted, shaking his hand, 'and Helmut?'

'Yes?'

I held a finger to my lips. 'Not a word to anyone.'

He looked shocked. 'Of course!'

★

Luisa was waiting in the van wearing an expression of undisguised disgust. She waited until we had rolled through the gates and onto the road before she launched her attack.

'I think you should tell me exactly what's going on, right now,' she simmered.

'Buggered if I know,' I replied, thinking hard and fast, plumbing the gearbox for something low and safe.

'Don't give me that,' she countered, lighting a cigarette with a shaking hand. 'Of course you fucking know, Martin. You're Mr Big Fucking Clever Guy. You know everything. Will you please drive like someone competent?'

I rummaged in the ashtray for a roach, looking all around me for a painless route through this inquisition.

'We've got to get out of this place. We've got to split, because whatever it is these Frogs are after, they're never going to believe that we haven't got it.'

'Haven't we got it?' she asked, quietly, with the poise of a patient Grüppenfuhrer.

I snorted. 'I don't even know what we're supposed to have.'

Her smile was smug. 'Yeah, right,' she said, 'it's drugs. What else would it be?'

I shrugged. 'I dunno – could be anything, but you're probably right.'

'And you don't have them?'

'Yeah, course I do. Does it look like I've got a ton of hash stashed in the back?'

'Don't be stupid,' she sniffed. 'Surely your friend must have told you what he was running from? Surely he told you where he had been, and what he had been doing?'

I was starting to sweat. Germans seem to have a natural ability to interrogate – I found it strange that there were no famous

German chatshow hosts – and Luisa was a mistress of the art. I chuckled in a silly, nervous way.

'Yvan tell me anything? You must be joking!'

'So he didn't tell you where he had come from?'

I wiped my upper lip with a clammy knuckle. 'No he didn't.'

You pathetic little man, said her eyebrows.

'Look, I laid it on him that he had been to Morocco, as though I already knew, like he'd told me when he was drunk and he said that he hadn't been but he was going to Casablanca to have a drink at Rick's Bar or something.'

'There is no Rick's Bar,' she pointed out. 'Everyone knows that.'

That was twice now that I had been pulled up on my English-language film history by foreigners. 'Yeah, whatever, but that was his plan.'

'How can you be sure?'

Why was she so interested? ''Cos he said so.'

'So why was he running to Morocco? What had he stolen? Where had he hidden it? Did you ask him that? Did he tell you?'

'For crying out loud! Do you think I tortured him or some-thing?' I shook my head with the dramatic disbelief of a teenager denying culpability to a careworn mother with video evidence. 'I don't give a toss where he'd been, what he's sup-posed to have done, or anything. All I care about is not being here when those bastards come back, and if you want to stay and argue with them you can. All right?'

I stamped hard on the brakes and coaxed the van around a hairpin that even the goats thought ludicrous. There were seven bends remaining to the valley bottom, eight minutes max in which to devise a way of retrieving the cocaine and hiding it in

the van without Luisa noticing. It was too little time in which
to devise a workable scheme, even without the added pressure
of a rolling interrogation, and while telling her the truth would
make life easier in the very short term, it would lead to an
unacceptable situation shortly thereafter. I would have to share
either the cocaine or the proceeds from its sale, and that was
something I was not prepared to do. I wouldn't leave her des-
titute, far from it, but I would leave her, and soon. She yelled
something in German.

I jumped. She had been talking and I hadn't been listening.

'I said you're hiding something from me. You know exactly
what is going on, and you're keeping the truth from me.' She
pointed at my eye with a talon-like nail. 'I will find out, you
creep, and I'll make you pay.'

I had never, ever won an argument with Luisa, and while I
was certain that sooner or later she would burrow her way into
my secret like a sharp-toothed ferret, the longer I delayed that
bloody moment, the better.

'You're all wound up,' I declared, pushing the Cowboy
Junkies into the cassette player. 'Chill with this for a minute.'

The first few notes of something miserable and calming
filled the cab before Luisa pressed EJECT. 'I am not fucking
wound up,' she seethed. 'I want you to tell me why we have to
leave the castle and why those Frenchmen made us go, and I do
not want to listen to this shit!' Her bracelet jingled, her hand
flashed, and the Cowboy Junkies hit the slipstream. I stepped
on the brakes.

'You are a fucking crazy, coked-up bitch!' I announced.

'And you are . . .?' she replied, with uncharacteristic irony.

There was a good chance that the tape could be saved, and
as I stepped out of the Transit I could see its clear plastic case
gleaming in the sun where it lay on the banked-up verge. I

picked it up – it was unharmed – and as I turned to walk back to the van I noticed a gap in the oaks that gave a sightline all the way down to the junction of the dam road – the road upon which I would travel to the *finca*, in which my treasure was buried. I climbed up onto the verge, peering between the trees to see if I could spot the ruin, but I couldn't. It was much farther along, past the junction, past the big, lone olive tree, farther even than the bright white Mercedes van parked in the middle of the track. I closed my eyes, shook my head, and opened my eyes again. It was still there. Some idly encountered nonsense of Theo's about line of sight slapped the stunned look from my unshaven face and pushed me from the verge back into the road. How could they possibly have found the stash already? Had I told somebody last night? Had I once again unconsciously spoken my thoughts? Had somebody seen me at the *finca* and sold me out? If they had found the stash, why were they waiting there? I raised my head. Why were they waiting there? I climbed into the van and rolled apprehensively towards the next hairpin, ignoring Luisa's continued harassment. Even if they were doing nothing more sinister than enjoying a little *pain*, *vin* and Boursin in the Andalusian sunshine, they had still managed to prevent me from retrieving my five kilos, and without the coke there was no point whatsoever in going to Cadiz. As I struggled to mould my soggy brain around the problem, the cracked road was taking us both down to the shallow, sparkling river and the road junction. A decision was needed, and having none available as the Transit lumbered towards the shady bridge, I made one. It wasn't a very good one, as things turned out, but just as some people are no good at rolling joints, I have never been very good at making decisions. I stepped on the accelerator, putting some direction and drive into our forward motion.

'We're going to Cadiz,' I announced.

Luisa started as though slapped. 'We're going where?'

'Cadiz,' I replied. 'You'll love it. It's very popular with, er, Germans.'

'Cadiz?' she cried. 'What the fuck are you talking about? I'm not going to Cadiz.'

'Oh yes you are.'

'Oh no I'm well bloody not.'

I glanced to my right as we sped past the road junction. Oh no, I'm *bloody well* not, actually. The Mercedes van was parked fifty metres or so down the track on the right, but I saw neither Jean-Marc nor his henchmen. We bumped across the bridge and around the sharp left-hander that led to the N340.

'Martin, I am not going to Cadiz. Stop the van,' Luisa insisted.

'Oh yes you are,' I repeated. 'You're coming because you can't stay here and I can't think of anywhere else for you to go.'

'I want to go home,' she cried.

'Home where? Germany?'

'No!' she yelled. 'My home in the castle. Back there. That is my home!'

'You can't,' I yelled back, 'because when they come back they won't just smash up the *casa*, they'll smash you up, too.' I took a long look in the rear-view mirror, and when I was sure that we weren't being followed I took a deep breath. 'Listen,' I continued calmingly, 'come with me to Cadiz, we'll stay in a nice hotel, with a bath or a shower or something. I've got two hundred k of pesetas, and about five g of coke. We'll do a little shopping, have a dip in the ocean and come back in a few days and those Frog bastards will have pissed off back to Paris and you'll be able to go back to your home. How's that?'

She thrust out her lower lip, and not for the first time I could see her as a petulant three-year-old.

'I want to go home,' she muttered, but she was coming.

I looked in the mirror again, hoping that Jean-Marc wasn't coming, too.

The further I drove from the castle, the longer its malevolent shadow grew across my contracting brain. It scared me to leave, probably as much as it scared Luisa, and it depressed me to admit that the fear was of my own making. The van raised little tornadoes of degraded polythene and yellowed newsprint as we sped along the litter-strewn road to the coast, and I tried to look beyond the neglected, untended citrus orchards to the uncultivated beauty of the landscape through which we travelled, conning myself that an appreciation of natural charm would bring about a natural high. Needless to say, it didn't work. Andalusia was my other woman, and she had lied to me. I had come home drunk with a gorgeous *gitana* nymph, and now, in the naked heat of the Iberian morning, I had awoken dehydrated and unslaked beside a wrinkled hag with a fake tan. It was only when Andalusia spoke to me that I remembered her charm, but right now that wasn't enough. The tinkling of diminishing goats bled through the heat haze like the sound of her earrings, and I put my foot down to be rid of her, to reach the cold honesty of the Atlantic coast.

Fuck it, I thought. I needed another line.

'Fuck what?' snapped Luisa.

'Everything,' I muttered, and she might have understood.

She lit a fag and bounced a long plume of smoke off the windshield. 'Cut me a line.'

I looked at her. 'I'm driving the bloody van. It's a little inconvenient right now.'

'So give me the stuff.'

I sighed. 'Luisa, you can't snort coke in a van full of slip-stream. It'll blow all over the place. Just wait a minute, will you?'

'Why is everything such a fucking struggle with you?' she wondered. 'Just pull the van over and cut us both a line, will you?'

I stopped in a garbage-tip lay-by and hacked four thin ones from my diminishing wrap on the back of a cassette box.

She consumed her crystalline stimulant noisily, then paused in appreciation as the rush dowsed her mind. This was her first taste of my new supply. 'This is very good. Wow! This is very, very good.' She leaned forward and levelled her sights on me. Close range, head shot. 'Who did you get this from?'

'No one you know.' It was the best I could do at short notice. It wasn't good enough. I watched her as she watched me, and I saw the events of the last few days playing behind her pupils as she watched the same movie through my eyes, and then, aghast, I saw her work out the ending.

'You bastard!' she announced, with some admiration. 'It's the Frenchie's coke, isn't it?' She shifted to her knees on the bench-seat and seemed to loom above me.

I bent to snort the remaining tramtracks, keeping an eye on her as I did so. 'Which Frenchie's?'

She raised an eyebrow in anticipation of triumph. 'You tell me.'

I shook my head. 'I don't know what the fuck you're talking about, Luisa.' I scratched my ear and folded my arms, uncrossing them when I saw her watching. She laughed cruelly.

'You're such a loser. Look at your guilty body language. I have hammered the nail straight on the head, haven't I?'

'You've *hit* the nail on the head,' I corrected, but she already knew it and her delight was beginning to curdle.

'Give me some more,' she demanded.

I opened my mouth. 'You've got the wrong . . .'

'Now!' she insisted. I could have told her to shove it, but we didn't have that kind of relationship. I took a deep breath and dug the wrap from my pocket.

'I hope you haven't been sharing this with anybody,' she said as I cut her another couple of lines.

'Course not,' I muttered.

Her nose reddened like a warning lamp as she sniffed, and seemed to pulsate as she sat back and let the alkaloid do its thing with her thought processes.

'You weren't going to tell me, were you?'

I stared with blurred vision at a distant road sign, then glanced sideways at Luisa. She was waiting for an answer, a Marlboro fuming blue between her pale lips, her lifeless brown hair falling straight about her suntanned face. She was twenty-six now, and she had had way too much fun in the last decade. It showed on her face, around her long-lashed brown eyes, and on her hands, and although she was still slim, with almost the figure of a mannequin, her chemical-plan diet had hardened the edges and sharpened the lines until you would cut yourself if you crossed her.

'Of course I was going to tell you,' I insisted, wincing as the tiny part of my brain that didn't do drugs banged on the door and yelled 'Idiot!'

Luisa smiled like a cobra. I grinned back like a rat.

'Tell me what?' she asked.

I was busted.

By the time we were halfway to Cadiz her tireless cross-examination had taught her more than I had wanted to tell and less than she wanted to know. She knew that Yvan had left me a kilo of cocaine, and that it was safely hidden away. She knew that I had left it behind because I didn't want to risk driving into a city I had visited only once before with such a jailable weight on board. She knew that we had about five grams between us, at least two of which were reserved as *muestra*, samples with which to tempt my buyer. She didn't know where the stash was hidden, and she didn't know why I was planning on selling the kilo wholesale. She also didn't know why I was such an idiot.

'A kilo?' She shook her head in disbelief. 'How much is that worth?'

'In sterling?'

'In whatever.'

'This quality, about fifteen grand.'

She laughed. 'You are *such* a loser. I can't believe it. You astonish me.'

I chewed my lip and focused on the white lines in the road. 'So what would you do with it?'

'Whatever. Doesn't matter. Give me some more!'

I thought about warning her of the dangers of overdose, but something heavy in her eyes stilled my tongue. I passed her the wrap, and after she had filled her nostrils straight from the packet, she outlined her business plan.

'First we weigh it all out, then we put our own stock to one side. I'm thinking maybe thirty per cent, say three hundred grams for personal use. Then we split what's left into two piles on a ratio of seventy–thirty. The first pile you step on hard – make it a fifteen per cent mix maximum, but spice it up with some speed and give it a good freeze – and you sell that to tourists at ten thousand a gram. The yield on that will be close on three hundred and forty thousand marks.'

Her maths was good – I'd already calculated the sterling
profit at one hundred and twelve grand, and Luisa was working
on three marks to the pound. Her logistical appreciation, however, was crap. 'You're talking two thousand eight hundred
grams. That's a lot of weight to shift.'

She looked up as though she had forgotten I was in the van.
'You'll manage.'

She swept her hair back from her face and wound down the
window, her head full of big houses and shiny cars. 'The
remaining one-eighty we'll use to develop a quality customer
base. You'll use a low cut ratio and we'll try to get something
that feels like it's over fifty per cent pure. I want to get something close to four hundred grams out of this and I'll price it at
thirteen, fourteen thousand a gram. They'll love it.'

I rubbed some of her careless spillage into my gums. 'Who'll
love it?'

'The ex-pats will love it,' she explained. 'And the doctors,
the lawyers, the property developers, the media people – all
those people who are too good for the Costa in all their big,
pretty houses out there in the *campo*. They get consistent quality and consistent price, and they pay more for it . . . I need a
new house. New car too. I'm not having this shitheap parked
on the drive.' Her hand was shaking as she lit up a Marlboro,
and she smoked it hard and fast, like a woman outside a court-
room, running up and down lists of strengths, weaknesses,
opportunities and threats.

'You really weren't going to tell me, were you?' she said,
when my name had popped up in two of her lists. 'What were
you going to do? Piss off and leave me? Keep it all for yourself?
And what would you have done with it?' She didn't wait for
my answer. She already knew. She sighed. 'Fucking loser.'

★

The landscape slid from dramatic to dull as we wound first westwards, then northwards, to the port of Cadiz. Coastal marshes and electricity pylons succeeded the olive groves and the crags, and I felt a genuine pity for the bureaucrat charged with the promotion of this fogbound coast as a tourist destination. They called it the Costa de la Luz – the Coast of Light – but if you sat between its dunes and the Atlantic, you would see the sun rising only on another continent. We had long since passed the broadcasting limit of the FRA so I pushed a compilation tape into the slot and sang along with PJ Harvey until the novelty wore off. Luisa hugged her knees and spoke only to question the truth and the detail of my story. What was it wrapped in? Was it exactly a kilo? Was it solid or powder, and at last, the question that wouldn't go away, the most important question of all: where was it hidden?

'It's safe,' I assured her, as though that would satisfy her. It didn't.

'I didn't ask you how it was,' she replied coldly. 'I asked you where it was.'

'It's hidden, under some rocks, in the *campo*.'

'In the *campo*?' she cried. 'Are you stupid or something? What if it rains?'

I closed my eyes. 'Luisa, it hasn't rained for sixteen months, and the gear is wrapped in polythene.' I glanced at the sky, but it was still blue, and Luisa wanted more nose candy. I pulled over and watched her scoop it straight from the wrap with a long little-fingernail. She loaded both nostrils, tipping her head back to keep it in as she waited for the powder to dissolve upon her mucous membranes.

'Let's have some,' I said as she sat frozen by the aftershock. I reached for the wrap, expecting her to release it, as etiquette dictated. She held on, her grip catatonic until the paper began to tear. We both let go at the same time, and the remaining four and a bit grams fell like summer snow upon the wasteland of the Transit's footwell. Luisa screamed and I threw myself across the cab, my clammy palms cupped to catch the coke, landing heavily in her bony lap.

When the dust had settled I looked up at her. Her face was that of an astronaut who has accidentally cut his lifeline and is drifting silently away into space. She didn't want to look down.

'Can you save any of it?' she whispered.

Unlikely. 'Don't know,' I replied. 'Don't move. How windy do you think it is out there?'

Her eyes moved slowly to her left. 'It looks okay.'

'Good. I'm coming round.'

I opened my door and stepped out into a day that was okay for wind-surfing, or kite-flying, or drying laundry, but decidedly unsuitable for salvaging small amounts of powder, and the wind, as is well known, is an instrument of the Devil.

I hesitated before opening Luisa's door, and as I did, a gust rushed in like a comedy sneeze and blew all my hope away. I took a deep breath and glared at Luisa.

'That's why we have etiquette,' I growled.

9

As the sun ripened and sank lower in the sky the options on the N340 became fewer and fewer, until finally I pointed the van down the narrow throat of land between the lagoon and the Atlantic that led to Cadiz. Furniture superstores and car dealerships lined the highway, obscuring the city as we closed upon its solid, grey walls. My heart leapt a little as an olive-drab cop pointed angrily at the van and directed me, with a sweep of his gloved hand, onto the opposite carriageway.

Luisa started, pulling her feet from the dashboard and nervously gathering up the litter strewn about the cab. I felt for my hash and she emptied the ashtray into a crisp packet, as like experienced balloonists we prepared to jettison ballast. We relaxed only when we saw the ambulance ahead.

'It's okay,' sighed Luisa. 'It's just an accident.'

We slowed down as we passed the scene, peering through the crowd of spectators to see what had happened.

'Looks like a kid on a bike,' observed Luisa, 'and a van.'

A drawn little middle-aged man stood shaking and smoking on the pavement a few metres from the crowd. A blue-uniformed cop stood at his elbow, his head bent in enquiry while a couple of teenagers gawped. The little man dragged nervously on his fag, shaking his head in vehement denial or disbelief.

'There is the driver,' reported Luisa.

I grunted in confirmation, strangely disturbed by the whole affair, then spotted a 1970s mock-art deco hacienda with a neon arrow flashing *cocktels*. It was called the Hotel Zipolite.

'That's the place Helmut recommended,' I announced, pulling up outside. 'Nip in and see if they have a room.'

She offered me a look of incredulity that suggested I had just asked her to go and try to do business with the head of the local organised crime syndicate.

'*You* go,' she replied.

I went, and booked us into a large double room with a cold floor, an en suite bathroom and a view across a council estate to the ocean. A wall of fog hid the horizon, and as I watched with a bottle of brandy in one hand and a litre of San Miguel in the other, the sun slipped behind it, turning it to pink candyfloss and stealing its careful menace.

Luisa knocked back a couple of painkillers and dropped onto the bed. 'What the fuck are we doing here?'

A significant day was slipping away, and even though I was watching it go I had failed to see what it was taking with it. 'Just chilling,' I replied slowly. 'Just killing time until the coast is clear.' I chanced a look at her. She was staring unhappily at the ceiling. 'Want to watch telly?'

She sniffed. 'I want to know where the coke is.'

I lit a joint and sighed into the fog. 'The coke's safe. Trust me.'

She sat up suddenly, scratching her scalp as the ants started their subcutaneous grooving. 'You've got it here, haven't you?'

I dragged a nail across the back of my neck. 'No.'

'It's hidden in the van.'

I rubbed my nose. Her ants had woken mine up. 'No it's not.'

Luisa scratched her arms, and then behind an ear. 'It's strapped to your leg, then, or round your waist. Lift up your T-shirt.'

I raised the hem and dropped it. 'You want to fucking strip-search me?'

She wrinkled her nose. 'As if.'

'So just fucking leave it to me, and I'll sort us out.'

'No you won't sort us out,' she screamed. 'You won't fucking sort us out. You'll sell it cheap to someone who will laugh at you and you'll piss the money away and we won't be any better off than we were before you got it, and you know why?' She caught her breath. 'You know why?'

I looked at her, hoping that my eyes were saying what my mouth couldn't. She jabbed a bony finger at me. 'Because you're a fucking loser, Martin, and you live in the gutter.'

We had rows like this all the time.

'You live in the gutter with me,' I pointed out.

'Not for much longer,' she breathed. 'Not for much longer, Martin. I'm not putting up with this any more. Why should I be forced to live like a bum because I like to get high? Why do I have to live like some hippy Goa backpacking student when we make so much money? I want to live in a house full of stuff and I want to drive a car that doesn't make me ashamed, and I'm never going to get that with you . . .'

'Oh yeah?' I challenged, taking a mighty swig of the *bobadilla*, my goat well and truly up and running, 'and I'll tell you what else you don't get with me. You don't get asked to pay for your drugs. You don't get asked to pay for your house. You don't get asked to drive anywhere because you can't fucking drive and you don't get asked to do a stroke of graft because, apart from anything, you're a bloody sociopath and you scare people!' She glared malevolently at my wavering finger. 'So things aren't that bloody bad, are they?' I concluded, somewhat obliquely.

'Fuck you,' she hissed, but she always had an answer for everything.

'Yeah,' I agreed, draining the bottle and heading for the door. 'Fuck me.'

Ordinary people were checking in as I crashed through the hotel's narrow lobby. Mr and Mrs Nextcard, doing normal things and leading regular lives. They stared wide-eyed at me as I passed, their faces so familiar that they could have been anybody. Why couldn't I be like them, I wondered, as I slipped into the night.

10

So Luisa wanted to leave me, did she? And where was she going to go? Medellín, maybe, or Beverly Hills? Was there anywhere else in the world apart from Colombia and my house where a bird could be kept in cocaine in return for zero effort? Hell, in Colombia the women had at least to milk the llamas, or something. From a strictly narcotic point of view Luisa was one of the most privileged women in the world, and she wouldn't be going anywhere until she found someone capable of keeping her in the weights to which she had become accustomed.

Which reminded me. I needed to score.

I dodged into a tiny bar in a street north of the Plaza Catedral, meeting the suspicious glares of the elderly clientele with a wild and dangerous look. Helmut and Mickey often spoke the argot, the *jerga*, of the Spanish jailbird, and I had learned from them the self-conscious, Brandoesque accent with which it had to be spoken in order to impress the depth of one's porridge upon one's audience. Just as every convicted halfwit in the UK left prison as a fully fledged Cockney sparrer, his Iberian counterpart swaggered home in unfashionable clothing speaking Spanish like a stroke victim with a mouthful of frozen peas. I ordered a shot of *anis* and concentrated my mind's eye upon the skinny reflection in the mirror behind the bar until I saw a pissed Sly Stallone mumbling his lines for an audition as Colonel Kurtz, and then I knew I was ready to impress them.

The barman was a fat boy, false and hearty, but his smile evaporated when I grunted my request for directions. He looked past me, fingering a zit in the folds of his neck.

'What he say?' he called to the regulars.

'Plaza de Candelaria,' replied a half-cut pensioner without shifting his gaze from the first lottery draw of the evening. 'Tell him it's at the end of the street.'

I looked up at the barman, waiting for him to pass the message on, but he granted me only the reversed nod with accompanying nostril flare that, on this occasion, could have been translated as 'Did you hear that?' or simply 'Out.'

Some people aren't impressed by a criminal record.

I necked the shot and left them to their numbered balls, feeling light-headed, unsteady and frustrated as I stumbled into the lamplit alley. Something unravelled deep in my gut, blinked and belched an acid spray against my colon, sending my knotty quadriceps into spasm and causing my knees to tremble. I stood for a moment with my brow pushed against the cool glass of a milliner's window, blaming my pain on that last glass of *aguardiente*. I felt the suction of every grease-filled pore on my forehead as I rocked against the smeared plate, sucking wind in the feeble gasps of an unnoticed heart-attack victim as I tried half-heartedly to keep at bay the rushing panic that had finally run me to ground in this dark and stinking warren at the edge of the world. Reflected in the window I could see the perverse absurdity of my position: twenty-seven, alone and shivering in an alleyway in Cadiz, like a TV junkie.

I held my breath as a cold wave of nausea smashed me against the window, then breathed easier as it receded. Too much alcohol had been consumed in too short a time as a result of there being no cocaine available to make life more bearable. It was pathetic, and it was ugly, but through the haze of pain and confusion gathered around me in the piss-stinking doorway of the closed shop I could see that I was still free to fuck up my own life.

'*¿Que hace, hombre?*' called the boys as they rolled past me in line abreast, out looking for the mythical virgins fabled to exist within the disco bars around the docks. Something light yet insulting bounced off the back of my neck and the laughter of the passing youths defined my status as adeptly as a sociologist's thesis. Bum. Down and out. Alcoholic. Addict. Still, I hadn't killed anyone, and that was something to hold on to.

I pushed myself away from the window, leaving an impression like the Shroud of Turin, and pushed on towards the light at the end of the street.

'*Aqui termina la fiesta*,' announced a peeling poster. 'The good times end here', and I'd always thought they were just beginning.

I pulled Helmut's folded letter from my back pocket and reread it. His jailbird buddy could be located through the Bar Tosca on the Plaza de Candelaria, and as I squinted, one-eyed, through the light of the traffic, I realised how misleading a pretty name can be.

I pulled the door open and entered an empty bar decked out like a South African's impression of a Swiss chalet. Serge Gainsbourg was chain-smoking himself through some eight-track melody and it struck me that Helmut's mate was working for a man of such reactionary tastelessness that he was likely to become fashionable.

'I'm looking for Tony,' I explained to the sour-faced barmaid. She shrugged. We were all looking for something. 'We spent some time together once. He said that if I was ever in Cadiz I should look him up. Here. In this bar.'

She said something with her eyes, underlining it with a

curled lip, then she sniffed and moved away from the bar. I stared bewildered into her wake. My Spanish wasn't that good.

'All she needs is a bloody good seeing to,' said a short, oily man in a shiny blazer. 'But she won't get it in here, will she?' He jabbed my elbow as he cackled, and just as I joined in, he stopped.

'Silvestre,' he announced, extending his hand.

'Gordon,' I replied, shaking it. 'You know Tony?'

He shouted up a drink as though he were buying time. 'Sad Tony?' he asked at last.

I moved my head through a range that was neither nod nor shake and shrugged. 'Is there any other Tony?'

Silvestre sipped his *manzanilla* and stared wistfully into the past. 'I suppose not. I remember Happy Tony, and Angry Tony and Silly Tony, but they're all gone now—'

'What about Ex-con Tony?' I interjected.

Silvestre looked at me, as though noticing my shabbiness for the first time. 'That's very good,' he opined, as though it wasn't. 'Ex-con Tony. He'll like that.'

Sad Tony turned up just after I had sniffed the perfumed male clientele, felt their razor desperation and looked to the frosty barmaid for help.

'El Tragico,' she frowned, nodding towards the door. I knocked back my beer and took a couple of deep breaths. I was meeting a man called Sad Tony in a gay bar called Tosca, and I had already indicated that he and I went way back. The bird-like patrons watched our meeting with keen interest, no doubt amused by Sad Tony's predilection for a bit of poor-quality rough. He stood next to me at the bar, a big, muscular forty-year-old with greasy black hair and the musky smell of a man who believed in the power of pheromones.

'I don't think I know you,' he announced in an accent developed by the judiciary.

'You don't,' I confirmed. 'We have a mutual friend.' I showed him Helmut's letter. He read it twice, smiling the second time, running his thick, golden fingers over the text as though he might feel through to Helmut's intentions. The smile was gone when he handed the page back.

'I haven't seen this man for years.' His knuckles, I noticed, were in full-time employment, the fresh scabs stacked up on old scars. I offered him a drink, and he asked for a Coca-Cola.

'So you're looking for some action, right?' he guessed.

I nodded, slowly and with some apprehension. It was important that the exact nature of 'some action' was clearly understood between us before he led me anywhere dark.

'Er, yeah, I'm definitely hoping you can sort me out with something,' I smiled. 'My girlfriend's back at the hotel.'

'And mine has sent you here with letters.' His grin was bitter enough to burn his lips. 'How is young Helmut? Is he happy?'

'He's all right,' I replied. 'He's got a body shop.' I didn't mention Mickey.

Sad Tony laughed briefly. 'He's got a body shop.' He lit up a Ducado and pointed at me through the corrupt haze, his voice a little louder and a little higher than before. 'Bleeding from beneath the horns of the bull I pulled him. I shielded his flame as it sputtered, and held his head above the waters as he was swept away. He was grateful then, oh yes, and he promised me that he would never forget me. Know what I mean?' The man was big, gay and mad, with a history of violence splattered across his fists.

I nodded. 'Well, maybe you should come down and visit him some time. He always speaks very fondly of you, and the times you spent together.'

He turned to face me, his chest spilling over his white shirt like a split horsehair mattress. 'He speaks of me? What does he say?'

I needed cocaine to carry me through this one. 'He says he owes you big time. He says he would have died inside if it hadn't been for you. He says that not a day goes by without him thinking about you.' Helmut was going to kill me. 'It was his idea that I came to Cadiz. With my long-term girlfriend. He told me to look you up. Maybe that was his way of break-ing the ice – you know these Germans: all formality.'

Sad Tony nodded. 'So you want to go somewhere else?'

I showed him my palms. 'I'd love to, but I've just got here and, as I said, my girlfriend is waiting for me back in the hotel. I just popped out to score, and I thought I'd have a look in here on the way. I'm in town for a few days.'

Tony knew when he was being blown out. He nodded, somehow looking even sadder. 'What do you want?'

I smiled, somehow looking even happier. '*Coca.*'

'How much?'

'Five?' Fuck it, I was on holiday. 'Ten.'

I followed him to a corner table. Silvestre watched us go, a dirty grin splitting his thin lips.

'Show me the money.'

I arrived back at the hotel some ninety minutes, three lines and four beers later, confident that Luisa would be so pleased with the three fat grams I would show her that all the pain and anxiety of our separation would be forgotten in a crys-talline instant. Loser? I'd show her who was a loser. Who else could have gone out and scored in a strange city with such alacrity?

I took the stairs two at a time for the first flight, struggled a little on the second, and crawled up the third. Cocaine is not the ideal drug for enhancing athletic performance. Panting for breath, I knocked on the door, banging loud enough to be heard over the noise of the TV. Get in, get sorted and . . .

The door swung inwards and two pairs of hands grabbed my lapels and pulled me into the room. I saw the TV, a single white sock like a fallen dove upon the floor, a moustache and then the wall. In extreme close-up. Someone was shouting at me, and someone had just won a holiday for two in Rio, and somebody else had a handful of my hair. There was no pain as first my forehead, and then my nose, and then my left cheek, and then my nose again were bashed against the wall. The third time my nose hit I tasted blood, and when I bit my lip the pain started. Hard, sweaty flesh held my face hard against the wall while my right hand was lifted high between my shoulder blades. I rose onto tiptoes to relieve the tearing pain in my triceps, and as I did so another pair of hands encircled my waist and unbuckled my belt, tearing my jeans down to rest on my boots.

'*Il n'a pas un calçon, le con!*' hissed somebody, and as my mind caught up with the situation I was spun around and bent double by a boot in my unclothed groin. I hardly felt the follow-up punch in the solar plexus and fell onto my side writhing and breathless. I stopped a kick to my temple with the back of my hand.

'Hold it! Wait! I'm going to be sick!' I gasped.

Rough hands dug nails into flesh and dragged me into the lavatory. My boots and jeans were pulled off as I clawed my way up the bowl and peered over the edge.

Blood dripped freely against the white porcelain before the first rush of vomit washed it away. My stomach spasmed as I retched, my eyes bursting in their sockets and my nose dripping like a leaky tap. Confused, unreadable pain messages reached my brain and screeched across my frontal lobe like the electric bees of an untuned television set. Beneath it all, the only decipherable signals I could pick up were those of the cool, hard marble floor beneath my bare knees and the porcelainware against my throat, but it was all enough to make a reasonable assessment of the situation: I was in very deep trouble indeed, and I wasn't wearing any trousers.

I wanted to keep vomiting long enough to think about my predicament, but my persecutors were impatient. One of them was giving orders, and on his command I was dragged from the lavatory, through the bedroom and a round of amplified applause and into the bathroom. There was another body propped against the wall beneath the washbasin, hands clasped and raised as though in supplication.

'Oh no,' I mumbled through split lips. 'Luisa!'

I reached for the edge of the bath as they lifted me, my hands trembling too much to grip, my brain trying to ignore the present and put itself in a position of apprehension. It caught up as they dropped me, realising with a foolishly calm detachment that they were going to try to drown me. I tried to call out to Luisa, but I couldn't think of anything to say before they turned on the taps. My legs were in the air outside the bath, and my head, hard against the yellowing enamel, was directly beneath the gurgling rush of water. The first couple of seconds of the cascade came as a refreshing relief from the pain in my face, but as the lukewarm water filled my nostrils and washed a mixture of blood and stomach acid into my throat, it became clear that my torturers were not trying to make amends. The hard little nub of the bathplug dug into my face just behind my right eye where that side of my head lay against the bottom of the bath. I wriggled against it, but a hard hand upon my left ear insisted that I remain still as the water level rose to submerge my nostrils and my mouth. A last, feeble gasp for air was thwarted by a well-timed punch in the ribs, so I held what little breath I had left in my blackened lungs and closed my eyes. I'm not a fighter – never have been – and deep, deep down I had always suspected that when Death turned up like an ill-suited double-glazing salesman, he would have an easy sale. Behind my tightly shut lids a radial wash of whiteness faded through red to black. The surprise and the embarrassment of my unscheduled departure overshadowed the fear of my imminent death. I smiled as I welcomed the salesman over the threshold.

My last lungful bubbled up through the bath and the drowning reflex sucked the same amount of pink water back in. I coughed it back out, and sucked it back in. Maybe I had been kicking around, and maybe I stopped, or maybe they were just good at torture, but they pulled me out at the best possible moment, jerking my head up into the tap and knocking me senseless.

I was in bed, in my old room in my mum's house, and I didn't want to get up and go to school. I tried to squeeze another sixty seconds of snug, dream-spun semi-consciousness from the blankets, wishing I could be anywhere but at home, in bed, on a cold schoolday morning. I opened my eyes. I was on the bathroom floor of a hotel room in Cadiz, and I was bleeding. I was also very scared. There were people standing around my head, and one of them said: 'Clean yourself and we will talk.'

A towel dropped onto my face, and I smelled a cigarette being lit. I dabbed squeamishly at my swollen, red face with the thin white towel, my whole body feeling like an overstuffed black pudding, and waited for the surge of pain that was lurking behind a broken blood vessel or a chipped tooth to light up and fry my brain. My hair was wet and sticky, and my cheeks felt hot and tight and shiny on either side of a nose through which I seemed no longer able to breathe. I struggled into a sitting position and hung my throbbing head.

Jean-Marc and his boys had tracked me down, and how likely was that? Nobody even knew we were here, for Christ's sake, except Helmut.

And Luisa.

She was kneeling beneath the washbasin in a shiny red dress that had ridden up to expose the length of a lean, brown thigh, her bare arms stretched to where they had tied her to the bracket. Wet black blurs beneath her eyes belied a face set in stubborn indifference. I sent her a cheap smile of encouragement, but when it arrived there was nobody at home to sign for it.

I wished I could have told her that I was going to bring this temporary situation to a successful outcome, but I couldn't, and I wished that I didn't trust Helmut more than I trusted her.

'Give him a drink,' said Jean-Marc.

I wriggled around so that I could see him and grabbed the brandy bottle from the sneering little Arab kid in the tatty shell suit. I would have expected a villain as debonair and designer-led as Jean-Marc to have changed into something more appropriate for an evening on the coast – white cotton pants with a pastel polo shirt, perhaps – but he had let me down. He looked tired, grubby and very unhappy. He leaned down and lifted the brandy from my feeble grasp.

'Didn't even know they made brandy down here,' he mused, reading the label. He passed the bottle to the Arab kid, and crouched down beside me on knees that cracked.

'Listen,' he said, 'I know why you're here, and you know why I'm here. Yes?'

I shrugged, unsure of my opinion and uncertain where to look. I decided to meet his eye like an ignorant, beaten puppy.

He pouted, lit a cigarette, then chucked the pack at me. I sparked one up and sucked in a lungful.

'That kicking,' he said, 'it was to show you that I will not be lied to, and stressful as I find violence, I will have my colleagues hurt you very badly if you do not tell me where you have hidden my property. Ideally, there will be no more nastiness.'

Fair enough, I thought. Deny everything. There was still the chance that he was unsure of the facts, and a convincing show of ignorance at this stage might have been enough to persuade him of my innocence. It was an assumption of one per cent hope cut with ninety-nine of the basest stupidity, and I made it.

'Listen,' I began. 'Jean-Marc . . .' I tried to rise to my feet but he held my arm and gently pushed me back to my knees.

'Tell me,' he said, with the quiet insistence of a responsible, caring adult.

'You're going to get mad again, aren't you?'

He sighed. 'That depends. Tell me.'

I could feel the eyes of the others upon my swollen face like peacekeeping paratroopers watching a drunk in a minefield. I took a deep breath.

'This thing you're after, the thing you think Yvan gave me—'

Jean-Marc held up a finger to still my tongue. He smiled quickly at his accomplices, and rose to his feet.

'Let me guess: you're going to tell me you haven't got it, right?'

I nodded vigorously. 'Exactly.'

He nodded back, his smile leaving his eyes and then his lips. '*Les gars,*' he said slowly, with an irked shake of his head. His boys perked up. 'Tap this bastard hard.'

I bleated like a little lost lamb as the two slavering wolves fell on me like badly dressed Assyrians and beat five years of my life from my internal organs while Jean-Marc watched a documentary about Mexico at maximum volume. When I came round I was curled in a ball on the wipe-clean bathroom floor, listening to the rush of my blood through my swollen ears and sucking on a split lip. Some parts of my body didn't hurt, but I couldn't find them as I scanned myself from top to toe for serious injury. My legs, though stiff and bruised, seemed to be all right, and my hands had escaped serious injury, although my fingers hurt where they had protected my head from Benoit's boots. My face and my jaw felt like they had been processed in a blender with twelve pounds of pig iron, but worst of all seemed to be my ribcage. Or else the cut on my head that made light painful. Or maybe my back. Certainly my kidneys were going to bleed when I next pissed, and my heart was already panicking. I coughed, just to see what would happen, and it hurt, the pain amplified by the rush of pure fear that knocked the denial from my mind and let it see just how ugly and serious my life had suddenly become. It seemed very likely that I was starting out on a very short, very uncomfortable journey through the rest of my life, and that I would be lying wide-eyed, swollen and fly-blown in the weeds before next Saturday night wearing a big, black, crunchy halo of dried blood.

I'd probably be found by goats.

'Are you hurt?' asked Luisa, like she cared.

I pulled myself to my feet and wrapped a thin towel around

my waist. 'What do you think?' I replied, with all the sarcasm I could muster. 'What about you?'

'Like you care,' she muttered. 'All you care about is yourself. You knew what could happen, and you knew I wanted to come out with you, and you just . . .', she paused, trying to sniff back the tears, but her nose was as corroded as mine, and they came anyway. 'You just fucking went out and left me here.'

She took a deep breath. 'YOU FUCKING LEFT ME HERE! YOU BASTARD!'

I stood before her, helpless and useless as she sobbed, seeing the situation entirely from her point of view. I couldn't remember the row that had ruined our night in romantic Cadiz, and not one of the weasels that lived in my head could come up with a valid excuse for leaving her alone in the hotel. I owed her an apology.

'Fuck your apology,' she replied, startling me. 'Untie my hands.'

'It's best if I don't,' I whispered. 'What happens if they come in? They might give us both another kicking.' I could smell brandy somewhere in the room. It was a good treatment for shock.

'Untie my hands now!' she growled. They had ripped a sheet to make her bonds, but the knots were much looser than I had expected them to be, and I freed her with a speed that falsely suggested competence. She wiped her eyes with her hands, smoothed back her hair and shifted to her knees, lowering her dress over her shoulder.

'Look what that scum did to me,' she hissed, pushing her left breast forward. An oval of uneven teeth marks the size and shape of a walnut shell surrounded her nipple, the inflammation already darkening to a sullen bruise.

'And here,' she added, lifting her arm to show another bite on her triceps.

I winced. 'Is that all they did?' It didn't come out the way I'd meant it to.

'What do you mean "is that all"? Isn't this enough?' she screamed.

She was shaking from fear, from shock, from cold and from fury, bound and bruised in a bathroom in Cadiz. I reached out and touched her arm, and she recoiled.

'Don't you *ever* touch me.'

'I'm sorry,' I mumbled, and I meant it.

'Sorry is not enough,' she replied. 'Nothing will ever be enough for this thing. Ever.'

She was right: maybe now was a good time to leave her.

'You're a fucking bastard. They kept asking me for their cocaine, as if I knew where it was. You should have told me. You should have told me where it was buried, and then none of this would have happened. Jesus Christ, it's less than a kilo. Is all this worth less than a kilo?' It would have taken me some time to do the maths, but Luisa wasn't waiting for a reply. 'You should have told me, Martin.'

'I did tell you,' I insisted. 'I told you it was buried, and I didn't tell you where for exactly this reason.' The aroma of cheap *coñac* was becoming a distraction.

'What reason?' Her lip curled. Her eyes were glowing like warning lights: if she didn't put at least a quarter of a gram into her bloodstream pretty soon, her engine would stop running.

'This reason. If I'd have told you where it was they would have beaten it out of you and then they would probably have killed you. It was better for me to keep it all to myself and let them take it out on me. What you don't know can't hurt you.'

I knew what she was thinking, and she was right.

'You're lying.'

'I'm not,' I insisted.

'Prove it,' she challenged.

I didn't have the time to waste arguing with Luisa. I needed to develop a strategy with which to negotiate with Jean-Marc, and as far as I could determine it would be one of total compromise. He would come in and ask for the cocaine, and I would tell him exactly where it was. Then he would kill us. The sink was full of broken glass, the smell of *bobadilla* evaporating from the shards.

'How did the brandy bottle get broken?' I asked, aghast.

'Over your head, you idiot,' sighed Luisa. 'Can't you smell your hair? You stink like a bum.'

Both Luisa and I had a greater chance of survival if I could persuade the Frogs that they would never find the coke without us. I could tell them that it was hidden away like a crock of Moorish gold in a place they would never, ever find on their own. I would volunteer to show them where it was, on the understanding that Luisa was dropped off somewhere safe and public. If I didn't come back, she would make the necessary calls and everything would end in tears. That way, both our lives would be saved and she would never know the true quantity involved. I ran the plan back through my mind, hoping to refine it but succeeding only in remembering it, or most of it.

'Are you deaf?' I jumped – Luisa had been talking. 'I asked you where the coke is buried.'

My face might have been filled in, but it looked blank. My swollen mouth hung open as I looked at her. She scowled.

'You have to tell me, Martin, can't you see?'

I would have told her anything for a cigarette, but otherwise I would have to think about it, and right now I was busy thinking about the little ball of polythene deep inside my Wranglers.

'If you don't tell me then I am nothing to them; I am surplus . . .'

'Superfluous,' I corrected her. 'It's "superfluous", although "surplus" will do, I suppose.'

'Whatever.' She shook her head angrily. 'If I knew where the coke was, then they wouldn't need you . . .' She thought about what she had just said and called the sentence back for modification. 'They would need both of us, I mean.'

Yeah, right. I suddenly wondered why they had thrown me back into the bathroom, and why they had left us together so long. I looked at the bathroom door, and wondered how many Frenchmen would fall over if I limped across and pulled it open. I needed a cigarette, though, and they could only say no. Then break my fingers for asking, but it was easily worth the risk for just one Marlboro. And maybe the chance to grab the wrap from the back pocket of my jeans.

'I'm going to get us a fag,' I said.

She forgot about saving her life for a moment. 'Good idea,' she replied.

I pulled open the bathroom door and cowered like a pensioner in my bloodstained towelling skirt.

'¿Qu'est-ce que tu veut?'

I looked up. The Arab kid was alone in the room, sitting in front of the TV. A coyote tiptoed along a shimmering desert track as though walking on broken glass.

'Allez, va-t-en dedans.'

'I only want a smoke,' I wheedled, 'or two, if you've got spare.'

He jumped to his feet and snatched the pistol from the top of the telly.

'Over there, on the bed,' he said, pointing with the gun.

'Thanks,' I smiled, nodding like a felt dog, 'cheers.'

I grabbed the pack and the lighter and backed towards to the bathroom. My jeans were lying by the bedroom door.

'Where are the others?' I tried.

'Downstairs,' muttered the kid, 'drinking cocktails. Now get back in there.'

'Can I get my jeans?' I asked politely. 'It doesn't matter if I can't. It's just that it's a bit . . .'

A flicker of anger crossed his face like the shadow of a crow. I was beginning to piss him off.

I waved. 'Okay. Doesn't matter.' It did, though.

I lit up two fags and stuck one in Luisa's mouth.

'Didn't you hear what the kid said?' I whispered. 'They're downstairs in the bar. This is our chance!'

She raised an eyebrow, squinting through the smoke. 'Chance to do what?'

If the only TV show she had ever seen had been *The A-Team*, she would have known the answer. I looked at her and sighed.

'To get away. To escape.'

'What are you talking about? I'm not escaping.' She said it as though I had suggested a white wedding. 'It's a stupid idea.'

'It's not a stupid idea,' I retorted, my voice a little higher and a little louder. 'Out there is an eighteen-year-old kid, on his own, watching telly. You're going to take that dress off, go out there, walk right up to him and tell him that you're cold, and that you want to be warmed up. Then you're going to throw your arms around him. Then I'm going to come out and take the gun off him.' I looked right at her and grinned. 'Then we're going to escape.'

Luisa looked at me as though I'd said something incredibly stupid, then tipped her head back and looked at the ceiling. 'Fuck off,' she sighed. 'This isn't a movie.'

I banged my forehead against the bathtub. 'Course it's not a fucking movie. It's real life and it'll all end in tears if we don't seize every opportunity we have to escape. There will be no second chances.'

'Just tell me where you've buried it,' she replied, still looking at the ceiling and sucking hard on her shortening fag.

I ignored her demand, my cheeks burning with rage at her stupidity, her insouciance, her poker-faced conniving to save her own sallow skin and abandon me.

She was watching me impatiently, blowing smoke like a train that was about to leave, and, looking back at her, I saw where she was heading. She had a deal. She had to have a deal. They had started on her, and even though at that point she truly had nothing to offer in return for her life, she had made a speculative deal with Jean-Marc. Furthermore, if she was willing to forgo the opportunity to escape, then her pay-off had to be more than life alone. The smoke was becoming intolerably hot so I lit another from its glowing dog-end.

'Give me one,' said Luisa. I tossed her the pack. 'Did you hear me?' she added.

'We've got a golden opportunity to get away from this situation,' I retorted. 'What's your problem?'

She exhaled a plume of blue. 'It's a shit plan. One of us will get shot, and anyway, they've got the van keys.'

'So what?' I protested. 'We'll wait for them to come back and I'll take the keys back off them.' I had swiftly increasing reservations over my ability to deliver on that last statement. So did Luisa.

'No you won't,' she sneered. 'You'll just get beaten up again. It's better that we go along with them.'

'Yeah, right,' I mocked, 'and then they'll kill us.'

Luisa pursed her lips and shook her head as though she had been in this situation many, many times.

'That depends,' she said. 'Just tell me where it's buried.'

'I took it to El Gatocin,' I replied, with perhaps too much haste and too little consideration. If Luisa were straight, then the whereabouts of the cocaine was her life insurance, and if I had lied on the declaration, then her policy would be null and void. By failing to disclose the true location of Yvan's poisonous legacy, I was effectively condemning my girlfriend to the short, sharp, barely felt hammer blow of a bullet in the head.

'Where?'

'El Gatocin.' I couldn't look at her. Weasel that I know I am, I cannot face the subject of my deceit if I do not believe wholeheartedly in my own lie. Look hard, and some perverse integrity will become apparent. 'Out along the river valley.'

Her eyes were hard upon me, urging me to share the secret, but I could not reveal the true hiding place. I could bleed her dry of promises and assurances but I couldn't exhaust her capacity for betrayal. She knew that I knew that, but she didn't say so.

'Where on the river valley?'

'About two klicks down, on the left bank, there's a *finca*. Some mad old woman lives there, and it's buried at the edge of her property near a *cal*-painted stone. Give the old bag my regards if you see her.' I would never give Antonita La Buena the chance to put her scrawny, leather hand on my forehead and tell me I was already dead, although I would be, if Luisa ever met her.

'Draw me a map.' She lit her third cigarette in five minutes. 'I need a map.'

'With what?' I replied. 'You don't need a map. I know where it's buried, and that's all that matters.'

'Whatever,' she sighed, rising to bare feet and smoothing her dress. She paused before the mirror and dabbed at her eyes with the corner of a wet towel. 'I'm sure we'll find it.'

I sat on the edge of the bath, absorbing the situation in bullet time. I wanted to shake her hand, to congratulate her on a job well done, to applaud a virtuoso performance. If Luisa had been a matador I'd have given her both ears. The trouble was that it was me who'd been stabbed in the back.

'I don't believe you,' I stammered, although I did.

She shrugged. 'I don't care. I'm going for a drink. I think you'd better stay here.' She paused by the bathroom door. 'How does it feel?'

She wouldn't look bad, I thought, meeting Jean-Marc for a drink in the bar. Dark hair, red dress, brown skin and her stage make-up repaired. 'How does what feel?' I replied.

'Being fucked,' she said. She didn't wait for an answer.

Jean-Marc and his spotty sidekick were laughing as they came back into the room and even though the bulk of my feelings towards them were derived from either blind hope or wide-eyed fear, right now I found their alcoholic good humour annoying. This hotel had been my choice, and it should have been me staggering through the door all margarita'd up, not them. What confidence I had gained from my feeble plotting had soon been overshadowed by the fear that I had let pass my best opportunity for escape. My mind was splitting into multiple spheres of worry, and I knew that no matter how I sang and danced for these bastards, it wouldn't save my miserable life.

As the shrivelling effects of the last line of coke were metabolised from my system I turned my spine towards the cold and waited for the tap on my shoulder.

'Let's go!' called Jean-Marc.

Luisa came behind them wearing fresh make-up, and as she stood by the door, hugging her elbows, I tried to meet her eyes and she looked away. 'Hang on a minute,' she protested. 'I thought we had a deal.'

Jean-Marc frowned. 'What deal?'

'You told me that as soon as we knew where the coke was, he would be surplus, remember?'

Jean-Marc was happy. He loved it when a plan came together, and he could afford a few moments to indulge his informant. 'So what do you suggest I do with him?' he asked.

'Drown him in the bath or something,' she replied. 'I don't know – you're the gangsters here, not me.'

'Luisa?' I cried. 'What the fuck are you talking about?'

She sighed irritably. 'Can't you shut him up?'

Benoit cocked a fist and I held up my hands in surrender.

'Don't you do something with a pillow over the head and then – *bang?*' she asked, making a girly gun shape with her fingers which I didn't find cute.

Jean-Marc approached her and put his hands on her bare upper arms. 'Listen,' he soothed, as though placating a neurotic child, 'let's take him with us for the time being. It will be much better and easier for us to get rid of him in a remote spot. Less mess, less chance of getting caught . . .'

Luisa was shaking her head. 'Why can't we make him eat sleeping pills and drink a bottle of vodka. That way it will look like suicide. He was sad because I left him,' she added, by way of a motive.

Jean-Marc glanced at Benoit, then back at Luisa. 'Got any pills?'

She nodded. 'I'll get them. I've got Mogadon, Imovane and Temazepam.'

Jean-Marc stopped her. 'What about the vodka?'

'There's that cheap spic brandy,' chipped in the Arab kid. 'What about that?'

'I'm wearing it,' I said.

'So can't someone go out and buy a bottle?' pleaded Luisa.

Jean-Marc shook his head. 'This is getting stupid. He's coming with us and we'll do it cleanly when we're out of town.'

He looked at me. 'Get dressed.' His voice seemed to come from very far away. Luisa picked up my jeans and rifled the pockets. She gasped when my ten-gram wrap hit the duvet, snatched it up and went into the bathroom.

'What's the point?' I mumbled.

'There isn't one, really,' mused Jean-Marc.

He was wrapping the pistol in an oil-stained handkerchief. 'Benoit will ride with you. *Liebchick* in there will ride with Youssan and me.' He paused in his careful cloaking of the hand-gun, then changed his mind and unwrapped it.

'Benoit: take this. Shoot him in the head if necessary, but wait until his van has stopped before you do it.'

Benoit sidestepped the piece and came up alongside Jean-Marc to take it. He pulled the slide back a little, peered inside, then let it click forward before dropping the magazine into his hand. A fat, sweaty copperhead winked at me before being reinserted like a cure-all pessary into the black plastic butt of the weapon. Benoit clearly did not need to be told where and how to shoot a man.

I hobbled into my trousers, wishing for a little more room in the crotch and a little less in the pocket. My hard-won ball of powder had gone, and with it all hope, and for the first time on this, the worst night of my life, I wanted to lie down and cry.

11

Outside in the damp night I waited in the Transit with Benoit while Jean-Marc, Youssan and Luisa went off to find the Mercedes. As it roared from a narrow side street I followed it into the traffic, miserably wondering how much blame I had to accept for my current predicament. Were there precautions that I could have taken that would have saved my life, or was I just unlucky? I hoped that I was unlucky, but deep, deep beneath the bullshit struggled a pale stem of truth that insisted it was only the idiotic and the indolent who blamed luck for their misfortunes.

The essential cause of all this, of course, was impetuosity, runaway impetuosity. I had gone charging in with the tunnel vision of a pricked bull, and I had been ambushed. It wasn't my fault: it just happened.

I was unlucky.

Three klicks out of Cadiz the Transit started wheezing so I flashed Jean-Marc a signal that I needed to pull over. The van needed fuel, and I felt like I needed to be sick. It was unfair to blame my predicament entirely upon impetuosity – if I hadn't displayed a certain alacrity then I wouldn't have inherited the cocaine in the first place. My mistake, I decided as I followed Jean-Marc into the Texaco, was kindness. It was my heartfelt concern for Yvan's family that had put this pack of hyenas on my trail, and now Wolf-Girl had led them to my lair. If I had done the traditional thing and paid a *campesino* to chuck the cadaver into the reservoir then I would have been whooping it up in some strobe-lit nightclub right now instead of sitting beneath the flickering neon of an out-of-town service station. Informing Yvan's next of kin was a kind, thoughtful and considerate act, and, above all, it was the most stupid fucking thing I had ever done in my whole, pitiful life. It was more than gravity that kept my head down as I pulled myself tenderly out of the Transit with the bright, orange lights of Cadiz at my back. I tiptoed over to Jean-Marc.

'Any chance of having some of my money back?' I ventured. 'I need some fags.'

'Give him some cigarettes,' said Jean-Marc to the Arab kid, looking at me the whole time like a child might look at a wounded earwig. The Arab kid lobbed me half a carton of Marlboro.

'You lot are a bit free with the fags, aren't you?' I remarked. 'Got any coke?'

Jean-Marc sneered and turned away, pausing to crush some other crawling thing with the toe of his boot. 'Half fill it,' he called to Benoit.

Back on the highway and as happy as a man with a hundred cigarettes I tried to make a friend of Benoit. For the sake of amicability I ignored the recent memory of his participation in my torture and hoped for a similar concession on his part.

'What do you think of Spain, then?' I asked him.

''S all right,' he replied.

'Yeah?' I took my eyes from Jean-Marc's tail lights and looked across at Benoit. 'It's a great place.'

He was staring through the side window at the passing traffic and the blackness beyond the rubbish-strewn roadside, too preoccupied to reply.

'Beautiful women,' I added. 'Gorgeous women. And lovely

weather. A little more rain would be a good thing.' He remained stubbornly mute, so I kept probing for the button that would turn him on.

'The jails here, so I've heard, are among the most progressive in the world.' I glanced across again, but his expression was that of a man with dangerous debts on a bus full of holidaymakers.

'They even allow conjugal visits,' I continued needlessly, 'which is nice.'

He sighed, then turned to face me. He realised now that I wanted to talk, and despite his own preoccupations about the present and the future he obviously felt that it would be a good thing and an honourable thing to allow me to discuss my passions. He rubbed his face and sniffed. 'Why don't you shut the fuck up?'

That hurt, and no retort would soothe it, so I bit my lip and looked at the road. Benoit yawned, scratched, picked his nose and fidgeted, his stretched nonchalance failing to cover his nervous tension. We drove for twenty minutes in painful silence, the creaking of the van and the crackle of tobacco sometimes audible over the clatter of the aged diesel engine. I had yet to find the atmosphere oppressive: Luisa had trained me to withstand this treatment for weeks at a time, but Benoit, used to the close contact of chattering men, was now missing the social aspect of our journey. He stared hard into my face, some bizarre jailhouse rule insisting that he caused me to begin a conversation. His gaze stuck to my stubbled cheek like spittle, but I ignored it. He'd told me to shut the fuck up, so the fuck up I'd stay shut. When the look alone failed to goad a response, he began grunting and chuckling and making little noises of surprise. At last he laughed out loud, stretching in his seat and repeating himself for emphasis. I ignored him, suddenly preoccupied with the matter of Luisa's treachery.

He must have read my thoughts. 'How the fuck did some-one like him end up with someone like her?' he mused, aloud. He spoke French with the flat, sinusy twang of the Midi, a place where the bread was *pang* and the wine was *vang*.

I fumbled for the cigarettes, aware that I had not yet won because he had not addressed me directly. The white line in the middle of the highway seemed to glow as it passed beneath the Transit, inviting me to hang my head from the driver's door and drag my nose along the rushing tarmac. I lit up and sucked hard, trying to smoke out all my cravings as my joints swelled and my subcutaneous layer began to vibrate with the itching hatchings of a thousand million brown and shiny crawling things. Outside, the *campo* slid by as dry and dirty as my ulcer-ated tongue, and I wished that I were out there, hidden in some fold in the earth, so far from the road that I could never be found.

I shuddered as I realised that Jean-Marc had probably arranged for exactly that to happen to me. It was too late to play the silly psychological games of bored men, so I threw in my hand.

'Tell me something,' I requested. 'Back there, in the hotel, what did she mean when she told him that they had a deal?'

Benoit chuckled and shook his head. 'How the hell did you ever manage to pull a bird like that?' he replied unhelpfully.

A white-painted post and rail fence fell in beside the road, and I noticed a shotgun-peppered roadsign that said 'Beware of Bulls' race past the van. Benoit saw neither. I spat my smoke against the bug-splattered windscreen. 'I gave her what she wanted, simple as that.'

'She's obviously not as demanding as she appears,' he grunted.

I was tempted to ask him how long it had been since he had

enjoyed a relationship with a woman lasting longer than the time his money could buy, but I saw no sense in losing blood over the issue.

'So what was the deal?'

'Oh, you don't want to know the deal,' he advised.

'Why not? Will it spoil my night?'

He shrugged like a bouncer. 'Okay. It's your funeral.'

After he had told me, I realised that he had been right. I didn't want to know. They had found her in the bar, all dressed up with nowhere to go. Jean-Marc had greeted her like an old friend, using his bonhomie and her shocked silence to whisper sweet nothings into her ear that the other customers would never have heard. He paid for her drink, and they slipped up to the room. Benoit sipped his beer and watched the reception desk. As soon as it was left unattended, he hit the stairs, leaving the Arab kid to watch the street outside the hotel. Up in the room, Benoit found Luisa and Jean-Marc deep in negotiation. Jean-Marc had thanked the Lord when he found Luisa alone in the bar, and his plan had been to hold her booty as collateral against the return of his booty. Luisa had rejected that plan as unworkable. It was crude and offered no room for manoeuvre on either side. As a business agreement it was as sophisticated as Yosemite Sam, and she couldn't work with him on those terms. Instead, she suggested a plan of her own. She would find out from me where the drugs were buried, and she would take Jean-Marc to that place. In return, he would give her fifty per cent of the stash, and he would kill me. Jean-Marc rejected her terms as ridiculous, and I was inclined to agree. Fifty per cent of the stash was two and a half kilos. He told her that ten per cent was the best he could offer, and to his surprise, Luisa accepted, but only on the understanding that he would shoot her lying bastard of a boyfriend some place where it really hurt.

The bathroom scene had been Luisa's idea. She'd seen it in some black-and-white movie and it had worked a treat on Montgomery Clift. The Arab kid had burst into the room an hour or so later. He had seen me weaving along the street singing 'Paradise City', and as I fumbled to put my key in the lock, they were ready for me.

He'd missed one detail, one dark and swollen detail. 'So which one of you bit her?' I asked.

Benoit scraped his tongue along his teeth. 'Not me,' he shrugged. 'She really hates you, doesn't she?'

'I know that,' I retorted. She was going to hate me even more when she turned up at Antonita La Buena's house and found the cupboard bare. I hadn't yet worked out how I was going to play my ace, but it was up my sleeve, and it was all I had. I felt that I should be angered by her treachery, but all I felt was confusion. Her deceit seemed too contrived, too premeditated to be the consequence of that row in the hotel room. Luisa needed me, if only as her dealer. No one could replace me on the terms she currently enjoyed and she was smart enough to know a good thing when she saw it. Killing me made no sense at all, and I wondered if they would let me have one last line.

'You're the one who's going to do it, aren't you?'

He was looking out into the night, and I saw the hairs on the back of his neck rise like the hackles on a cornered terrier.

'You're going to kill me,' I repeated. 'Admit it.'

He wound down the window and pushed his face into the warm slipstream, mopping his brow on the sleeve of the night.

I laughed: a fake, cynical little snort. 'Come on, Benoit, admit it. You're going to kill me.' I took a drag on my fag and hissed the smoke between my teeth. 'At least be man enough to admit it, you fucking *lache*.'

Benoit looked at me for a long moment, then opened a fresh packet of cigarettes. 'Just fucking drive, will you?' he sighed in reply.

I felt my heart contract and my bowels loosen. Some time in the near future this man was going to cock that Heckler and snap down the blinds on my life. Ridiculous, I thought, but, absurd as it seemed, it was true. My tongue stuck to the roof of my mouth and as the blackness seeped into the cab I felt the air thin out, the oxygen consumed. Like a drunken midnight swimmer I began to gasp, suddenly and fearfully aware that I had swum out beyond the stretched reflections of the lights on the shore and that I couldn't make it back.

'Speed up,' said Benoit. 'Keep close to them.'

I stepped on the diesel and shook my head slowly. This was my first encounter with dangerous criminals in over fifteen years of casual drug abuse and lawbreaking, and it seemed both inappropriate and unjust that so severe a sanction should be imposed upon me for what was technically my first offence.

'It's not fair, you know,' I whined to Benoit. 'I didn't know that stuff belonged to Jean-Marc, and he never fucking asked for it, and now I'm going to get killed . . .' My vocabulary was suddenly overwhelmed by a flash-flood of self-pitying emotion and, for the first time in as long as I could remember, I started to sob. The notion that I could die was like an abstract work of art the size of the *Sagrada Familiale*: it could be seen, examined and understood from a distance, but close up it made no sense at all and succeeded only in upsetting the senses. My death was the destruction, the annihilation of a universe, and as such it was beyond understanding. My mind shut down for safety reasons and I felt my body shrink a little in the discomfort of my seat. 'It's not fair,' I muttered.

Benoit shrugged. He figured it wasn't his problem.

'You don't have to kill me.'

'You didn't have to tell that mad bitch where it was buried. You could have told us. To be honest, you've played this situation like a bit of a jerk.

 'You would still have done me in.'

He didn't reply, but he'd given me an idea. I could rip the carpet from beneath Luisa's painted toes and tell Jean-Marc the true location of the cocaine, but that wouldn't necessarily save my life. Jean-Marc would not wish to be rid of me until he had the cocaine in his hands, and there, in a spot chosen for its remoteness, he could have me laid to rest with ease. Now that Luisa had shown her colours I could no longer rely upon her to look after my interests, and the only way I could realistically hand the cocaine to Jean-Marc and live was as part of a team. I should have brought Helmut with me, I thought ruefully.

'There has got to be some other way out of this,' I protested, to nobody in particular. Nobody replied.

I wound down my window and let the night into the cab. It blended with the blackness in my head and urged me to take Benoit with me when I died, right now, at high speed, via that roadside boulder. It didn't help.

'Why do I have to get shot over this?' I asked.

'You don't,' mumbled Benoit.

'But I will, won't I?'

He folded his arms and hung his head, looking up through his eyebrows at his boss's tail lights.

'You see,' I cried, 'you can't answer me, can you?'

He raised a hand and rubbed his cheek so that I couldn't see his face. I laughed, but there was no joy in my triumph.

'What a big, fucking man you are, huh? What a big villain you must be. You're going to kill me, blow my fucking brains all over the sierras because some twat with more money than you tells you to, and you don't even know why, do you? You don't even know why you're killing me, except that your boss is too clever and too chicken to do it himself. What does that tell you about yourself?' I ranted, and effectively, for I saw the colour rising from his boil-scarred neck. I had never goaded a violent man before, but it came easily to me and somehow eased the aches and pains engendered by my enforced abstinence from my medication. I wasn't even sure why I was winding him up, but the bitter words were burning my tongue and I had nothing to lose by letting them fly. I wished only that I could back my tough talk with a matching walk, but that shortfall wasn't going to stop me now.

'I'll tell you what it tells me about you, *mec*,' I continued. 'Tells me that you're a peasant, a bit-part player, a servant. You're one of those dumb bastards who think that being a bouncer gives you power, that being a henchman makes people respect you, that your poxy little pistol makes up for your poxy little dick . . .'

If I hadn't had my window open then Benoit's punch would probably have put my head through the glass. I'd had enough kicking for one night, and by now I knew that a punch in the jaw came with delayed-action pain.

'Fuck you,' I sneered. 'Do something big next time, like using that big gun on me, or won't your boss let you? I bet you're into body-building, too.'

'Stop the van,' said Benoit.

'Fuck you,' I replied, glancing at him from the corner of my puffed-up eye. He stretched in the seat, pulling his backside up from the vinyl and tugging the pistol from his jeans.

He cupped the weapon on his lap.

'Stop the van,' he repeated.

'Fuck you,' I insisted, and this time it hurt. Some hard and pointed part of the pistol seemed to crush my ear against my skull as he snapped it against the side of my head and I winced as ripples of pain rolled across my eyes. He hit me again in the same place, with the same piece of metal, and I swerved across the carriageway. All I had to do now was to grab the gun and boot him out of the van.

'Stop the van.'

I stepped on the brakes and the Transit shuddered to a halt, then stalled.

'Keys.'

I ignored him, and he hit my ear again. Behind the pain, which had dulled with repetition, I felt my mind sway towards unconsciousness as something warm ran down my neck. I handed him the keys, and he climbed out of the van.

'Out,' he ordered, appearing at my door, and with one hand holding my broken ear I slid down from my seat. My knees were weak and it took little effort on Benoit's part to tap me onto the dusty shoulder of the deserted road. He squatted down beside me and whispered into my good ear. 'I don't need to tell you this, but I will: there are two things you need to know about Jean-Marc. One, he detests liars. He takes it personally, as an insult to his intelligence. Considering the circles he mixes in, it's an inconvenient attitude, and that leads me to number two. Jean-Marc is a very angry man, but, as you have guessed, he has never killed anybody. He reckons that on this trip he will kill someone, and if you ask me, it is something he needs to do, for the sake of his reputation. He knows that he's got it in him, and I do too, but where we come from there's a lot of people who think he's all mouth and pussy. This is something he needs to make good.' He prodded me with the pistol. 'Personally, I don't give a fuck about you but if I were you I would make it a firm policy from now on to tell the truth, and nothing but. That way you'll make it easy for him to hold on to his cherry.'

We looked up at the same time and saw Jean-Marc's tail lights reversing towards us along the shoulder. Benoit stood up.

'You want to see my dick, you fucking pansy English PD?'

'What's the matter?' yelled Jean-Marc.

I struggled to my knees and squinted through the red glow of the Merc's rear lights to see if Luisa was showing the same level of concern. She wasn't.

'*N'importe quoi,*' called Benoit. 'Just showing him how things work.'

'*Connard,*' he shot back, and I fancied that some of the shrapnel caught Benoit. 'Let's get a fucking move on, eh?' He gunned the engine and drowned out any possibility of reply.

'Get back in there,' said Benoit. 'I'll drive.'

The stars seemed to move across the light blue night sky as I wobbled around the van and pulled myself into the passenger seat. Our headlights fluttered in the dust cloud of Jean-Marc's impatient departure, and I had hardly lowered my well-kicked backside onto the bench seat before Benoit stepped angrily on the gas and lurched into his wake. I closed my eyes and rubbed gently at the crushed and swollen gristle blossoming on the side of my head like a flower too ugly to bloom by day. The shock was wearing off and the adrenalin was ebbing, leaving pain in their stead as God's reminder that I was still alive.

12

I was dreaming hard and fast, breathless and mumbling with the headlights of the passing traffic flashing across my face. My body was temporarily out of order, slumped in the front of the Transit, and my mind was bent beneath the sun, stooped low on a dusty hillside in Bordeaux.

There were some grapes that weren't worth picking. They spoiled the wine, this old Arab was telling me, because they lay too close to the earth and too far from the scratched and bleeding fingers that sought to pluck them from the vine. It was the art of the *vendageur* to recognise the grapes that would spoil the vintage, for the *noblesse* of a bottle depended not on the grapes crushed within it, but upon those that were excluded. I stopped listening for a moment and looked at my lecturer. He was no more French than I was, with his grey eyebrows and his old man's beard and his desert tan, yet he seemed confident of persuading me of his credentials. It was all about purity, he said, and that was the truth, although it struck me that the French talked a lot of bollocks about wine. Luisa talked a lot of bollocks, too, but I could see her through the trees on the other side of the room, and she was trying to tell me something. I smiled at the girl sitting next to me and passed her the joint. She said something as I stood up, but I didn't hear. Luisa was waiting for me. Her boyfriend didn't know that she was there, nor did he know that I was going to save her from him, to whisk her away to a place where the sun always shined and the drugs were free and the music could make you cry. The problem was that I couldn't make it all the way over there, not yet. I needed to sit down for a while on the empty armchair next to the corpse on the sofa. His shoulders, his hair and his face were dusted with several grams of the whitest, the purest cocaine, sprinkled upon him perhaps by his old friends and customers as a homage to his services. I sat down on an armchair next to the sofa, smiled at the body and leaned across to lick the powder from his cold cheek, but as I lowered my face to his my nostrils tingled with the cold smell of Alpine snow. It melted on my tongue, its crystals of ice rather than cocaine hydrochloride, and as the meltwater ran across a dry eye and over the bridge of a broken nose I realised that I knew this man from somewhere.

'I've come from the past to fuck up your future,' he mumbled.

I was licking my arm to remove the taste of his face from my tongue.

'I don't think I've got one,' I replied.

'Not now, you haven't,' he smiled, his eyes staring ahead and his body still.

'I got to go and meet this German bird,' I told him.

He smiled again. '*Jusqu'ici, tout va bien.*'

I lit up a fag. 'What's that s'posed to mean?'

'We should go travelling together,' he replied. 'Buy a camper and drive to Nepal, have fun, have adventures. We should live a little.'

I lit up a fag. 'Why?'

His eyes turned to meet mine, the whites like antique ivory and the pupils dry and hard. 'Because life's too short.'

I thought about it, but I couldn't answer. My attention was directed towards a weight, perhaps a boot, pressing angrily against my side. Something heavy and pointed, like a pair of pliers, dug into my skull above the hairline and my jeans had shrunk to crush my crotch in a denim vice. I lit a cigarette and tried to lift myself out of the armchair. The world span away, and I squeezed my eyes shut, remembering and then forgetting the words of the girl as I stood up. That world was gone for ever, and an acne-scarred assassin was driving me out of chaos and into purgatory. Or maybe I was going straight to hell.

I opened my mouth and felt my lip split open, the stinging pain soothed by a spill of blood against my teeth, and I looked around the cab for something to drink. My body probably craved water, but my mind had long since disavowed my corporeal needs. I wanted brandy, or vodka, or whisky, and though my bones craved calcium, and my wasted muscles screamed for complex sugars, I wanted cocaine, or amphetamine, or diamorphine. I settled for nicotine. The filter kept sticking to the cut on the inside of my lower lip, and as I pulled it off the pain rolled like backed-up rainwater along the gutter and up the downpipe to splash against my brain.

Outside, in the darkest hour of the longest night, a dog barked briefly as we rolled through Alcala de los Gazules, our passage unseen by any of its inhabitants, the echoes of our engines bouncing off the whitewashed walls and reverberating through the *naranjas* to be heard by only the hounds and the *burros*. Out to the east lay the Sierra de los Melones, and beyond that the castle and the end of the story. I looked up at the stars and felt something crumble and settle a little lower in my gut. I found Orion standing legs astride across Andalusia and remembered a night when Luisa had taken advantage of an

acid tab to make the constellation the first letter of the word
'Hope'. She had spent hours on her back in a leaky rowing
boat finding the remaining letters of the word and had tri-
umphantly spelled out her discovery for me until I too saw
Hope in the heavens.

It was Hope that was keeping me in my seat now – that and
the fact that Benoit was squeezing nearly seventy miles per
hour out of the Transit. Hope would whisper sweet reassur-
ances into my battered ears, rub my back and mop my brow,
pat my hand and lead me right up to the gallows, where she
would suddenly see that she had made a terrible mistake and
would flee, leaving me alone with the priest and the rope.
Hope would tie a bandage around my eyes and leave me in the
care of her blind cousin, Faith. Hope, though she would never
admit it in public, was a distant cousin of Death. I knew all of
this, and although she was no great temptress, her company was
pleasant and reassuring, and she was welcome for as long as she
wished to stay.

We were several kilometres beyond Alcala, following a twisting road higher than anything around it when we passed a long,
low, *cal*-painted building with yellow lights splashing into the
road. A great cheer came from within, and I saw Jean-Marc's tail
lights brighten and then dim as he stopped. Benoit pulled alongside, and as he wound down his window I looked across and saw
Luisa sitting between Jean-Marc and the Arab kid.

'Do you think they're still serving?' asked Jean-Marc.

'So what if they are?' replied Benoit. 'You can't be thinking
of going in there?'

Jean-Marc rubbed his nose and grinned. 'Why not?'

Benoit slumped in his seat, shaking his head. 'Who's going
to watch these two?'

I'd already spotted the Bolivian gleam in Jean-Marc's eyes.

The bastard had dipped his nose in my bag, and now he wanted to dance the night away.

'They can come in with us,' he smiled, looking across at me. 'You'll behave, won't you?'

I needed a drink more than freedom. I nodded meekly.

'See?' said Jean-Marc. 'Let's go. Lulu wants to celebrate.'

Outside the early morning was so strongly scented with pine that even my ravaged nostrils could detect the resin on the cool air. Above and all around the sky sparkled as though every star in the northern hemisphere had invited a southern cousin over for the evening, their brightness diminished only by the warmth radiating from the bar and the cold glow of the waning moon. Hard-working fingers threw the harsh staccato chords of the rhythmic *toque* out for the stars to join in the *baile*, and as we approached the door a couple snogging before a parked Peugeot looked up and smiled. It was a very bad time to stumble across a party.

13

We found the table farthest from the action and seated ourselves. I had smiled plaintively at everyone I passed, but the few
who had noticed our arrival had eyes only for Luisa.

The *patron* pushed his way through the throng to take our
orders, his bloodshot eyes appraising us suspiciously as he licked
the sweat from the ends of his moustache. His bar gasped
beneath an atmosphere of Ducados and disorder, the ashtrays
untouched and the floors carpeted with olive stones and dog-
ends. A chant had risen from the crowd, as though they were
demanding an encore, and their raucous bullring chorus made
conversation difficult.

'What's the party for?' I yelled.

'Santo Niño,' he confirmed. 'Religious thing. What can I
get you?'

Jean-Marc leaned across the table and put a hand on my
arm, his big mouth smiling while his eyes made threats.

'Let Lulu do the talking,' he barked. 'It's good for her to
practise her Spanish.'

Luisa shouted up a round and the *patron* departed through a
corridor in the crowd that gave a sightline to the floor. At the
top of a circle of whooping, shiny-faced drinkers two gui-
tarists, one as green as the pines on the slopes and the other as
old as the hills, thrashed out a rhythm on Sevillean guitars with
nods and smiles and sighs and grimaces as the skin around their

nails was eroded from their digits. The old man seemed to be suffering the less: his apprentice screwed up his brow and shook his MTV haircut to the left and to the right as he pushed his arms and his fingers through ever denser layers of numbness and pain.

This seemed to be a spontaneous event, for neither the men nor the women appeared to be dressed for a party, even if they were drinking for one. A couple were dancing the fandango in the centre of the circle, whirling through the smoke and stamping to multi-layered handclaps from the cheering audience. In keeping with local tradition the girl, a brown-eyed twenty-year-old with ponytailed hair as dark as her low-lidded eyes, wore jeans, a T-shirt and a shell-suit jacket. Her partner wore the shell-suit trousers and a T-shirt that declared *Raide Gauloises*, the padded thump of his trainers drowned out by the percussion of the crowd. Despite his outfit, he knew the moves.

So did she, and although she was no looker, the confidence with which she stamped on the polished flagstones and the haughtiness with which she dismissed the eager entreaties of her partner imparted to her a desirability, a beauty from beyond the physical boundaries of her own body. She clapped her hands beside the golden stud in her ear, and stepped away from the desperation of life, whirling and stamping to the sound of cascading guitars, as her suitor grinned, giving her the wide-boy eyes and promises of a born loser. Scowling, she spun away, attainable but untameable, like the high limestone country of the sierras, looking dark-eyed upon the citrus-studded valleys and the green waters of the dying rivers below. I was in no mood for a party, but as I watched her dance I felt something break inside me and spill its liquid centre across my heart and down my spine.

I looked at Benoit. 'Bit of culture for you.'

'She's good,' he allowed, his eyes like spinning plates on sticks. 'Can you two dance like that?'

Luisa and I, dancing? 'We only know the first twelve steps,' I yelled, but he didn't understand.

'What's he saying?' demanded Jean-Marc, waving Benoit closer, and as they shouted at each other in French I looked hard at Luisa. Our drinks had arrived, and raising my *coñac*, I proposed a toast.

'To Luisa! Traitor, murderess, and soon to be ex-girlfriend.'

'*Olé!*' yelled the crowd.

She was chewing her thumbnail, her cocaine eyes darting from Jean-Marc to Benoit to the Arab kid and back again.

'Fuck off, Martin,' she growled.

'*Listo!*' they cried.

I necked my drink and grabbed hers. 'No, Luisa, you fuck off. I'm finishing with you, right now. It's over. You're chucked. Our relationship is over. You're on your own. Understand?'

'*Viva la machina!*' they roared. '*Viva!*'

I looked over my shoulder, but they weren't cheering for me.

'Don't be ridiculous,' hissed Luisa.

I slurped her brandy. 'You'll never last without me. Even if that wanker gives you your cut, you'll never last. No one will put up with you. You're a fucking lunatic.' I rubbed my nose. 'Too much of this . . .', I sniffed, '. . . it's fried your brain.'

She held up her hand in an exaggerated gesture of barely repressed fury, her bangles reflecting the candles on the table. 'Don't you worry yourself about it,' she snarled, through clenched teeth.

'*Bravo!*' they exclaimed. They were beginning to piss me off.

'Thanks to you, I haven't got much left to worry about, have I? I can't believe you tried to get him to drown me! You're like some bloody praying mantis or something.'

She let Jean-Marc out of her sight just long enough to toss me a sideways glance. 'Praying mantis?'

'Yeah, praying mantis,' I nodded. 'They kill their mates.'

She grunted and swung her eyes back to the Frenchmen. 'But you're not my mate,' she said, 'and it's black widow.'

'*Ole! Ole! Ole!*' cheered the crowd. '*Viva la fantasma!*'

She rose suddenly and addressed Jean-Marc. 'I'm going to get a hit. You coming?'

Jean-Marc turned away from Benoit and let his eyes take the long route to her face. 'Why not?' he grinned, winking at me.

The guitarristas beat the last chords from their glowing instruments and threw their hands in the air in a victorious flourish: every song finished was another battle won, but the crowd left them sitting like Vietnam vets in an empty airport, for their cheers were for the girl. Her performance over, she seemed to shrink, the fire in her eyes extinguished and her confidence fleeting as she nervously acknowledged their congratulations. I smiled at her, but she didn't notice.

'I'd shag it,' commented Benoit.

The Arab kid grinned, perking up and turning to see what Benoit would shag. His delight turned to disappointment as he spotted her across the bar, and he turned back to his beer. 'She's a skinny pig,' he declared. 'You can have her.'

I finished Luisa's brandy and shouted up another round.

Benoit looked at his watch. 'How long we been in here?'

'Five minutes. Something like that,' I shrugged. The crowd wanted more from the girl – everyone but the Arab kid wanted more from the girl, but before she could be bullied into another performance an old man in a half-suit and flat cap stood up and stretched his frayed cuffs towards the *guitarristas*. The elder of the two musicians rose to his feet and smiled at his supplicant, bowing in recognition of an equal.

Half-Suit was half-cut, but he remembered this song only when his spirit was too weak to resist the call. Three generations around him were still attempting to persuade the girl to dance for them when they heard the first wavering line to his *seguiriya*, and his first note stilled their tongues and turned their heads. It was time for the early morning to take a sombre turn, and as the old man sang with the voice of a muezzin they hung their heads and listened to the God-awful truth.

If you cannot save me, then do not cry for me,
For your tears cannot soothe me,
And if you cannot plead for me, then do not grieve for
  me,
For your words will not save me,
For I must die, as you must die,
And our clever lies
Have betrayed us both
And our clever lies
Have killed us all.

El Duende was in the house. That dark and elusive spirit, beloved of both El Camaron and Lorca, had slipped in through door and dragged a song from an old man's throat. I looked down at the floor as he sang, fearful of looking up and meeting his watery, bloodshot eyes. He knew as well as I that there was one more in that low-ceilinged, rock-built mountain *jerga* that night. Maybe he had counted the bodies and then counted their shadows before arriving at a discrepancy, or maybe, like me, he had felt the draught of its passing freeze the marrow from his brittle old bones. However he had done it, he had detected the presence of El Duende, and he knew that it was I who had brought him into the room.

Jean-Marc's hairy hands landed heavily beside me on the table.

'Luisa is unhappy,' he announced.

'Get used to it,' I muttered. 'She's a miserable bird. A great, big, melancholy albatross. You'll see.'

'I don't want her to be unhappy,' said Jean-Marc, 'because she is going to show me where you hid my property.'

I dragged a fag from the box. 'Why don't you let me show you where it's hidden?'

He put a hand on my shoulder. 'I asked you to, and you lied to me. I detest mendacity. I never, ever give liars a second chance, for if you lie to me, it's because you think I'm stupid, am I right?'

I nodded. He was right: I did think he was stupid.

He nodded back. '*Et voila!* Now Luisa says that you've stolen her drink and you've said some bad things, and you've upset her, so I'd like you to go back to the van and wait with Benoit. How's that?'

I shrugged and began to rise. Jean-Marc pushed me back into my chair and put his mouth close to my ear. 'One other thing: if everything goes well tonight, there doesn't need to be any unhappiness. As far as I understand it, your ex-fiancée only wants you out of the way so she can move in with her new boyfriend. I know she's going on about having you shot and stuff but that's women all over.' He tightened his grip on my shoulder and came close enough to lick the sweat from my cheek. His voice smelled of brandy, tobacco, mint and cocaine, and it trembled as he spoke. 'But fuck with me and I'll empty that beautiful gun into your body. Understand?'

★

The *guitarristas* were swigging on bottles of *mosto* as we left, and the crowd was trying to persuade the girl to dance again. I followed Benoit into the night, wondering what Jean-Marc had meant about Luisa wanting to move in with her new boyfriend. Surely they weren't getting it on, were they? The very thought turned my stomach. Outside the sky was still dark in the west, the valley thick with shadows, and in the distance the street lights of four villages sparkled on the far slopes like handfuls of jewels cast upon a black velvet blanket. What lay between them and me was impossible to tell: crags, edges, rivers, forests, all were hidden in the darkness, and it struck me that within twenty paces of this unfortunate bush I could be as invisible as the land. If I kept moving, they would never find me, and once I was far enough away I could hide up, grab a few hours' sleep, before heading to Bloody Mary's house. She had been waiting to score from me in Dieter's Place when I had walked in that morning with Jean-Marc, and I had promised to visit her. She would have cash in the house and she owned a car, and one way or another, I would leave with both. I would recover the cocaine and flee to the coast, where I would disappear for ever beneath a dirty sea of banknotes. It was a brilliant plan, and all I needed was the courage to run away. I looked across at the glittering villages, and for a moment they seemed to float above their background, so near that I could reach out and pick the gems from their hearts and leave each a little darker, as was my wont.

All I needed was a little bravery, a handful of guts, a pair of balls. All I needed to do was run, but Benoit heard my thoughts and grabbed my arm.

'Get in,' he growled.

I climbed in and lit up a cigarette.

'Can I put some music on?'

He shrugged. 'Okay. No rap.'

The FRA was playing 'Guitar Man' by the King, a song about escape, daring, perseverance and reward. It meant little to me, although, as a big chicken, I could relate to the bit about the poultry truck.

I was pondering Jean-Marc's suggestion that there would be no need for any unhappiness when Luisa appeared at the window like an escaped lunatic.

'Out!' she yelled. 'Out now!'

Benoit covered his cratered face and groaned.

I wound down the window. 'What?'

She had clearly ingested a lot more cocaine than the recommended daily allowance, and she wasn't out to gloat on it. 'So I'm an albatross, am I?'

I sighed and looked absently into the dark Spanish hills, wondering if this was the first time they had heard a conversation open this way. I nodded. 'Yep.'

She shook her head, smiling in disbelief. 'How do you figure that?'

I wished my head was only half as fucked up as hers. 'Go away,' I told her. 'Go back inside and dance with Charles Aznavour. Pretend you're the only gull in the world, and he's the only buoy. Go on.'

She took a deep breath and wobbled. 'Why am I an albatross?'

'Because you hang around my neck and you bring me bad luck, that's why,' I exploded. 'We had it good – we had the perfect situation. We were blessed and you bloody sold me out for a sodding kilo of cocaine.'

'It was five kilos, you lying bastard.'

'Five kilos then. Whatever. That's not the point. You're supposed to be my girlfriend. You're supposed to be on my side instead of trying to get me killed. What do you think you're playing at?'

I'd walked into it and she was smiling like a happy trapper.

'You really want me to tell you what it's all about?' she said slowly, in a tone that suggested that I didn't. 'You really want to know the lowest line?'

'"The bottom line",' I sighed. 'It's "the bottom line".'

She shook her head impatiently. 'The only person I have sold out is me,' she began. 'For three years I have wasted my life waiting for you to prove that you're something better than the loser you are. Three years! Do you know how much money has passed through your hands in that time? Do you have any idea where I could have been by now if I had that kind of money? You sicken me. Every time I see myself in the same space as you I feel cheaper and sicker. You lie and you cheat and you tell stupid stories to people and you give your money away to other losers and I watch you fucking my life up and I hate you. I hated you so much I became indifferent to you, and then I hated you even more, and I hate myself for hating you because you are nothing, Martin!' She drew breath and let another salvo go. 'You're nothing. You are despised by everybody, and I am brushed with the same tar. You have no friends, because nobody respects you—'

'It's "tarred with the same brush",' I interrupted.

She rolled her eyes. 'That's another thing I hate about you . . .'

'I do have friends,' I protested, dragging her back to the point. 'More friends than you.'

'Go on, then,' she urged. 'Name one.'

'Henrique.'

She laughed. 'El Stupido? That halfwit who hangs out with you only because no one else takes him seriously.'

That was fair. 'Theo.'

'He thinks you're a loser. He says you suck up to him when you haven't got any coke. He despises you.'

I opened my mouth and closed it again. I didn't like the way this argument was going.

'Who else?' she demanded. 'Is there anyone else?'

'Helmut?' I heard myself ask.

She laughed out loud, slipping her shoulder out of her dress and cupping her bare left breast with her right hand. 'See this, idiot?' I felt Benoit's gasp upon the back of my neck. 'German teeth did this, not French.'

'You bitch,' I whispered, my eyes upon her nipple but seeing only the cascade of unnoticed incidents tumbling like wind-blown photographs.

'Oh yes,' she nodded, covering herself. 'A bitch is what I am and that's the way Helmut likes it. German men appreciate domination, and Danish men, too.'

I threw an angry look at Benoit, who was eagerly trying to understand the conversation. He raised his eyebrows and smiled before switching his gaze back to Luisa. Maybe she had been bitten elsewhere.

I didn't want to ask her about her domination of Danes.

'Which Danish men?'

'Lars,' she replied indifferently. 'Henrik. Not just Danes. Mickey.'

I had been cringing in the face of a furnace blast of shame, but the last name slammed the door.

'Mickey?' I gasped. 'Metal Mickey?'

She tipped her head to one side. 'So I was out of it at the time. It happened at a party.'

'Which party?' There weren't many parties around here without my name on the guest list.

She shrugged. 'I don't know. Anyway, you weren't invited.'

I dropped my head into my hands. 'You and Helmut. How long?'

'Oh, thirteen months or so. Everybody knows, except you.'

Everybody knew, except me. The best part of my mind really didn't want to argue any more. It wanted to limp away into the deepest shadows and hide beneath the heaviest rock until everybody had died. I was standing dazed in the rubble of my life, and I'd been noticing the cracks for months. I'd thought they were there for decoration. I shook my head and stared at my reflection in the windscreen, wanting to change the subject.

'Trying to get me killed is a bit extreme, isn't it? Why don't you just elope?' I glanced sideways at her like an unfairly kicked dog.

Her gaze was steady. 'Because that's not the only reason we need you out of the way, Martin. You have probably never noticed that our business is characterised by uncompromising extremes of behaviour. You deal in cocaine like you're running some dopey hippy cooperative, and you leave yourself vulnerable to takeover. Helmut and I have been ready to take your business for months, only we have not had the means to do so.'

I laughed, despite being entirely unamused. This was a plot of solitary construction, and even though his fidelity as a friend had been severely compromised, I could not accept that Helmut would sanction my slaughter. He was German, admittedly, but he was still just a dope-smokin', peace-lovin' hippy. He didn't even eat meat.

'You're off your head,' I told Luisa. 'Helmut wouldn't get involved in something like this. This is all your idea.'

Her smile reflected the starlight. 'You're off you're head,

actually,' she replied. 'How do you think these men found us? By chance, perhaps?' She chuckled like a villain. 'Who recommended the hotel, idiot?'

The chill that shivered my spine was part shock and part dread. The treacherous bastard had also recommended Sad Tony, and I could easily imagine what a bad bugger he could be when properly motivated. That reminded me.

'Helmut's queer, you know,' I advised her. 'That coke you're abusing: I bought it from his ex-boyfriend. I hope you're using protection.' It was my best shot, and it fell way short.

Luisa tossed her head. 'He never seemed queer to me. Maybe he'll let me watch some day.'

She had an answer for everything, and now she was pointing at me.

'What's that film, the one with the Mariachi guy?'

'*El Mariachi*,' I sighed. 'So what?'

She rubbed her nose, still smiling. 'I used to dream of some black-clad assassin like him arriving and accepting my commission, and when your stinking French biker friend turned up, I thought my dreams had come true.' An altercation at the door of the bar interrupted her revelations. Jean-Marc had been caught pissing on a local's car, and the night was riven by drunken recriminations of angry men. Jean-Marc, unable to speak Spanish and utterly unconcerned, yelled unintelligibly as he walked back towards the van, a bottle in one outstretched hand and a cigarette bouncing on his lips. Luisa tilted her head and looked hard at me, as though for the last time. 'Maybe they have,' she said.

An hour or so later we were descending in slow convoy through a forest of pine beneath a sky that was neither dark nor light. I squeezed my eyes shut enough to squint through the gaps in the grey blanket of the pre-dawn through which we rolled, braking and changing down, braking and changing down. Some time soon Jean-Marc would turn right onto the brown track down to El Gatocin, and I had no idea of what I was going to do about it. Benoit was tired and miserable: the dawning of a bright new day was unlikely to show to him the glory of the coming of the Lord. I wondered how likely it was that I would be meeting my maker before lunchtime.

Heavy aches were running like tanker trucks full of nitroglycerine from my knuckles and along the tunnels of my veins to my shoulders, where they emptied their cargo in explosions of pain before trundling back to my hands. My lips throbbed from their wounds, and somewhere above my right temple something was violently insistent that I kept my eyes shut. Beyond the pain, however, lay the shame, and that hurt most of all. I was nothing: I was zero, and I didn't count. If I gave Jean-Marc what he wanted, he would probably kill me. If I refused, he would certainly kill me. If I commented upon his choice of hosiery, he would probably kill me. For as long as I was in his custody, I had no rights, and all the answers to all my questions lay in what was left of Sad Tony's generous deal. All I needed was a hit, a snort to spike my brain and let out all the stale air and the bad feeling, a brand-new coating of brilliant white against which to effect some clarity and some contrast. Every nerve-end in my body needed its share, every synapse gaping like a fledgling in the nest, screaming like the world's longest maternity ward. Seeing my weakness, my brain began to tease me with hypotheticals: would I prefer a line of coke right now or a pistol?

The answer was A.

A line of coke or a faithful girlfriend?

A again.

Cocaine or freedom? I bit my lip. The answer was always going to be A. I stopped scratching my scalp when I felt the blood under my fingernails and started rubbing my tongue along the back of my teeth to make up for it. When my tongue started bleeding I figured I'd probably have a go at another part of my scalp, and so on until I could get some therapy. The answer would always be A.

'*Jusqu'ici, tout va bien,*' muttered Benoit, and then it wasn't. We rounded a long, sweeping bend with pine-clad slopes above our right, their dark green tops below us to the left, and there, poised on the steep downhill entrance to the *camino forestal* that led to El Gatocin, was the Mercedes van.

As it began its slow descent to the valley floor, I considered the possible consequences of my lie to Luisa. Jean-Marc would be unlikely to see the funny side of my deceit, and while I fully expected him to react violently, I hoped that he wouldn't kill anybody until he had the cocaine in his possession. That was my one advantage, and it was one with which I could negotiate a deal. Unable to trust Luisa, I needed a friend who could watch my back while I went digging, or better still, a friend who would dig for me while I sat somewhere safe and public.

Then I remembered that I had no friends, except Henrique, who hung out with me only because nobody else took him seriously.

Night lingered longer in the valley, the pre-dawn light between the resinous evergreens a smoky grey, the air moist and scented. On the valley floor a neck-high layer of mist rested upon the river, spilling in places across the wide, grassy banks between the tall trees. Jean-Marc had parked at the end of the track, and I could see him far below, pacing around as though trying to keep warm while awaiting my arrival. I lit up a fag as we rounded the last bend and fixed a big, creepy smile to my face as I stepped out of the van.

He was blinking hard and scratching at phantom itches, wired like a Russian reactor on Sad Tony's coke. I sucked on my throbbing thumb and smiled at the bloodshot Frenchman like a scared dog.

'This ain't the place.'

He stared at me, blinking hard and fast. 'What do you mean?'

'I mean this ain't the place,' I repeated. 'Don't worry, though, because we're not very far from the right place. If you just follow—'

'What do you fucking mean, this ain't the place?' shouted Jean-Marc and the pigeons panicked, scattering from the tree-tops and drawing spirals of river mist into the vortices of their flapping wings.

I shrugged and Jean-Marc spat.

'Get that *Boche* bitch out here,' he yelled. I shuffled my feet, sucking nervously on the butt of my Marlboro.

'Give me that fucking pistol,' he hissed. I couldn't see Benoit, but he seemed reluctant to hand over the gun.

Jean-Marc swayed a little. 'I said bring that gun here now!' he yelled.

This time Benoit did as he was told, and the curious calm of resignation crept like hemlock from my feet to chill my stomach and freeze my heart as I watched Luisa pushed protesting from the van by the Arab kid.

'Shut your mouth,' barked Jean-Marc, his lips drawn back across his teeth. 'One of you fuckers is lying.' He snapped back the slide on the pistol, dropping a round onto the sand at his feet.

'Which one of you fuckers has lied to me?' he yelled. I took two hard drags on my butt and dropped it. No words came to mind. Luisa twisted herself free from the grip of the Arab kid and stood facing Jean-Marc, her fists clenched and her nose as red as his.

'Fuck you!' she screamed back at him. 'Fuck you, because no one's lying about nothing.'

Anything, I thought.

Jean-Marc held the pistol at arm's length and squinted along the sight.

'Oh yeah?' he raged breathlessly. 'Is that right?' The muzzle swung round to point at my heart. I moved to the left. It followed. I looked past it, past Jean-Marc's sweating face and into his dilated eyes. 'Is that right?'

I opened my mouth, then closed it. I shrugged, then opened my mouth again and closed it.

'Is that fucking right?' screamed Jean-Marc, and the Arab kid moved quickly behind the van.

I glanced at Luisa, quickly and furtively as though it were against the rules, and locked on to the look on her face. I'd seen it a million times before, every time she'd caught me out. It was not a look she had often caught from me.

'It's him,' she screamed. 'He's the fucking liar! He told me it was down here. Blow his fucking heart out!'

I could hear everything, smell everything and taste everything, but all I could see was the foul little mouth of Jean-Marc's pistol. It rose and fell with his heartbeat, as though nodding its consent to Luisa's bidding.

'Fucking kill him!'

Jean-Marc tightened his grip, shifted his weight and raised the weapon. His eyes darted from me to Benoit and back again. He shook his head. 'I can't do it,' he announced at last. 'I want to, but I can't.'

Luisa laughed, a short, sad little snort of pity and disgust.

'Fuck you, you fucking amateur,' she sneered, shaking her head.

'No,' countered Jean-Marc, 'fuck you.'

A hammer fell upon a nail, a branch was broken from a dry tree, a Bible was dropped on a tiled floor, and Luisa was punched three times backwards, her left hand groping behind her to find the soil that would break her fall, her cry of shock catching in her throat. A burst of startled birds exploded from the scrub as her head bounced off the dusty ground, and her knees came up to her chest as she scratched at the earth and tried to rise. A dark-mouthed cylinder of dull and smoking brass rolled towards her, the cartridge trying to rejoin one of the bullets that had smashed her sternum and torn her trachea before ricocheting off her spine and sending fragments up into her head. Her eyes widened and her mouth fell open showing bloodstained teeth as she looked first at Jean-Marc and then, as if by accident, at me, the realisation growing that she was about to die. There was no blame in her eyes, nor any anger, just the jaw-dropping shock of an awful embarrassment, a terrible surprise, like a kid discovering for the first time the dangerous relationship between petrol and matches. She rolled onto her side and arched her back, her brain fighting against the darkness, her left hand clutching now at the air in the space where she thought her wound must be. Her agonised amazement became fear as she focused clumsily on something very close to her face, and she didn't see Jean-Marc as he stepped back and fired again, the round knocking a clod into the air near her right hip. He fired again, and this time he hit her in the side of her chest, sending a spray of red into the cool morning air. Luisa rolled onto her back, gurgled, and died.

'*Ca plane pour moi,*' grinned Jean-Marc, with a little swivel of the hips. He lifted the pistol again, his breathing fast and heavy, but Benoit stepped forward and pushed his arm down.

Jean–Marc shrugged and let the smoking gun dangle from his finger by the trigger guard. Benoit took it from him and made it safe before stuffing it into his waistband. 'Pick up your cases,' he told Jean-Marc, pointing at the ejected brass.

The killer's eyebrows rose above his flushed face. 'You pick 'em up.'

'You are a very little man,' said someone, and I felt he was talking to me. The earth was moving from side to side, and I was shaking my head, and almost out of sight I could see that the Arab kid was doing the same. Luisa's heels drummed against the dust in some obscene Stygian fandango, and I remembered how we had hit every shoeshop on the Costa in search of those shiny red shoes. Death grinned at me, then snatched her up by her scarlet dress, hitching it up to her urine-stained crotch, leaving her life and her dignity to be mourned by the half-muffled ringing of the silver bangles around her limp and trembling wrists. The ground beneath her was so soaked in her blood that it could no longer be absorbed; it ran in streams to collect in the hollows and ruts of the track. By noon it would be black, and a square metre of Spain would be forever angry.

I stumbled backwards, sitting heavily in the dust, digging my nails into the dirt as though the proof that this had really happened lay buried below the surface.

Something light and small landed in the dust beside me.

'Have a *clop*,' suggested the Arab kid.

I opened my eyes and stared up at him like a moron.

He pointed at the packet. 'Have a smoke.'

Goats were probing along the river bank as I was led back to the Transit, and I sat shivering and smoking in the passenger seat, seeing Half-Suit's face in the stains on the windscreen as

Benoit and the Arab kid dragged Luisa into the weeds. Jean-Marc changed his shirt from a soft leather-look holdall and sauntered across to me, his affected nonchalance failing to conceal his flushed face and shortened breath.

'I had to shoot her, didn't I?' He only half-expected a reply, and when none was offered I could hear him smile as he turned away. 'If I hadn't shot her, I would have had to shoot you, wouldn't I? Then I'd never have got my stuff back, would I? Shouldn't have taken me for an idiot, should you? Fucking well know now, don't you?'

He was asking a lot of questions, I thought, as he turned away, unzipped his fly and pissed on the track, marking his territory like an animal and underlining his triumph. Benoit jumped into the driver's seat, his hands still dripping with the river water he had used to wash away Luisa's blood, and started the engine.

'I don't know what you're playing at,' he declared. 'I warned you of this last night.'

Jean-Marc's red nose appeared at my window.

'Take me to the cocaine,' he said.

I nodded.

'Back up to the road?' guessed Benoit. I nodded again, and the Transit climbed out of El Gatocin, leaving the rising sun, the goats and the flies to find the body of the woman we had killed.

14

Once upon a time Bugs Bunny had been tied to a railroad track by Yosemite Sam. I can't remember what he'd done, but there he was, lashed to the downstate track while the mustachioed psychopath stood on the upstate track, a-chucklin' and a-tappin' his boots and a-checkin' his pocket watch. Along came the upstate train, dead on time, and off went Sam, his pulverised remains bringing early retirement to the traumatised engineer. I felt like the rabbit.

I extended my hand and levelled it against the artificial horizon of the dashboard, checking to see if the numbness in my head went as far as my fingers. It didn't: I was shaking like a man on a fuzzy tree, my mouth as dry and dirty as the floor of a Spanish bar, and I could hear the panic where my veins ran behind my battered ears. Luisa was dead, but the message wasn't getting through to where it mattered most. A whirling, roaring storm was raging in my head, and all routes in and out were cut, the wind gusting like punches and the rain falling like catlicks from the jagged, flashlit sky. In the distance, swinging in the gale and blinking in the rain, a neon sign flashed the message 'Maybe Not' through the hurricane. Maybe Luisa wasn't dead. Maybe they were blanks. Maybe it was all a trick. Maybe it wasn't, but maybe she was still alive, unconscious and bleeding to death in the dawn's early light. Maybe I could persuade Jean-Marc to take her to hospital . . . There was another sign struggling to survive the storm, sparks flying downwind as it shorted in the rain. 'Last Words' it flickered, and Luisa's had been unfortunate.

The sunburned sewer through which scumbags like us scurried was supposed to be awash with betrayal, deceit and self-interest. The effluent of civilised society, it ran down in streams from the moral high ground, but even down here, it still came as a bit of a shock to find out that your girlfriend was screwing your apprentice and plotting your murder. It took time and strong spirits to come to terms with such treachery, and I had neither. Luisa had gone from surly to treacherous to dead in the space of one short summer night, and now she was gone for ever. Maybe if I had trusted her with the truth it would have been me swelling by the river, shocked and lifeless, and Luisa would have been aching in my place. I wondered how I felt, and unable to get a reply, I wondered how Luisa would have felt if it had been me wearing Jean-Marc's ballistic piercings.

What would she have said?

Luisa would have said, 'Fuck him.'

So fuck her, I thought, in French, so Benoit would understand.

I didn't want to think about Luisa any more, and Benoit seemed keen to fill the silence with something that would drown out the whispers in his own head. I spilled a little small talk, just to see how he soaked it up.

'Who does the cocaine belong to?' I asked. He considered his reply for a moment, then decided that I had earned one.

'Big man in Paris,' he said.

'Jean-Marc?'

He snorted. 'I said a big man.'

'So why's Jean-Marc come to get it?'

'Because it's his fault it came here in the first place. He's the one who lost it, so he's the one who has to find it. That's why.'

'And you work for Jean-Marc?'

Benoit laughed. 'No, I do not work for Jean-Marc. I am here to represent the man who owns the merchandise that Jean-Marc lost.'

'How did he lose it?' I wasn't really that interested in the answer, but talking was better than thinking, especially at this dark hour.

Benoit changed down and gunned the van up an especially steep section. 'He made some unwise appointments . . . *merde!*' He cursed as the van stalled and used both hands to pull the sagging handbrake as high as it would go. As hill starts go, on a steep and crumbling dirt track, it was tricky, but the van started on the second attempt and wheezed forwards like a broken old *burro*.

'He gave the consignment to one of his bastard kids to deliver to the cutting house. Said he felt responsible for him, reckoned the kid deserved a fresh start after coming out of prison and finding that his *pute* mother had died while he was on the inside . . .' The van almost died again but Benoit paused and kept it alive.

'This van is shit,' he announced.

'So what happened to the kid?' I asked, as if I didn't know. The kid had met Yvan, simple as that.

It wasn't, though.

'You tell me,' grinned Benoit. 'You saw him last.'

It meant nothing, and yet it meant everything: it changed events not one little bit but redefined the colours in which they were painted. I felt that perhaps I should have been more shocked by the revelation, but my mind was so numb that, although weighty and in some way significant, the news that Jean-Marc and Yvan were father and son was like a rock dropped down a deep, deep well. Still falling, and gathering momentum, it had yet to strike, and when it did, the splash would be only faintly heard and the ripples most likely unseen.

'What is wrong with this stupid fucking van?' cursed Benoit as the Transit stalled again. He twisted the ignition and pumped the gas, then turned to me. 'What's the matter? What's wrong?'

I knew what was wrong, but I couldn't explain it to him, not even in English. Something long and wiry under the bonnet had to be yanked to one side, and then the van might start. Helmut had performed this operation on the castle hill, and twice the Transit had recovered.

'Open the bonnet,' I said, 'and only turn the key when I say.'

Jean-Marc and the Mercedes van had pulled up behind us, Yvan's dad yelling over the blaring horn.

'*Arrête tes conneries!*' yelled Benoit in angry reply.

''*Ta guele, connard!*' screamed back Jean-Marc and as I lifted the battered bonnet of my van he stepped out of the Mercedes and stormed up to Benoit. The Arab kid climbed out of the Mercedes and stood watching the red-faced argument, and for a moment our eyes made contact. Antonita La Buena had looked at Yvan in the same way.

I found the cable but my command to turn the key was lost in the shouting between my captors. All the tensions and acrimony of two long nights and one long, hot day together had finally reached their critical mass on the dawn of the second, and Benoit could no longer contain his meltdown. It is a wonder to watch Frenchmen arguing. They face up at close range, too close for punching, and try to crush each other with

a combination of vitriol, volume, incoherent logic and garlic.
Jean-Marc stood his ground like a red-nosed Napoleon as
Benoit chested him and let rip.

He told Jean-Marc that he resented his assumption of power
and challenged his qualifications for carrying out a job that he,
Benoit, had been doing since he was thirteen years old. He
waved his hands in the air and announced that he found Jean-
Marc laughable, pathetic even, with his strutting around like a
cockerel and his stupid Parisian superiority. He also found
him to be dangerously irresponsible, and his arrogant, smart-
arsed behaviour likely to put them all in a Spanish prison for
twenty years. Jean-Marc tried the how-dare-you-talk-to-me-
like-that response, but when it was clear that his authority
was likely to be punched out of him he resorted, rat-like, to
picking on the details of Benoit's argument. This was a peasant country, he argued, closer to the Third World than to
Europe, and no one would bother to investigate the death of
a couple of foreign junkies. It happened all the time down
here, he insisted, because life was cheap. Benoit, resorting to
rural idiom, told him that he was even more stupid than his
trousers if that was what he thought, and with neither fore-
thought nor reflection, I decided that it was time to leave
their squabbling company. Leaving the bonnet raised, I stepped
over the side of the track and onto the wooded slope leading
back down to the river, hundreds of steep metres below. I
walked slowly and steadily with knees bent against the fall
line, my veins already full of lead and my muscles like broken
glass. I looked back after a couple of dozen steps, and already
the slope and the dark, dripping pines had hidden the vans
from view. I turned to my left, following the contour, hearing
my captors suddenly aware of my absence. Their shouts, much
nearer than I had expected, echoed through woodlands, but

their weak promises and violent threats weren't going to bring me back alive.

'*Il est là!*' called the Arab kid, and my heart raced as I hobbled on, moving parallel to the track and back towards the clearing. I had no idea how far a pistol bullet could travel, nor how easy it was to send one accurately through a forest towards a moving target, but my TV experience told me that it was probably pretty straightforward. Like a punch in the head from a drunken skinhead, you never heard the bullet that hit you. I deduced from this that if I could hear them shooting then I was probably safe, although it seemed wise to keep increasing the range between us. The track appeared above me and to my left, slanting downwards to cross my path fifty metres ahead. I paused, breathless, suddenly and gut-suckingly terrified at its edge before glancing back to the yellow curve. The vans were just there, less than a hundred metres away, and I was here, unseen. I glanced right, then hobbled across the track and onto the steep facing slope. The Frogs would expect me to head downhill, and the Scout Handbook said that the searchers never look up. The deep carpet of pine needles was as slippery as snow, and my heart was smoking like my Transit's clutch as I slipped gasping against tree trunks and stumbled on cones as big as pineapples. My thighs felt as though the muscle had metamorphosed into molten rock, and I was sure that my lungs were bleeding as I crossed a crest and came upon the corner of a goat track. I fell to my knees among the raisin-like droppings and sucked deep, deep breaths of cool mountain air. My mouth felt like it was stuffed with hot, soggy cotton wool, the saliva condensed to wet clay, and my nose seemed incapable of drawing enough oxygen from the atmosphere to meet the demands of my gasping body. I held my breath, straining to hear the sounds of pursuit over the throbbing of blood in my ears, and as I listened the baying of a lost and angry hound echoed through the evergreens.

'You're dead,' screamed Jean-Marc, 'I'll kill you! I promise I will kill you! You're dead already, you little fucker! You're dead, you hear?' Turning in circles of fury, he howled his oath into the woods, over and over again as though repetition might bring realisation.

When I took my hands away from my ears, the cursing had stopped. Hidden high above me in the dark foliage a bird argued melodically with another, and their polite bickering was all I could hear. I rose, slowly, cautiously and painfully, stooping low to peer between the trunks, but I couldn't see the hoods for the trees. I stumbled onto the goat path, choosing the downhill route against a weak and feebly protesting better judgement.

Downhill was easiest.

Downhill seemed more likely to have fags.

Downhill was the direction of my future.

I emerged from the forest and wobbled on aching legs across the rocky river bank to the water's edge, too tired and preoccupied to look around for an ambush. I needed to wet my head and soak my throat, and having drunk from a whirlpool I fell back to the safety of the forest and sat down with my aching spine on a fallen pine. In the prehistoric, fog-bound swamp of my mind, strange, primitive, single-cell organisms within it were trying to evolve into complex thoughts and reactions, but the barren, poisoned environment in which they dwelled was too toxic for healthy development and they stumbled into the slime, their last words merely gurgles as they went under.

Luisa had gone.

Luisa had been shot.

Luisa had been killed.

Luisa was dead.

Even carved in granite those words would never carry their back-breaking weight.

I had witnessed Luisa's murder, and the words had failed.

Luisa was dead.

I looked deep down into the darkness for some flicker of feeling, some pain, some sorrow, some guilt, but there was nothing, not even a missed heartbeat. I closed my eyes and saw her head bounce in a puff of dust as she went down and tried to rise again, the cracks of Jean-Marc's murder weapon like rents in a canvas that let the darkness pour through. I felt the heat of her spilled blood radiating across my face as it ran in winding rivers to drain into a black and silted lake. I smelled the warm spray of her last gasp as she stared at me and beyond me with those wide, surprised and terrified eyes and heard the drumming of her fingers and her heels as her lights went down and the life fled her punctured body.

Luisa was dead. It was no less than she deserved, but even though that thought sounded right, I wondered how long it would be before I truly believed it.

15

It felt like the afternoon when I woke, my brain wearily shoving the shutters and letting the pain come rushing in. It seemed likely that nothing good would come of sitting still, and even though I could think of nothing good that would come of moving, there was always the chance of a drink in the latter option. I rose on shredded muscles, dragging myself up through the sticky tears of a rough-skinned pine, and stumbled along the river bank, wobbling from rock to rock and reaching out for the flood-tide debris of broken trees and displaced beer crates to steady my passage. On my left ran the river, its easy fluidity mocking my painful progress at its side. The soles of my boots were as smooth as the rocks over which I slipped, and my hands bled from the spite of vegetation. Beside me, the river dozed, like a tourist on an air-conditioned coach passing a *campesino* and his *burro* on a steep mountain road. I ducked low to squeeze between a rock and a hard place and twisted my head just in time to prevent a broken branch from spiking my eye, but not fast enough to avoid injury. Stabbed in the cheek, I flinched and lost my footing, fell forward and sprawled against a boulder the size of a small car. The river woke up and laughed as it slid happily between the tall, dry rocks of the rapids.

'Bastard!' I yelled, but the river kept laughing. I threw a rock at it, but missed. I wondered how long it would take me to die if I just gave up, here and now.

As the sun slid into the Atlantic somewhere west of Cadiz I sat on a flat rock above the torrent sucking the nicotine from a broken cigarette and trying to work out a route to the road bridge. I could either climb the crag at my back and walk along the top or I could try to find a ledge that would take me along at river level. The alternative was to sit on the slab and sob like a spellbound prince, but I could find no tears in my beaten, dehydrated carcass and so I just sat there beneath the first stars with the roaring of the river and the riveting of the frogs. You never know how bad things can become, even when they might already be at their worst. The remaining effects of my last drink and my last snort were being drawn from my body, their ragged fingernails dragging carelessly along every nerve they passed. I felt sure, however, that things could be much worse. My body was beaten like a dirty carpet, and it felt like the only places there were no scabs were where the blood had yet to dry. I lit another fag and blew a plume of blue into the night air. It had been a long, long time since I had been as straight as this, and if this was what life without drugs was like, I hadn't missed out on much. Maybe this was as bad as it ever got, or maybe this was nothing compared to what was coming, but I didn't really care. All I knew was that when the last numbing effects of the shock and the narcotics left my system I was going to be the only one who mattered in an uncaring world of pain. Nobody was going to offer me succour, or sympathy, or shelter from the storm, and I was as comfortable here, with the heat being sucked from my bones by this altar-like rock above the roaring river, as I would ever be.

Every now and then a drop of the river ricocheted off a wet rock and splashed against my face ten metres above as though reminding me of its powerful presence and capabilities.

'I'm here,' roared the river, like a Californian waiter. 'What can I do for you this evening?'

I ignored it, concentrating on the glow at the end of my cigarette.

'I'm just a hop and a skip and a jump away. Come on in and let me take care of you.'

There were loads of bats, I noticed, the insectivore night shift in the same factory that employed the swallows, the swifts and the sand martins.

'You just lie back and let me pour into your body, filling your lungs with my coolness and washing away all your fears and worries. You'll never look back. How about it?' I flicked my dog-end over the edge and watched as the glow diminished before being snuffed by the roaring blackness. If it could be that quick . . .

'It can!' cried the river. 'I'll tap your head against a rock so quickly that you'll never feel a thing. One second you'll be alive with pain and worry, fear and regret, with no future and an unspeakable past, and the next you will be free, and, best of all, it's a great rush!'

The river was a dangerous, smooth-talking bastard, and there were probably warnings in the guidebooks. I needed a drink, and the unfamiliar discomfort of hunger had seized my gut as I set out with a half-hearted determination to prove to the river that I had better offers to consider. My eyes had become accustomed to the light of nearly half a moon and the tips of my boots seemed stiff enough to pick out a route along the canyon wall in its silvery light. I had never climbed on rocks before, but in my happy past I had occasionally shared a spliff with the rock-climbers who scrambled on the crags beneath the castle, and in return for the smoke they had given me some advice: rule one, I recalled, insisted that one always kept three points of contact, and as I took deep, slow breaths and stretched out along the cooling rock I stuck diligently to this sensible advice. A long, horizontal crack allowed easy progress high above the river and I shuffled along with toes deep inside it, taking my time to find good handholds and trying to remember some of the other tips the long-haired, white-handed, jangling rope-monkeys had given me. The crack began to rise, forcing me to climb higher, and then narrowed until only the very tip of my pointed boot could make any purchase. Handholds were becoming scarcer, too, and I recalled now the warning to think ahead while climbing. The rock had bulged outwards, and my left hand was stretched so far up ahead of me that I was spreadeagled against the pregnant boulder and unable to see my feet, and worse, any further footholds. My knees began to tremble, not as an effect of fear but rather as a cause, and as I probed blindly with my right boot for something that would support my weight, my left, better suited to line-dancing than rock-climbing, slipped.

I jerked my right towards the unseen crack from which the left had slipped, but it missed. As I scrabbled for the mythical second chance I lost my grip and slid down the bulge, my decline impeded solely by the friction of my fingertips against the smooth rock. I tensed my body and squeezed with every muscle, trying in vain to turn myself into a human limpet as gravity reeled me in. To fall is to pass into the unknown, for very few people know the properties of a fall: how long, how fast and how fatal a drop can be are subjects of fascination for most men. Some even believed that the fall itself could kill you. I had seen men peering over precipices or leaning over the parapets of multi-storey car parks declaring that a faller would be dead before he hit the ground. Unlikely, I thought, as I was tugged with little jerks towards the edge. What killed was not the fall, but the landing. The sweat on my face froze as I realised that nothing I could do would prevent my rapid descent, that every movement I made towards gaining a hand- or a foothold would only accelerate my downfall. This moment seemed to be ironically representative of the past forty-eight hours, and the cool thing to do would have been to relax and let go, to deny Death the pleasure of seeing me squirm. As an invertebrate, however, it was my nature to squirm until at last, with no great haste, I slipped from one treacherous element into another, plummeting into the rapids like a black sack of trash. In a freeze-frame flash I saw myself falling, and remembered rule number three: don't fall off.

The river said something that I didn't catch as I entered, plunging feet-first in a rush of bubbles into the muted darkness, waiting for a submerged rock to drive my knees into my pelvis before the drowning reflex filled my lungs with pure mountain spring water and laid me down to sleep upon the river bed. I probably thought of Luisa, and I might have suffered the embarrassment that is the red-cheeked and incongruous accomplice of accidental death, and perhaps I shrugged, for I truly never expected to surface from the whirling, rushing maelstrom of the rapids. I dug my chin into my chest and covered my face with my hands as I was spun through the muffled thunder, bouncing off hard objects and trying to find something with which to rediscover gravity. I knew I was losing because I was going down and down, deeper and deeper until, rock-bottomed and disorientated, I broke the surface, hearing again the roar of the river and gulping in lungfuls of air and water as I was carried spluttering and gurgling through the foam, my arms flailing and my head tipped backwards, my cowardly knees and my useless feet banging painlessly against unseen rocks. I felt at last how cold the water was, its icy fingers on the back of my neck as it tried to drag me back down. I fought against it by kicking it and beating it with my hands, opening my eyes for the first time and seeing the stars above the canyon before sliding feet-first over a long, smooth rock and down again into the whirling, whispering confusion below the surface. Water rushed up my nose, causing me to gag, and when I opened my eyes again I was moving backwards downstream and there, wheeling above the crag from which I had fallen, silhouetted against the pale night sky, was something black and malevolent, like a man-sized rook. I gasped and fell backwards, piking through a torrent of white to splash down less than a second later in a wide and shallow pool with islands of rock and a sandy bottom. Whimpering like a lost puppy, I realised I could stand, but after a few steps in the chest-deep water I fell forward and thrashed my way to the nearest beach. Something scarpered through the black bush as I dragged myself up the luminous white sand. I sat down heavily, resting my back against a boulder and brushing the water from my hair, trembling with shock and shivering with cold. I had survived, but my cigarettes hadn't, and that really, really hurt.

16

I stood up and shook the blood back into my limbs. I knew where I was: Lago de Cristal, a one-time beauty spot favoured by teenaged lovers and spaced-out daytrippers nowadays known as the *estanche cafe con leche*. The nickname lost a little in translation, even if the pool did resemble a cup of cold coffee with a dog-end floating in it. It was a long hike up from the road to the lake, but with the right company and sufficient stimulants it often made for a good day out. Girls would get stoned and strip off, and the blokes would perform acts of aquatic bravado between the rocks and the waterfall that fed the lake – the same waterfall, I realised with a shudder, down which I had just arrived. I had never heard of anybody even attempting to ride the fall down into the splashpool and it was ironic that I, the most garishly plumed chicken of them all, had been the first to do it. I had argued with Henrique and his mates here last summer that it was probably possible to ride the fall on an inner tube, and remembered how keen I had been to demonstrate how it would be done had it not been for my bad arm. El Stupido wouldn't have let me: the fall alone, he insisted, would be enough to kill me and then the force of the falling water would spin my broken body around and around at the bottom of the pool like a cat in a twin-tub, and that would be that. His mates agreed, claiming that I would probably be dead before I hit the bottom. I shivered. They were wrong, but they would

probably never know. I walked painfully around the edge of the
brown pool, stepping over the remains of fires and the clanking,
crunching detritus of the dozens of disposable barbies that had
been enjoyed here by my short-sighted and uncaring peers.
Some fool had even dragged the bench seat from a wrecked
Volvo three klicks from the road and set it up facing the falls.

I shook my head as I slumped into the deep, creaking vinyl.
I could conceive of no other object as alien and inappropriate
to this once beautiful setting than the back seat of a Volvo, and
yet, as I stretched out on its dusty length, it was as welcome as
a condom machine in a Ugandan whorehouse. I watched the
bats hunting above the pool, conscious that the falls seemed
somehow louder by night than by day, aware that I needed to
continue my descent and feeling the artificial warmth of the
vinyl pressed against my wet back. I deserved a rest, I decided,
and it was important for me to regain my strength before going
on. If I had been in the high mountains, such a decision would
have been fatal, but down here it was merely uncomfortable. I
kicked off my boots and let the warm water drip from my bare
toes.

I dreamed of bears, and blood, and Luisa danced that twelve
step fandango, telling me as she span between life and death
that the choice was all mine. I knew for a moment what she
meant but then a bear knocked her down with a muddy paw
and lay down beside me, warming me with its deep fur. My
comfort was reduced by the need to push the bear away and to
pull Luisa into its place, but I was too tired to move and too
weak to close my eyes as I watched her head bounce from the
dusty track over and over again . . . I sat up, suddenly awake.
The bear sat up and looked at me with wide, fearful eyes. I
yelped. The bear turned into a dog and growled in dismay

before leaping from the Volvo seat and jogging into the undergrowth with its hackles raised like a porcupine's quills. I looked
around me, quickly and with a dropped jaw, like a sentry awoken
by the sound of a dagger being drawn. It was light, though only
just, and the waterfall seemed quieter than last night. I scanned
the spaces between the trees and the rocks until I was satisfied
that I was alone but for the dog, and I knew that dog.

'Carlito,' I called. 'Come here!'

No movement stirred the undergrowth, but I knew he was
there.

'Car-*lee*-to,' I sang, 'here boy!' To call Carlito 'boy' was a
little patronising: the dog was at least fifty and he did whatever
he liked.

'Carlito,' I wailed. 'I'm in it right up to my neck this time.
Don't muck me about – I need you.' A willow warbler with a
bill full of writhing green caterpillars looked at me with the
pity of a busy mother encountering a wino on her way home
from the shops. I bent down and tossed a rock into the bush.

'I've blown it, Carlito,' I called. 'I'm as fucked as you.' I
picked up my boots and poured a mugful of water from each.

'Remember Luisa, Carlito? Remember her?'

Dogs have very good hearing. It is never really necessary to
shout at a dog for the sake of being heard, so I lowered the
volume and rested my thumping head in my hands.

'She got shot, Carlito, four times from this close. I saw her
go. I was there. There was nothing I could have done, you
know . . . even now, like afterwards, I can't think of a single
thing I could have done. One minute she's yelling at that Frog
bastard to blow me away, and the next she's bleeding in the
dust, and there was nothing I could have done.'

A lost gust raced around the pool, stirring the trees and
flashing silver through the leaves, while high overhead a

northbound airliner reflected the fire of the rising sun like the Devil's coach and four. I desperately needed a cigarette, and a drink, and a long, fat line, although I was beginning to consider a boycott of the cocaine alkaloid on the grounds that it was more trouble than it was worth. I had been buying, selling and ingesting the stuff for the last five years, and it seemed that all the trouble I had never experienced had simply been paid into a high-interest hassle account that had matured last Friday night with Yvan's arrival. Today had to be Thursday, and in the space of one week my brittle little world had been smashed like a Sevillean voodoo snowshaker.

Carlito slunk out from beneath the bushes, pausing for a hard scratch behind his ear. He had his own problems and he didn't care for mine. When his flea-wrangling was completed, he shook his tatty hide, snapped at a passing fly and gave me a condescending look.

'You coming or what?' he muttered.

I stood, carefully, scared to stretch in case I tore something, and followed the dog down the mountain. Carlito walked some way ahead and it seemed meet that I should remain a respectful distance behind him. I was an immigrant and he was indigenous, and I could not refute his precedence in the natural order of our descent. Most of all, however, I remained behind him because he seemed to know where he was going and I needed to be led, even if only by a middle-aged dog with some kind of itching skin complaint.

'Hey, Carlito!' I called. 'Where we going?'

The dog ignored me, pausing only to pee recklessly against a cactus before continuing down the narrow, winding goat track to the flood plain below. The sun had yet to rise above the high ridge to the east but the quality of light had improved to allow the oranges to glow on the dark, distant trees, and before it dipped behind the western skyline, I would be out of the wilderness and back among the quick. I wondered how long Carlito had been living up at Lago de Cristal. It was a long climb for a low dog, and far from the bins from which he made his living, but then Carlito was only truly safe when he was certain that he was alone.

In an hour and a half of painful progress we had passed from the mountains to the flood plain, and as we descended the sun climbed higher and the chill of last night became a fond memory. Right now there were well-dressed people waiting for trains all over Europe, heading into offices, shops and factories, reading newspapers, sipping skinny lattes and avoiding eye contact, and I was following a fat, scabby dog down a goat track in Andalusia as part of an unconsidered attempt to escape from a psychopathic Parisian killer and his two unhappy henchmen. It didn't seem right that I was having all the fun.

Twenty minutes of self-pity later I saw the bridge, its modern span stretching across the valley as though the river were of secondary importance. Its long shadow reached as far as Esmeralda, a low-roofed, well-built *chirringuita* in a grove of shady poplars on the bank of the river. Open for only a few weeks of the year, it was never a place one planned to visit. Like a leaping trout, or a kingfisher, it was a riverine feature that one chanced upon, and when the beer was cold, it was more delightful than any number of brown fish. This morning, however, it was closed, its door and serving hatch barred and bolted. Carlito pissed casually against the sun-cracked wood and trotted up the dappled track towards the road. I sat on the stained step of the little bar and chained the six butts I had found in the dust, sparking them up with the Arab kid's lighter.

'Thanks, Carlito,' I called after the broken-hearted mutt.

Instead of bringing pleasure and relief, the second-hand

smoke delivered the reminder that this adventure was not yet over, and that sudden pain and a slow death were closer now than they had been this morning. That I had, almost unconsciously, fought so hard to stay alive so far surprised me: I had always fancied that I would snap like a cornstalk when the scythe arrived, and yet here I was, running for my life like a fox in a shrinking wheatfield. I lit another dog-end and decided that I must have been more scared of dying than I thought. The will to live was no more than the fear of death, and for a moment too long Luisa's confused and terrified eyes looked down at me from the trees as I saw her lose the chase. Why had she cursed him like that? Yelling insults at an angry, drug-crazed gangster with an automatic was neither big nor clever, and look where it had put her. Something soft and weak and sentimental was trying to tell me to break out the weeds, to tear my hair and wail at her passing, but its keening was a mere irritation. Whatever Luisa and I had ever shared had been used up and discarded a long, long time ago.

She had arrived at the castle like a tomahawk, sharp-edged and blunt, spinning and fast moving, closing on the cowboy she had pursued from the Costa. He was too fly for my liking: first he was a photographer, and then he was a screenwriter, and then he was a DJ, and then he moved on, leaving a bar tab with Dieter and Luisa embedded between my shoulder blades. The only true love, she told me, was unrequited, and I replied, somewhat lamely, that I knew what she meant, as we sat on the ramparts blowing smoke into the curved rays of the rising sun.

She was hugging her tie-dyed skirt to her knees, but she stretched out a bangled arm and touched me for the first time.

'You do know,' she announced. 'I can see it in your eyes.'

The sierras favour only a certain kind of love: there is little room along the ridges and in the corks and through the groves

for the Californian variety with its floaty dresses and its fluttering eyelashes and bell-bottomed jeans. Andalusia demands
a love as hard as the crags, as withering as the sun, as lethal as
the bulls. Love is defined by the land and its people, like the
music. It is passionate, forceful and violent, and its pleasure is
measured only by the gaps between the pain. Love is a bastard
born of rape, raised in bondage and let loose on a naïve society to destroy convention and defy the Commandments, to be
cited in court as the reason why we have to have rules and
sanctions. It has a certain beauty, a tangible desirability tainted
with the knowledge that like a teenaged whore it will ruin
your reputation and steal your wallet, and when all is lost, the
memory of love is all you're left with. Luisa and I never found
this love, but we had cocaine, and that, of course, was very
similar.

I lifted my damp backside from the step and followed Carlito's
fading paw prints down the lane to the blacktop. I hid in the
chaparral for nearly an hour as the first dozen cars passed me,
squinting up the road to try to recognise the next. The thirteenth car was an overwaxed yellow Datsun, its chrome fittings
gleaming in the morning sun as it roared towards the bridge.
This flamboyant ZX belonged to a man I knew I could trust, a
lone eccentric with a pool of honesty and integrity so deep and
clear that I had never dared bathe in it for fear of contamina-
tion. I rose and stood at the roadside, waving hard with both
hands. Carlito emerged from a clump of tall purple flowers,
shook the seeds and the pollen from his moth-eaten hide and
stood beside me like a nonchalant commuter as the car roared
to a growling halt in an explosion of dust and smoke. Carlito
shook his head and sneezed.

'Two for the price of one?' asked the driver, his combination of shoulder-length curly hair and a flat cap strangely unnerving. 'It's a special offer or what?'

'Alberto!' I smiled. 'It's so good to see you!'

He peered across the passenger seat like a man about to offer a lift to a lunatic. 'Climb aboard for the drive of your life.'

Carlito and I raced for the front seat. Carlito lost, and I extended my hand to Alberto. He tapped my palm through kidskin gloves as though handshakes were unimportant, or unhygienic.

'Alberto,' I said, 'I need to get to Bloody Mary's house in La Mendirosa. You know her? Red-headed *Inglesa*, bit lairy, nothing special to look at. Can you drop me there?'

He shrugged. 'Sure I can. Got to lighten the load a little first, though. You ready for a near-death experience, or have you just had one?'

I strapped myself in and laughed. Alberto was a genius even if he did look like a serious version of Bon Scott. The unmarried only child of a government inspector and the illegitimate daughter of a Gibraltarian condom smuggler, Alberto was the smartest, fastest and most professional *contrabandista* between Malaga and Cadiz. His one-man tobacco-distribution service was cheaper, more frequent and more reliable than any offered by the legitimate outfits, and he even gave away T-shirts, lighters and other promotional gifts. He used fast boats, false bottoms, big dogs and black *burros* to bring his contraband in, and it had long been rumoured that the only man who knew for sure where the ends of Franco's secret tunnel between La Linea and the Rock lay was Alberto. The grand master of innovation and evasion, he seemed to know every track, footpath and goat trail in the land, and everyone who lived along them. Apolitical and unopinionated, he saved all his passion for his hatred of drugs, and that broke my heart. Alberto was one of those people who seemed to fit twenty-five hours into every day, not least because he suffered from chronic insomnia and claimed not to have slept for eleven years. In those 4018 sleepless nights he had mastered the black art of electronics, built his own satellite receiver and learned every language broadcast from space. He had inherited a pirate radio station from a distant relative who was doing time for ETA, but had abandoned its revolutionary output in favour of an easy-listening blend of classic rock, popular flamenco and home-made advertisements. Since nobody within earshot of the FRA would pay for publicity, Alberto gave it away, advertising births, deaths and marriages, special events at local bars and matters of agricultural interest. He also made room in his busy schedule for odd corporations like Turtle Wax, Decca and Heckler & Koch, and he had no issues whatsoever with tobacco advertising. I smiled and sat back as the Datsun accelerated, glad to relinquish the responsibility for my destiny for the next couple of hours. I picked up a soft-pack of Winston from the central console.

'May I?'

Alberto slipped the clutch and the car growled. He nodded, holding out a leather-gloved hand. 'Consistent quality, consistent flavour.' He dropped his shades onto his nose and eyeballed Carlito among the empty plastic bottles on the back seat.

'How are you today, pal?' Even though his mother had spoken the language of the Rock, Alberto still pronounced the second-person pronoun as 'jew'.

Carlito sniffed and returned to his genital ablutions. Alberto grinned and pushed his glasses back into place, then slipped me a sideways glance. 'Pal for Action Live!' he announced.

I didn't care, but I was in his car, smoking his cigarettes, and I owed him. '"Pal for Active Life",' I corrected.

'Absolutely!' he agreed. 'No wonder top breeders recommend it!'

I sighed and turned my battered face into the cool breeze as we wound up the twisting, potholed road, smoking the accelerated cigarette down to the butt and then lighting another. Alberto glanced down at the pack as I scrabbled for a third, but even though he was the last person to be tight with cigarettes I realised that he might think I was taking advantage of his generosity and hesitated, my fingers trembling above the cellophane, my swollen eyes turned towards his.

He looked away quickly. 'Go ahead!' he urged. 'They won't kill you.'

'Thanks, Alberto,' I mumbled. Part of me wanted to look in the vanity mirror to see what Alberto had seen, but another part counselled that vanity was a privilege I couldn't afford. Alberto was clearly dying to know what had happened to me, but professional courtesy prevented him from asking. I sucked slowly on the butt and wondered what I had to lose by telling.

'I bet you're thinking I've had a bit of a kicking.'

Alberto studied the road. 'Er, no,' he replied uncertainly.

'Yes you are,' I countered.

Alberto shook his head. 'Not.'

'You're saying that it's not crossed your mind that I might have been involved in some violence recently.'

'Nope.'

I sighed. It was possible that he was telling the truth. 'So what were you thinking?' I asked.

Alberto took a breath, opened his mouth, then closed it again. 'I was thinking that you can't get quicker than a Kwik-Fit Fitter.'

I shook my head. 'That's bollocks.'

'Now you mention it, I gotta admit that you do look like shit,' added Alberto.

'Got beaten up,' I replied. 'How bad do I really look?' I had to ask, because there exists a certain satisfaction in the declaration 'You look like shit' that occasionally prompts people to say it when it isn't strictly true.

'Like shit,' affirmed Alberto. 'Really bad, like old, stamped-in shit, like you should be dead or in hospital or something.'

'Oh God!' I groaned. 'What about my face? How bad is that?'

Alberto set his mouth and looked at me with some sympathy. '*Hombre*,' he said, 'it's your face I'm talking about. You saying there's more? Who did this? Guardia Civil?'

I thought about it for a moment, watching the aloes whizz past the car. 'No,' I replied. 'It was rock-climbers.'

Alberto emitted a long, low whistle. 'Rock-climbers?' he said, shaking his head. '*Bastardos*, eh?'

I nodded. 'Oh yeah, jangling bastards,' I agreed.

We dropped Carlito, at his barked request, beside a line of beehives on the side of the road, then accelerated over the ridge and into the next valley.

'I bet he gets stung bad,' opined Alberto, and I nodded wearily. I didn't feel like talking, and Alberto must have felt my reticence.

'Put the radio on,' he suggested.

It was a good idea. I punched the button and wound up the volume.

'. . . comfort, security and above all power. The Toyota Land Cruiser: all you need and more. This is Janis Joplin and Bobby McGee,' announced Alberto, from way up in the mountains.

'That was clever of me,' declared Alberto. 'I was just thinking about her.'

I looked from him to the radio, and back again. 'How the fuck do you do that?'

'Happens all the time,' he replied.

'I'm don't mean your rock'n'roll telepathy,' I sighed. 'I mean this . . . this remote-broadcasting thing.'

'Tapes,' he explained. 'I stay up all night and make tapes. Make sure that they correspond with the real time of day, and then I'm free to fuck with the forces of customs and excise. As long as they think I'm broadcasting on a pirate frequency, I'm an Interior Ministry problem.'

Every night, before signing off, Alberto told his listeners that the lights were on. He never told them that there was nobody home, and now I knew why. It was clever, but I couldn't help feeling disappointed.

Ten minutes later we stopped at a long, low, *cal*-painted building on the western slope of the next valley with nothing more than a faded tin A-frame advertising long-deleted ice creams to identify it as a bar. I struggled from the car and hobbled into the shade, my clothes becoming damp again although it was not yet nine in the morning. I watched the shimmering road anxiously for any sign of the hounds while Alberto unfolded a square metre of stockingette and wiped the dust from his yellow bodywork. Partly satisfied, he refolded the duster, popped the boot and lifted a cardboard box onto his knee, balancing it while he slammed the polished lid shut.

'At Alberto's, we know the best time for business,' he grinned, and I followed him into the darkness of the bar. He dropped the carton onto a stool and leaned against the bar beside it. I blinked what little light there was into my eyes and studied the bottles beyond the polished zinc bartop. It was never, ever, too early, and Alberto was singing in German about a little white cow eating sweet green grass.

'. . . and we thank her for her cheese,' he crowed, until interrupted by the swish of the fly-curtain.

'*Cafe?*' asked the owner, shaking Alberto's hand and staring at me with frank curiosity.

Alberto turned and followed the gaze. '*Cafe?*' he echoed.

'Er, yeah, lovely,' I replied, 'and *aguardiente* as well, please?'

Alberto shrugged. He was the only true teetotaller I knew. 'He's okay,' he whispered to the proprietor. 'He got beaten up by rock-cimbers.'

The owner tipped back his head and grunted. '*Coños*'

Alberto looked back at me, winking as though he knew the score. 'Come and sit down,' he said, but I didn't want to cramp his style.

'You're all right,' I reassured him. 'I'll just go and wash my hands.'

The proprietor's wife, a hard-core *señora* in a lilac shell suit, didn't turn as I passed the washing line where she was hanging shell suits out to dry. I hurried across the dusty yard beneath the cool shade of the almond trees and shut myself in behind the tin door of the lavatory to consider my situation.

I hid my face in my hands, I stretched, I shook my head and I scratched behind my ears, trying to ignore the alarmist chirruping of the sparrows and the feeble struggles of a dying fly caught in a spider's deathtrap. I needed to gather my thoughts, to analyse my circumstances, make projections for my future and formulate a plan, but all I could think of was that thimbleful of aniseed liquor and a good hard suck on a Winston. I pushed open the door and took a seat at the bar. There would be plenty of time for reflection at Bloody Mary's house.

★

The proprietor was busy refilling his cigarette machine with Alberto's contraband fags, and the smuggler was examining the guts of a Walkman while a small boy watched in wonder.

'He's a genius,' I smiled at the kid, 'like McGyver.'

The kid turned, smiling politely, the smile coagulating when his eyes crossed my face. He reddened and looked away.

'You know,' I continued unnecessarily, 'McGyver, Canadian bloke off the telly, fixes anything.'

'Can you, Alberto?' asked the kid. 'Can you fix anything?'

Alberto dropped the carcass into one little hand and the cover into another. 'Not this I can't,' he muttered. 'It's totally fucked.' Kids warranted no special treatment from Alberto.

The proprietor looked up from the Ducados Lite. 'You sold it to me,' he cried. 'You told me it was top quality.'

Alberto scratched his head. 'It was. What tapes have you been playing on it?'

The proprietor looked at his son. 'What tapes have you been playing on it?'

The kid looked at me. I shrugged.

'Looby and Bella,' he mumbled, 'and First Date.'

'Ah,' sighed Alberto. 'Crap music. Cheap tapes. You see?'

'The First Date tape wasn't cheap,' argued the proprietor. 'It was close on three thousand from El Corte Ingles. That lot were all the rage a month back.'

Alberto shook his head. 'Doesn't matter how popular they are. Doesn't make them good.'

'He's right, you know,' I added. 'The tape might have been expensive to buy, but the quality of the music is still rubbish. Burns out a Walkman just like that.'

'Same with VCRs,' said Alberto. 'People think they can play any old movie on a video recorder and it'll keep going for years, but it won't.' He walked across to the bar and sipped his coffee. 'Why do you think the Americans keep making crap movies?'

I shot down my *aguardiente* and tapped the bar for another.

The proprietor moved like a robot. 'Why?'

Alberto smiled and looked at the floor, a patient smile on his thin lips. 'Okay, let me ask you another question: who owns the movie companies in the USA?'

'I dunno,' grunted the barman, filling my glass. 'Warner Brothers? The Mafia? The government? Mickey Mouse?'

'Worse,' whispered Alberto. 'Sony.'

The proprietor blinked. 'Sony?'

'And who makes the video recorders?'

'Sony?' tried the proprietor.

Alberto turned his palms towards God and shrugged. 'You want a good VCR, you see me. I can get you a French one – a Thomson – and the French make very good movies. Until then . . .' He made a face like a goldfish and turned to me. '*Hermano*, let me show you something. You will not believe your eyes.'

I knocked back my drink and was dragging myself to my feet when the kid hissed, 'Guardia! They've gone around the back!'

I heard the doors of their cruiser slam shut, and then they pushed their way through the curtain at the rear of the bar, scoping the dark room even as their eyes grew accustomed to the shade. I risked a look at Alberto, and he was all smiles.

'*Buenos dias, señors*,' called the first into our tense little situation, looking like a trainee accountant in khaki. 'How's it going this morning?'

He had his eyes on everyone as he replaced his prescription aviators with a pair of round spectacles that reminded me of Helmut.

'Excellently,' beamed the proprietor.

'Fantastic,' exclaimed Alberto.

'Great!' I enthused.

'What happened to you?' asked the second cop. He was big and ruddy, clearly the brawn element in the team. He folded his arms, his big face in shadow and looking forward to illumination.

'Domestic,' I replied, with the appropriate amount of sheepishness. 'Girlfriend's brothers.'

'They're rock-climbers,' added Alberto.

'*Cafe, señors?*' suggested the proprietor.

The big cop was still staring at me, wondering, perhaps, if he knew me from somewhere. I smiled in the guilty way that guilty people do.

'You from the Rock?' he asked.

'No.' I shook my head, and noticed that my hands were shaking as well. So did the cop. He was about to push the point, when the arrival of another car dragged his attention to the doorway. There was an urgent yet playful blast of the horn, and the kid rushed outside, yelling '*Tia!*'

'Shopping,' the barman shrugged. 'Malaga. Anyone want anything?'

The cop turned back to me. 'So where you from?'

I lit a fag and inhaled. 'I'm English. I love it down here.' On the outside I was smiling and sucking in smoke, and on the inside I was screaming as I was blowing it out. The last thing I needed was the interest of policemen, but I was becoming the life and soul of the party. Any minute now they were going to ask me for my papers.

'Down where?' asked the accountant.

'Here,' I replied, 'in Andalusia.'

He raised his eyebrows. 'In Andalusia? But these people are

all bandits, communists and peasants,' he smiled coldly, defying contradiction. 'Isn't that right, *Patron*?'

The barman smiled back and shrugged.

'And all this is just an extension of all that,' he continued, pointing to the south and, presumably, the Sahara.

'There's more water in Ceuta,' observed the second. I laughed so hard I dropped my fag, and as I bent down to retrieve it from the floor the proprietor's wife came in from the back.

'*Hola*,' I heard her call, then, '*Hasta lluego*.' It was a casual and inaccurate way to bid her husband goodbye.

The first cop pushed his glasses onto his nose and sipped his coffee. 'You speak Spanish very well. What do you do for a living?'

'I'm a teacher,' I replied. Shadows of disbelief fell across their faces.

'In a school,' I continued needlessly. 'I teach Spanish and French.'

As the women and the child left I crossed to the bar and tapped for a refill – you never know when it's going to be your last. The badge above the cop's pocket identified him as Morales. Good name for a cop.

'Language or literature?' he asked.

I smiled. 'You cannot teach one without the other, but principally language.'

The second cop sighed and turned to Alberto. He could smell intellectual homosexuality from a kilometre away. 'That your motor out the front?'

'So you know some Spanish poets?' presumed Morales.

'Some,' I concurred.

'Who is the best, in your opinion?'

'Machado,' I replied. 'Who do you think is best?' This was turning into one of the petty duels that I used to enjoy in days gone by. It was a bit different when I was straight, worried and in pain.

'The lion goes from strength to strength,' enthused Alberto. 'Two-and-a-half-litre turbo injection, all rebored and everything: the drive of your life.' He was still advertising his ride as he passed through the beads. I wished I could join him. My inquisitor leaned forward and pointed at me.

> When his beloved died
> he thought he'd just grow old,
> shutting himself in the house
> alone, with memories and the mirror
> that she had looked in one bright day.

> Like gold in the miser's chest,
> he thought he'd keep all yesterday
> in the clear mirror intact.
> For him time's flow would cease.

He leaned back against the bar, his palms turned upwards, smiling. 'Antonio Machado. Died in France of consumption, I believe.' He frowned, rubbing his chin in a charade of feigned forgetfulness. 'What was that poem called?'

I focused on the floor and tried to stop my head from spinning. My stomach had fallen away as I had registered the first line, and my nervous system was trying to follow through the same hole.

'It's called "The Eyes",' I croaked. 'He forgot what his wife's eyes looked like.'

I knew exactly what Luisa's eyes had looked like. They were dark, so dark that you couldn't see where the pupil ended and the iris began. The whites were blemished with the tiny tracks of broken blood vessels, but the lashes were long, dark and thick. The sun and the smoke had riven tiny cracks in the skin around the corners and, more often than not, dark, bruise-like smudges had shadowed her lower lids. The last time I saw her eyes they were no longer seeing me, but looking right at me. How could a man forget what his wife's eyes looked like? I sighed. I was engaged in a duel and had yet to fire my shot. My opponent was waiting.

> As a man, I won't repeat
> the things she said to me.
> The light of understanding
> has made me more discreet.
> I took her away from the river
> soiled with kisses and sand.
> The sabres of the irises
> were stabbing at the breeze.
> I behaved as what I am.
> As a true-born gypsy.

I shrugged and looked at the cop. He was still standing.

'Lorca, of course,' I muttered. 'Died in Granada. Shot in the arse, I believe.'

The cop split his mouth into something like a smile. '"The Faithless Wife",' he said. 'Interesting, considering your position.'

I caught my breath and held it against my fluttering stomach. Prickles of hot sweat burned my lip. The bastard had cast me in his own little detective movie. I blinked and stammered like a guilty little man. 'What position?'

He looked at me for a moment. 'I suspect that you are in the position of the faithless husband. Am I right?'

It took me a moment to appreciate that he was barking up completely the wrong tree. I smiled, and nodded, and maybe I blushed a little.

'You can see why you're a cop and I'm just a teacher,' I said.

'Machado never understood El Duende, did he?' sighed Morales. 'But Lorca, it lived in his genes . . . "In all countries death is an end," he said. "It comes, and the curtains are closed. Not in Spain. In Spain, they are raised . . . A dead person in Spain is more alive dead than anywhere else in the world" – that's something to look forward to, is it not?'

Who was I to argue? I nodded sagely and tapped for another *aguardiente*. The barman made a mental calculation as he filled the glass. I lit a fag, then offered the pack to Morales. He took one and lit it with a Zippo engraved with the badge of the US Marine Corps.

'Tell me one thing about English education,' he said, pausing as his oppo came back into the bar.

'That is a beautiful car he's got out there,' declared the big cop. 'Clean as a whistle.' Alberto loved to show cops around his car because that way he could ensure that they would never find his secret compartments. It was truly a terrible shame that the mad-haired smuggler had such a naïve abhorrence of drugs.

'In England,' began Morales, 'you have—'

He was interrupted by the roaring protest of displaced gravel and the creaking of brakes. He blinked and looked towards the door as two vans pulled up outside, their drivers slamming the doors and shouting at each other in bad-tempered ignorance of the solitude of their surroundings.

'French?' asked Morales.

I nodded, for my tongue had swollen in my throat. I knocked back the *aguardiente* and stood closer to the cop.

The Arab kid entered first, pulling the curtain aside and letting it drop. He sat heavily at the first table, neither looking around nor noticing the Guardia and me. He looked worried, upset, and as the argument continued outside he pouted, shook his head and lit up a cigarette.

The curtain was dragged noisily aside. I jumped.

'. . . then just piss off back to Châtelet,' blustered Jean-Marc. 'You're no . . .' He spotted the two cops and smiled, then saw me. His eyes widened and the smile clattered to the floor as he spun around.

'Noisy bastards, aren't they?' muttered the big cop to Morales, and even if they had spoken French they wouldn't have heard Jean-Marc's warning.

'Something's pissed them off,' surmised Morales, nodding in response to Benoit's ugly smile.

'You fucking blind or something?' hissed Benoit to the Arab kid, his chair scraping on the flags as he sat at the table. Jean-Marc sat back and smiled pleasantly for all to see.

'Shut the fuck up,' he growled, his face like a ventriloquist's dummy's. The obvious quality of his expensive clothes only heightened his appearance of unwashed shabbiness. The growth on his sunken face, the dark rings below his bloodshot eyes and his greasy, uncombed hair betrayed the urbane gentleman and exposed his grubby roots. Even Benoit, with his lunar complexion, looked nobler than this yellow-toothed sewer rat.

The Arab kid glared hard at Benoit from beneath a thundercloud brow. Benoit stared back, defying him to have a go. The cops tried not to stare.

Jean-Marc held three fingers in the air. '*Café, por favor, et cognac?*'

The barman raised his eyebrows, his glance flicking towards the Guardia. '*Coñac?*'

Jean-Marc dropped his arm. '*No cognac, merci, gracias. Café.*'

Benoit and the Arab kid were still staring each other out.

Jean-Marc was still smiling. 'Are you two fucking crazy or what?'

'I've got nothing to be ashamed of,' growled the Arab kid.

'That spotty bastard hasn't been out long,' decided Morales's colleague. He turned to the barman. 'Do my coffee first.'

'In England,' persisted Morales, 'you learn only French in the schools. Is that right?'

I looked past him. Jean-Marc was smiling at me. His nose was glowing, and my hands were shaking. I nodded. 'Er, yeah, that's right.'

'Oh no it's not,' argued Morales. 'You should learn Spanish. Spanish is more widely spoken than French, is it not?'

Jean-Marc clasped both his hands together as though gripping the butt of his pistol, his forefingers extended and touching at their tips to make the barrel. He rested his chin on his cocked thumbs and pondered me from behind his gun. I needed to think, and the cop wasn't giving me any time to do so. I knew that somewhere in this roadhouse lurked the opportunity to bring salvation upon myself, glory upon Morales and custody upon my pursuers.

'You're right,' I concurred, 'but you're preaching to the converted. I hate the French.'

The only snag was Alberto. If I cried wolf, no one would leave. The Guardia would call for back-up, the bar would be crawling with cops, and when they'd searched the vans, they'd probably search Alberto's car. Then they would find Alberto's contraband, and Alberto would go down.

'I think the Russians are the worst,' opined Morales. 'We have a lot of trouble with the Russians here.'

There was a chance that they might let Alberto go, but it was unlikely, and if they busted him, then his car would become the property of the state. They might even repossess his house, and I would be responsible for the downfall of this kind and crazy man.

'Oh no,' I disagreed, shaking my head and returning Jean-Marc's stare. 'The French are much, much worse than the Russians.'

Behind all this idle chatter a decision was waiting to be made. I made it: Alberto's welfare was not my problem. My welfare was. The law could decide. I took a deep breath and turned to face Morales.

'Listen. Those three guys who just came in . . .'

Morales turned and looked at their table. Jean-Marc lowered his hands and gave a friendly nod. It suddenly struck me that there might be some shooting, but I had faith in the ability of two well-trained cops either to disarm or outgun three incompetent thugs.

Morales looked at me. 'The Frenchmen? What about them?'

The curtain at the rear of the bar rattled and Alberto came in, struggling with his fly.

'A man's gotta do what a man's gotta do,' he smiled, clapping my arm with a wet hand. '*Hermano*, we got to go!'

'Nice meeting you both,' I smiled to the cops. Alberto pushed through the curtain and I made to follow him.

Morales called me back. 'What about these Frenchmen?'

I paused, less than a fist's throw from Jean-Marc. 'Oh yeah.' I smiled. 'This one just said that they had nothing to worry about from a couple of country bumpkin coppers like, er, you two. See what I mean about the French?'

Morales's smile evaporated and his oppo swung around to see who fancied him.

'See you later,' I waved, and limped out into the sunshine.

★

'That was too close,' I muttered as we rolled towards the wooded valley. 'Look at my hands.'

Alberto grinned. 'What do you think of that cop?'

'Morales?'

Alberto nodded. 'Yeah, Matteo Morales Silvestre. He's from Aragon. New. I've never met him before today. What do you think?'

'He thinks he's smart,' I started, then my mind caught up with my mouth. 'You mean you know the other one?'

'*Claro*,' he confirmed. 'Eight hundred Winston a month and the odd case of *cubanos*. Trouble is, he isn't sure about his new partner, either. That's why we . . .'

I stopped listening and gazed out at the short-sleeved cork oaks and their piles of dirty laundry lying stacked at the shaded roadside. Alberto gunned the Datsun across a hump-backed bridge over a bed of dry rocks and accelerated towards the next ridge. Something about his driving was making me feel ill, and I wound down the window to wash my face in the slip-stream.

We emerged from the shade of the wooded valley out onto the rocky slopes of the ridge, and it was as though somebody had opened the oven door. I wound up the window, closed my eyes and let the air-con take over. Maybe Machado had a point, I thought, as the memory of Luisa darkened my mind. Already her face was losing definition and I wondered how long it would be before she left me for ever.

'Who left you for ever?' asked Alberto. I looked at him as though he had read my mind.

'You just said "she left me for ever",' he said.

I made a mental note to make my mental health a priority some time in the future.

'Luisa,' I mumbled. 'She's gone.'

Alberto stared straight ahead. 'Hey, it's your business, man. None of mine.'

It made sense to confide in Alberto. He was weird, but he was also cautious, clever and discreet. That he considered me a friend showed a deficiency in his wisdom, but then who was I to criticise a man for his powers of judgement. As long as no drugs were involved, Alberto would do whatever he could to help me, and I would have betrayed him in a minute if the act of treachery could have put me one step further from the darkness.

The road wound up into the mountains, its short straights following the contours between bone-dry fields and joined by hairpins at their ends. The valley was already far below, the cool shade of the corks hidden by a shimmering haze, the twisting road down from the bar clearly visible in the mid-morning sunshine. Alberto stopped the Datsun on the gravel verge of a wide bend and jumped out of the car.

'*Agua dolce*,' he explained, gathering the empty five-litre mineral-water containers from the rear seat. 'Pure as a mountain spring.'

He hopped over the roadside and disappeared, following a well-worn track through the scrub to a distant spring, famed, no doubt, for its curative powers, or supernatural properties, or, occasionally, its flavour. I had heard of a secret spring up near Olvera that rendered barren women fertile, and another, near Ubrique, that cured horses of worms.

I climbed out of the car and standing at the edge of the deserted road, dropped my jeans to check on my injuries. From the waist down, I was a born loser. Ugly orange abrasions criss-crossed the yellow bruises on my bony shins, and my aching thighs were stamped with dark blue contusions. My T-shirt hid my swollen tackle, and as I lifted it to examine the damage, a rolling whisper made me look up. My eyes were met by the horrified faces of a carload of *campesinos* encountering the ugliest flasher they had ever seen. I managed to drop the shirt as they glided past, silent-running in neutral to save fuel, but standing at the roadside with my jeans around my ankles, wearing cowboy boots and a wan smile, I felt that the damage had already been done.

I terminated the examination and lit a cigarette. The smoke curled around my face like poison gas, and I felt the nicotine enter my overloaded system with all the comfort of a lethal injection. I took another drag, holding the smoke, then coughed it out as a cold sweat broke along my twisted spine. I dropped the butt and crushed it against the dusty road. No satisfaction. I needed a joint, or a line, or, ideally, a half-dozen of those DF118s that Theo had given me so long ago. I stared across the valley, following the road as it snaked across the facing slope and wondering how many DFs it would take to put me into a pleasant eternal slumber, free from worry, from pain and from guilt. A car crossed the opposite ridge and began its descent, the sunlight bouncing from its windscreen and a faint plume of dust trailing in its wake. I was still feeling sorry for myself when another car appeared opposite, its windscreen flashing the first. I watched as they descended towards the sanctuary of the corks, deep in the valley where they could hide, unseen by the angry sun, and embraced . . .

They weren't cars. They were vans. I hobbled around the Datsun, ignoring the scream of my thighs.

'Alberto!' I called into the shrubs. 'Leave the bloody water and come quick!'

There was no reply. I scoped across the valley again. The

white Mercedes was in the lead, three turns above the corks and maybe five minutes away from me.

'Alberto!' I yelled. 'Quick!'

He had to be able to hear me. How far away could the spring be?

'Alberto!'

I leaned through the passenger window and withdrew a fag from the pack on the seat. This time it didn't taste so bad.

'Alberto!'

It was possible that he had descended out of earshot. Convenient walking distances were often considerably greater in these parts than elsewhere in western Europe. Holiday companies must have loved Andalusian clients.

'Alberto!' I yelled again. 'Come quickly, your car is on fire!'

I gave him a second or so to come to my rescue, and then I tried to steal his car, but he had taken the keys with him.

Maybe he was wiser than I thought.

I hobbled to the edge of the highway and looked across the valley for the vans. Both had entered the woods, and soon they would be accelerating against the gradient towards me. Maybe not. Maybe they would appreciate the cool shade of the corks as I had, and would stop for a picnic, or a fight. Unlikely, I decided, just before the white van broke through my weak, self-willed wall at the edge of the woods and changed down for the long, serpentine, uphill drag. I sucked what strength I could from my fag and shuffled around the Datsun to lean through the driver's-side window and press the horn. It did the trick – Alberto must have thought his car was calling him. He appeared at the top of the trail, breathless and wearing a worried expression. Mine must have been better.

'What the hell is going on?'

I held his door open. 'We got to go, Alberto, and quick!'

His narrow brown eyes locked on to mine, but he moved towards the car anyway. 'What's going on?'

I helped him stack his water on the back seat and hobbled around to the passenger side. 'Just drive. I'll tell you.'

Alberto sighed, shook his head and turned the ignition. The Datsun roared.

'You in some kind of trouble with these rock-climbers?' he asked. 'Where's your girlfriend?'

I closed my eyes. 'Alberto, please drive the car. I'll tell you the score when we're rolling.'

Alberto stared straight ahead, gunning the engine as though he might drive away, or maybe not.

'She's gone off with these rock-climbers, hasn't she?' He smiled and turned to look at me. I saw myself in his scratched mirrors, and I looked uncomfortable.

'Let her go,' he continued. 'If you truly love something, let it go, and if it truly loves you, then it will return to you, right?'

I struggled for words, but Alberto took my silence for acquiescence.

'I know you want to run to her and bring her back to you, but that's not going to happen. She needs some time to get her feelings into perspective, and if she decides that life is better without you, *hermano*, then your life is better without her.' He looked me up and down curiously. 'You've never been a rock-climber, have you?'

I could feel the vibrations of the Mercedes like the hammer blows that would close my coffin.

'Alberto!' I yelled. 'Please fucking drive now!'

He tutted and put his supercharged sports coupé into first. 'Okay, already.'

'Can't we go a bit faster?' I asked.

'Are you sure we're driving to a place you want to be?'

replied Alberto, an eyebrow cocked above the rim of his shades. 'Am I driving you into more misery and discontent? Is that something I want to do?'

'Just drive, will you?'

'Yeah, right,' he snorted. 'Drive you right back to Luisa.' He slid his gloved hands around to five to one. 'Like she wants me to.'

Given the time, and the relevance, I would have quizzed him on that comment. We cruised over the ridge and began the descent into the next valley. Alberto, who had never had a girlfriend in his life, was still lecturing me on the best way of resurrecting mine while pursued by homicidal Frenchmen driving vans. I had to laugh.

'You may laugh,' allowed Alberto, sanctimoniously, 'but for you, she is as dead as Janis Joplin.'

'I know,' I agreed quickly, twisting my neck to scope the road through the passenger-side wing mirror.

I made up my mind. 'Alberto: speed up, and listen. Luisa really is dead.'

He smiled and nodded. '"That's better, see?'

I shook my head and fumbled for his fags. 'No—'

'Who the fuck is that?' interrupted Alberto. 'Who the fuck is that lunatic?'

He pulled himself upright, dragging on the steering wheel with two gloved hands and peering into the rear-view mirror. I looked back. The Mercedes van was so close that it filled the rear windscreen.

'Speed up!' I screamed. 'He's going to ram us!'

Alberto stuck lead on the gas and the Datsun surged ahead, but this was no road for speed trials. I looked back, and saw the Mercedes regress before regaining ground as Alberto slowed for the next bend.

'Alberto, I'm really sorry to drag you into this, but we really got to split,' I began. 'The men in the van killed Luisa, and if they catch me, they'll kill me too.'

Alberto looked like he was concentrating on the road ahead, but his jaw muscles had tightened and the blood had drained from his face.

'I'm not exaggerating: if they catch me, they'll kill me, and that's that.'

'And me too,' he surmised.

I felt bad about that, but he was right. 'Er, yeah, probably,' I admitted. 'Sorry.'

Alberto sighed. '*O Madre Dios.* Put the radio on.'

The FRA was playing 'Sympathy for the Devil'. It was better than 'Hi Ho Silver Lining'.

'Luisa's dead?' asked Alberto impassively.

I shifted in my seat in order that I could see them coming. 'Yes she is. Speed up! They're gaining on us.'

'*No problemos,*' he muttered, dropping into third for a wide hairpin and accelerating out of the bend. 'You sure she's dead?'

The Mercedes was hidden for a moment by our dust before bursting through the cloud like a charging bull.

'Am I sure she's dead? What's that supposed to mean?'

'I mean how can you be sure she's dead? She may just be pretending to be dead so you don't go after her.' He glanced in the rear-view mirror. 'This guy is a good driver, or a crazy one.'

Alberto, I decided, watched too much satellite TV.

'She's dead, and I know she's dead because I saw her get shot, and the man who shot her is driving the van that's chasing us.' I glanced ahead and gripped my seat. 'Slow down!'

'You see?' he sighed, like it happened all the time. 'Guns don't kill people. People kill people.'

'What's that got to do with anything?'

He raised a gloved finger. 'It's an observation, and now you know it's a truth.'

He changed down and braked, taking the sheer-sided corner by its outer edges and racing away as the van followed his line and kept its distance.

'Is this a business matter?' enquired Alberto.

'Yeah, sort of,' I replied.

'And they *shot* Luisa?'

'Yeah, five times, except one of the bullets missed.'

Alberto let a long, low whistle out through pursed lips. It was beginning to sink in. 'You got to kill these bastards.'

'Yeah, right,' I muttered. 'Watch that corner!'

Alberto wrestled the speeding car through the switchback and toed it towards the next bend.

'You do know that car adverts are total bollocks, don't you?' I asked. 'You can't really drive along mountain roads at those speeds. You know that, don't you?'

He glared at me, taking it personally.

'Just an observation,' I added.

We were climbing now, a steep gradient that levelled out as it approached a blind bend.

'This is a bad place,' declared Alberto. 'People always driving off this corner, because there's no sign. People come racing up the hill, excessive speed, no sign, and then no road.' He slowed down to twenty before taking the bend. 'They should put a sign there. It would be a major contribution to road safety.'

The road ahead descended in a gentle curve down to the stone bridge across a dried-out *arroyo*. I looked back in time to see the Mercedes skid around Alberto's treacherous bend. It wobbled dangerously before regaining its hold on the road, and a few moments later the Transit followed. The bend took the driver by surprise, and as he tried to make good his over-compensation he skidded across the gravel and accelerated off the tarmac. I watched my Transit hang in space for a moment, as though Wile E. Coyote was at the wheel, and then it dropped onto the steep, boulder-strewn slope, landing in an explosion of dust that could be felt rather than heard.

'My bloody van's just gone over the edge!'

Alberto shrugged, barely glancing to his right as the Transit emerged from its shroud and began accelerating towards the valley. 'We'll see it again at the bottom,' he said. 'Might need some work done on it, though.'

Thorny succulents were brushed and crushed as the van bumped and rattled down the rocky slope, the dust plume at its rear like the smoke trail from a burning bomber.

'He's fucked, isn't he?'

'Maybe not,' replied Alberto. 'If he can keep her pointing downhill, and keep his braking nice and smooth, maybe he'll be okay. If not, he can always jump.'

As the van continued to gather momentum, I wondered how anybody could remain calm enough to keep their braking nice and smooth while hurtling down a steepening mountainside towards a ravine. Alberto checked for the Mercedes in the rear-view, and slowed down. Already below us on the mountainside, the Transit was taking the straightest line to the bottom, and I tried in vain through the dust and shrubs to see who was driving.

'He's not in control,' opined Alberto, as my van glanced off a boulder with a spine-snapping thud. The nearside wing rose in the slipstream like an air brake before being swept back and torn from the Transit in a spinning flash of black and red.

'He should jump,' said Alberto, 'before it turns.'

An idle and inappropriately appointed part of my

subconscious, like a fashion journalist at an execution, wondered how Alberto had come to know so much about the
management of unplanned off-road driving. TV, answered
another part, and on TV, anything automotive that went over
the side of a cliff ended up in flames.

'Yeah, before it explodes,' I added.

The nose of the doomed van had turned slightly to the left
of the fall line, tracing a curve across the tightly stacked
contours.

'It won't explode,' snorted Alberto, 'it's diesel, but he is now
on the highway to hell. Watch this.' He pulled over, but left the
engine running.

Fifteen metres from the ravine the Transit lost its grip,
rocking first from four wheels to two, and then back to four as
it tried to traverse the slope. The next time its uphill wheels left
the ground, they didn't go back, and the blood-red beast of
burden teetered on two wheels before dropping onto its side in
a screeching, shrieking cymbal crash of breaking glass, spinning,
smoking rubber and deformed steel. A torn-off wing mirror
flashed the sun across my eyes, spinning away from the wreck as
it rolled across its broken back and punctured side to bounce on
buckled wheels and fall, like a tortured bull, with a last gasp of
steam and a gush of hot oil from its ruptured sump, onto its side
and drop from view into the ravine.

Alberto did the scalded bit with his fingers, sucking in his
breath in a long whistle. 'That's going to need a lot of work
done on it now.'

'And the driver . . .?'

'What do you think?'

I was becoming incapable of thought. 'Didn't explode.'

Alberto rolled his eyes. 'They don't, as a rule.' He checked
the rear-view. 'Where are his *compadres*?'

I scanned back up the road but there was no sign of the Mercedes. 'Must have stopped,' I suggested.

Alberto slipped the Datsun into first and rolled towards the bridge. 'Maybe,' he grunted. 'Want to see the wreck?'

I grabbed the pack of Winston with white knuckles and squeezed one out. Did I want to see the wreck? Did I want to see what was left of the driver? I tried to consider these questions for a moment, but caught my breath as something deep within my sunken chest cavity ruptured. Cool vapours filled my lungs and a substance heavy and cold, like mercury, surged through my veins, displacing the thin blood and flooding my cortex. My body had realised before my mind that it was time to stop struggling and enjoy the slide. I laughed.

'Yeah, let's go see my van.'

Maybe the driver was still alive, smeared against the roof. Maybe he was still conscious, staring with widening eyes at the narrowing sky, feeling the numbness creeping towards his heart. I wished Luisa could have seen him, bereft of choice and beyond mercy, and I hoped, above all, that the driver was Jean-Marc. Alberto stopped on the stone bridge.

'Where is it?' I asked, looking along the bone-dry bed.

Alberto gunned the Datsun across the bridge and up the road. 'We'll see it from up there,' he said, 'and if you want anything from it, that's the nearest place.'

We parked on the shoulder of a bend, and there, maybe two hundred metres below us, on its side, lay the Transit, oozing juices like a crushed beetle. Across the ravine and above us, where the facing slope met the road, was the Mercedes van, and less than halfway between that and the Transit a tiny dust cloud betrayed a figure struggling downhill. Alberto placed a metre of dark green pipe with a battery pack on the roof of his car and unscrewed a cap from the front. He didn't wait for me to ask.

'Back-up tank sight from a T-95,' he grinned. 'Bought it on the Rock. The Russian Army hasn't even got these. Check this.' He pushed a couple of buttons and turned a dial marked in Cyrillic script. 'Laser range-finder. *Magnifico!* On a clear day you can see for ever!'

That depended upon how long for ever was.

'There's a spotty guy running down the slope,' breathed Alberto, squinting into the rubber eyepiece and twisting another dial. 'Range . . . seven hundred and seventy metres.'

'How long before he reaches the van?'

Alberto adjusted the position of his huge and unwieldy monocular. 'Hang on,' he muttered, slapping the latest Russian military technology. 'It's packed up. Piece of shit. I've lost him.' He looked up, squinting into the haze at the distant figure. 'I'd say five, maybe seven minutes. Take you less than one to reach the van from here.'

It was a dangerous opportunity, and one which seemed utterly singular. This was probably my last remaining chance to try to recover my passport, driving licence and jacket from the van, and the longer I stood here considering my chances, the smaller they became. On the other hand, however, passports could be reissued, driving licences bought, and the jacket . . . the jacket had last week's takings stashed in the lining.

'Whahay!' whooped Alberto. 'He's fallen over!'

I took three strides and slid down the slope towards the wreckage. Within moments the convex mountainside opposite hid the dust trail of my competitor, and I shimmied down the last few metres on my backside. The van was broken across a boulder, its side stoved in and the roof bulging like a compound fracture, the red paint flaking and revealing the vulnerable, shiny steel beneath. A breathless terror at what lay in and around the driver's seat gripped my spine and tried to pull me away from the cab, but something stronger tore its skinny hand from my backbone and thrust me forward. I wanted to see the driver dead, or better still, dying. I had but a few moments to witness his death, to look into his eyes and see Luisa looking back. I had nothing to fear, for my heart was beating hard and his, at best, was faltering. I was strong now, and he was weak. I had won, and he had lost, and yet the slap on my back was not powerful enough to propel me to the door. I made a rapid compromise and skidded around to the back of the van. I lifted the door upwards and stepped back as the weight of the cargo knocked the second door hard into the dust. A claw-like hand bounced upon the panelling, the ring on its finger making dull metallic contact with the door. I leapt backwards, gasping. Whatever it was, it was dead, and it was neither Jean-Marc nor the Arab kid. I crouched down at a distance to look into the loadspace, my hands hard upon my knees like a kid looking into a wasps' nest. The back of my van was full of corpses. Alberto's whistle pierced the nightmare and I turned upon my blistered heels and scrambled up the slope to his car. My heart-beat hammered in my ears, drowning out the song of the crickets, the warnings of the larks and the three shots aimed at me by Benoit. I stumbled into the Datsun and dropped my head into my hands as Alberto accelerated up the hill.

'You were lucky!' he cried, clearly excited and coming at the experience from a different angle to me. 'That was close, man! I saw the smoke from his pistol before I heard the crack! One of the bullets hit one of the boulders back there! Fuck!'

I heard his words, but I saw only that cold, heavy hand with its knuckle-duster ring falling hard against the van.

'They killed the cops,' I panted.

Alberto dropped a gear. 'They killed the cops?'

'Where's the fags?'

The car stopped at a precarious angle on the mountainside, its lovingly tuned engine humming as it patiently awaited its master's next command.

'They killed the fucking Guardia?' breathed Alberto, his face pale and dusty. He was beginning to annoy me.

'Yes, they killed the fucking Guardia,' I confirmed, fumbling a cigarette between my trembling lips. 'Their bodies are piled up in my van. Dead.'

'Why they put them in the van? Why not leave them at the bar? They crazy or something?'

'I don't know,' I blustered. 'Why are you asking me?'

Alberto leaned over me. 'What about Ramon?'

I sucked the smoke down deep and held it. 'Can we get moving and discuss this somewhere else?'

'Ramon? Did they kill Ramon?'

'I don't know,' I replied, looking into the wing mirror. 'Who the fuck is Ramon?'

'The *patron* of the bar we just left.'

I shook my head. 'I don't know. I didn't see him. No. Fuck it, I don't know. Maybe . . .'

The Datsun rolled forward, the driver's eyes hidden behind mirror shades.

'This is very bad stuff,' he said, 'I think they must have killed Ramon.' He sniffed and shook his head. 'Don't worry about it.'

We climbed to the ridge and descended the next valley in shocked and fearful silence. I kept my eyes upon the wing mirror and let the better part of my mind dwell upon the irreparable damage I had caused Alberto. Early this morning, as I had followed Carlito down from the waterfall, Alberto had started the day as a well-connected smuggler going about his daily business. Now it was not yet noon and he had become implicated, through no fault of his own, in the deaths of two policemen and a local businessman. Trouble loomed in front of me like a freak wave, its face bulging with irrefutable accusations and undeniable evidence, and if I couldn't paddle up it I would be crushed beneath it. I glanced at Alberto. If he noticed, he didn't acknowledge me. I didn't like the way he had just said, 'Don't worry about it.' It sounded like the end of a friendship.

17

Imagine fleeing the country on a cross-Channel ferry. Imagine leaving everything behind, letting nobody know, catching the 00.45 from Folkestone and heading to a new and poorer life in an alien land. Imagine leaning on the stern rail with a plastic glass of Stella and watching those white cliffs diminish in the moonlight, then watch aghast as your wallet and your passport slip from your pocket and tumble into the wash. The loss was irrevocable, and I dropped my head into my hands. This was becoming too much to bear, and I needed a drink.

'Let's pull over at the next bar and work out a plan.'

Alberto put a little too much gas into a tight right-hander and struggled to point the Datsun back onto the road. He was angry now, and flaking.

'I think we need to have a drink, get a story sorted out, and go to the cops,' I continued. 'I don't think—'

'What you think happened today?' interrupted Alberto, his voice the fractured crust on a magma of anger.

I flicked my dog-end into the woods. 'I think those Frog bastards shot up those cops—'

I had more to say, but Alberto cut me short. I think I was beginning to annoy him.

'Then what did they do?'

I stared through the fly-splattered windscreen, but saw nothing but blackness. 'I don't understand.'

Alberto was hunched over the wheel, his Roman nose nearly touching his kidskin driving gloves. 'Then what they do?' He repeated. 'They walk out or what?'

I did not want to play this grim game but Alberto was trying to make a point, so I humoured him.

'Er, yeah, they walked out, I think.'

'Wrong!' he retorted, with a single shake of the head. 'They put all the bodies in the back of your van. Yeah?'

I nodded.

'Then they drive your van off the mountain, by accident, I think.'

I nodded again.

Jean-Marc would have been at the wheel of the Mercedes van, and it was reasonable to assume that Benoit had been driving the Transit. Considering the animosity evident between his two lackeys, Jean-Marc would have kept them out of each other's faces by ordering the Arab kid to ride with him. Benoit had left the doomed Transit with the ease of a man stepping off a tram, and it was logical, therefore, to assume that my pursuers still numbered three.

Three plus the entire law-enforcement resources of the Republic of Spain.

'So what we've got here is your van, with your stuff in it, and three, maybe four, bodies and no you.'

He was right.

'And two of the bodies are Guardia Civil, and they're very sensitive around here about Communists killing Guardia Civil.' He gave me a sideways glower. 'It's a local historical thing.'

I wondered where he had come up with the Communist reference.

'And you think you can walk into the Guardia post and . . . and say what?'

I took a deep breath. This was undoubtedly going to be the wrong answer. 'I'll tell them the truth.'

The Datsun whined as Alberto dropped it too many gears. He cursed as he stirred the box. 'And what's the truth?'

'That these three French bastards kidnapped me from a hotel in Cadiz, made me drive out here, shot my girlfriend four times down by the Guadiario, tried to shoot me, then shot those cops and the barman . . .'

'Why they kidnap you?'

'Because they wrongly believe that something I have belongs to them.'

Alberto groaned and shook his head. He suddenly knew the score. 'It's a fucking coke thing, isn't it?'

I studied the 'W' in 'Winston'.

'It is, isn't it?' he persisted. 'It's a bloody stinking cocaine issue. *Bastardos!* Jesus Christ! Fuckers!' He shook his head, really angry now. I didn't know what to say, so I said nothing.

'You know how much I hate that stuff,' he raged. 'I hate it. You know how many times people ask me to carry it? Ten, fifteen, twenty kilos from Sagres or from Algeciras, and you know what I say?' He didn't wait for me to guess. 'I say, "No thank you very much, because I hate that stuff, and if you ever ask me again you will never see me again." That's how much I hate that stuff. You know something? That stuff is made by devils, by Santa—'

'Satan,' I interjected.

'You know how much I hate that stuff. It fucks you up. It takes all your money. It takes all your friends. It breaks up your family. It makes you into something worse than a cockroach. It makes people kill, and it gives smuggling a bad name. It is evil.' He touched his sweating brow on the steering wheel in some autoreligious gesture of supplication. 'Oh Jesus! Oh Jesus am I fucked?'

Jesus would have heard what happened from His dad by now, and He would have confirmed Alberto's worst fears. The Devil's spore had touched his hands and now they were covered in blood. He was indeed fucked.

'It's that fucking dog's fault,' he raged. 'Should never have picked that fucking dog up. Nothing good ever comes from any contact with that cursed hound.'

That observation, I felt, was unfair. Carlito had played no part in the deaths of the Guardia, nor Ramon, if he were indeed dead. It was a primitive, knee-jerk reaction around here to blame the low-slung hound for every disaster from sour milk to tax increases, and it was unreasonable to do so. If anyone was a jinx, it was me, not the dog, and somebody had to show enough common sense and objectivity to speak up for him.

'Bastard dog,' I agreed. I needed a drink. 'Can't we pull up somewhere to discuss this?'

The dark shadow of some low-flying thing swooped across the car. My weak heart skipped a beat, but Alberto had seen it too. Under any circumstances other than these he would have questioned its source, but demons and rooks were irrelevant now.

'What is there to discuss?' He was being wilfully obtuse.

I humoured him. 'Er, the fact that we're both fucked. The fact that the last people to see your mate and those cops alive was his missus, his son and his sister-in-law. The fact that the last time those people saw their husband, father and brother-in-law alive he was in the company of two cops and us. The fact that the two cops, along with said husband et cetera are now deceased and we are at large. The fact that no one but us and those Frog bastards knows the truth. The fact that through no fault of our own, we're both seriously fucked.' I let loose a sardonic sideways glance. 'Did I mention that already?'

The car had decelerated with the gravity of my observations. I could see Alberto's mind whirring like a zoetrope. Nice guy slapped. Nice guy slapped. Nice guy slapped. 'Let's find somewhere cool to have a drink,' I said, for right now I was prepared to trade a beer and a shot for the next fifteen years of my life.

Alberto dropped the car into second and toed the accelerator. I checked over my shoulder for the Mercedes van, somehow knowing that it wouldn't be there. Maybe I gave movies too little credit for their reflection of real life. We crunched off the road onto a bone-dry *camino forestale*, its compacted limestone surface heaving a dust trail that made the Datsun look like a crop duster as it wound its way high through the corks. Long, long ago, Henrique had advised me to never, ever make Alberto angry, and even then I had understood that this was a matter of respect rather than a warning. Alberto was known as a man of patience and understanding, and to goad him was akin to poking the eye of a friendly horse. No one but the irredeemable did it.

I had poked him hard, and he rubbed his eyes, saying nothing, until the car stopped at the crest of the shaded hill. I followed Alberto as he slipped through the trees on foot, sucking on my swollen thumb and wincing as my beaten muscles expanded in the midday heat.

'See that white house?' said Alberto, pointing at a thumbnail scratch on the side of the next valley. 'That house belongs to Concepcia Rafaella Costas, the cousin of Pepe. Further down the track you find an obvious fork that will take you over that ridge and into the next valley. From there you will recognise the house of the *Inglesa*.'

I looked at him. 'It's fucking miles away!'

Alberto shrugged. 'No, not really. It's the heat – makes everything look distant. It's safer that you take the old path than the road.'

'Old path?' I protested. 'What old path?'

Alberto pointed at a little-used rabbit run barely discernible against the tobacco-brown forest floor. 'This path,' he replied. 'It goes down the mountain here and up the mountain there.' He sighed. 'It's easy, and it's better for you.'

My free ride in the Datsun had come to an end. Alberto's disappointment was nearly tangible as he hummed some fatalistic melody almost inaudibly into his moustache, and I searched hastily for the words that would make our parting sweeter, or perhaps even postpone it until he dropped me at Bloody Mary's door.

'Alberto, I'm sorry,' I started, which was big of me. 'I never wanted any of this, for Christ's sake. Do you think I would bring this down on anyone? It's all a series of . . . I dunno, ridiculous coincidences.'

He was going to have to split. His innocence in this matter would be weightless against the momentum of the investigation that the *junta* would initiate. It was the end of this life for Alberto, and I wondered where he would go.

'I'm a fucking smuggler,' he replied, kicking a fircone the size of a rugby ball into the valley. 'I got plans, contingency plans, plans I never thought I would have to use. I plan for the future because the future's got plans for me.' He looked hard at me, and I failed to return his stare. 'You sure those were Guardia in the back of your van? I mean, you didn't spend very long down there, and you got . . .' He was clutching now, and even I didn't need much more than a couple of seconds to recognise the blood-soaked corpse of a cop, especially one with whom I had traded verse less than an hour before.

'It was Morales, the new one. It was him, and that's that.'

Alberto's mouth was the same shape as his moustache. 'You'd better get going,' he said, leaning into his car. 'Here's some water, and here's some cigarettes.'

I took the plastic jug and the carton of Winston and watched as he climbed into the driver's seat. He couldn't leave me standing here.

'Alberto!' I cried. 'You can't leave me standing here! Who's going to go with me? I'll never make it on my own!'

He checked his turn somewhere between points two and three, looking at me for a moment as though trying to remember a long-lost line. Then a sad smile cracked his thin lips as though he knew better than me that neither of us had any choice.

'*Vaya con Dios*,' he suggested.

18

It took me the rest of the day to find my way out of the valley and it was dark before I crossed the ridge and began my descent towards La Mendirosa.

Bloody Mary's house stood in a wide meadow riven by a shallow, sparkling stream. The nearest blacktop was three klicks to the west, and the nearest village another ten from there. Bloody Mary cherished her solitude, and on a fine day there were few locations better placed in which to be lonesome. Her house had been the property of the same family since the thirteenth century until she took the deeds, the lucky beneficiary of a stupid dispute between two now deeply regretful brothers. The terraced fields upon which Bloody Mary let her apprehensive neighbours grow their vegetables were serviced by an irrigation system of dressed stone said to be three hundred years older than the house and built by Arabs. The satellite dish on the southern gable gave her Sky, and the smartcard she'd bought in Gibraltar made it free. The perfection of the location always made newcomers think they'd been there before, or maybe just dreamed about the place, and even Bloody Mary, returning from another night of bitter recollection and acid consumption, was said to find the place familiar.

The fairytale notion that this lonely cottage was my pastoral home seized my imagination as I approached the valley floor. I ignored the gasps of my bleeding feet and wallowed instead in the self-indulgent fantasy that this was my return, the end of the road and the closing of the circle. My trials were past and my travails were complete, and all that awaited me behind that oaken door were comfort, peace and contentment.

Scattered bats, the cicada chorus and the fat moon were the only witnesses to my arrival. Warm light, fed by a throbbing generator, slipped through the curtains and fell in the dust around the house.

'He's here, he's here,' called the cicadas, 'here without a clue.' I paused on the threshold and considered my strategy for the first time. I'd had all day to devise and test a plan, but my mind had been on other, less pressing matters. It was a shame, because a straight Bloody Mary was bloody scary, and I'd be lucky to see a crack in the door without a good cover story. My pitch, I decided quickly, would be that of a flat-broke gambler holding a prial of threes: I'd show her two cards, and let her guess enough about the rest to speculate upon my success. Her stake in my future would be a yellow Toyota Starlet with hand-painted flowers on the side, and her reward, when she recognised it, would be wisdom.

And maybe her car back.

I knocked three times, cringing in anticipation of my reception, but neither welcome nor challenge was issued. The drone of the TV rose and fell like waves on an abandoned shore, and swallowing the embarrassment of the unexpected caller I laid into the heavy, studded door with my boots before moving around to the curtained window and beating on the glass like an air-raid warden.

When this failed to provoke a response I assumed that Bloody Mary was either out or dead, and climbed in through the bathroom window, breaking a china cat and a bottle of something sticky and pungent. The bathroom door led onto a short, dark passageway, the end of which framed the living room. I crept forward and poked my head around the door. To my left, an unlit kitchen area, with a table and a sink, and to my right a bright, uncared-for room with bare, whitewashed walls, a grubby sofa, a couple of awkwardly positioned straight-backed chairs, a bookshelf full of paperbacks, and the disturbing buzz of the TV. Goosebumps broke out along my spine as I stepped into the room, sniffing heavy sweetness from the still air. Bloody Mary was lying on the floor between the sofa and the TV, a pool of blood near her head and a pair of pink, fluffy slippers on her feet. She wore the shapeless velour of a lonely soap addict, and the undisguised bruises of an unloved heroin addict. She had rewrapped the wrap and blown out the candle before collapsing, leaving everything as neat and tidy as one could expect from a guilty junkie. I lit up a Winston with shaking hands, wondering obliquely how so short a fall could cause an injury that bled so much. My legs seemed unwilling to take me any closer to the scene, so I bent across the sofa to examine the body. The wine bottle nestling beside her wizened face said 'Sangre De Toro', a single drop hanging from its mouth above the pool on the tiled floor. It seemed that only Bull's Blood had been spilled, and my mission had suddenly become a little easier.

Bloody Mary, bitter, iron-faced ex-wife of a Northern serial killer, had made the smartest decision of her unfulfilled life and left for dreamland, knocking over a bottle of *tinto* in her rush to be gone. Whoever found her would rightly predict a verdict of misadventure, I decided, and then the corpse coughed. I fell backwards as it lifted itself onto its hands and groaned. Still alive, and unconscious of witnesses, she vomited onto her wipe-clean floor with the fury of one who dreamed she was in heaven and woke up in hell.

Still retching, she looked up, and I stared aghast at a face eroded by an excess of everything but joy. She was as surprised to see me as I was her, and she blinked hard, dragging her gaze back from the locked gates of Xanadu, her mouth open and her chin flecked with vomit. Her dyed red hair hung like two legs of *jamon negra* from the sides of her head, resting on the shoulders of her green leisure suit in a disturbing demonstration of what went wrong when one ignored the basic rules of fashion. We raced to find an appropriate greeting. Bloody Mary won.

'I'm expecting company, you know,' she belched.

I tried to look friendly and harmless. 'I'm really sorry to just turn up like this,' I smiled.

'Oh, it's you, is it?' she asked, scanning the darkness for accomplices. 'Come in, quick.'

'I'm already in,' I announced.

'Triffic,' slurred Mary. 'Shut the bloody door and get a mop. I appear to have been sick.' She rose from all fours to her knees, looking down at herself in stoned disbelief before hitting me with the expectant look of a petulant schoolgirl. 'What the bloody hell's happened to me?' she asked.

It was a good question.

Bloody Mary was a dog-eared page ripped from the back of a cut-price volume of true-life crime and pinned to a cracked wall just off the tourist trail in the shadow of Montecoche. She had a smile like a fresh bruise and hair the colour of spilled wine that she wore with the swagger of a disappointed woman of half her forty-nine years. The cheap gold with which she manacled herself reflected a skin flushed from flight and cured by the same sun that had hidden behind the Northern clouds as Mary had watched the corruption of her unambitious life.

Bloody Mary's husband had killed prostitutes on rainy nights in the Lake District in the 1980s. Nobody knew whether he was on a mission from God or just passing the time, because he said not one word after his arrest. He had killed seven before they caught him, and high-ranking cops had queued up to interrogate him.

'Why did you do it?' was a common enquiry, as was 'How many more?' and 'Where are the bodies?' Another popular question was 'Did the missus know?' but Bloody Mary's husband just smiled and rubbed his beard. They sent him to Ashworth Special Hospital to watch it grow longer and, on the advice of the CPS, closed the file on his red-headed wife.

Bloody Mary sold her story to a Sunday tabloid, scooped up the silver, and ran. She stopped running when she reached the bottom of Europe, and bought a tidy little two-bedroom place on a development in Calahonda. Her arrival caused a stir among the overheated, understimulated residents of the Costa's Britbelt, and it took her three months to realise that anonymity was unlikely to be found among the largest British ex-pat community in the world. She moved inland, thinking she could hide in the narrow streets of the hilltop village of Matamoros, but her ancient home soon became the Andalusian equivalent of Lizzie Borden's house, providing quality Kodak moments for coach parties bored with White Towns and *burros*. She lasted two years in Matamoros before selling up and moving out to La Mendirosa, where at last she found the solace she both craved and abhorred.

I went into the kitchen to fetch a broom and a couple of towels. Mary had wobbled into the bathroom to wash out her mouth, ineffectively, it seemed, from the volume of cursing rising over the thumping of plumbing. Exploiting the opportunity created by her absence, I had a good look around and found her car keys in a bowl full of shrivelled oranges.

Mary padded back and fell heavily onto the worn-out sofa. 'Fucking cat smashed me Chanel,' she muttered, lighting a Cartier with a gold cigarette lighter. She looked up at me, blinking, as though noticing me for the first time.

'Jesus! They gave you a good going over, didn't they?'

'Who did?' I asked quickly.

Mary opened her mouth to reply and changed her mind, but it was too late.

'Who gave me a good going over?'

She shrugged. 'How should I know? Some big bastard you let down or ripped off, no doubt. I'm surprised it don't happen more often, the way you carry on.'

It was a good recovery, but it wasn't good enough. I searched her eyes for the truth but the smack had so muffled her body language that she simply stared back like a cataleptic.

'Nice works,' I said, changing the subject before she could devise a rescue strategy.

She followed my gaze to a silver syringe steeped in a glass of steaming water.

'It's antique,' she said distractedly. 'Twenties. Belonged to some poet, apparently, so you keep your grubby hands off of it.' She lay back on the sofa and clocked me with one bloodshot eye, trying to count how many beans she had spilled. 'You going to stand there all night or what?' She shifted her gaze to the window, suddenly unsure. 'It is night, isn't it?' she asked, as though the darkness outside might be for her alone.

'Yeah, it's Thursday or Friday or something,' I confirmed. 'You asking me to mop this up?'

She sighed as though she were wasting time. 'What do you think? We have to maintain our standards, lad. Can't go leaving pools of sick on the front-room floor. We're not Scotch, you know.'

Scottish, not Scotch, I thought, but I wasn't going to correct her. The last person who had taught Bloody Mary anything was currently in Ashworth Special Hospital comparing facial hair with an arsonist from Wiltshire.

I dropped the towels onto the cooling contents of my hostess's stomach and swept it from the room. The front door, it seemed, had been unlocked all along, and as I stood in its frame, leaning on the broom and blowing smoke into the night, I considered my latest problem.

I couldn't be certain that Mary had spoken to Jean-Marc, and I couldn't see how I could ever know for sure. Asking her straight out wouldn't work because she would tell me only what she wanted me to know. Neither torture, which would probably have been quite gratifying, nor seduction, which would certainly have been quite horrifying, were within my limited abilities, and the simple truth was that it didn't really matter whether she had met Jean-Marc or not. What mattered was that she was prevented from seeing him again, and no matter how long I stared into the darkness, I could see only one way of bringing that to pass.

I wiped the apprehension from my mouth with the back of my hand and returned to Mary with a smile on my face. 'Can I ask you a favour?'

'You can ask,' she replied, her eyes locked on the TV.

'Can I stay the night?'

Mary shifted her weight and gave me a long, quizzical look. She thought she'd blown it with that comment about the kicking, let the *chat* right out of the *sac*, but I was still here, standing in her parlour, clearly even dimmer than she thought. She smiled like a spider.

'You can stay, but it'll be out here on the sofa, mind. There'll be no funny business and you'll have to work your keep.'

'Fair enough,' I said. 'What do you want?'

She pointed languidly at the empty wine bottle lying on the floor. 'You can pick that up for starters and fetch us another. There's glasses out in the kitchen somewhere.'

I uncorked a fresh bottle of *tinto* and found a couple of dusty, ill-matched glasses. 'I've had a terrible couple of days,' I announced, sitting uncomfortably on a straight-backed chair.

She nodded, her attention focused on a man with a paintbrush.

'You would not believe what I've been through since I saw you in Dieter's Place.'

Bloody Mary frowned and held up her hand. 'Do us a favour, will you, duck? Shut the fuck up while I'm watching *Home Front*.'

I wondered if that was how she used to respond to her husband when he said he'd had a bad day. I poured the wine, lit a fag and watched a woman with a cordless drill, trying all the time to ignore the acid anxiety rising in my gullet.

'Do you ever watch *Home Front*?' asked Mary during a commercial break. 'It's dead good. I wish those experts would come down here and give this place a seeing to.' She was indulging herself in opiate dreams of normality, staring into the suburbs and wishing, like me, that she had a Next card. Most people I knew got high and watched MTV, or porn, but Bloody Mary watched soap operas and make-over shows, and I could see why. This blandness beamed from outer space allowed her to look back at a land to which she would never return, to imagine the life that her husband had taken from her, a life that was over and done.

Pitying her life, however, wouldn't save mine. She had as good as admitted that she'd seen Jean-Marc, and instead of levelling with me and striking a deal, she had tried to cover her clumsy tracks. That fact proved that she was against me in a situation where my life was at stake, and that put me in a very difficult position. I had no more intention of staying the night at La Mendirosa than I did of bunking up with Benoit, but it was important that Mary felt that I was in no hurry to leave. Her nearest neighbours, who blamed me for their daughter's delinquency, lived just over a kilometre away, a distance that Mary could cover on foot in half an hour. If I simply upped and left in her car, it was feasible that by fording the shallow river and taking the broken back-tracks her neighbour's big four-wheel drive could be at the Matamoros crossroads before me. It was necessary, therefore, that my departure should be witnessed by no one, and that it should be effected as soon as possible.

'Got any hash?' I asked, as a man on TV hammered nails into a floor.

Bloody Mary was hugging a cushion. 'No,' she replied curtly, her attention already distracted by her dilemma. Her reason insisted that she remained straight until she had delivered me to Jean-Marc and claimed her reward. Her desire, however, was to squirt more heroin into herself, and she couldn't do that while she was watching over me.

'Got any coke?'

'No I bleeding haven't,' she confirmed. 'My useless fucking dealer stood me up. All I got is smack.'

I appeared to consider her reply for a moment, then shook my head. 'I haven't done any smack for ages. It'll just knock me out.'

'So?' asked Mary, no longer quite so occupied with suburbia.

'You look like you could do with a good kip. A little hit will do wonders for your injuries, you know.'

With me safely tied to the mast, Bloody Mary could reward herself with the knockout she'd been craving since she came round from the last one.

I sipped my wine. 'I'm tempted.'

Bloody Mary was delighted, and she could only guess how pleased Jean-Marc would be to find his quarry wrapped in an Afghan duvet.

'Go on, then,' sighed Mary, hiding her relief behind an indulgent smile. 'I'll do you one up.' She turned to the works.

'Allow me, please,' I insisted, rising. 'I'll do one for you first, then I'll do mine. It's good etiquette.'

She was a self-taught addict, a mature student, and she hadn't expected this. She covered the wrap with one hand and the syringe with another. 'Tell you what,' she said quickly, her back to me, 'I'll do mine and you do yours. Okay?'

I frowned. 'Why?'

She turned to face me, her eyes gleaming. 'Why not?'

'Because it's bad form,' I sighed. 'It means you don't trust me.'

She looked at me, trying to read my intent. I looked back, trying to hide it. She shrugged. I'd won.

'Okay,' she said, 'whatever.'

Knocking up a shot for a middle-aged woman was both disturbing and strangely banal. The equipment she used was untainted with the squalor and expediency common to the works of most smackheads I'd met, and the background talk of emulsion and Formica imparted the feeling that I was mixing nothing worse than a stiff gin and tonic. I pulled up a low stool and sat at the coffee table behind Mary's line of sight. She had it all laid out within easy reach: a tarnished spoon, a wrap made from the overexposed pages of a hard-core porn mag, its garish inks dulled like an overrubbed fetish, and a dented Jif lemon. Her spoon was bent to balance, and using the tip of a paring knife I pushed a gram of the powder into its bowl. I studied the flecked brown heap, suddenly and acutely aware that Bloody Mary's sorrowful life was in the spoon, on the tip of the knife, in the bag and in my hands. She would shoot whatever I gave her, hoping, perhaps, that I would succeed where she had consistently failed. I snatched a glance at the edge of her tired face, the bunched, dyed hair lying like horse's tails on the cushion. She was watching TV, but every other sense was focused in anticipation of the hit. The *Home Front* experts had come up with an ingenious design for a partition made from egg boxes, and I was trying to remember how much heroin made an overdose. I needed a little time alone, a moment or two in which to look myself in the eye and see my sanity reflected.

I stood up, grabbing the empty Volvic bottle from the table.

'Where you going?' croaked Mary.

'Get some water,' I replied. 'Need water for the brew.'

I left the spoon with the syringe and slipped into the bathroom. The tang of vomit hung in the air as I locked the crooked door and let the taps run gushing into the washbasin. I slid back the door of the medicine cabinet above the sink and rifled through the Timoteis and L'Oreals for something with which to tranquillise my central nervous system. The choice seemed huge: Nembutol, Seconal, Mogadon and T-Quil, but the bottles were mostly empty. Mary's cabinet was a disgrace. I pocketed the last of her Mogadon, soberly aware that she would have no need for repeat prescriptions after tonight.

The mirror on the cabinet's door was old and cheap. The poor-quality silver coating had oxidised behind the glass and black spots crept across the reflective surface like a degenerative eye disease. The face it reflected looked just as worn out. It was gaunt and half-bearded, framed with long, lank hair that was neither dark nor fair. The lips were swollen, with a scabbed yellow contusion at one corner, and the nose was scored with narrow, black scratches. A dark crescent rose from the left eyebrow, its slopes shiny and red, and beneath it the bloodshot eyes stared back at me from the deepening epicentres of two spiralling storm systems. The last time I'd seen this man he had been standing in a blandly furnished hotel room in Cadiz. His face had been lit by the distant fire of the setting sun, and the worries balanced on his creased brow had been borne by the optimism in his eyes. He had been certain that the problems he had fled were but temporary disruptions to his life, matters from which distance would preclude confrontation. He had been wrong, and now that bruised forehead overhung the sunken eyes like a crumbling, frost-shattered cliff face, eroded from within and held back only by the irreversible momentum of the actions it had initiated.

I beheld the face of a murderer, and despite years of subconscious preparation, I was unready. I had thought that I understood both the theory and the mechanics: I had played cops and robbers, putting perps down with cold precision. I had played war, cutting down imaginary stormtroopers in their dozens and finishing them off with my pistol. I had watched men shot with a gasp on TV, coin-sized holes in their white shirts, and later, at the movies, I had seen other men blown backwards in an explosion of blood, fabric and smoke as better-researched rounds knocked them down. I thought I knew the force required to drive a knife into a picket's back, or the necessary tension to turn a rope around a student's throat, or the hand—eye coordination needed to put two slugs of forty-cal into a bank robber's thoracic cavity at thirty paces. I had read about the despatch of the Nubian, I had seen Judith behead Holofernes, and I had believed that I had comprehended the cold-blooded determination and the hot-hearted fury necessary to commit such acts. I had been wrong. Art had failed death much as religion had failed life, leaving me unprepared for either. Maybe it was a good thing too, I thought, as I studied my face for the remains of anything worth saving. I imagined an infinite tunnel of mirrors through which I could look back upon every day of my life so far. I could have searched through my ageing faces for the first sign of trouble, tracing the hurricane in my eyes to the distant reflection of a passing butterfly. This killing had to be justified, and in the one room in my mind unpeopled by lunatics there was a table, and on the table was a single sheet of paper, and on the paper, in big black letters, was the justification. Bloody Mary would have betrayed me, given the chance, and would have shrugged as I struggled to talk myself out of the death she had brought upon me. I was abroad in a new world where values were rounded up to the nearest hundred, where actions spoke a bloody sight louder than words. Shit happened, and I was in it, with the choice to kill or be killed.

I took several deep breaths and looked around the room. The table was bolted to the floor. The walls were padded. The room was not unoccupied by lunatics. I closed my eyes for a long time, and when I opened them again that God-awful face was looking at me from the mirror, the face of the final murderer that Mary would meet in her pitiful life. There was someone else in the bathroom with me, too, someone terrifying and familiar, a face visible in the blinking of an eye, and, as I whirled around, gone. I clasped the pills to my chest with sweaty hands and searched the room for evidence of his passing.

Something was disturbed, left slightly out of alignment, as though two identical photographs had been cut in half and expertly matched, leaving only the tiniest inconsistency in their conjunction. Morales would have known who it was, as would that old man back in the mountain bar. El Camaron would have known, and when it came down to it, I knew too. El Duende was in the house, but he was to be expected in these parts. I filled the plastic bottle and turned off the taps.

'You better not have stunk my bathroom out,' warned Mary as I shuffled back into the room. She squirmed on the sofa, trying to squeeze every last comfort from the stained and sagging cushions.

'You've missed all the action,' she announced. 'They did a bloody lovely job on that house. Colour scheme wasn't really to my taste, though, and I don't think the family really liked it, either.'

I grunted, concentrating on the preparation of her lethal injection, trying to supersaturate a teaspoonful of water with a fatal quantity of heroin. The resulting solution looked strong enough to shut down a steelworks, and I wondered how long it would take to stop Mary's hardened heart. I would stay until she passed out, I decided, dragging the brew through a clean cotton-wool ball. The opiates and whatever they were cut with would perform their mischief with or without me, and, as Jean-Marc had once observed, there was no need for me to see such sadness.

'Get on with it,' urged Mary, echoing one of the voices in my head. She had kicked off a slipper and slapped up a vein on her foot. Time was moving too slowly for her as I tried to delay the moment, like a reluctant executioner waiting on a call from the governor.

'Buggering hell!' cried Mary. 'That all for me?'

'It's just well diluted. Leave it if you want,' I shrugged, hoping now that she would. I was hesitating on the edge of my fall, looking for alternatives, trying to find a reason to spare her miserable, treacherous life. Reason, however, thrust me onwards, insisting that short-sighted compassion would deliver me to my own death, but reason was brutal and flawed. Unconsciousness would serve me just as well as death, as long as I moved fast. Suddenly there was no need to kill Mary. All she needed was a hit strong enough to dump her on the leeward side of coherence for the four hours I reckoned I needed to dig up my treasure and disappear on the coast. Background noise returned and time seemed to regain its former momentum as relief welcomed me back from the brink. I still had hold of the syringe, its dripping point a blur in my trembling hands. A quarter of the quantity I had boiled up would suffice to knock her out, and my conscience would be clear.

'What are you grinning at?' snapped Mary, snatching the syringe. 'Waiting for me foot to fall off?'

I opened my mouth and raised my hands, and Mary shot the lot into her leathery vein.

'Are you the fiend who would send my soul to hell?' she whispered, as the plunger touched the bottom. I didn't know what to say.

She shook her head. 'It's Shakespeare, int it? *All's Well That Ends Well* or something. You're supposed to be the bleedin' teacher, aren't you?'

'I taught Spanish,' I told her, 'not English.'

Bloody Mary sighed sadly. The heroin hit her brain before she could tidy up, and the syringe dropped to the floor like a spent cartridge.

'Jesus Christ!' she gasped, before words failed her and she slipped into Coleridge country.

I turned her onto her side and watched her for ten minutes or so, using the time to chase a little brown dragon down a tinfoil valley. The sweet vapours both nauseated and numbed me, like a bottle of Cinzano outside a youth club disco. In a week remarkable for acts of excessive stupidity, I still retained the ability to surpass myself. The woman lying beside me was dying – she was doing it in a fun way, but she was still dying – and it was pretty much my fault.

As the momentum went out of her first runaway rush, Mary surfaced, wearing the face of one who had forgotten her passport.

'What about you?' she gasped, her eyes flicking back and forth as she realised her mistake. 'I thought you were having some too. It's important, 'cos if you don't, and I do . . . I should have let you go first . . . Jesus . . .'

She was gone, hanging on for dear life, all alone in the front car of the world's scariest roller coaster. I left her to it, and moonwalked around her house in search of items of worth. In the next numb hour or so I gathered together close on fifteen thousand pesetas, a knife, a cigarette lighter and some gum. I put the money in my pocket, the rest in a carrier bag, and left my broken hostess fading away on her stained sofa. I let her keep the poet's syringe.

The car started first time, and I crawled guiltily away from La Mendirosa, wondering if I'd just committed manslaughter, or some degree of murder. It was important, I thought, to keep reminding myself that at the exact moment she had snatched that syringe my intention had been merely to knock her out. It was her junkie greed and urgency that had finished her off, and that could have happened any time.

Serial Killer's Wife Found Dead From Overdose.

Who was going to care? I lit a Winston with her gold cigarette lighter, flicked on the headlights and shrugged. Maybe she'd thank me one day.

19

The nearest *pueblo* to La Mendirosa was Matamoros. Built along a saddle between two peaks, its whitewashed buildings were stacked in the protective shadow of its once mighty castle and spilled down the slopes like dropped sugar cubes. Six routes of varying quality and importance met in the steep streets, putting Matamoros on the road to everywhere. Its strategic importance as the crossroads between the mountains and the sea had enabled it to profit as a commercial centre, and until recently the biggest Saturday market in the region had been held on the southern edge of the town, trading mostly in goods of uncertain provenance. Before the introduction of motorised transport it had made sense for traders and buyers to make the journey into town on a Friday evening, thus ensuring that no time was wasted when the market opened before sunrise on Saturday. With a healthy mix of *contrabandistas*, *bandidos* and *gitanos* rolling into town every Friday afternoon, a sense of *fiesta* had developed, and over the centuries Matamoros had become the broken home to a disproportionate number of bars and bawdy houses. Governments and supermarkets had progressively eroded the market from 1939 onwards, and today it was a tepid event involving carpets, produce and cheap shell suits. The bars, however, and the tradition remained, and every Friday night Matamoros rocked.

I cruised cautiously into town, anxiously aware that it had

been nearly ten hours since I'd last seen a cop, and he'd been dead in the back of my van. It was more than likely that all leave had been cancelled in the local nick and that voluntary overtime had been sanctioned. Cops hate cop killers, and the Guardia had always felt vulnerable in Matamoros. I passed through narrow, *cal*-painted streets lined with promenading Spanish youth, feeling both suspicious and conspicuous as I sat without ID in my stolen car. The claustrophobic sense of being trapped was emphasised by the rows of impossibly parked hatchbacks huddled on the non-existent pavements and those still touring the town in search of a space hooting their horns and cranking up the bass. Giggling girls traded good-humoured insults with gelled Romeos, continuing the banter even when both parties were in different bars, their uproar punctuated by the frequent reports of cheap fireworks. Streams of urine and spilled booze rolled through the gutters, and as I concentrated on avoiding the drunken pedestrians, I noted the occasional po-faced black widow shaking her head at the outrages committed on her property. A rental car, leaving just as the evening was picking up speed, headed back for the Costa and left me a spot on the Plaza del Santo Cabro, right outside Quetzal, one of the busiest disco bars in town. It had been twelve hours since I'd had a drink, and Bloody Mary's accidental overdose meant there was no longer any need to rush. A quiet couple of drinks and some tapas would give me the time to consider the recent past and make plans for the immediate future, and who could say when the next opportunity for a beer and a shot would arise?

I put most of the car into the space and made a hasty exit, hurrying through the streets head down and smoking, my hand on my brow in the manner of a fugitive. The Transit and its bloody cargo would have been found by now, and I was concerned that my face would be staring back at me from posters in every window and on every wall. I focused on the shiny pavement and headed downhill, away from the centre, and against the tide. I knew a discreet little bar, where the eyes were rheumy and the uptake was slow, a place where the fugitive could enjoy tight-lipped sanctuary for as long as his money lasted. It wasn't far, but the Friday-night flow was against me, and as I dropped my guard and looked through the crowd for a passage, my gaze crossed that of a bob-cut blonde twenty metres distant. We looked away at the same time, and as her face disappeared in the crowd I tried to rebuild the image of her face in my mind. I'd seen her recently – she was English or maybe Belgian, thirty-odd, with nice eyes and a nasty mouth, but she was no one I'd shared any pleasure with . . .

Something in her expression had indicated recognition, and confident that she would be more mentally efficient than me, I started looking for an exit from the street. My scalp and my stubble prickled with the sting of nervous sweat as my body acted on cues that my mind had yet to detect. An unknown threat was closing on me, and as I stepped into a doorway a split-second rent in the crowd showed me two frowning faces with eyes swinging like sabres, now less than ten metres away, weaving their way towards me, apologising as they pushed their way through the drunken mob.

Suddenly I knew where I'd seen these faces before, frozen in the harsh light of the Photo-Me booth and stuck into the passports that Henrique had nicked from the car at the *chiringuita*. Sarah something and someone Murphy – how much time off work did these people have, for Christ's sake? They should have been back in the office by now waiting for their postcards to arrive and not bothering to tell anybody about their holiday because no one cared. I'd seen them somewhere else, too, recently and in person, but I couldn't remember where. What were they still doing here, and why were they after me? There was no way that they could have known that I had their passports. It was impossible. Henrique was fiercely *Andalus*, and while that confirmed a certain flakiness, it guaranteed that he would be as mute as the sierras if questioned. Now, however, was not the time to question their motives. They'd seen me, they wanted me and that was enough.

I ducked into the nearest alley and started running, my shoulders hunched in anticipation of the fingers that would feel my collar. A sharp left turn took me down a ravine-like *callejone* shiny with the spillage from the watered geraniums that festooned every high balcony and sill. The result of tonight's lottery rolled from blue screens behind every open window I passed, the suspense and the applause punctuated only by the walls between the houses. Lapdogs yelled indignantly from behind studded oaken doors as I jogged by, and a shrunken geriatric in a flat cap and a cardigan croaked a polite but wary greeting. This was the long way back to the car, but it was more scenic than the direct route. I was still smoking, I noticed, as I turned left again and tried to trot up a crooked stairway, and it struck me that a man seen running with a lighted fag is truly in flight. At last, gasping, and not yet confident that I had shaken my pursuers, I emerged in the crowded Plaza del Santo Cabro, where I had left the Toyota.

Its position, right outside the hippest bar in town, made it a natural leaning post for various dark-haired suitors, but that was the least of my problems. I felt for the keys in my pocket and sidled around the square beneath the looming tower of the church, cursing my bad luck and already missing the drinks I had never met. My nerves were breaking along my bones like a messed-up, on-shore storm swell, and a couple of measures of something strong would have calmed their surging and allowed me to concentrate on future trials. I paused for a moment at the foot of the church steps, tempted to turn around and head for the nearest bar. It would only be one or two quick ones, and what harm could it do? I glanced at the Toyota: it was near enough to spit at, and I might never be this close again if I turned back. Drink was a wonderful thing, I had to admit, but was it worth the potential loss? I shook off the burden of indecision, straightened my backbone and turned towards the car. I could get a drink anywhere and any time, except in jail, I realised, as one of the kids leaning against the Starlet stood upright and placed his peaked, chequer-banded cap upon his close-cut head. At the same time, his oppo appeared from within a cluster of girls, grinning white-toothed beneath his bumfluff moustache. Two cops – Policia Local – in front of me and two tourists coming up behind me like a pair of Terminators. Panic became a diuretic to my will, but my mind raced ahead of the numbness to drive my legs up the steps to my right. The church door was the only door, and my shaking hands turned the big iron ring without feeling. When I breathed again, it was to inhale the incense and tallow fragrance of the Catholic Church.

20

The light of a hundred candles reflected from the gold and the treasure with which the vaulted room was decorated. Painted saints and cherubs stared down on me in utter disbelief as I looked from one face to another in open-mouthed wonder. In all my time in Spain I had never been inside a church, and the opulence entranced me. That something so rich and so intricately designed could exist in the heart of a hill town seemed ludicrous, like finding a jewellery box stored in a shed. Huge white columns like the stripped trunks of cork oaks ascended into heaven, supporting a ceiling painted with golden stars across which flew blonde angels. I wiped the drool from my chops and stepped across the nave to lurk in the shadows of the side aisle. I needed to find another way out, a back door that would let me approach the car from a different angle. I was thinking in whispers as I patrolled the precincts of the church, awestruck at the iconographic beauty of the building. This is what churches were supposed to look like: the austere monochromes of the parish churches of my distant memory had a certain nostalgic beauty, but this place possessed enough to make a Christian of me, I thought, running my hands across the time-polished grain of a chair carved in the form of a kneeling angel that had to be worth five hundred quid of anyone's money.

It was perhaps fated that I should find myself hard-pressed in this perfumed temple of penitence and reflection. Like most cowards, I professed a disbelief in organised religion while keeping my thoughts about the existence of God to myself. Personally, I thought it was a load of old bollocks, but publicly I hedged my bets. I was like a self-serving ligger, sucking up to the performer while disapproving of his agency. I wanted to be on all the guest lists, but I didn't want to pay. Unfortunately, the winged doormen would have looked me up and down and proclaimed that, dressed like that, in a hair shirt and broken boots that had fled all responsibilites, I wasn't coming in. I couldn't argue. I was what I wore, and pride, the sovereign ring of the spiritually poor, wasn't going to let me beg.

I found a curtained alcove, and behind another curtain a locked door. It seemed architecturally possible that this door led to a side street, but I was strangely uncomfortable about rummaging through the drawers of the shrouded table to find a key. I crossed the altar and tiptoed down the other side aisle, trying to place my new pursuers in the context of my predicament. They must have found out that I had handled their passports, and the only way that could have happened was if Henrique had spilled his guts. That considered, I couldn't work out what they wanted with me. Was Murphy going to give me a kicking, or was he planning on pointing me out to the police? The former seemed most likely, for he was a big bugger with a fighter's nose, although looks could be deceiving, as I often hinted darkly when trying to impress girls.

Perhaps the stolen passports had been retrieved from the Transit, and the connection had been explained to them by the Guardia. That too seemed unlikely. The Guardia would have simply returned the passports and told the hapless tourists to piss off back to the Costa. I sat heavily on a pew, suddenly very, very tired. These two idiots were nothing more than an irritating side issue demanding more time than they were worth, like a pair of mosquitoes in a mamba-infested tent.

I tipped back my head and looked up at the ceiling. Its wide symmetry effected a promising tranquillity on my soul, as though the building itself were inviting me to unburden myself. I let my head roll forward.

No way.

Now was not the time to undergo epiphany, and this little branch of the company was ill-equipped for the job. Turning my soul into something worth saving would have been a job for regional headquarters even before the events of the last week. Now it would need direct referral to head office, and the best this place could expect from me was a deal. It had to be simple, since I was in no position to make detailed demands, and it had to be realistic. I stood up and pointed at Jesus.

'Get me out of this, and I'll make an appointment to meet up in the near future. Let me get to the car and get out of this village, and I promise you I will come to your office and talk serious business.'

It wasn't meant to come out that way, but it didn't really matter, because if He did exist, then words were unnecessary, and if He didn't, then I could have said the Lord's Prayer backwards for all the difference it was going to make.

I was a drug dealer, and I thought like a drug dealer. If I sold salvation like I sold cocaine, then I would expect the discerning new customer to demand a free sample. I wouldn't give it to him, but then my business wasn't based on love and trust. I left the offer in the air between us and turned towards the door. It was worth a try, and miracles happened every day . . . The clatter of heavy iron on aged oak killed my fancy. I caught my breath and stood as still as a statue, only my heart moving. The door was opening, and someone was coming in.

Trembling, I reversed up the side aisle, and ducked into one of the two confessionals, wishing that I had a gun. A gun would improve most situations. I wouldn't have to shoot people, but I could entrance them, hypnotising them with the unblinking, oiled eye to perform my will. I'd seen it on TV, and I had been in the front row on Jean-Marc's opening night. He had made a girl think she was dead.

Purposeful, confident feet were approaching, the shoes of a man with a mission, and I was hiding in the ecclesiastical equivalent of a broom cupboard. It seemed appropriate to put my hands together, lower my face and mumble. I heard the door click, creak and clunk, and I smelled garlic and wine.

'In the name of the Father, the Son and of the Holy Spirit,' said the voice with the weariness of a man sent to cut down a forest with a penknife.

I hesitated to reply. The last time I had been to confession had been the first time, and even then I had lied. The responses were weak and dusty from disuse, but as I cleared my throat, they fell from my lips unbidden.

'Er, bless me Father for I have sinned,' I mumbled, shaking my head in disbelief of what I was hearing. 'It has been, er . . . quite a long time since my last confession.'

Another sigh greeted this admission. Why did they make this procedure so difficult? I sighed in reply, my ears pricked towards the church door.

He was waiting for me to begin, and I didn't know what to say. I could have told him how glad I was that he was a priest and not an assassin, but it seemed inappropriate. I couldn't just apologise and walk out: it would look suspicious and was exactly the sort of behaviour by which I would be remembered.

'You should have prepared yourself for confession before coming in here,' grunted the priest.

'I know,' I nodded, 'it's just that, er—'

'What?' He was impatient.

'Look, Father,' I began. 'What's the point of all this? I mean, is there any?'

'The point?' spluttered the priest, not knowing whether to use a question mark or an exclamation. 'You come in here to ask me the point? Have you not been taught?'

'Oh yeah, I was taught once, but it was ages ago and I just want to know if there is anything to be gained from doing this.'

Like a copper, it is a priest's duty to read you your rights and to lay down the law. He cannot assume that the sheep in his flock are always aware of what they are doing, or why they are doing it, and if asked a question so basic as to be almost mocking, he must answer it with grace and clarity. That's what I thought, anyway.

He thought for a moment, then coughed, clearing the phlegm from his throat.

'What is the point in confession?' I felt for him. He had probably nipped in here from the dinner table, expecting a five-minute tale of infidelity, or petty theft, and instead he had walked into a theological ambush. 'Confession of one's sins is the one means by which one can be freed from their burden and reconciled with others, with the Church, and with God. Confession is a fundamental part of the sacrament of penance and reconciliation. As a sinner, you have offended against God, you have loved yourself more than Him, and you have injured the community of man and the Church. Confessing your sins is one of the steps towards becoming reconciled with God, with your fellows and with the Church. Understand?'

I didn't know what a sacrament was, but the rest seemed pretty straightforward.

'Do you accept that God made you?'

Did I accept that God made me? Assuming that God existed,

then it still seemed a little simplistic to see myself as God's little bundle of joy, and it seemed a little too convenient to explain my current status as God's will. That sort of thinking belonged across the water, in the desert. I told my unseen tutor that I didn't understand.

'You are two beings,' he explained. 'One, the man, was made by God in His form. The other, the sinner, was made by you and you alone. Your sinful self has overgrown the man that God made, as poison ivy covers the beauty of a statue. Your sins are the leaves upon that ivy, your sinful will the stem and trunk that are wrapped around the stone. God abhors the ivy, and if you condemn it as a strangling weed, then you are joined with God. Destroy what you have made, so that God can save what He has made. That is the point of confession. But you ask me too if there is anything to be gained from this, and I tell you now that the answer is no, if what you seek to gain is material. Confession gives you nothing that you can hold, or hoard, or spend, or save. The act of confession is an unburdening, an unloading of the weight of sin and guilt that crushes your conscience. You carry the stains of your sins like dirt on the palms of your hands, like mud in your eye, like infection on your tongue, like a thorn in your thumb. Confession cleanses and sterilises, and prepares you for penance.'

'Penance?'

I heard skin on skin, and a sigh. The priest had put his head in his hands. There would be no dessert for him tonight. When he spoke, it was slowly, with weary resignation. 'There is no point in confessing your sins unless you are truly repentant. If you are going to go out and carry on doing whatever it was until next time you confess, then you have wasted your time and God's — and mine — by coming here. If you confess, you must be truly sorry and determined to change yourself from the inside, to return to God with all your heart and turn away from the evil in which you have taken root. We call it conversion of the heart, and the first act of a true penitent is one of contrition.' He sniffed. 'I take it that you'd like a recap on the nature of contrition?'

I sniffed, and he took it as a yes.

'Contrition, you won't remember, comes from the inside. Only you and God alone know the authenticity of your contrition. You can tell anyone you like how sorry you are, but He knows and you know how much you mean it, and this is important. Perfect contrition is the best, and this arises when your sorrow is for the betrayal of God's love. If you are truly sorry for your sins, and you are sorry above all because you have let God down, then we call your contrition perfect, and this alone is enough to grant you forgiveness for your everyday sins. Big sins – mortal sins – are harder to beat.' This was bad news.

'If, however,' he continued, his gruff voice rising to preaching pitch, 'your contrition has arisen out of self-interest, such as the fear of eternal damnation, then this we call imperfect contrition. It's not ideal, but it's better than nothing. It shows a certain appreciation of one's sinful nature. What you have to ask yourself is why you're sorry, and how much, and then, and only then, can we think about absolution. Got it?'

'Yes,' I replied. 'Thank you. There's one more thing.'

'Ask me.'

'Confidentiality. You can't tell anyone else what I confess, can you?'

'That is correct. I am bound by the Church to observe the sacramental seal, which means that everything you tell me is kept secret. Nothing you tell me will ever be repeated to anybody by me. You can be confident of that.'

'Thanks.'

'There's something else you should know,' added the priest. 'Confession is an uplifting experience. The unburdening is as physical as it is mental. Absolved of sin, you would leave here feeling stronger, lighter and happier. It's what you would call a natural high.'

My blurred attention snapped back into focus at that news, but there was nothing I could truly confess to man or God at this time. How could I be penitent and contrite, and then drive the ten klicks from here to the reservoir and dig up five kilos of the powered sin that had brought me here in the first place? As the priest had suggested, I would be wasting my time, God's time and his time.

'Can I confess in any church?'

'You may.'

'Any time?'

'Within reason. If it's been such a long time since your last confession that you've forgotten why we do it then it would probably be best to make an appointment, or at the very least turn up after, rather than just before, dinner.'

'Okay.'

'So are you ready?'

'To confess?'

'Of course.'

I covered my mouth with a stained hand and shook my head. I took it away. 'There are some things that have happened for which I am truly sorry – repentant. Want to hear about them?'

'Go ahead.'

'I don't think I need to go into too much detail. If God is about, then He already knows. I'm just going to list them.'

'All right,' said the priest.

'And remember the sacred seal, or whatever it was.'

'Of course.'

'Right then, here we go.' I took a deep breath. 'Number one. I have a four-year-old son in England whom I have never seen. I abandoned his mother while she was pregnant, and I am sorry for doing that. I ran away because I thought that staying with her would ruin my life, and now it's sort of ruined anyway. That's one. Next: I have committed an act of greed and, well, theft, I suppose. In fact, I've committed lots of thefts. I nicked a car, just now . . .' I was heading off on a ramble, so I dragged myself back to the main road. 'We'd better take one thing at a time.'

'Whatever,' said the priest, wishing he'd put a tape in the video.

'Okay. Here it is: I took something from a dead thief. I didn't kill him, he just died. I took it and I hid it, and when the man it belonged to asked for it back, I told him I didn't have it. I told my girlfriend where it was . . .' A grunt of exasperated disappointment came from behind the screen. '. . . but it turned out that she was having an affair with my best friend and wanted rid of me. She betrayed me to the Frenchman.'

'Hang on a minute,' interrupted the priest. 'Who's the Frenchman?'

'Jean-Marc,' I replied. 'He's a bastard.'

'I remind you that you are in a church.'

'Sorry. He's the man to whom the stolen goods belonged.'

'And your girlfriend told him where the stolen goods were to be found?'

'Right.'

'So did he find his stolen goods?'

'Er, no. He didn't. The thing is that I never trusted my girlfriend enough to tell her where the stuff was really hidden. I lied to her, and told her they were somewhere else. When we got to where she thought they were, and found out they weren't there, the Frenchman lost it big time.'

'And what did he do?'

I took a deep breath. 'He killed her. Shot her. Four times. She wanted him to kill me, been trying to persuade him to kill me for ages, but he didn't. With me dead, he'd have had nothing.

There was a very long pause, punctuated only by the distant yells from a different world.

'Is there more?'

'Oh yes,' I nodded. 'Loads more. I asked a friend to help me, a good, decent man, not much of a churchgoer, but a good man all the same. Things went very badly wrong. I shouldn't have involved him. Some other people got killed, and his life has been destroyed, and then tonight, before I nicked the car, a woman who I think probably wanted to die anyway got killed as well – in quite an enjoyable way, as it happens, if that helps, and, er, I sort of had something to do with it.' I rubbed the scum from my lips with the back of my hand. 'It's been a busy old week, one way or another.'

I stared at the screen. The church was filled with a roaring silence. I heard the wet sound of the priest's lips as he moved them.

'There's loads of other stuff, too,' I added, when the silence became too much. 'It feels like I've been running for years, running from bills, letters, responsibilities, from the conse-quences of things I have done that won't go away, from memories—'

'Wait,' interrupted the priest. 'Unpaid bills are a long way down the list at this stage. I think we should concentrate on the mortal sins you described. You said your girlfriend was killed. Do you feel any responsibility for her death? Do you feel perhaps that even though you didn't pull the trigger, it was your actions that brought about her murder? In the eyes of man, of the law, it is the Frenchman who is guilty, but in the eyes of God you share the blame. Do you see that?'

It would have been easy to agree, but for once I didn't feel like lying.

'To be honest,' I replied, 'I find it very hard to feel any remorse. If I'd told her the truth, I'd be dead right now, and she probably would be too. Deceiving her hasn't made much difference at all.'

'Do you feel any sorrow for your girlfriend's death?'

I turned my ears inwards and listened hard for violins. I heard music and the usual voices, but no fiddles. 'Not really.'

'I see,' said the priest. Outside the church somebody was having too much fun with a novelty car horn.

'How would you feel?' I asked, detecting his disappointment. 'Your girlfriend is having an affair with your best friend and plotting your murder so she can take over your business, then she betrays you to a mutual enemy and gets killed. You try feeling sorrow. It's not that easy.'

Nor was it that easy for a Catholic priest to imagine himself in my apparently unrepentant circumstances. He tried for a short while, then changed the subject.

'You mentioned a child, a son, abandoned in England. You said you were sorry about that. Tell me why.'

I'd never really thought about why I regretted leaping from a foundering family. I wasn't even sure if the guilt I occasionally felt was real, or simply expected. It was the done thing in my society to spill over the sides to anyone who would listen. We all had our feeble reasons for outstaying our welcome on the Costa, and a pair of sympathetic ears could be found on every out-of-season barstool. All you had to do was give an equal hour of understanding for every hour taken. My sob story had always been about the nervous breakdown that ended my teaching career and caused me to flee my shake-and-bake family to this self-imposed exile from which I could never return. God knew how guilty I felt about leaving the kid, but the boy was better off without me, or so I said.

The problem was that God knew exactly how guilty I felt, so I could see no point in lying to his agent.

'I don't know why I'm sorry,' I mumbled. 'Don't even know if I'm sorry. It's the done thing, though, isn't it?'

He ignored the question. 'What about these stolen goods? What are your intentions towards them?'

As I've said, I can only lie effectively if I can believe my own story, and the notion that I would leave five kilos of cocaine buried seemed so preposterous that I was momentarily lost for words. My confessor noted my silence.

'Okay. We'll skip over the matter of the man whose life you have ruined for the moment and go straight to the last thing you mentioned. This woman who died tonight, this woman whose death you say you sort of had something to do with: did you kill her?'

I covered my mouth and considered the question. Did I kill her? Was I the fiend that sent her soul to hell? The emptiness I had felt when I asked myself that question less than an hour ago had become a hollowness, a void where something vital had once existed and that was now filling with a dense, black horror. Conscience had got a gang together and had caught up with me on the corner of Easy Street, and now I was going to get a kicking. I knew the truth, conscience knew the truth and God knew the truth, so it didn't matter what I said. I took a deep breath.

'No, I didn't kill her,' I replied.

The denial hung on the screen like spittle, infectious and repugnant. From our separate sides we watched it drip into the darkness, and then the priest sighed.

'Why did you come here tonight?'

'To confess,' I lied. 'To get these things off my chest—'

'You're a liar,' interrupted the priest angrily. 'You might have come here for forgiveness, but you did not come to confess. You can try to deceive me, but you will not deceive God who sees, and has seen, everything. You have no intention of giving up your sinful ways and you have shown no remorse for the sinful acts you have committed. You seek to justify your actions, to cast your crimes as the necessary means towards an end which is wholly sinful—'

'Hold up a minute,' I protested. 'Aren't you supposed to grant absolution instead of making me feel even worse? Isn't that what this is supposed to be all about, listening with a neutral ear and letting me clear my conscience?'

'Did you think it would be that easy? Did you think you could spill your soiled burden all over the floor of this church and leave with a straightened back?' He laughed sadly. 'When God comes for you, you'd better be waiting. You'd better be down on your knees and waiting.'

Maybe this unseen priest sensed that he and I were in competition, that we were both trading on the same turf. We both sold products that promised everlasting joy, only mine were cheaper and had fewer strings attached. Either way, he seemed to have taken a dislike to me.

'Can't you just give me a blessing or something?'

He laughed again, or maybe he sobbed. 'No, I cannot possibly give you my blessing.'

He swallowed, and I heard the sound of smooth hands drawn across a stubbled face. He took a long breath and held it as though he were carefully selecting the right words. When he spoke again he was calm and detached.

'I'll give you something you can take with you when you leave. It's something that works well with children and the mentally incompetent, and I think it will help you. Before you say or do anything, at any time, for any reason whatsoever, stop and ask yourself: what would Jesus say?'

'What would Jesus say?'

'There you go,' he said softly. 'You're getting it already. What would Jesus say? It immediately makes things easier, doesn't it?'

'So what would Jesus say right now?' I challenged him.

He thought for a moment. 'I would not presume to know what Jesus would say, but I would expect Him to say that you should leave this church now, and that you should put your life in His gentle hands, and that one day He will lead you into another church with the honest intention of renouncing your sinful past. Go now, and I will pray for your immortal soul.'

It was more than I'd expected.

21

I slipped out by the sacristy door, feeling small and embarrassed. I was a worm, a cockroach, a weasel, but I was still one of God's creatures. Staying close to the wall, I walked down the side street to the square and peeked around the corner to Quetzal.

The huddled figures in the alley to the right were up to no good, a sure sign that the cops had gone. I scanned the square for Murphy. He'd gone too. The car was thirty seconds away, the keys were in my hand. I followed the edge of the square around to the bar, promising myself a smoke as a prize. The lads in the alley looked out of the gloom in fearful surprise as I crept past, then turned back to their dealing when they saw that I wasn't going to spoil their fun. My hand was shaking as I pushed the key into the lock and I whispered thanks as it clicked up. I slid in and switched on, the car filling with the high-altitude lunacy of Bloody Mary's Peruvian pipe music as I revved the engine. I was nearly there. I slipped the car into first and drove it away, rolling out of Matamoros and into the blessed darkness of the mountains, a contraband cigarette between my chapped lips and wondering what the hell Jesus would have said.

Looking back across the twisted, fantastic landscape of the past week, it seemed impossible that I could have made it this far, and yet here I was, in Mary's car, less than ten klicks from the cocaine and lost to the world. I would pick it up and head straight down to the coast. If I was quick about it, I could make it to the Bulldog Bar before closing time and persuade Trigger to follow me out to the airport at Malaga. I would dump the car in the long-stay car park, grab a lift back into Torremolinos with the saturnine barman, and crash at his place until my face healed up. It would be easy, and I deserved it to be easy. I punched EJECT and tossed Mary's tape into the slipstream. Not everything from the foothills of the Andes was worth keeping. I span the dial to the FRA, but all I heard was the dragged-gravel static of Alberto's fast exit.

Helmut had once told me that the secret to success was the disciplined pursuit of short-term goals. I wondered which of his short-term goals Luisa had been, but the pain lasted only a moment. Helmut was history: shit happened. Right now, my primary ambition was the disposal of the cocaine. The short-term goals on the twisting road to its realisation were fairly easily attained. One: drive to the abandoned *finca* by the *barranca*. Two: dig up the coke. Three: drive to the coast. Four: lose Mary's car at the airport long-stay. Five: crash at Trigger's place. I'd tell him that I just fancied a few days by the beach. Six: wait until my face had regained its charm, then knock out a couple of dozen gram-wraps in order to generate a cash flow. Seven: rent a car, or maybe a motorbike. Bikes seemed like more fun. Cars were safer. Eight: rent a holiday apartment in Fuengirola or Torre with a conveniently located payphone. Nine: buy up the cutting agents. Tourist tooters on rented scooters had little idea of what they were buying. That the quality of the substance they were buying with their holiday money was at least double that of the scouring powder they were used to buying back home rarely registered. They knew what they liked, and they liked what they knew, and I was more than happy to oblige. Cocaine was like scrambled eggs: some liked it with added cream, some insisted on a dash of Worcester sauce and others liked them speckled with pepper. Serve them a single egg, scrambled and cooked in a teaspoonful of melted butter, and, regardless of the dish's purity, they would send it back. They wanted a freeze: I would give them a cut of Procaine. They wanted a rush: I would give them a cut of speed. They wanted a good gram for their money: I'd give them a fifty per cent cut of lactose, a tasteless and usefully dense powder usually added to baby food. The little wrap of party powder that they would carefully slide into their wallets and handbags as they left their rooms and hit the throbbing streets would be a lot like the average album: a couple of hits and seventy per cent filler, and it would still be better than the rubbish they were used to. Even being generous – they were on vacation, after all – I could turn those five kilos into twenty and save a weight for samples and personal use.

The retail price of cocaine was currently hovering at around eight thousand pesetas, or forty quid, a gram, thus putting the value of Yvan's life at eight hundred thousand pounds. I laughed out loud: eight hundred thousand quid! I didn't need to recheck my maths – in a world of uncertainty and shifting parameters, mathematics are the only constants. If you can't cope with the numbers, you'll never handle the weights. It was just a great shame that it was effectively impossible to shift five thousand grams of four-stepped cocaine on my own. Twenty thousand grams gave me twenty thousand opportunities to be busted, and under the present circumstances it seemed wise to follow the route of least risk. I would cut and fold five kilos into ten, and let nine of them go at fifteen thousand pounds each. The remaining kilo I would turn into one and a half, and two-thirds of that I would trade for a passport, a wallet full of credit cards and a driving licence. The remaining five hundred grams I would trade along the strip, and in two weeks, or however long it took to be born again, I would drive north in a second-hand car with one hundred and fifty thousand pounds. It seemed like a reasonable plan, exactly the sort of scheme Luisa might have devised.

I lit a fag, the flame reflecting my haggard face in the windscreen. How easy it had been to slip back into the groove, to take up where I had left off. There were hoards buried all over these hills and not one lay untouched as a result of contrition. One made amends after one had liquidated one's assets, when one could afford to be contrite. I could hear the stupidity in the back of my head, yelling out like some mad old witch that the only chance I had of saving myself was to turn away from the road to the *barranca*, to leave the poison where it was buried, to walk away from the five thousand grams of concentrated sin, so black that it was white, and take instead the one single ounce of good intention that outweighed it. A ghostly beam fell across my hand as the moon appeared between the trees, and I swerved through the shadows until she was once again hidden. Nothing was going to persuade me to give up my cocaine.

At the castle turn a temporary 'Road Closed' sign had been erected. I didn't even touch the brakes, driving past the turn-off like any other Algeciras-bound motorist. It was possible that the road had been closed in order that it could be resurfaced, but it was most unlikely. Notices of intent would have been posted months ago, and the knowledge that the *provincia* was going to spend money on a road that didn't lead to a marina or a golf course would have delighted everybody. The road could have been closed because of a landslip or a flood, but either natural disaster required rain, and it hadn't rained here for over a year.

I checked Mary's rear-view. No one using headlights was following me. I knew why the road was closed, but like a conscientious scientist, I didn't want to believe it. The road was closed because of me, because of Yvan, because of his cocaine. The road was closed because the Guardia were searching the castle, but it wasn't going to stop me from recovering what was mine. I took the next right off the main road, following a dusty single-track lane past hand-painted signs warning of plagues and boils through dark brush where the burned-out carcasses of stolen cars and the evidence of joyless liaisons with unparticular girls littered the verge. I parked on a dog-leg and leaned against the bonnet, smoking a Marlboro and turning my ears into the night air. The valley was heavy with the smell of woodsmoke – I had taken it for river mist in my headlights – and even as I listened for voices and movement, tiny smuts spiralled down like black snowflakes to land on Bloody Mary's car. I stubbed the fag, satisfied that I was alone, and stepped into the brush. When I had foreseen my headshot death, I had fallen on ground like this. How long would a corpse lie undetected in this highway hinterland?

Long enough, I figured.

Soot continued to fall from the starless sky as I found a narrow path heading downhill and in the right direction. Moments later, I winced my way past a thorny bush and stood on a wide beach of pale, river-rounded rocks. The slopes of the castle hill lay across the river, the castle buildings hidden by the convex topography, the contours buried beneath bands of moonlight and shadow. The river, narrow for as long as the sluices stayed shut, bisected the bed and was less than knee-deep as I waded across. The scrub on the far side was somehow cleaner and more wholesome than that on the roadside, and within ten minutes I reached the road along which I had ridden Yvan's big motorbike so long ago.

My feet, rested by the kneeling and the driving, had woken up as I crossed the river and registered their disapproval by morphing the nerves that served them into the jagged throats of broken wine bottles. I winced as the pain sent my calves into spasm, and tried to bribe my busted heels with the promise of cocaine. They didn't seem to think it would work, but they reserved judgement and allowed me to hobble along the track and through the weeds to the *finca*. As soon as I saw the low walls and collapsed roof, I dropped into the undergrowth and waited, my ears twitching like a feather-mouthed fox listening out for pursuit. I gave them five minutes, but they weren't coming, and then, with my heart beating so fast that it was taking all the oxygen I could burn just to keep it going, I crawled breathlessly into the ruin. The fallen roof did not let in enough of the night to see by, and it was in the yellow flame of a lighter held in trembling hands that I found the rubble under which my stash was buried.

I pushed and pulled one-handed at the pile until my fingers touched the gritty T-shirt in which I had wrapped the drugs.

It hadn't been rained on.

It hadn't been eaten by goats.

It hadn't been stolen from me. I owed Jesus for this little miracle, but I'd pay Him some time in the future. I pulled the little bales out and found the one which I had cut, flicking a pile with a fingernail onto the back of my hand and sucking it into my brain as a man in a desert would take his first water. I felt the bitterness at the back of my throat, the gentle numbing of the nasal passages and the first real smile I had experienced since meeting Sad Tony, back there in Cadiz. My skin seemed to shrink to fit my body as my pupils widened to let in more light and my nerves lit up like urban freeways. Moving faster and with more grace than before, I pulled off my boots and poured four or five grams into each. My feet deserved a little pick-me-up. Unexpected but not altogether unreasonable thoughts began to crowd my brain. My hair needed cutting. Maybe I'd have it dyed at the same time. Elvis blue, perhaps. I would need to buy a decent Walkman once I had settled on the coast, maybe one that played CDs, and I needed new clothes. I would need to rent a pad with satellite TV. My thumb required medical treatment, and a visit to an expensive dentist wouldn't hurt. I needed a whole new wardrobe and a new pair of boots. It seemed like a good time to start thinking about the little things in life, now that the big things seemed so certain.

The moon remained hidden as I retraced my route, her head cast down in shame because my grin reflected the distant sun more brightly than her pock-marked face. I was still winning, my feet were numb, and I was ninety minutes from the Costa.

A puff of white dust burst around the T-shirt as I laid it on the bonnet of the car, the powder falling to blend with the coating of soot that had covered the paintwork since I'd been gone. The air still smelled of bonfires, bringing about a curiously nostalgic yearning, as though I were missing a party somewhere. I stabbed my index finger through the hole in the open packet, snorted up the pile I withdrew and rubbed the rest into my gums. I tipped the knife and the gum out of the carrier bag I had taken from La Mendirosa and used it to wrap the cocaine as I struggled to find a good hiding place within the fragile steel shell of Mary's hatchback. At last, and with little confidence, I decided that my booty was safest stashed beneath the rear bench seat. If I found myself in enough trouble to warrant a third-party search that involved lifting the rear seats, then I was as good as busted already. I checked for the moon, but she had seen nothing. It was time to head for the seaside.

22

I sped back towards the main road, consumed by a familiar but not altogether comfortable euphoria that only the thought of Luisa could dampen. I watched the speedo rise like my blood pressure, seventy, eighty, ninety, one hundred k.p.h. with the thumping dance beat of a raver's radio station to rock me down to the sea. Except this road didn't lead to the sea. The shotgun-peppered 'Give Way' sign flew past me like a balloon in the jetstream as I stamped on the brake pedal. An umbrella, a sunhat and a pile of magazines lost their grip on the parcel shelf as the car fishtailed towards the T-junction in a dragster-like shroud of dust and rubber smoke. I thought of the scrapyard at Jimena, the severed struts and peeled-back roofs through which mustachioed firemen had recovered molten bodies at junctions such as this, and as the car rocked gasping on its suspension only halfway across the southbound lane, I took a hand from the wheel and punched myself hard in the head as a hatchback sped past, heading north, the indignant white faces of its occupants turned to inspect me. I breathed out, found first, and headed for the coast.

Waiting at the level crossing on the outskirts of Los Molinas I checked the rear-view. I had been seeing orange sparks at the edge of my vision for hours now, but I had put them down to some new psychophysical optical disturbance, rather like the rook I used to see in the back of the Transit. As I watched the dark mass of the mountains behind me, however, I clearly saw a shower of sparks spill over the ridge, like the wind-blown fire from a fallen Roman candle. I wound down the window and looked back, but darkness had reclaimed the heights. It looked as though an invisible Titan had taken an angle grinder to the ore-bearing rocks, carving himself a niche in the topographical folklore while spraying sparks all over the bone-dry *campo*. I recalled the smell of burning on the night air, and the soft showers of smut that had dusted my hair with carbon back at the river, and I was close to connecting these with the visual phenomena when I looked in the mirror and saw the police. Right behind me, so close that all I could see was the word 'Policia' side-lit in soft blue. A long, dirty train of empty aggregate wagons was clunking and squealing across my front at walking pace, and I wished with all my heart that I could open my eyes and find myself in any of them, regardless of their destination. Behind me the beeps and bursts of the police radio could be heard over the scraping of the passing train, and the blue light flashed just twice, its reflection mockingly played back from the windows of parked cars.

The shotgun cop had left the car, crossing the rear of the Starlet and coming up in my wing mirror. I swallowed hard and wound down the window. I was nicked.

The cops were friendly enough and seemed quite apologetic about arresting me. Unfortunately for me, my girlfriend and the restaurant on the Costa where I had booked a table to celebrate her twenty-first birthday, regulations stated that any foreign national unable to prove their identity could be taken into custody until such time that a person could be found to vouch for them. As far as the two cops were concerned, I *was* John Bedford, nephew of Ms Mary Bedford of La Mendirosa,

and they saw no reason to believe otherwise. Under normal circumstances they would let me proceed with a warning to keep
my passport handy at all times – after all, if the Guardia had
stopped me there would have been fixed penalties, jail-time,
magistrates and everything. Recently, however, there had been
a spate of quite unusual incidents which had left the Jefes with
no choice but to tighten security all over the district. I had once
seen a poor-quality monochrome photograph of a condemned
man – a Communist spy – talking with the firing party who
would shortly perform his execution. I wondered what he had
been thinking as he listened to their nervous, detached chatter.
Was he formulating a last-minute escape plan? Was he begging
to be put through to the God he had cut off, or was he simply
aghast at the ludicrousness of his situation? Right now I knew
that his mind had been utterly empty. The thoughts that made
it through were out of date by the time he had read them, the
cerebellum closing down like an embassy under siege. Yes, I
could smoke. No, they didn't want one. I must have heard
about the fire?

'Looks like a bloody volcano,' observed the older of the pair,
nodding towards the mountain.

'What happened to you?' asked the younger, the radio mike
dangling as he waited for instructions.

'Rock-climbers beat me up,' I shrugged in a matter-of-fact
way. 'You lot should do something about them.'

'You haven't been soaking druggies in petrol and torching
them, have you?' grinned the other.

My stomach shrank to the size of a nut and I blinked hard,
biting my lip. 'Uh-uh,' I smiled, shaking my head. 'Why?'

The cop flicked his heavy-lidded eyes back towards the ridge.
'Trouble in paradise. That was a commune up there, bunch of
hippies, foreigners mostly – no offence.'

I saw the universe shrink with no loss of weight to become one tiny ball of blackness. I raised an eyebrow. 'What happened?'

'Dunno,' shrugged the cop. 'All I know is that three of them had petrol poured over them and some nutter set them alight. Burned the whole bloody place down. Still burning – look.'

He pointed as another plume of sparks blew westwards into the Montecoche.

'What were you doing on the *barranca* road?' asked the young cop.

I sighed. 'Hoping to find some flowers to pick for my girl-friend,' I replied. 'Not that it matters much now.'

The radio interrupted the interrogation. 'Bring him in,' was the upshot. I was no longer responsible for my destiny.

The old cop drove Mary's car back to the fortress-like police station at Matamoros, and as he swaggered into the poster-plastered reception area it was clear that he had nothing exciting to declare. At last, and with an encouraging lack of urgency, they checked me in. I placed almost everything in my pockets in a plastic bag, signed the guestbook, and was shown to my room. The custody officer, assuming that I couldn't speak Spanish, touched the first two fingers of his right hand to his lips as he stood in the doorway. I offered him a cigarette, and he took it, lit it, and passed it back to me with a wink. I stood before the bunk and nodded my thanks as the keeper of the flame locked me in. Cocaine-induced formication had me scratching like a chained hound as I paced the precincts of my room, the judicial version of a Formule 1 motel: clean, modern, pleasingly minimalist and probably designed by Germans. The white walls were coated with some shiny, slip-pery substance intended, it seemed, to deter graffiti. A single course of glass bricks ran the width of the cell at ceiling height, and above my head the muted glow of fluorescent light was diffused from behind suicide-proof opaque perspex panels. Interactive experiences were limited to the use of the seatless stainless-steel toilet bowl and the operation of a heavy-duty rubber room-service bell. The lettering of the metal sign that had at one time warned against flippant use of the button had been defaced beyond recognition by the overlaid declarations of the cell's desperate, defiant and nonchalant former residents. I read the deepest-carved with indifference: I could add little. It was, I observed with a curiously detached objectivity, the first in a series of government accommodations in which I would pass the foreseeable future. I should have been depressed, dejected, even terrified, but a chemical spill on the appropriate lobe was preventing the emission of those emotions. They would well up behind the crystal dam, becoming deeper and denser, their essence concentrated until impenetrable by light, and when the pressure forced the breach I would be drowned in darkness. The cocaine was worth fifteen years. That alone would take care of my basic needs until I was forty-two. The bodies in the van would ensure that Spain continued to look after me until the day I died, and then she would see me interred in an unmarked grave within the walls of her embrace. I had drunk my last beer and kissed my last girl. I had tried, and I had failed, but now that I was caught I could see that sadness was not the only witness to the surrender of my future. Standing shyly in her shadow was the sweetly smiling figure of relief, and behind them both, wheeling like a man-sized rook, soared El Duende.

Life, for me, began at twenty-seven.

I sat on the wipe-clean mattress. Sooner or later some striped cop would ask if the prisoner's car had been searched. They might even have been searching it at that moment. As soon as the shock of their discovery wore off, they would be down to fetch me. Just as in the church in Matamoros, I doubted that any of the uniforms in this nick bore sufficient braid to carry the responsibility of my interrogation, but they would pass the time until the suits arrived by taking my photograph and my fingerprints. They would run a check on me with the Regional HQ at Estepona, with Interpol, with Gib and with the Guardia Civil barracks at Ronda. Sooner or later, by chance or by design, my face would fall alongside the photo from my passport. They wouldn't even need to find the cocaine.

I thought back to that Tuesday morning so long ago when I had stood in my wrecked front room, half-cut on *aguardiente* and buzzing on Yvan's coke, watching Luisa trying to tidy up the mess. Even then, a voice I had ignored had sung some improvised *canto jondo* that lost its meaning in translation. The essence, I realised now, was that it was all over, even then, and all I had been doing since was delaying the inevitable. I wondered if our home still existed, or if it had been destroyed in the fire that had leapt from those writhing bodies, and I thought of the peeling poster in Cadiz that had warned me: *Aqui termina la fiesta.*

It was time for bed.

23

His flies were undone, and he was shouting at me.

'*Vamonos.*'

My tongue had swollen and my throat felt like a burned-out car. There had been no dreams, and as I sat up I rubbed my eyes, trying to recall my last known position.

Inside.

I needed a drink. The low-flying cop needed me to move my arse. I groped for my cigarettes, fumbling to plant one between my lips. The cop told me I didn't have time. The car – Mary's car – and the coke. I rolled my head, my face and my neck through my hands and stood up.

'Where we going?'

The cop scratched his armpit and pointed at the door. 'Let's go.'

This is the first day of the rest of my life, I reassured myself as I walked past the closed doors of the other cells and waited while the cop leaned past me to punch a four-digit code into a lock. I would adopt a silent routine until I knew what they knew, and then I would spill my guts. I blinked, and in the split second of darkness I saw Alberto laughing at one of his own jokes. Only yesterday, up in that mountain bar, I had been ready to sell him out as easily as he had decided to help me. Now, for whatever difference it made, I would stand up for him. That he might never know was unimportant. My story would begin with Jean-Marc, and it would end with Jean-Marc, and if they couldn't catch him then they could have me.

'Next right,' said the cop.

We stood before a closed door. The cop knocked, calling out at the same time, 'Prisoner.'

The door opened on to a room similar in layout to the cell in which I had spent the night. The same high window of glass bricks, the same shiny white walls, the same rubber panic button. There was no bunk, no graffiti and no lavatory, and in the centre of the room stood a table, its legs bolted to the floor. A big, silver ghetto blaster stood on the table like exhibit A. I wondered if they thought I'd nicked it.

A career cop in a new day's uniform sat facing me, beckoning me, and as I shuffled into the room he pointed politely at an empty chair.

'Sit down, please, Mr Bedford. I'm sorry to have woken you at this early hour, but I need to ask you some questions, okay?' He had the dark, gel-dependent hair of a ladies' man, and he smelled of something rugged and masculine.

I gave him a look that said I knew he was taking the piss, but his earnest expression did not change. 'Go on, then,' I grunted.

He shuffled a sheaf, span a biro, and pressed the record button on the ghetto blaster. He told the tape the time and date, and introduced himself and my escort to the ghetto blaster, in universal police style.

'Your name is Bedford John,' he declared. 'Please confirm this for the tape by saying yes if you agree.'

I agreed.

The cop smiled. 'Señor Bedford, please understand that you have nothing to fear if you have committed no offence.'

I smiled back, feeling a lot better.

'My name, as you heard, is Estrellada, and I am investigating three suspicious deaths that occurred at approximately eight-thirty last night at Castellar Alamanunja, and the subsequent fire which badly damaged the castle. Do you know what I'm talking about?'

I shrugged casually and replied carefully. 'The officers who brought me here for forgetting my passport mentioned that there had been a fire and some people had been killed.'

'Okay,' nodded the cop. 'You speak very good Spanish, by the way. How come?'

It was the only compliment I received these days and it was always accepted with gratitude. I told him I was a teacher, and he raised his eyebrows high enough for me to read the unspoken words in his eyes.

Poor kids, they said.

He asked me if I knew where I was between eight and nine on Friday night.

I smiled. 'I was having dinner with my aunt.' The alibi seemed curiously Dickensian, but it amused the cops.

'As one does,' grinned Estrellada, obliquely, as his colleague sniggered.

I looked blankly back at him. He made a conciliatory gesture with his shoulders.

'Have you never heard the expression "to dine with one's aunt"?'

I shook my head. 'No.' This was one of those things that belonged in the weird box with the Witch's Path. 'Is it something bad?'

Estrellada laughed out loud. 'No, no . . . Doesn't matter, I'm sure it will check out. Did you know of the castle?'

I shrugged again. 'I'd heard of it, but I never went there. It's not really my scene.'

The cop nodded. 'What scene is that?'

I thought fast and answered slowly. 'A closed scene. All eco-warriors and open-toed sandals. All foreigners – no offence meant. So what happened?'

Estrellada gave me a three-second appraisal, and decided that I was not the man he hoped I was. He thought for two more seconds, and then he told me.

'There was a body shop up there, run by a German national. As far as we understand, a local man arrived at the castle in a state of great agitation and carrying a jerry can of gasoline. He was followed in by at least two other men, and a violent argument broke out. We are working on the assumption that the German national, his assistant, who was registered disabled, and the local man were somehow subdued by the others, tied up, and doused with the gasoline.' Estellada looked me in the eye. 'You can guess the rest.'

I raised my eyebrows, suddenly aware of the lack of oxygen in the room.

'We think,' sighed Estrellada, 'that this incident is related to the murder of two police officers and a local bar owner earlier in the day.' He rubbed his eyes as though he'd been up all night, then gave me a plaintive look, as though he expected me to have all the answers.

I pouted, and shrugged. 'Not very peaceful round here, is it?'

Estrellada's eyes widened as though I had spoken treason aloud. 'No, no, no, no,' he countered. 'Violent crime is very rare indeed in these parts. The Costa and the hinterland enjoy some of the lowest crime rates in Europe. You can rest assured that the chances of becoming a victim of violent crime, or indeed any crime while you are down here, are much less than you could expect in your home country. Absolutely yes. Two of the victims were known criminals and we feel sure that their deaths are tied up with some sort of organised crime. The average tourist has absolutely nothing to fear.'

'Is it safe to go rock-climbing?'

He sat back and gave me a look. 'Is it ever safe to go rock-climbing? You a rock-climber?'

I shook my head. 'No way.'

'So you have nothing to fear.'

'Okay,' I conceded.

'What happened to your face?'

'This?' I looked into his dark eyes, loath to mention the rock-climbers again. 'I was beaten up, outside the bus station in Malaga.'

'By whom?'

'Don't know. Thugs, probably.' I touched my throat. 'They took my crucifix, too.'

That last bit was good: it was the detail that encouraged belief.

'Did you report it?'

'Not until now,' I sighed. 'What's the point?'

'You know the point,' replied Estrellada, 'but you're better off reporting the incident at the police station in Malaga. All I can do is send my report to them.'

I waved my hand in a dismissive gesture. 'Whatever.'

'So what were you doing down the *barranca* road last night?'

'I was looking for flowers.'

Estrellada gave me a long, doubting look. 'In the dark?'

Something about me stank – I could see it in Estrellada's tanned face – but he was investigating two triple homicides and a fire, and I was either innocent and stupid, or guilty and extremely clever. Either way, he saw that he was wasting his time by continuing the interview and dismissed me with the ominous assurance we would meet again.

'I'm sure that everything you have told me will check out,' he smiled. '*Hasta lluego.*'

Leading the way back to my cell I hid my surprise when I saw Henrique shuffling towards me, his face a cartoonist's impression of indignant persecution. His lower lip led the way, his narrow, hunched shoulders prodded from behind by a cop who would never respect his rights. Both his wet brown eyes and his bumfluff moustache were pitiful, and as we met at the locked internal gate, I nodded a cautious greeting. He had splashed out on a new outfit, all designer labels and lager stains, and he nodded back wearily, with none of the surprise or shock I had expected from old acquaintances.

'You hear about the fire?' he sighed.

I nodded. 'What happened?'

Henrique shook his mullet. 'Don't know. I've been down on the Costa since last week. Only came back here to pay my fines off, and the bastards nicked me for possession.' He looked furious, and rightly so.

'Possession of how much?'

Henrique glowered. 'Too much, and they're gonna bust me for the rental car. What about you?'

'A mix-up,' I replied. 'Bureaucratic nonsense.'

Henrique's escort finally remembered the code for the gate and our conversation ended as we were pushed in opposite directions.

'*Suerte!*' I called, as though I had luck to spare.

Back in my cell, and unable to sleep, I let my mind entertain me by projecting images of flickering flames across the spit-stained ceiling. The hard rain that had drenched me was falling on others, dripping from their faces and pooling in rainbow puddles around their bodies.

Helmut and Mickey were dead, and that was fine.

An unnamed local man was also dead, along with Luisa, Ramon, Morales and his fat colleague.

The castle stood in ashes, and the Guardia were looking for at least two men. It was possible that Helmut and Mickey had been murdered by gypsies, tramps or thieves, in circumstances entirely remote from my own situation, but it seemed unlikely. I didn't need to see the evidence to know that the last, smoke-filled, blood-boiling scene of Helmut's life had featured Jean-Marc, and I had a horrible feeling that I knew the unnamed local man.

There was something else, too: Henrique had been down on the Costa, in a rental car, with drugs and a suit that had been rejected by *Miami Vice* for being too flash. Where did a three-time loser like Henrique find enough money to party on the Costa and then come back here to pay his fines off? Fines were paid off at five hundred pesetas a week around here, and the only people who ever paid them all off in a lump sum were lottery winners and successful criminals. Henrique, as far as I knew, was neither. I watched every second of every minute of every hour bud, bloom and die before they came back for me. The fear was like a wet westerly gusting against my spine, cold and insistent, chilling my bowels, robbing my legs of feeling. How long would it take Estrellada to establish my true identity? I had not yet been charged, and so they had not yet taken my photograph, but I would be easily described.

My story was a snail, crawling on a straight razor.

What would they find when they went knocking on Bloody Mary's door? A corpse, choked by her own vomit, wide-eyed and breathless in the dawn's early light?

Cadavers could neither accuse nor deny, and I would swear that she seemed fine, if a little depressed, when I left her. Yes, I knew about her habit but who was I to criticise after all she had been through? They did know who Mary Bedford was, didn't they? They knew what her husband had done, didn't they, and they knew what she had to live with? I was the only relative who ever cared about her, and if I hadn't been banged up in here on a totalitarian technicality I might have been able to make it back to La Mendirosa in time to save the poor woman's life. No one was jailed in England for forgetting to carry their passport, and, after all, I was white, wasn't I? It seemed to me that the only way they could make this terrible situation better would be to let me go home and put my poor aunt's affairs in order . . .

It wasn't much, but it was all I had, and it would work only if Mary was dead. The image of that bent teaspoon piled high with her sweet brown addiction dispelled all doubt: Bloody Mary was dead, and circumstances had made me partly responsible. I had slipped the already loosened straps of the moral straitjacket and dropped through the floorboards of society to splash down in the sewers, my yellow eyes blinking hard in the darkness and my newly developed whiskers twitching as I crouched ankle-deep in the effluent of civilisation. I had descended to Jean-Marc's level, and if we ever met again it would be on equal terms. It seemed to be a lousy choice: prisoner or criminal, sectioned or sanctioned. I could accept the chains, the ropes, the strings and the threads that would bind me into society, the numbers, the photographs, the files and the catechisms, or else I could choose the freedom which ultimately promised restraint. I could choose to live within Eden and select something to sate my appetite from a set menu, or live without and eat whatever I could catch. I could graze with the sheep or run with the wolves.

I wanted to graze with the wolves.

I wondered what Jesus would have said.

24

It was light outside when they came for me again, and it was
with both relief and resignation that I walked down the hall to
my next interrogation.

I was escorted past small women with mops to the same
interview room as last night. The door was opened for me, and
I was prodded towards the same chair, before the same table.
The ghetto blaster had gone, and this morning's cop was a dark
man in his forties with sad eyes, slick hair and a moustache that
gave him the look of an Iraqi spymaster. He was not alone, and
as he pointed at the chair, his guest turned to greet me.

'Sleep all right, did you?' said Bloody Mary, through the side
of her mouth. She turned back to the cop. 'Yeah that's him.
Look at the state of him.'

The cop glanced up at me and smiled at Mary. She looked
remarkably good for one who should have been dead, despite
the green leisure suit. I'd never injected heroin myself, but I
could have sworn that a thousand milligrams was enough to
switch off the lights. Mary caught me looking and chucked me
a smile like a man wearing a bulletproof vest. I raised my eyebrows and my palms as though I didn't know that she knew
what I knew that she knew. The cop cleared his throat, shuffled
a pile of forms and picked up a pen. 'So you are happy to confirm that Señor Bedford is your nephew and that he is resident
with you for the duration of his stay in Spain?'

Mary nodded, still looking at me. 'Yeah.'

'And you confirm that you gave Señor Bedford your permission to drive your car on the night of the sixteenth July – last night?'

'Yeah, that's right,' replied Mary, leaning forward to tap her ash.

'Do you have your vehicle registration document and a current insurance certificate?'

Mary leaned down and picked up her bag. The carton of Rothmans that leaned alongside it was straight off the boat. 'Here.'

The policeman inspected her documents, ticked some boxes, and span the sheet of paper over to her. 'Okay. Sign here . . .' Mary scribbled, '. . . and here . . . and your initials here . . . and here . . . Thank you.' He looked at me. 'Señor Bedford?'

I rubbed my hands on the back of my jeans. 'Yes?'

'It is my duty to inform you that the law requires all persons, regardless of their nationality, to carry appropriate identity papers with them at all times. If you are driving a motor vehicle, then you are also required to carry proof of ownership or the appropriate authority from a rental agency, a valid driving licence, and proof of adequate and up-to-date insurance. Failure to comply with these requirements carries a maximum penalty of fifty thousand pesetas on each count, imprisonment or deportation. Do you understand?'

I nodded. 'Yes.'

'I have no wish to ruin your holiday,' he smiled, 'and I wouldn't want you to leave Andalusia with bad memories, but I do require you to attend this police station at some time within the next seven days and present your passport and your driving licence. Sign here and here.'

I signed. He gave me a copy. Out in reception I signed again, and they gave me back my stuff. We were shown out into the sunshine, passing three cops and two indignant, jangling rock-climbers they had arrested.

I truly did not know what to think, but Mary did. We drove out of the police compound and parked on a dusty verge at the edge of town, looking down on a wide valley of dewbound orchards and houses scattered like broken china against the shadowed earth.

'Before we go anywhere,' she announced, 'you and me are going to have a little chat.'

They were ominous, rain-laden words, and I started looking for cover.

'I'm really, really sorry about last night,' I began. 'I've been a bit off my head lately and I know I've been a bit out of order nicking your car and stuff.' I was even prepared to own up to the theft of her cash, as soon as she asked. She didn't.

'If I'd been worried about the car I'd have left you in there,' she said, appraising me with a look that was half pity and half amusement. She stuck a Rothman between her narrow lips and held out her hand. 'Lighter.'

I dropped it into her palm and she sparked up.

'Housekeeping.'

I handed over the slightly sweaty wad of pesetas I had stolen. She stuffed the money into her handbag without counting it and tried a long shot.

'Where's the charlie?'

I scratched my nose. Dead giveaway. 'What charlie?'

'Don't fuck about, lad. The coke you nicked. Where is it?'

I fumbled for a fag, sweat beading my upper lip. 'I don't know what you're on about. Are you saying I've nicked your coke?'

Mary laughed, a dry, humourless rasp. 'Very good. If you weren't so fucking unbelievable you'd be quite convincing.'

'I really do not know what you're on about,' I spluttered.

'Okay,' she said, with a studied nonchalance, 'have it your way. This is mine: on Thursday night your charming French mate bought me a drink in the Quetzal. Turns out you're not mates after all. Turns out you've ripped him off, and he's saying big *mercies* to anybody who can help him retrieve his property.'

She clocked me sideways for a reaction. She didn't see one.

'So I told him that the extent of my help depended on the nature of the property and the quality of the *merci*. You with me?'

I stretched my mouth and raised my eyebrows. She took it for a nod.

'Turns out the Frenchman fancies his chances with me, so he tells me everything, which took some time and a few drinks since we were talking in two languages. The upshot, it seems, is that you've done his nephew in, nicked a bloody great kilo of cocaine and done a runner, which explains why you stood me up last Wednesday. Still with me?'

I shook my head wearily. 'It wasn't his nephew, it was his son, and I didn't kill him. I was with Mamout at the time. Ask him.'

Mary raised her scratched-on eyebrows. 'Mamout? Theo's rent boy? You're with him now? Jesus! No wonder your bird is shagging all over the *campo*!' She touched her crucifix in delighted disbelief. 'I don't give a toss about your depraved sex life. I want to know what you've done with the cocaine.'

'You knew about Luisa?' I cried. Her infidelity was becoming a local legend, spreading across the *campo* like the shadows of the sierras. 'Why didn't you tell me?'

'None of my business,' shrugged Mary.

'Yeah, well, I'll tell you something you don't know about Luisa,' I muttered darkly. 'Luisa is dead. Shot four times by

Sacha bleeding Distel. That's the kind of bloke you're dealing with.'

This revelation hit her hard, derailing her train of thought and spilling her nonchalance. Gynaecide was her specialist subject. Blowing smoke through the window gave her the opportunity to look away and gather her thoughts.

'Who says I'm dealing with anybody?'

'So what are you saying?'

Mary sighed. 'I'm saying that you should cut the bullshit and confide in your Aunty Mary. If you want to live, that is.' She blocked my apparently redundant protest of ignorance with a wrinkled finger. 'I'm not finished yet. I've had a long, hard think about your situation, lad, and it looks to me like you're pretty well buggered. You've got no friends, no money and no car. The arse is falling out of your trousers and you look like shit. You've got in way out of your depth and you're punching above your weight, and frankly, even if you told him he could have it all back, I reckon your French mate would kill you just for all the trouble you've caused.'

I opened my mouth and she raised the finger. 'Wait. You can talk when I'm done. Your only choice, sunshine, is to keep on running, and to do that, you're going to need help.' She turned to face me, a fag in the corner of her mouth and one eye closed against the smoke. 'Ask me who's going to help you.'

I sighed and looked away. 'Who?'

'Your old Aunty chuffin' Mary, that's who,' she cried, slapping me on the leg and causing me to jump like a nervous girl. 'Keep it in the family, kiddo!'

Bloody Mary's proposal was as simple and as sensible as they come. She would drive me to wherever the cocaine was hidden and keep watch while I retrieved it. I would give her half, and she would drive me to the coast. I would disappear. Bloody Mary would go home. The end. I wondered why she wanted to help me.

'I don't,' she replied. 'It's all a matter of economics, lad. Think about it. You've got a kilo of coke, right?'

Absolutely.

'You're going to be happy to give me half in return for a ride to the coast, right?'

'Suppose so.'

'What would Charles Aznavour give me? One tenth? A few wraps? A couple of hundred quid? A candlelit dinner for two? I'm not helping you, I'm helping meself, kiddo, just me and no one else. What do you reckon?'

I took a few thoughtful drags as I gave her proposal the consideration it deserved. She was letting me load the works all over again, giving me another bite on her rotten cherry. I met her eyes and nodded.

'It's a deal.'

Bloody Mary stared through her fly-splattered windscreen, a winsome smile on her narrow mouth as she remembered something she had loved and lost. She held on to the memory until it hurt too much, then dropped it and turned to me.

'Let's go,' she said.

We swung into the wake of a tour bus, heading eastwards and downwards and away from the coast.

'Wrong way,' I told her.

'Not to my house it isn't. You think I'm going to show myself on the Costa looking like this?'

I choked on my smoke. 'We're going back to La Mendirosa?'

'I need to change,' she replied. 'I know that personal hygiene and deportment are entirely unknown quantities to you but I've got standards to maintain, all right?'

Doubt began to cloud my mind and I wondered if I could trust her. Maybe I said it aloud – it wouldn't have been the first time – or maybe she read my mind. She stamped on the brakes, leaned across me and opened my door.

'Go on, then. If you don't trust me, piss off. Go on.'

I would have loved to, but there was a problem. My cocaine was under the back seat.

'What are my options?'

'Fuck off, or come home with me.'

I had had better offers, but not recently. I pulled the door shut, studying her face, trying to read her intentions. Maybe she could be trusted. I shrugged. 'Let's go.'

Mary must have been woken by the local copper early this morning. He would have asked if she had a nephew called John, and if he had been given permission to borrow her car. Mary's mental arithmetic was pretty good, and she would have backed me up. The cop would have given her a lift to the nick, and if she hadn't had time to change then she would have had no opportunity to discuss my future with Jean-Marc. I scratched at my teeth, feeling for the skin with which I had been snatched from judicial oblivion and wondering if there was enough left for the rest of the adventure.

At this hour, when the cool, night-scented air pooled in the shadows of the big pines and the sky was crossed by commuting rooks and the chalky streaks of northbound jets, all things seemed possible. I had even walked out of prison a free man. I wondered for an absurd moment if I had imagined the dead cops in the van wreck, but such fancy was idle and inane. It seemed most likely that there had been no evidence recovered from the wreckage that identified me, and since the unregistered van wore Spanish plates, there was no need to go looking for Englishmen. The only witness was the barman's wife, and thinking back, I realised that she had neither seen me nor spoken to me. The only assistance she could have provided to the investigation into her husband's murder would have been the confirmation that Alberto had been accompanied by one other person. The kid had seen my battered face, but how long would it be before the social workers allowed the police to question him? Estrellada had even commented on my injuries and his failure to hold me proved that I was still an unknown quantity in this case. It would be impossible, however, to solve the criminal equation without establishing my value. My absence from the castle would eventually be noted. My description and that of my poor dead van would be recorded as a matter of procedure, and our house searched. They would find the photograph of Luisa and me, red-eyed and shiny-nosed at the Santa Llena *feria* and they would bang it hard against the wires to see if anything interesting fell off. My release from Matamoros police station was a fluke, the fortunate consequence of parochial human error, and any minute now Estrellada was going to add me to his calculations and gawp at the result.

My worry burst into a sickly panic as a dark shadow flashed across the road before the car. Mary saw it too, and she leaned over the wheel to see what had blotted out the sun. The dark underbelly of a helicopter banked low across the valley to our right, the down draught from its whining rotors stirring dormant dust devils from the barren slopes.

'Them again,' muttered Mary. 'Over my house all last night, and now they're back again. Do you think I could get any sleep?'

I sighed and lit a fag. Bloody helicopters were too much. I watched it until it disappeared behind the curve of the valley, the disc of its rotors reflecting the sun like the wings of a dragonfly.

Today, anything was possible. I punched the radio and stabbed up the FRA. Empty static filled the car like the spray from a fire extinguisher, dowsing my optimism and reaffirming the dread of last night. The tidal roar said as much about Alberto as a breakfast show news report.

'It's gone,' said Mary. 'Looks like they finally caught him.'

We were at the dusty turn-off to La Mendirosa, and Mary changed down into first for the descent. The track was wide but deeply rutted, and it was easy to ground a small car on the boulders that thrust like bones through the fractured earth. Mary bit her lip as she negotiated a clear path, choosing her moment with care and precision.

'So is there exactly a kilo?' she asked casually.

'*Mas o menos,*' I replied. 'I'll show you.'

'You'd bloody—' She let it drop, her attention seized by whatever she had seen in the rear-view.

I half turned to see what had spooked her. 'Who's that?'

A dark hatchback had turned off the highway and was descending the track in our dusty wake. 'Buggered if I know,' she said. 'Either they're coming for me, or they're lost. This road doesn't go anywhere except my place.'

My scalp had started itching. I scratched too hard and too long. 'What sort of car did the Frogs have?'

'I dunno,' shrugged Mary. 'Didn't see.'

'How many Frogs were there? Two?'

'Three.'

'Three?' I cried. 'How come?'

'What do you mean?'

I shook my head. She was probably wrong, and it didn't matter. It was becoming increasingly likely that I had allowed myself to be driven into a trap, and I couldn't work out where I had gone wrong. Trusting Bloody Mary, when I knew she had communed with Jean-Marc, had probably been the first of today's mistakes, and it was just as likely that I was going to be forced back into hiding in the very near future. I felt like a rat harried into a corner. I looked around again, and the car was still behind.

'Stop panicking,' chided Mary. 'It's probably just some lost tourist. They come down here all the time, realise it's a dead end, then piss off back to the main road.'

'Supposing they're not tourists?'

'Well why don't we just stop and wait for them?' suggested Mary, like some B-movie blonde. 'If they're tourists, we can tell them that they're on the road to nowhere.'

'Brilliant,' I muttered, 'and what if it's Jean-Marc?'

She shook her head. 'It's not going to be him. How would he know where we were?'

Yeah, right. How would he know?

I had an idea. 'Is there a turn-off, somewhere we could pull off and hide until he goes past?'

'Nope.' She winced as the sump scraped across a boulder.

I had been in a state of numb disbelief as I left the nick this morning, and I could not recall any of the other vehicles in the car park. It was possible that I would have noticed Jean-Marc's van, but this dark hatchback rang no bells at all.

None at all.

Not a single one.

Ting-a-ling.

Right up at the front of my brain, in the area to which I had been denied access since my judgement had become suspect, in the back-up control room, there was a record of a dark-coloured hatchback seen moving across the front of my vision. That was all that could be confirmed. Time and place were not available. I would have to check my own records.

'It's just tourists, trust me,' growled Mary, looking in the rear-view.

I could recall a car passing in front of me. Two white faces . . .

'When we get to your house I'm going to leg it round the back and over the river,' I decided. 'You go indoors and wait for them to arrive. If they're tourists, fine. If it's anyone else, tell them that I'm still at the police station.'

We were on the short straight down to the house. The sun had rolled over the ridge and burned away the mist, a spotlight on Bloody Mary's barren plot. I would remain in hiding until the visitors had gone, and I would spend that time rescheduling my short-term goals. One of the new ones involved persuading Mary to stay put while I did a runner with her money, her car and the coke. It was something that required imaginative planning.

We rolled past the genny shed and past the dusty fig tree, and just as it became too late to do anything but scream I looked up. I wanted to yell out for her to stop, for everything just to stand still for a moment and wait for me to catch up, because everything was moving too fast for me to cope and something was totally wrong. Two figures were coming towards the car, peeling around the front as Mary was shouting something and I was trying to push the lock down even as they were pulling the door open and dragging me out into the dust and they had my T-shirt up around my neck and they were throwing me to the ground. I rolled over, squinting into the glare, one hand shading my eyes and protecting my face as I looked up at the triumphant grins of Benoit and the Arab kid. I squirmed in the dirt like a speared snake to hiss at Mary. 'You fucking bitch!'

She held my gaze, slackjawed and shaking her head as

though she'd just seen someone struck by lightning. 'Honestly, I didn't know!'

Jean-Marc was close by. 'Get him inside, quick!' he yelled. 'There's someone else coming.'

They dragged me to my feet, their fingers digging deep into my flaccid triceps.

'How am I supposed to know who it is?' Mary was shouting in English as Jean-Marc pulled her from the car.

She hadn't done much tidying up, I noticed, as I was thrust through her back door. Photographs, books and an unusual number of chiffon scarfs littered the floor, and as Mary was pushed inside, she gasped, 'Oh my God! I've been burgled.'

There was a wet crack and simultaneous gasp as Jean-Marc backhanded Mary and sent her sprawling. 'Shut the fuck up and get over there.'

I could feel the look she gave her assailant, but she kept her mouth shut and crawled over to kneel beside me.

'You stupid cow!' I growled. 'Now look at us!'

Benoit was focused but nervous. 'On your knees. Hands on head. Face the wall.'

I did as I was told. 'You're going to be gutted when you find out where the coke is,' I muttered to Mary, as though it would help.

'Shut that bastard up,' warned Jean-Marc. 'Put something in his mouth.'

The Arab kid ran up on squeaking rubber soles and snatched back my head.

'Eat,' he grunted, stuffing a fetid tea towel into my mouth. I sensed that Benoit was close behind me, and I was certain that nothing would distract his supervision. The others were pre-occupied with the hatchback.

'Can you see them?' hissed Jean-Marc.

'Yeah, they've stopped.'

'What are they doing?'

'Nothing.'

'What do you fucking mean "nothing"?' yelled Jean-Marc.

'Nothing,' shouted the Arab kid. 'They're just . . . wait . . . they're turning round.'

I had changed my mind about the dark hatchback. I wanted them to visit.

'They've gone.'

'Gone?' asked Jean-Marc. 'Sure?'

'Gone,' he confirmed.

I felt myself shrinking inside my body as the blood rushed from my extremities to laager around my vital organs. I closed my eyes, bowed my head, and held my breath. The first of a finite number of very hard things was heading my way.

As it turned out, the first thing that hit me was a cushion, but the intent was behind it.

'Get up and sit here,' ordered Jean-Marc, his voice a mixed bag of fury, malevolence, amusement and satisfaction.

I rose and turned, walking across to the table with my eyes fixed on his sunburned face.

'Don't be giving me looks now,' he warned. 'You want to be nice to me.'

I dropped into the chair, my body gripped by a leaden fatigue. 'What's the point?'

What was the point? There wasn't one, as Jean-Marc had pointed out, way back in Cadiz. Maybe I had bashed my head in the right spot as I was dragged from the car, or maybe the sum of my experiences at last added up, but as I studied the bubbled, flaking surface of the wall and listened to the anxious bickering of my captors the interference had been lifted from my vision just long enough for me to see the truth, and the truth was that my world had come to an end. Nothing I could do now could prevent my death, for it had been determined eight days ago and I had been too thick to see it. I had to die, and my estate would pass to my murderer. The cocaine radiated ill health and bad fortune like stolen rods of Russian plutonium, and even if I had succeeded in shaking the Frogs from my back, it would probably have continued to infect me and bring misfortune down upon all who came within its sparkling circle of malicious influence. It was beautiful, wonderful and dreadful, and its ownership of my will was so complete that, right now, if I had been given the choice between cocaine and freedom, the answer would still have been A.

Jean-Marc stood at my side, leaning on the table with both hands, so close that I could see the stains on his cuffs and smell the sweat and the petrol on his shirt. His van was a diesel.

'So where is it?'

'Outside. I'll go and get it,' I said. 'Tell me something, though, before I go.' It was fifty–fifty whether he would. This bit always happened in movies, just before the denouement.

'What?' asked Jean-Marc.

'Where did it come from, this coke? What's its story?'

'None of your fucking business,' he replied. 'Just go and get it.'

He was prodding me onto the plank, pushing me towards the lynching tree, denying me those extra few minutes in which to formulate a plan that would make us all happy.

'Let's talk for a minute,' I pleaded. 'Let's have a little drink, and a chat, and see if we can work something out. There's a bottle of Baileys under the sink.'

Jean-Marc raised his shoulders in an exaggerated sigh of frustration. 'Just go and get the fucking cocaine, will you?'

I made my hands into fists. 'I want a guarantee.' This was pathetic.

'What do you think he's going to do?' asked Benoit. 'Let you go?'

I turned to face him. 'Why not? What harm can I do him? It takes a big man to show mercy. I'm not going to tell anyone . . .'

Jean-Marc grinned past me at the Arab kid. 'What did I tell you? The Lord indeed moves in mysterious ways. Go get this idiot's stuff from the van.'

The Arab kid jogged from the house, happy to escape into the fresh air.

'What's going on?' shrilled Mary, all hunched up on the sofa like a widow.

Jean-Marc slapped me before I could think of a reply.

'Do you think I like doing this?' he yelled. 'Do you think it's easy for me?' He bent down, his foul mouth a tongue's length from mine. 'You force my hand! *Merde, quoi!* You, that idiot Art Garfunkel lookalike, your stupid bitch, the world is full of dogs . . .' He was becoming overheated and obscure and it was a couple of seconds before I realised what he had said. Alberto did look a little like Art Garfunkel, and even though there wasn't much left to break in my liquid heart, I felt something snap, fizzle and fade.

An unnamed local man.

'How many bodies is it now?' I asked. 'Seven, eight? You aiming for two for each kilo? Is that what it's worth?'

Jean-Marc wiped his mouth and pushed me hard in the chest. 'Each has been your responsibility,' he insisted. 'If it had not been for you, no one would have forced me.' He smiled.

'It's all your fault, but you leave me to live with the consequences.'

The sequence of events that had put me back at the wrong end of the French automatic was suddenly obvious. Once he had realised that I was unlikely to breeze into a bar of his choosing in Matamoros, Jean-Marc must have decided to pay another visit to his German informant up at the castle. Helmut would have told him everything he knew, for betrayal is like a severed artery that once opened cannot easily be closed. This time, however, Helmut would have been very poor value for money since he had no idea where I was, and he was preoccupied by an argument with a lunatic in a flat cap with a jerrycan of petrol.

What mad demon had whispered in Alberto's ear persuasively enough to put him on the road to the Devil? What inconsistent and illogical thoughts had driven him to the commission of an act so insane? He told me that he was a smuggler, that he had contingency plans, and I had understood these to involve an act of silent disappearance. Where was the subtlety in arriving at the castle in a supercharged banana with a gallon of gas and a Zippo? I sat down heavily and let my head drop into my hands, swaying with the nauseous vertigo of sudden guilt. Alberto knew I was at Bloody Mary's house, and before he had died, he had betrayed me, the words spilling from his throat until the flames cauterised his treachery. How much pain had he suffered before giving me up, and how much more had the act of betrayal incurred?

I looked up at Jean-Marc, too tired to make a face. 'The Art Garfunkel lookalike: his name was Alberto. Did you give him a break after he told you?'

He scowled. 'Told me what?'

'That I was here.'

Jean-Marc laughed out loud. 'That mad fucker? He told me

you'd gone to Africa on a speedboat. Laughing his head off he was, before I shot it off. Crazy bastard!' He rubbed his eyes as though they still stung from the smoke, then pointed hard at Mary. 'She's the one who told me to come here.' He slapped a brown paper bag, folded and unused, onto the table. 'Kid from the shop brought it to my room this morning, just in time, as it happens. Five minutes later and I'd have been on the road back to civilisation.'

I unfolded the bag and read a carefully printed note. 'Dear JM,' it said, '*rendezvous La Mendirosa (mon maison) ASAP. Information important de Martin. MB.*' She had made the effort to betray me in French. I tossed the note onto the table and shook my head, remembering the carton of Rothmans Mary had brought into the police station, and knowing exactly where she had bought it. She must have asked the cop who had driven her into town to wait outside while she ran into the shop, scored her contraband smokes and wrote our death warrants.

'You stupid cow,' I told her again. 'We were out of here, safe, sorted. Now look at us!'

'It's "*ma maison*", by the way,' added Jean–Marc, 'but I got the message. I'm just sorry that I'm not going to be able to reward you in the manner I promised.'

'Oh, she'll be happy with what you're going to give her,' I assured him, looking hard into Mary's watery eyes and seeing her reasons. I shook my head. 'You sad old cow.'

'Don't worry about me, kiddo,' she replied. 'Anyone mind if I smoke?'

Jean–Marc gave me an impatient shove, and I rolled with it. 'What can you do?' he asked. 'It's done. You have to accept what's happened and move on.'

How much pain did a well–aimed bullet carry? I had

watched Luisa writhe in the dust in breathless disbelief after being hit, and all I'd seen in her eyes was surprise. Executed efficiently, a killing could be physically painless, and there had to be some comfort in that. The agony existed in the waiting, but only if one had not accepted death as one's saviour. Maybe, in the Soviet-style shop of choices through which I now browsed, it was time to choose death. Death was packed in a tasteful box branded 'The Big Sleep'. The ingredients were listed as 'oblivion 99%', 'relief 0.9%' and 'pain 0.1%'. There were no sweeteners, but the product carried a lifetime guarantee. 'You owe it to yourself', said the blurb, and I knew I could afford it. Death cured all the known effects of life and was the obvious choice in a confused world, and yet right here, and right now, I wasn't buying it.

'I have an idea,' said Benoit. 'We can leave him here if we can find somewhere to lock him up. That shed with the generator: maybe there's a lock on it.' He paused to check that his boss had caught his drift. 'If we can lock him in somewhere, chuck in some water and whatever, we'll be out of here before they can raise the alarm.'

I looked from one to the other like a new guy on a building site. 'You're having a laugh, aren't you? You're not going to lock me up.'

Jean-Marc's attention had wandered. He grabbed me by the throat and pulled me to my feet. 'Just go and get my fucking property now.' He pushed me away, fumbling in his breast pocket, then inexplicably, unless one believed in last requests, he offered me a Marlboro and lit it up. 'Go and get my gear,' he said evenly, 'and I'll lock you up. Deal?'

He was lying. I shook my head. 'I've got a better idea.'

He closed his eyes and took a deep breath. He really wanted to kill me very badly.

'First of all you empty all the bullets from the gun and give them to me. Then Benoit and I will go and get the gear. I'll give it to Benoit and he'll bring it back to you while I run away.' I was making it up as I went along, and while the plan was okay so far, it failed to address one of Jean-Marc's main concerns. I thought fast. 'You're worried that I'll turn you in to the police, and I can understand that . . .' Unassisted by cocaine, my brain ran at low revolutions. I looked at Jean-Marc.

He raised his eyebrows. I had stalled. 'Just go and get it,' he sighed. 'Don't make me set fire to you.'

His eyes darted to the door as two loud cracks split the valley. Benoit turned quickly, tense and frowning, some sewer rat instinct preparing him to fight or flee. He moved a step closer to the door, his hand moving across his front to pull his pistol from his jeans. He glanced at Jean-Marc, his eyebrows raised in a question that his boss couldn't answer, and suddenly everybody in the room knew what was about to happen. An ionising charge of nervous static crackled through the air in a fractured second as mouths dropped open and wide eyes swivelled to the door.

I heard a breathless grunt and the thud of a boot against the door as two figures burst through the sunlit gap. The first moved fast to the right as the second came straight in, colliding heavily with Benoit and and knocking him violently to the floor. They were shouting loudly and in English, their vocal noise deliberately increasing the terror and confusion in the room.

'ARMED POLICE! ARMED POLICE! GET ON THE GRIND GET DINE GET DINE GET DINE ON THE FUCKING GRIND!'

If they were the police, then they were the RUC, but Jean-Marc didn't question the authority of a remarkably unofficial-looking shotgun. He raised his hands and moved backwards, nodding furiously as though he understood what they were saying.

'GET ON THE FUCKING GRIND OR I WILL SHOOT YE . . .'

'. . . *SUR LA PLANCHEE SUR LA PLANCHEE* – DINE STAY DINE STAY DINE.'

One of them was a woman. Both of them wore baseball caps and had covered their lower faces with bandannas. I saw Benoit take a kick in the jaw and watched Jean-Marc crumple to his knees at the bidding of the sawn-off.

'You sit in that chair,' said a tall man with narrow eyes, in an Ulster accent that falsely suggested compassion, before pushing me down and running to the sofa with a large black pistol held in both hands.

'ITE,' he yelled. 'ITE OR I WILL SHOOT YE!'

Mary shuffled out on her knees, her hands in the air and her eyes wide with the apprehension of sudden death.

'Spoilt for choice now, aren't you?' I called.

'YOU GET ON THE FUCKING FLORA! GET ON THE FLORA!'

I thought they'd told me to sit in the chair, but I didn't argue. They were the only people who knew what was going on. She was wearing jeans, and she was out of breath. Her partner kicked Benoit hard between the legs then grabbed Jean-Marc and dragged him into the centre of the floor.

'HANDS ON HEADS! *LES MAINS SUR LA TETE! LES MAINS SUR LA TETE!*'

Everyone complied. I almost saw the whites of Jean-Marc's bloodshot eyes as they widened in fear. He knew as much as I did about what was going on. Or maybe less, I thought, watching the male assailant put his foot on Jean-Marc's head.

'*QUI EST ARMEE? QUI EST ARMEE?*'

'They've got a pistol,' I called out. 'Either him in the blue shirt or the spotty one.'

I heard a gasp as another boot went in and then the clatter of metal on stone.

'I got it!' yelled the woman.

'Shoot the one in the blue shirt,' I yelled. The woman kicked me in the ribs. I winced as I heard more pain being dealt to the French, then bit my lip as a denim-clad knee fell upon my arm. The hard point of a pistol pushed into my hair and pressed against my skull.

'Where's the coke, wee man?' he whispered.

'The what?' I gasped. It was still the wrong answer and it didn't matter whom I told.

'Where's the gear, you little fuck?'

'I'll show you, I'll get it, I'll get it,' I burbled.

'Speak French, do ye?'

I nodded, and was dragged to my feet. 'Translate this: STAY DINE ON THE FLORA.'

'*Gardez-vous à la planchée.*'

I translated the instructions that followed, not enjoying the experience as much as I would have expected. The French were having even less fun, but their terrified discomfort as they turned their cheeks and placed their hands behind their backs brought me little satisfaction.

'Listen to me,' started Jean-Marc, trying to remember the words to the song that he thought would save his life, 'listen, listen, listen . . .'

The boot was on the other foot now, and a blow from its toecap knocked the proposition from his head. Mary protested that she was nothing to do with anything, but a mixed shower of threats and abuse persuaded her to keep her head down and her gob shut. I followed her example, trying hard to control my breathing and subdue the tattoo of the pulse in my ears as the big Ulsterman moved from body to body, lashing thumbs and wrists with plastic cable ties. Foreboding had risen from its natural source in the rocks deep beneath Mary's house to bubble through her floor and drench the bellies and the brows of we four losers, helpless captives to a destiny now beyond our control. Our fates were subject to the unwritten laws of the business we had failed at, and not one of us could deny that justice was coming. It was an occupational hazard: the sailor drowns, the pilot burns, and the drug dealer suffers massive invasive trauma to the back of the head. I knew that I would not be leaving at the same time as the others, but I hoped that I would be able to look into Jean-Marc's eyes as he said *adieu*.

'Hey, Jean-Marc,' I called out. 'Luisa was right all along. You *are* a fucking amateur!'

'You shut your mouth and come with me,' growled the big guy, dragging me to my feet and out through the door. 'D'ye recognise me?'

His baseball cap was pulled down to his pale-blue eyes, and his bandanna sat on the bridge of his nose. It could have been a trick question.

'No,' I replied. Something clicked in my aching head as I was suddenly granted access to my cached memory files. In rapid, disordered sequence I saw Helmut's pretty blonde, two white faces in a speeding hatchback, Mr and Mrs Nextcard checking in to the hotel in Cadiz, the sunburned face in Dieter's Place, the forced smiles in the stolen passports and the big guy with the cruel-mouthed blonde, searching the darkened streets of Matamoros for his elusive quarry. Of course I recognised him. I even knew his name, and that of his girlfriend. Until six or seven minutes ago I could have had a decent stab at what they both did for a living, but I would have been wrong. One thing I knew for certain, though, was that these two were not cops. They talked the talk, bursting in like Crockett and Tubbs, and they wanted us to believe that they walked the walk, but I was willing to gamble every gram in Mary's car that they were worse than the rest of us.

The big white Mercedes van had been hidden around the side of the house, and now it rested like a hamstrung bull on three slashed tyres. The Arab kid lay wheezing in the dust beside it, his entire abdomen black with blood and flies. If it hadn't been for his mortal wounds, one might have thought that he had been knocked down by the passenger door, which hung open above him. He had been shot as he leaned in to retrieve my effects, the heavy bullets whizzing like wasps through the cabin before punching him into the dirt. My jacket, Luisa's denim and her embroidered bag lay piled on the passenger seat above his trembling body. Jean-Marc had made sure that his nose alone would be on my trail by removing all evidence of my identity from the Transit, and in an instant I knew why my face had been unknown to the police.

Murphy looked down and away as he dragged me past his gurgling, gasping victim, swinging me in a powerful arc to slam into the bonnet of the van. I sucked wind and slumped as far as his ungiving grip would allow, my hands jerking in spasmodic, flinching gestures of self-protection as he took one hand from my scruff and tore the bandanna from his face. He leaned towards me, his face a scum-flecked grimace as he kneed me twice in the groin and cracked my cheek with his forehead, his breath hot against my nostrils. He relaxed his grip, and I stumbled away from him, the oncoming pain still just a hum on the tracks. Two steps later it hit me like a freight train, knocking me writhing into the dust. I tried to curl up, but his knee landed heavily on my wrist.

'Where is it now?' He stabbed the muzzle of his pistol into my palm.

'I'll show you,' I whined.

He pushed harder on the automatic, the blue steel stretching the skin beneath its rifled mouth to tearing point, the tiny, complex bones below beginning to grate together. I bit my lip to offset a pain only slightly worse than the agony of waiting for the blast that would destroy my hand.

'Don't show me,' he suggested through clenched teeth. 'Tell me.'

I arched my back in a vain attempt to relieve the pressure. Maybe the bastard was trying to stab me. Maybe he wanted to keep the noise down, but I would accept as much pain as he could give me before I told him where the coke was. Ten minutes ago, my death had been certain: I had known it as soon as Jean-Marc and Benoit had started talking about locking me up. Now I had been given the chance to keep on living, and the coke was the asset with which my future could be bought.

'Can't tell you, you'll never find it,' I gasped through cracking teeth. 'Can only show you.'

I felt a pop and a rush of heat across my pinioned hand. My persecutor recoiled at the same time, rising to his feet and kicking me.

'You're a dirty bastard, so you are,' he muttered. 'Get up.'

I rose, cupping my broken hand like a wounded bird, staring into the bloody palm like a horrified gypsy. My poisoned thumb had burst open and black blood ran along the lines of my head and my heart to drip onto Mary's sterile plot. The same blood had spurted onto Murphy's face, and he stood breathless with disgust, rubbing its acid stain from his lips. I could see his luck changing as it dried on his cheek.

Suddenly he stiffened, sniffing the air like a breathless fox.

'Get that side door open quick!' he barked, propelling me towards the van with a push that almost floored me. I looked around, following his anxious gaze across the narrow sky, and trotted to the van. As I reached it, I heard the whine of the Guardia helicopter, its direction of approach hidden beneath the layers of echo and counter-echo effected by the steep valley walls. Murphy reached the Arab kid as I slid back the door, and swung him by a shrunken arm and a wet leg into the black space by the side of Yvan's motorbike just a moment before the chopper clattered overhead. He watched it until it had gone, its sweet-smelling exhaust falling softly upon us, then turned to me, still trying to wipe the blood of my thumb from his face.

'So where is it?'

I shook my head. 'It's not here. I never brought it here. We have to drive to it.'

'So get in the fucking car,' he suggested. He reached into the van and stuffed a black handgun into the Arab kid's waistband.

'Can I get my stuff? In case we get stopped?'

He nodded, and I grabbed the bundle from the passenger seat of the van. As I turned, I spotted something soft and black and leather stuffed in the side pocket of the van door. I snatched it, inspecting its contents as I hobbled to the car. No money, no credit cards and no family photographs. Just a poor-quality picture of a trainee accountant on a laminated card with a Spanish flag and a gold emblem. Matteo Morales Silvestre, killed in the line of duty.

Murphy yelled something to his accomplice and two shots popped inside the house before she emerged backwards through the door, wreathed in blue smoke. She was breathless and excited when she reached the car.

'Get in the front and pull your seat all the way forward,' she ordered, pulling her bandanna down to reveal a hard, blonde face. I did as I was told, with a trembling bladder. She climbed into the back and Murphy took the wheel.

'Slotted?' he asked cryptically, bouncing his question off the rear-view.

'They'll give us no more trouble,' she replied evasively. 'Let's get out of here.'

It didn't work: Murphy was still staring at her.

'I gave them one each through the back of the knee, Derry style,' she explained, as though it were something laudable. At least she was flying the flag.

Murphy tutted. 'Wait here,' he sighed, opening his door.

'Where you going?' cried Sarah.

He swivelled so that she could see his expression the right way round. 'I'm going to finish the job properly. Watch Dopey here.'

'What's the point?' protested Sarah unhappily. 'They didn't see our faces. Let's just go.'

I'd seen their faces.

'Where's their weapon?' asked Murphy.

'Inside, in the fruit bowl. It's empty. I wiped it down.'

'What about the woman?'

'Look, Murph, I'm not going to shoot her with a twelve-bore, am I?' Her vocal cords were stretched with the stress of it all. 'She's all cuffed up and she's not going anywhere. Can't we just get out of here? What's the point in putting them on the sheet? Let's just get going while the going's still good.'

It was a shotgun argument, and some of the load hit the target. Murphy settled in his seat and turned the ignition.

'Fuck it,' he muttered.

'Have we got the gear?'

'He's taking us to it now.'

I shook my head as I tried to keep up. The situation is very poor indeed when it can be improved by one's abduction by Irish terrorists, and these two had delivered me from certain death. The Lord, as Jean-Marc had so rightly observed, indeed moves in mysterious ways.

25

I sat very still, my bleeding hand thrust into the sleeve of my jacket, shaking as each broken fragment of history tumbled into place. I had never questioned Yvan's reasons for crossing two countries and one frontier with eleven pounds of stolen cocaine, and while I had been acutely aware of its provenance, I hadn't considered its destination. The idea that he might have been delivering it to somebody had never crossed my mind, but these two hadn't simply stumbled upon the opportunity to acquire five kilos of nosebag. Yvan must have arranged a rendezvous somewhere near the castle but his schedule had failed to take account of his expiry date. As far as Bonnie and Clyde were concerned, he simply hadn't shown, and if they were as professional as their live firing exercise had indicated, they would have done what all the smartest dealers do when things don't go according to plan. They would have gone home, drawn the curtains and watched TV.

Freedom is a sick child for the kilo dealers: it needs constant care and supervision to keep it alive. It is threatened by sudden changes in temperature, and excessive heat can be as fatal as unnecessary excitement. It likes everything to be boring, predictable and safe, and if the wind changes direction, or a rook lands too near, or the milk has soured, then its guardians will take it home. As long as it is alive, there will be another day, but when it's gone, it's gone. Murphy and Sarah should have wrapped their freedom in a blanket and taken it home thirty minutes after Yvan failed to show, putting it to bed with the cash until the next opportunity arose.

Suddenly I knew why they hadn't taken their cash home. Henrique had nicked it while they were lunching at La Mirador. I remembered that night in Dieter's Place when he had given me the passports and tried to buy five grams from me. He must have been loaded, and that was why he had spent the last week down on the Costa. That was why El Stupido had returned to Matamoros to pay off his fines like some Superfly criminal lottery-winner. That was why these two hadn't gone home . . .

'Jesus Christ Almighty!' invoked Murph in a yell that shattered my fragile thought process. 'What's he hiding under that fucking coat?'

The sharp end of the shotgun jabbed my scalp and drove my brow into the dash.

'Pull over, for fuck's sake!' yelled Sarah. 'Did you not search him?'

Moments later I was standing with my hands on the warm bonnet of Mary's car in a settling dust cloud while Sarah squatted beside me and went through the personal effects I had recovered from Jean-Marc's van. Like the guy polishing his glasses at the barber's, I had tried to explain that I was hiding not a loaded gun, but a bleeding thumb, but no one took my word for anything these days.

'Hey, Murph, check this.'

I glanced around. She was holding up my passport and the roll of 10,000-peseta notes I had hidden in the lining of my jacket the day I left the castle. She was also holding her own passport, and Murphy's too.

'I can explain,' I winced.

'Don't bother,' she sneered, ruffling the pages of mine. 'Martin, is it? Funny – I had you down as a Wally.'

I was sweating as we resumed our ascent from La Mendirosa. The prickly electrical discharge of three overworked and partially informed minds filled the air between us with negativity as we performed mental arithmetic with inaccurate calculus. They thought I had broken into their car. They thought that I had stolen their money. They were hoping I still had it. They were going to ask me where it was. They weren't going to believe my response.

Murph raised his eyes to the rear-view. 'Is he the man?'

I heard Sarah sniff. 'Seems like it.' It wasn't often that I was referred to as the man.

'Want a fag?' She was addressing me, and I took the proffered Benson.

'I don't suppose there is any chance that you've got the rest of our money as well, is there?'

I shook my head. 'Honestly I haven't. I promise you.' I almost added that I knew who did, but it seemed inappropriate. 'That money is mine. Look: it's all small, dirty bills. Most of it probably comes from Thomas Cook.'

'So what?' demanded Murph. 'And how come you've got our passports?'

'I found them,' I lied.

'Don't lie,' warned Murph.

'I'm not,' I lied again. For the time being I was safe, my life protected by my knowledge. My worth could be weighed in kilos, and as soon as they knew what I knew, the balance would be zeroed.

'Look, Martin,' suggested Sarah softly. 'We know what happened between you and Jean-Marc. We know why he made us come up here for the meet, and we know what he had planned. I don't think any of this was your idea – I accept that – and I think you just did what any of us would have done.' She droned on in a tone that she thought was reasonable and persuasive while I tried to work out if she meant Yvan when she said Jean-Marc. I put it to the test.

'Look,' I spluttered, 'Jean-Marc turned up on his motorbike the other Friday right out of the blue. I didn't know he was coming – I hadn't seen him for years. He was sick – dying as it turned out – and all I know is that he told me I could have his stuff when he went. That's all I know.'

'Yeah, well, it was our stuff he was giving away,' growled Murph.

'The bike wasn't yours.'

'It was our money that bought it.'

Two sniggering truths emerged, confessing that the game was up. The first was that Yvan had done business with these two before, probably smaller loads, and probably legitimately, or as legitimately as the international drugs trade would allow. The second, and by far the more amusing, was that Yvan had represented himself as Jean-Marc. It wouldn't have stood up to close inspection, but as a ruse it was enough to have brought the heat down on his dad if things had gone wrong for these two. I had read an article a long time ago that chronicled the lamentable deterioration of *la famille française*, but it was only now that I saw how bad things had become.

'The point,' explained Sarah, 'is that we have a problem, and a simple solution, a deal, if you like, or an offer.'

'Ask her what it is,' ordered Murph.

I asked her.

'Give us our cocaine and the rest of our money, and as far as we're concerned, you can piss off. In fact, as long as you haven't already spent too much of it, I'll even bung this lot back so you can get as far away from here as you like, so I will.' She held my roll of notes before me like a carrot. 'You with me, Murph?'

He hadn't really been listening. Anyone round here would have confirmed that one didn't feed a pig under a new moon.

'Absolutely,' he nodded in ready assent.

'So what do you think?' she asked.

'Fine,' I grunted.

'So you have got the money?' cried Murph indignantly.

'Not on me,' I answered truthfully, 'but I know where it is.'

'Is it with the coke?'

I shook my head.

'Don't push him, Murph,' warned Sarah. 'It's a stressful situation for him. He's a bright fella. He knows what to do.'

One out of three wasn't bad, but Sarah was convinced that she had my measure – I could imagine her describing herself as a good judge of character – and for as long as it suited me I would allow her to talk me round.

'Car's still there,' announced Murph, as we rounded a bend in the dark shadow of tall pines. 'We should dump this one over the edge.'

He pulled up on the outside edge of the track, just alongside the same dark hatchback that had followed Mary and me down to La Mendirosa.

'Best leave it just where it is,' recommended Sarah. 'Supposing one of those bloody helicopters sees you push it over?'

'Slash the tyres then,' suggested Murph.

'Just bloody leave it, why don't you?' cried Sarah. The strain was beginning to show. 'Let's just get out of here.'

Murph gave her a look.

'Look, none of them are going to make it up here with

bullets in their kneecaps, are they?' she reasoned, nodding towards La Mendirosa.

'I should have bloody slotted them,' grunted Murph.

The little Renault hatchback offered far greater travelling comfort than Mary's old Toyota, and I could see the sense in using a hire car for drug smuggling. We accelerated away from the faded Starlet and its poisonous, blood-soaked cargo, driving too fast and too aggressively for this old, unfinished track. Bloody Mary was going to have to change her name. Despite courting Death like a starving whore she had slipped its embrace yet again and remained the only inhabitant of La Mendirosa who could still do the hokey-cokey, one of several joyous dances she would perform when she looked under the seat of her car. Lucky Mary.

'Which way at the top?' barked Murph.

'Left,' I replied with no hesitation. 'Watch that rock!'

There was a shriek of surrendering steel, and the car scraped to a halt.

'Fucking brilliant!' yelled Murph, punching the centre of the steering wheel. He put the car into reverse, but the scraping was worse as he tried to inch backwards. 'Get out of the car, there's too much weight.'

I was laughing as quietly as I could as I climbed out of the Renault. It seemed that whoever came into contact with this cocaine was doomed to suffer some automotive mishap on a dirt track. I pictured a trail full of moaning Bolivians with their baskets of coca leaf standing beside a broken-down bus on some Andean mountain road way back in the consignment's green and salad days. I briefly considered doing another runner, but I felt that Murph was the kind of man who could hit moving targets.

'There's oil running out from underneath,' called Sarah. 'I think something's broken.'

With only sixteen stones on its suspension, the Renault recoiled from the rock upon which it was impaled, but it was immediately obvious that it was bleeding to death. Murph stood with his hands on his hips, looking from the car to the sky and back again. An expensive piece of work on his tanned left forearm testified to his loyalty to HM Queen and country, its quality enhanced by the tattiness of the jailhouse tattoo on his right that identified him as a Dunlevin Volunteer. He kicked the rock that had killed his car and cursed.

'We'll have to go back and get the other one. All of us. Push this one to the side first. I'll come back up here with a tow-truck later.'

'Why don't we just leave it here?' asked Sarah, as we headed the few hundred metres downhill to Mary's Toyota.

'Because it's rented in my name, so it is,' he replied irritably, 'and you didn't slot the Frogs. We'll get rid of him and then I'll come back up here with a tow-truck and hope that we're all long gone before anyone discovers them.' He spat. 'This whole op's been a total fuck-up.'

'Would have been worse if you'd chucked that car over the edge,' said Sarah.

Twenty minutes later we had passed the broken Renault and were heading towards Matamoros in Bloody Mary's Toyota. I was as certain as I could be of their priorities and their intentions, which were the acquisition of the coke, the retrieval of their money and the disposal of the witness. Murph was more frightening than Jean-Marc had ever been, for he was a professional. I had no doubt that even if Sarah did want to spare me, he would override her decision and take irreversible action with her shotgun. Killing me would be a sensible, reasonable act, for I was able to identify them both by name and by face, and so posed an uncontrollable risk to their lives and their freedom for as long as I continued to live and breathe. Despite their belief that I had conspired with Yvan – Jean-Marc to them – to rip them off, they weren't hung up on the respect culture of the genitally underdeveloped. They wouldn't kill me for showing them up, or for their losing face, or even for pissing them off. They would kill me because it would give them one less thing to worry about, and that was what worried me.

Sarah was free with the fags as we passed Matamoros and headed down towards the coast. Fear was no longer an effective weapon, for there was no threat worse than that of death, and it served their purpose to gain my willing cooperation. If they were really good, they might even have persuaded me to dig my own shallow grave in the weeds.

Every now and then one or the other would have a guess, trying to find out if they could free up the passenger seat.

'It's buried, isn't it?'

'You buried it in the woods last night. We saw you coming out of the woods.'

I had little spare mental capacity to engage in conversation so I acted as though I were depressed, worried and preoccupied with my future. They took it for sullen indifference.

'I saw you take this car from Matamoros last night,' admitted Murph. 'We followed you, and we saw you coming out of the side road up here. We saw you get arrested at the level crossing, and we saw you leaving the nick this morning. We know exactly where you've been and what you've been doing, so don't try to kid us.'

I shrugged.

Sarah changed the subject. 'Why did you go to Cadiz, then, Martin?' she asked. 'Do you want another fag? Help yourself.'

'You're not making us drive all the way over there again, are you?'

I felt that I was subject to a new and inhumane variation of the tried and tested Mutt & Jeff technique as Murph and Sarah tried to annoy a confession from me. They probed, they tested, they threatened and they cajoled, but the edges of their interrogation tools had been dulled by inanity and softened by their lullaby Ulster accents.

A pair of large white vans waited at the barrier across the road to the castle, their sides unmarked. I thought of the bodies they would carry off the mountain, zipped into sterile PVC sacks like sun-blackened *jamon negra*. The only one I really cared for was Alberto, who should never have been there. Antonita La Buena had predicted Yvan's death and the destruction of the castle – the north wind, she had warned, would bring a spark onto the castle, and it hadn't taken an especially bright one to burn it back to the rock. I had forgotten what she had said would happen to me, but I wouldn't have hesitated to recommend her services.

Murph turned onto the *barranca* road and pulled over, looking at me as though I could tell him something. The skidmarks from last night lay like a pair of crushed mambas on the hot surface.

I looked at Murph. 'It's not here.'

He bit his upper lip and grimaced. 'He's fucking us about,' he growled.

Sarah took a deep breath. 'If it's not down there, Martin, where is it?'

I sighed. 'I've told you a hundred times that I've got to show you, you dumb fuck.'

Murph punched me hard on the cheek, and without thinking, I punched him back.

'Fucking stop it right now!' screamed Sarah.

'He's fucking us around, you silly bitch,' yelled Murph, grabbing me by the scruff of the neck and bouncing my head off the dash. 'I think we should slot him and cut our losses.'

'Murph,' panted Sarah, 'hold up. Think about it. Do him now and we've got nothing. Think about it.' I had the feeling that she laid a placatory hand on his arm, but all I could see was plastic. 'Tell us where it is, Martin,' she urged.

I tried to shake my head. 'I can't. I've got to show you.'

I could see how this line was beginning to annoy them. Murph tried to dent the dash with my head, then abruptly released me.

'Fuck this,' he muttered, shaking his head and climbing out of the car.

'Think quickly, 'cos I won't be able to stop him,' hissed Sarah as he came around the car, nostrils flared. He pulled the door open and dragged me out.

'Time to die.'

He meant it. I changed my tune. 'It's at the ferry terminal.'

'I don't care.' He shoved me hard in the chest and I fell over. He looked quickly up and down the road, then pulled his pistol from inside his bomber jacket. A thin flicker of blood dribbled from the corner of his mouth where I had hit him. His tongue darted out and licked it.

'It's at the ferry terminal, I promise you.' My promises had the value of Weimar Republic deutschmarks, but they were all I had with which to buy my life.

'Bullshit.' He snapped the slide back and let it drive a round forward.

'It's at the foot–passenger terminal. In a locker.'

'Murph!' Sarah had climbed out of the car.

'It's not in any fucking locker,' he decided. 'We got to call this whole thing off.'

'It's at the terminal, in a locker, the money, five kilos of cocaine, less a little, in a Puma bag.' I looked around at the beer cans, the broken glass, the used prophylactics and discarded clothing among which I was to fall. It was ugly and apt that I should end up here, dumped with the garbage of shame. The universe was about to end. It wouldn't hurt. 'The locker hasn't got a key – it opens with a number, and the number is written on the wall of the bog. That's what I've got to show you.' I tried to rise, but Murph pushed me to my knees.

'Which ferry terminal?' asked Sarah, her bandanna still tied around her neck.

'Algeciras.'

'Which bog?'

'Gents, nearest the exit, middle stall, left–hand wall, around the hole.' I stabbed north, east, south and west in the air.

Murph scoped the road and grinned. 'Cheers for that.' He no longer needed me.

'Wait!' I yelled.

'Fuck off,' he sneered, leaning into his aim, the muzzle gleaming like a silver lining. The elegy matched my resting place. Sarah turned away, hiding her face in her hands.

'Which locker?' I cried.

Sarah spun around. Murph raised the weapon and looked at her, then me.

'You don't know which locker,' I told them. 'That's what I've got to show you. There's fucking hundreds and hundreds of lockers, three sizes, and all of them look the same. You could just ask the security guy to show you which locker if you give him the number, but he's going to ask you what's in the bag, and then he's going to open it to prove that you're not lying, and then you're fucked. Those docks are crawling with cops – always are. Your only chance is to take me with you and let me show you. Take it or leave it.' I looked at her, then at him, and then at her again.

Murph made his weapon safe and pocketed it. Life had run through my hands like a wet rope, but I'd got a grip on the last metre. I didn't know how long I could hang on.

'Told you to think fast,' said Sarah. 'Get in the car and take us to the locker.'

I climbed to my feet with shaking knees. 'I need the toilet, so I do.'

Algeciras smelled sick in the late-morning air, the bad breath of Franco's ill-sited refinery held close to the shimmering streets by some malevolent trick of the atmosphere. Saturday morning filled the dusty avenues with kids on bikes and scooters, while the pavements remained the territory of gossiping women and reflective men. I watched them watching us from the open front of a suburban bar as we passed, and wondered at the absurdity of the momentary meeting of our separate orbits. They stood and sipped sherry, and five metres from their shiny shoes, I struggled to save my life.

As my captors revised the details of my execution, I concentrated on the achievement of escape plan number one. If it worked, I would be free, and if it failed, I would slip seamlessly into escape plan number two. This, the less sophisticated of the two, was that I would simply run for it while yelling for help. What was important was that I placed myself in an environment where there were more witnesses than Murph had rounds, and anywhere was better than the *barranca* road. I hoped that the ferries weren't on strike.

'When we get there, you're going to take us straight to the bog, and then to the locker,' explained Murph. 'I'm going to be all over you like your boyfriend, and just so we're all clear before we get started, have a look at this.'

He fumbled in his jacket pocket, withdrawing something wicked that clicked and gleamed.

'Try anything at all and I'll stick this straight through your spine. What I do with you afterwards won't be your problem, but you can be sure that I *will* get away with it.' I didn't question his confidence.

Escape plan two had been spiked with a five-inch flick knife with a stiletto blade. I'd often wondered if anybody older than sixteen carried them any more. Now I knew. He could cut my spinal cord and carry me into the bog like some spaced-out junkie. The few who noticed him dragging me across the terminal concourse would only pause to wonder why a decent fellow like Murph was involving himself with a loser like me, and they might make a half-hearted decision to try to follow his example and reach out to those drowning in the dregs. Some detached part of my brain was amused by the notion that by killing me in public, Murph could inspire the good people of the Costa del Sol to do more for those less fortunate than themselves. The rest of my brain was horrified.

'Left,' I said, and we turned into a street that could have led to any dockyard in the world. Salty chain-link fences surrounded compounds and bonded warehouses, their air of disuse enhanced by the overgrown railway line that ran alongside the road. The queue for the terminal stretched half a kilometre from its gated entrance, and we joined its end, becoming the rattle on the tail an angry snake of dusty cars piled high with tarpaulin-wrapped booty from the First World.

The ferry port rose boldly against the blue like a stronghold of control and efficiency, the white stripes of its concrete facia glowing like a sergeant's chevrons. I was encouraged by this, my first view of the port. I had never used the ferry terminal in Algeciras before because it had a bad reputation among those whose opinions mattered to me. The port of Algeciras was the gateway to Africa, and obversely, the threshold of Europe. The rusting ferries that crossed the dirty zone brought penniless illegals into the country, the majority of whom were swept back into the sea by Spanish Immigration and a vigilant company of Guardia Civil. They supplemented their diet of pleading refugees with the occasional plump student back-packer caught delirious with relief at having managed to sneak five hundred grams of Moroccan hash past the overworked Algeciras Customs. Possession of a rucksack and a questionable haircut at the port was almost enough to guarantee a charge of conspiracy to import illegal substances, and with a head like mine, one stayed away.

Murphy was unimpressed to be at the arse end of a line of homeward bound North Africans, and I could feel the heat of his ire radiating from his ruddy cheeks.

'Stay calm, Murph,' soothed Sarah. 'It'll soon be over.'

My breath had become short as I scanned the honking, smoking confusion of cars for an opportunity. My withered adrenals responded to a nervous demand for one final all-out effort and wrung themselves dry of adrenalin, sending my stomach into freefall and turning the spit on my tongue to steam. I asked Sarah for a fag, and she heard the apprehension in my voice.

'Take it easy,' she suggested unhelpfully. 'We'll soon have you on your way, or maybe you'll fancy having a nice celebrational drink in one of the bars we passed.'

'*Celebratory*,' I said.

'For Christ's fucking sake!' swore Murph at a swollen carload of confused Berbers. 'They got the whole pissing family in there! Get a move on, you old bastard!'

I sucked greedily on the Benson, and played my hand.

'Go up the outside,' I said. 'This lot are all lining up to get on the ferry. We're just going to Left Luggage. Jump the queue.'

He waited for enough time for my suggestion to become his own idea, then swung out of the queue and raced for the gate.

'Go right to the front,' I urged, as we entered a huge car park. 'There's a drop-off point right by the doors.'

Murphy licked his lips and accelerated towards the terminal. He needed no further encouragement for he could smell the cocaine, as close now as if he were sitting on it.

'Over there!' cried Sarah, spotting a space as a yellow Mercedes swung out of the taxi rank, leaving a gap open only to fellow members of the minicab mafia. Murphy wouldn't have known or cared, cutting a diagonal across the forecourt and pulling into line as the cabs rolled forwards. Gibraltar loomed forbiddingly ahead of me, its detail hidden in a petro-chemical haze, and to my right, between the edge of the car park and the angular mountains of containers at the southern end of the bay, I could see trawlers riding the sparkling sea. My heart went cold as I realised that I had run as far south as Spain would let me go.

Murphy took a deep breath and looked hard into his rear-vew. The coast seemed clear.

'Here y'are,' he muttered, passing his pistol discreetly to Sarah. 'Wrap your jacket around it. Shoot him through the seat if he tries anything.' He looked at me, wiping his mouth with the back of his hand. I wasn't the only one running on adrenalin.

'Don't move. I'm coming round to let you out. Try and be a bit clever.'

I watched the wing mirror like a meerkat watching for a hawk. Indignant taxi drivers made sure that I didn't have to wait long. Murph pulled open my door.

'Out. Let's go.'

I looked up at him and smiled. 'Okay.'

He took me by the elbow and tried to steer me away from the car.

'Hang on, Murph,' I said. Sarah had climbed out of the back and into the driver's seat. 'I got bad news and I got good news.'

He looked like he was taking it hard so I spoke fast.

'The bad news is that it's not in the terminal. I made all that up. The good news is that it's right here, under the back seat, wrapped in a carrier bag. Have a look.'

His whole body swelled with homicidal rage, then shrank back as he regained control of his emotions. Murphy was a man trained to keep the best till last.

'Who's the clever bastard, then?' he growled. 'Get back into the car.'

I looked around and climbed in. There was no need to argue.

'What's going on?' asked Sarah, her voice cracking.

Murph dropped out of sight. Sarah twisted to look at me.

'What's going on?'

I smiled at her, then past her. She frowned, and turned to follow it. I couldn't see, but I imagined that the frown was smeared into a face of horror.

'*No puede aparcar aqui,*' said the guard, his big hands hooked into his shiny leather belt.

'Murph!' called Sarah.

A shadow fell across my lap as the second cop came up on the passenger side. I grabbed my bundle and climbed out of the car, pausing only to dump something I couldn't carry on the dash.

'*Sus papels, por favor, Señora,*' asked the first.

Sarah tried to be blonde and pretty but came over as worried and sweaty. 'I'm really, really sorry, Officer,'

He sighed. 'Your papers. Your licence. Your insurance. Your registration. This is your car?'

The other cop was asking me the same thing. I replied in broken Spanish.

'Here is my passport, Officer. I am a hitch-hiker. These people are English also. They give me a ride to Algeciras. They are nice.'

The cop looked at my photograph, and then at me. He recognised lowlife when he saw it. 'What happened to you?'

I shrugged like some lairy cider drinker. 'Fell over,' I replied. 'Several times.'

'Got any hash?' he asked.

'Hashish?' I raised my eyebrows. 'No. I have no hashish.'

The other cop was losing his patience with Sarah.

'Tell me, is this your car?' His exasperated questioning drew the attention of my interrogator.

'Take her to the jeep and show her the sheets,' he called. He looked down at my jeans. 'Turn out your pockets.'

I pulled the linings out like ears and shrugged.

'Open the bag.' He poked with undisguised distaste through the rumpled tissues and cracked make-up in Luisa's handbag. Now was not a good time to find out that Luisa kept a secret stash. 'This your bag?'

'No, *señor*,' I replied respectfully. 'It is the bag of my girl-friend which I will be taking to her in Ceuta. This is her jacket also.'

The cop nodded. 'All right. Piss off.'

I thanked Murph for the lift, skipped around the car and melted into the waves of embarkees pressing towards the long rows of ticketing booths. Sarah stood weeping crocodile tears at the side of a Guardia Land Cruiser as she was shown the lami-nated A4 sheets that said 'You're nicked' in eight languages for those rude enough not to know when their goose was cooked. Murph stood sweating by the Starlet, patting his pockets and pretending to have lost his passport. Until two hours ago, he would have been telling the truth. A green and white VW pulled up alongside, bored cops arriving at the incident like wasps around a dropped ice cream. One of the newcomers sidled around to the driver's side of the dusty Toyota and nosed inside. I moved quietly through the tide of migrant workers until I heard Sarah calling my name. I paused, ignoring the jostling, and then I turned back.

'Can't you tell him?' she wailed. 'He says they've got to take us in because we haven't got the right papers. Can't you say something?'

I glanced back to where Murph was being invited to join Sarah at the Land Cruiser. Bursting into girly tears had clearly worked wonders for her in the past at moments of crisis, and right now she was looking at the kind of crisis that went on and on, like chronic dysentery. The Guardia, I had been reliably informed very recently, weren't like ordinary policemen. They levied on-the-spot fines on those who travelled without the proper documentation, and they were especially suspicious of foreigners driving cars that weren't registered to them. Even the most half-hearted search of this car would turn up a shotgun, a

9mm automatic, five kilos of cocaine, and Officer Morales's warrant card, planted for dramatic effect on the dashboard as I left the car. A registration search would send a Land Cruiser down to La Mendirosa, where the flies would lead the cops to one dead Arab, two bleeding Frogs and one Bloody Mary. The subsequent investigation would swiftly turn up two handguns registered to deceased officers of the Guardia Civil, and by then Sarah and Murph would be deep inside a black hole of judicial process one simply couldn't blub one's way out of. I looked at her, her fringe ruffled and her eyes puffed up, and I recalled her expression as she had turned away back at the lay-by on the *barranca* road, covering her face as Murph took aim on mine. The cop was arguing with the despatcher, trying to pass the collar of a lifetime over to the two who had just arrived on the scene. Bribery didn't work with this lot, but sweet-talking in Spanish sometimes turned a bad situation into a lucky escape. All you needed were a few of the right words.

'Please say something,' pleaded Sarah.

Any minute now one of those cops was going to find something remarkable in Mary's car. I struggled to find the right words, wanting to speak not just for me, but for Alberto too, the best friend I never had.

'*Vaya con Dios*,' I suggested. Alberto would have liked that.

I turned and slipped into the crowd, crossing the concourse like a man with a purpose in life. A twelve-storey ferry was ready to slip anchor, and five more minutes would put me on it.

I could handle Africa.